Early Praise
HOUSE OF LARGE SIZES

"An extraordinary family story, rendered with delicious irony, mingled with kinky sex, Haitian magic, and suspense. It takes a great author to do that with style. Ian Graham Leask did."

—Bob Van Laerhoven, author of *Baudelaire's Revenge*

"Ambitious and startlingly brave, *House of Large Sizes* is a big-hearted novel that tells the story of sexual addiction and emotional growth. Set in the Twin Cities, London, and New Orleans, Ian Graham Leask brings these places to shimmering life even as he delves into the private desires of unforgettable characters who call these places home. This is a novel that is transatlantic, transgender, and above all, transformative. Storytelling at its best, this is a timely and necessary book."

—Patrick Hicks, author of *The Commandant of Lubizec*
and *The Collector of Names*

"'You cannot hide in a laugh, only in laughter' Ian Graham Leask writes in *House of Large Sizes*. The truth is, there's nowhere to hide in this fiction, even if there's plenty of room to laugh. Leask has written a rollicking rickshaw of a novel, hauled around by the author's profound intelligence, acerbic wit, and deep morality. This novel is sexy and sad, too. The work of an expert storyteller uninhibited by any pretense. Do yourself a favor and hide away in these pages for a while."

—Peter Geye, author of *Wintering, The Lighthouse Road*
and *Safe from the Sea*

"Ian Graham Leask's HOUSE OF LARGE SIZES is that rare find, a novel that combines the pulse of compulsive readability with the grit of psychological acumen. At once funny, sharp, wise, and even shocking, HOUSE OF LARGE SIZES makes us examine some of the most pressing questions of our time, inc_____ _____ __ _____ ı in literature and in life. This is a nc

lue Girl and *Ex Utero*

February 2017

STILLWATER
PUBLIC LIBRARY
Stillwater, Minnesota 55082

"Dark, sultry and in-your-face, *House of Large Sizes* packs a punch that is engaging, vivid and at times, not for the faint of heart. Ian Graham Leask's compelling and twisty story masterfully explores the sinister underbelly of New Orleans, as well as the turmoil that hides in the dark corners of the human heart."

—Allen Eskens, Barry Award-winning author of *The Guise of Another*, *The Life We Bury* and the forthcoming *The Heavens May Fall*

"*House of Large Sizes* is a house of secrets and the people broken by those very secrets. It's a house of desire and addiction, of tragedy and meanness. A glass house where everyone throws stones, and yet, this accidental family strives to find hope and connection as they follow the trail of a discovered son and a lost brother. Pulled by both design and desire, they are crashed together in pre-hurricane Katrina New Orleans. *House of Large Sizes* drags us into the darkest days of transgenderism tangled in fetish and sex-work. An almost mythic walk through the valley of the shadow of death as they attempt to not lose track of why this accidental household of fractured people still desire life."

—Venus DeMars, musician and artist, founder of "All the Pretty Horses."

Praise for
THE WOUNDED

"...Ian Graham Leask's *The Wounded* is a dense, complex, and richly rewarding collection of stories, always engaging, always challenging both the intelligence and moral sensibilities of the careful reader..."

—Tim O'Brien, author of *The Things They Carried*

"...Ian Graham Leask demonstrates an extraordinary eye for the rituals of male coming of age, replete with the struggle between atavistic brutality and startling tenderness."

—Jonis Agee, Author of *Sweet Eyes*

Also by Ian Graham Leask

The Wounded and other stories
about sons and fathers

HOUSE of LARGE SIZES

A NOVEL

IAN GRAHAM LEASK

CALUMET
EDITIONS
Minneapolis

**CALUMET
EDITIONS**
Minneapolis

Printed in the United States of America.
10 9 8 7 6 5 4 3 2 1

ISBN: 978-939548-45-0

Book and cover design by Gary Lindberg

In memory of Veronica

Acknowledgements

This novel was conceived of, and its first draft written, prior to the Katrina Disaster. Thanks to all those who wanted to remain anonymous yet who generously shared with me their experiences and opinions about voodoo in Louisiana. Some of them are sadly no longer with us. Thanks to David Burke, Susan Kimberly, and Venus DeMars, who "kept me straight" on the realities of gender reassignment. Thanks to my readers and editors over the years, especially Rick Polad and Steve McEllistrem for their staunch eyes for detail, Gary Lindberg for persuading me to publish and be damned, despite his dislike of foul language, and Christian Tyssier for checking my French. And special thanks to my lovely partner Susan, who for some extraordinary reason puts up with me.

"Hell is the centre of evils and, as you know, things are more intense at their centres than at their remotest points."

–From *A Portrait of the Artist as a Young Man*, James Joyce

HOUSE of LARGE SIZES

A NOVEL

IAN GRAHAM LEASK

1

Terrance Langley told his clients that dwelling in the past was like keeping inflammation in the body—it would eventually flare up and kill you. Luckily, his clients could not see inside him; if they could they would gasp at the untidy bundle of regrets he hauled up the mountain of his life. Of late, he wished he had endured a little further through the English educational system and become a psychiatrist instead of a psychologist. To be this age and forced to listen, for an inadequate salary, to the whining and victimhood of immature egos was withering his soul. He'd had it up to his balls with the inner child.

It was only Monday and he ached to get home to Vera and spend every second with her, to eat and drink and laugh. Even with the office window closed, he could hear Big Ben, the old bell in Whitehall, chiming lugubriously through the backed-up day. Yet when he was at home, time whooshed him forward as if some malevolent god selected him for torture, hastening bedtime with its insomnia and impotence; its time-bomb of nightmare, either his, or more usually Vera's. Bedtime came before he could spend the promised hour at his desk, writing, or walking to the river with Vera to sit and watch the brown water drift by. After the ten o'clock news, he would yawn and she would cry and they would retire to the beautiful bedroom of their former passions to wait out the night like small mammals in a primordial forest.

Compassion for his clients, now dried up by the recent threat of Vera's relapse, had to be at least faked, and faking he could always do. An old faker with love handles who couldn't seem to keep his fingernails clean—fraudulent on all levels; hence the nightmares, the whiskey, the habitual loss of identity in outlandish fantasies about literary glory, the seduction of Holly-

1

wood actresses, and flashbacks to a time long ago when he had found the love of his life, only to be ripped in half when he had to abandon her. He was a Don Quixote look-a-like with shriveled pudendum and swelling prostate, barely coping in a constant mode of damage control.

In an effort to escape the doom of Vera's scheduled visit to her oncologist, Terry pushed his spectacles into his hair, clasped hands behind his head, and imagined a future wherein his novel, successfully published and lauded as the first great work of the twenty-first century, allowed him to stop counseling fruitcakes and go on the lecture circuit. He vaguely heard the receptionist, Minnie, answer the telephone in the adjacent office, but his mind remained in his novel, a novel about the pure realism of what gathers in our navels and gets streaked on our underwear, that realism illuminating how we produce romance, spirituality, and philosophy in our evolutionary quest for survival. The critic in the *Times Literary Supplement* would describe him as a prose poet possessing a benign eye for existential truth and a gift for subtly unlocking the fruits of his encyclopedic intellect. He would write the perfect review of his own book as an introduction, the reviewer as well as the reviewed, rather like Jehovah in his ability to beget himself and then sacrifice himself to himself.

There would be memorable characters, shaped by his long experience with human nature; yet his dramatus personae would codify fully realized classical archetypes. The best novel ever, loosely based on the earliest written story, yet truly a book of life—the inner life, the dream of how we see ourselves. It must be a novel of inner voice because that's where we articulate the great bulk of our existence; but it wouldn't be pedantic and obscure like the masterwork of that windbag, Joyce. Terry Langley would settle for a one-hit wonder like Lowry's *Under the Volcano*, or that poor O'Toole bloke's *Confederacy of Dunces*. But please, almighty Thou-Who-Doesn't-Exist, may I reap some benefit from my life's work before I'm too dead to appreciate it?

Minnie called through the office, "Terry! 'Oy! Wakey-wakey! International call for you."

Terry sighed loudly.

"Don't be grumpy, Terry," said Minnie. "And by the way, you have Monica in five minutes."

"That bloody malingerer! Wasting taxpayers' money!"

"Shush. You'll be in trouble again."

"Some of these people don't want to get well, Minnie."

Laughing, Minnie said, "Don't keep international calls waiting."

"Come in and find me Monica's file, then. They don't pay me enough to multi-task."

Minnie laughed again. Terry rubbed his face, picked up the receiver, and punched line three. "Good afternoon. Terrence Langley speaking."

"Terry?"

One word with two syllables told him the caller was a North American male, trying to disguise the depth of his voice.

"Yes. To whom am I speaking?" The formality in his own voice made him want to slap his own wobbly chops.

"This is George. George Pym. I was nine years old when you stayed with us in Minneapolis."

Terry's synapse leapt into party mode. "Blimey. That was thirty-odd years ago." His scalp numbed. Yesteryear rushed into the present.

George continued, "A bit over thirty-two to be accurate... 1972."

"Where are we now, 2004? Time's wingéd chariot, eh?"

"This must be a shock, Terry, but we need to talk."

"I'm pleased to hear from you, George. I remember trying to teach you football but it wasn't your forté. You kept sitting on the ball and resting."

"You were nice to me. I'm still not very athletic."

"And your family was very kind to me."

"Especially my mother."

"Ah, yes. I imagine this call has something to do with that."

"It sure does."

"Of course."

"She called the child Gilbert because she thought it sounded English."

Terry received an electric zing through his body. Outwardly unruffled, he said, "My child, presumably?" It would be a question of explaining: Vera darling, remember I told you I went through a rather wild period...

"I gotta tell you, there's no question about the paternity. However, other than teasing him a bit about not looking like the rest of us, and my mom throwing it in his face that he's a bastard, he doesn't know for sure, and doesn't know much about you."

"Well bugger me. Gilbert Pym. And he's thirty-two, you say? How interesting."

"Gilbert Langley Pym."

3

"Clever of her—a magnificent name. But I don't have any money."

"Nobody's after money. Gillie's not doing too good at the moment. He was doing real good for a while and suddenly he turned into a jerk."

"Of course, he has my genes."

George laughed, and the full, male richness of the voice made Terry smile. You cannot hide in a laugh, only in laughter.

"You're a funny man, Terry."

Minnie came into the room shaking her head, immediately picked up Monica's file, and placed it in front of Terry. Her black lipstick had all rubbed off and now she looked quite pretty, aside from the silver studs between her chin and bottom lip and the safety pin in her eyebrow. Terry winked at her. Minnie scowled and left.

"Sorry, George, I was just repelling a Visigoth."

"Huh?"

"No matter. I have an appointment shortly, but do go on."

"You've gotten left out of Gillie's life for three decades, Terry, but now we need your help."

"How on earth did you find me?"

"Internet, and a lot of guesswork. Mom remembered that you studied psychology. So I searched your name under English psychologists and, boom, there you were at the Holborn Clinic in Covent Garden."

George pronounced Holborn phonetically, but instead of correcting him, Terry said, "I didn't know we had a web presence."

"The world's shrunk, Terry. No hiding place."

"I assure you, I was not hiding."

"That's nice to know. But you probably should be hiding from my mother. I do."

"How is our Nina?"

Nina, Nina, Nina. Terry's genitals swelled at the flashing recollection of her bouncing breasts. There was a yellow couch; he'd sit on its arm with her straddling him.

"I haven't seen her since Christmas," said George. "She's out of her mind. Breaking the hearts of geriatric Hells Angels in Coon Rapids."

"Hasn't changed much, then?"

George cackled.

Oh please God, preserve those colossal American breasts sticking hotly in my face like the pillars of paradise. It's what Muslims are promised after all—an eternity of potency and beautiful women. "And your dad? Michael?"

4

"Dad didn't make it."

"Oh dear, I'm sorry. What happened?"

"He died about twenty years ago."

Vanished now was the attempted disguise in George's voice. Sensing deep discomfort, Terry didn't pursue details, but said, "I didn't know. Your mum and I didn't stay in touch."

"She implied you did—for a while at least."

"No. I always wondered, but after a while… you know."

"It's all, as I remember you saying, water under the bridge."

"You always were a clever lad. I'm alarmed that you recall my axioms."

"Dad wasn't much of a talker. He used to work all the time at the bakery or tinker in the garage, as I'm sure you remember."

"I do. I remember the maple icing he'd put on his doughnuts. Marvelous. But he couldn't understand why I hated cinnamon."

"Dad said you taught him that all Brits hate cinnamon."

"Genuine Brits, anyway. We suspect cinnamon lovers of psychotic deviancy."

"I remember a lot of what you said."

"I hope I didn't muddle you."

"You assured me that the darkness of my school years would ease up in adulthood, and that's what got me through high school."

"I don't recall being so wise."

"And you explained that every pretty girl needs a plain friend and that the trick was to go after the plain friend if you wanted to get laid."

"I'm cringing."

"It was good advice, but a bit wasted on a nine-year-old."

"Those were ridiculously permissive times, I'm afraid. Sorry about that."

"I remembered it later and passed it on to Gillie and he married a very plain girl who's now divorcing him. And I married the beautiful one for appearance's sake, then taking your advice a step further, shelved the pursuit of girls and went after their boyfriends."

"I see you've turned into a fine bull-shitter, George Pym."

"I've had great teachers."

"George, what does Gilbert look like?"

George remained quiet for some uncomfortable seconds before saying, "His hair is thick and stands up like summer wheat. He has hazel eyes and

5

the form of Adonis. A lot like you, Terry, except, as I recall you have a big nose and his is more normal."

"Cheeky sod."

"His looks get him into trouble. He got into fights as a kid, so he has scars on his face. He put himself through college with the help of insurance money we got when Dad died. He earned a degree in Architecture, but he's just like the rest of us in this family in so far as he's a classic underachiever. He runs a lot these days, stays in shape, and dresses like an off-duty mountaineer. He smokes weed sometimes and drinks too much beer."

"How's his eyesight?"

"Good, I think."

"I'm thankful not to have passed on my myopia."

"He has a different kind of vision problem—more of that later. He wears his hair too long—to stop it sticking up, you know—and sometimes ties it back in a ponytail."

"What an excellent description, George. Thank you."

"No, thank *you*."

In George's 'thank you,' Terry detected an immature joy at being praised. Terry remembered the withdrawn, obese nine-year-old George with his mother's dark hair and blue eyes, and what a dismal nightmare of a childhood the kid was undergoing when Terry dropped on the Pym family like a horse-hidden Greek. Terry repressed a cruel impulse to ask George if he still wet the bed. He remembered teasing the boy with the nursery rhyme: *Georgie Porgy pudd'n and pie, kissed the girls and made them cry. When the boys came out to play, Georgie Porgy ran away*. He would never tease a child now.

George was saying, "Anyway, you have a son called Gilbert and he's in need of a dad right now 'cos I can't do any more for him. I got my own problems."

"Why doesn't Gilbert know about me?"

"It's a long story, perhaps for later, but basically Mom wanted your baby. She thought it would bring you back. Dad was devastated but wanted to keep the family together. It worked out though. He and Gillie became close, and Gillie, even twenty years later, still isn't over his death. After it was clear you wouldn't return, or she couldn't find you, or whatever, Mom stopped talking about you. But she did go out and try and replace you— which at the end of it all Dad couldn't take. Gillie's had some tough breaks recently, which I'll explain, and I'm not sure how he'll react to knowing about you. He's in a mess and we have to tread carefully."

"You seem to know a lot about counseling."

"Only 'cos I been in it all my fucking life."

"Does Nina know you're contacting me?"

"Yes. Be very afraid."

Terry laughed, and George said, "I'm serious. She's something else. Went on a diet and stopped smoking, because she thinks she might see you. We can't let that happen."

"You'd better tell her I'm happily married, George."

"That won't matter to her. She's stuck back in the seventies."

"Sounds like you've all lost the plot."

"There is no plot."

Minnie stood in the doorway, hand on rotund hip, her expression saying *get off that bloody telephone and attend to mad Monica.* Terry covered the receiver with his hand and said, "Minnie, be a love and remind Monica of the virtues of patience."

Minnie's face stretched in a miraculous show of incredulity. The dropping bottom jaw, dragged down no doubt as much by metal as by surprise, pulled the cheeks and lower eyelids with it. "Terrence Langley, you're terrible."

"I'm fielding a life and death situation here, Minnie. Now please be my Cerberus and reschedule her."

Minnie backed out of the room, shaking her head. "Gawd Almighty, the things I do for you."

Terry exhaled a long stream of air. There would be time enough now for a full revelation of facts. "All right, George, tell the story." He brought the cordless phone over to the black leather couch, attached the sucker cord to his tape recorder, and after finding the tiny plug hole in the phone with his terrible eyesight, he lay down and listened.

* * *

Terry pulled on his overcoat in the reception area where Minnie applied fresh black lipstick and adjusted her piercings. He asked, "Where are you off to tonight?"

"Meet me mates."

"Tell me, Minnie, do I look fatherly to you?"

"You're *old* enough to be my father." She laughed. "Dirty old lech."

"You're projecting again."

"Too right," she said, coming around the desk to stand in front of him. Smiling, she tapped him in the sternum with a long black fingernail. "We all know your reputation, so keep your maulers off."

"A reputation exhausted decades ago, I'm afraid."

"Ah, don't give me that. You can still charm their knickers off."

"Oh, Minnie, when are you going to save me from myself? Be my Dulcinea?"

"Who's she when she's at home?"

"An archetypal object of desire, attached to the romantic psyche of a well-intentioned old Dago."

"Well, we all know where objects of desire lead geezers like you, don't we?"

"Indeed we do, my delightful little dove…"

"Blow jobs and buggery on Hampstead Heath," Minnie laughed. "Now get home to your missus."

Terry put his free hand over his heart and said, "Ah, the refreshing reserve of the younger generation."

Minnie, looking up at him like a Gothic Puck, gave him a little push toward the door.

"And mad Monica? Was she discomforted by her postponement?"

"She knows you don't like her. You better watch it—she calls you Mister Numb Nuts."

"She does not."

"Oh, yes. I smoothed her over, of course—tomorrow at noon."

"Shit. Can't you transfer her to Sajita? She can identify better with the pre-menopausal. Give me someone more challenging?"

"That's what you all want. You all only want to treat the interesting ones. It drives me bonkers. Don't forget your mantra—mental illness isn't spectacular, it's dull. You've got a full day tomorrow, so no more mucking around."

"Yes, Minnie dear, I shall obey."

"Go on now, shove off, Mister Numb Nuts."

* * *

8

Terry failed to notice London until he began crossing Waterloo Bridge. A man tired of London is a man tired of life. He swung his briefcase, measuring the exchange of weight as the tape recorder and book therein slipped from end to end. The book, bought during a late lunch break in Charing Cross Road, infuriated him. A first published work, nominated for a Booker Prize and winning other prizes for best first novel and most promising this, that, and the other, was authored by his friend and rival, Marty Kelso. Kelso, a sneaky little swine of a bus driver with whom he swapped manuscripts until a couple of years ago, had beaten him to the punch.

Terry's intention, to throw the book unopened into the river and watch it sink, quarreled with his curiosity—plus the fact that he'd had to pay full price for it. The little bastard hadn't even told him; he'd be gloating, driving around in his ridiculous bus. Oh well, just ignore it—leave it unread. Marty would finally ring, disguising his triumph, unable to wait, asking about the progress of Terry's literary masterpiece in his piping little voice. "Oh, forgive me Marty, for not getting to the book yet. Is it the one we work-shopped in Crouch End?"

It was nearly five o'clock, darkening, and Terry's bus, packed with commuters, idled in traffic two hundred meters behind him. He wore no hat so his Samuel Beckett hair blew sideways in the wind. May as well walk home for all the good the bloody bus does. This town's an anthill. The unreal city, Elliot called it. That other poem—Prufrock—especially now... yes, I understand now. Dear oh dear. Septic tank who wanted to be one of us. James too. Auden went the other way. Ha! He did indeed—boat race like a Sharpei.

For a man of such complex thought, London had become a cattle prod of excess stimulation, and to have so much going on all at once, just when he planned on winding down his career, wasn't fair. To be confronted with parenthood and the return of Vera's disease at the same time seemed like ample proof that the cosmos meant him harm.

And the humiliation of Kelso's popular success! Bloody fluke! But this is life, Terry thought, steadying himself. Adversity keeps it interesting, and then you age, falter, fail, and enter eternal negation. But surely not, surely there's the promise of salvation as reward for the painful struggle of existence. Receive me unto thy kingdom, oh Lord, that I may not perish and be no longer Terry.

Terry saw an alarming vision of himself twenty years hence, a tall stooped creature in a dressing gown, even thicker spectacles, behind which drooped bloodhound eyes, shuffling around mindlessly in a nursing home, smelling of piss. Don't be afraid of this vision, he pleaded to himself—embrace it. Cobblers! If only I was one of those who can rest in the faith of a life hereafter. But no, there's a different hell in that; it's they, the believers, who'll destroy the human race to further their faith. I am a sad wretch wracked between intellect and fear.

Rain in the wind. Sod it. Walk to the Elephant & Castle and catch pneumonia. That would just about do it. Can always wedge onto a bus in the event of a deluge.

He stopped and looked down into the river. You have a son called Gilbert and he's in need of a dad right now. Terry looked at Savoy Pier to his right. The Queen Mary of Glasgow moored there. A train rattled south over Hungerford Bridge and beyond. At the bend in the river, the illuminated monstrosity of the London Eye brought false festivity to the sky over Westminster. A launch decorated with fairy lights cruised up-river with a few huddled tourists in the bow, clasping white cups. Big Ben hammered out the hour.

Terry remembered when he had need of a father and there wasn't one. I have a son, albeit on the other side of the world, but I have a son and that son needs me. As if Vera doesn't have enough trouble. Oh, by the way, darling, I know symptoms of your cancer just returned, but I'm off to America shortly to meet my bastard son.

Terry gazed down into the river and saw that it had stopped moving.

There's a moment, just before the tide turns, when the rubbish floating in the Thames drifts nowhere, floats still. And is it a metaphor, a moment of blinding clarity? You're joking—step into the vacuum of the turning tide and it's the same old trash, boring and meaningless. But you should be chuffed to have seen it after all these years. Fill in that blank of experience— you saw the river stop.

Retire and finish your novel. Just do it. If that cunt Kelso can do it so can you. You've had enough dysfunction. Notebooks and folders litter the house, awaiting your attention. Langley's brilliant unpublished manuscript was not keenly sought after by University English departments in America—because there was no bloody manuscript. If he died, squatters would wad scraps of masterpiece to burn in the fireplace. Ah… the whole idea seems tame now anyway compared to the story George Pym just told—a story that, if rendered fictionally, would be considered implausible by the intellectually anemic, the politically correct reviewers who laud only novels of popular simplicity and meaningless innovation. Lazy bastards—another indication of the final stage of the Viconian cycle. No critic would believe the Pym story. Too Dickensian, they'd bleat, too complex… Baaaaaaaaaaaaaah! Useless wazzocks sitting on pompous arses, passing judgement on their betters. Any writer—even a bus-monkey—is superior to a critic. Baaaaaah! Better not put that in your novel. Cantankerous old plonker. Baaah! You are yourself a microcosm of the Viconian Cycle—decadent cynicism, the ripe carbuncle on the bum of civilization. Are we entering the period prior to cultural collapse? We're in the last days, brothers and sisters… come to Jesus! Submit to Allah! Look at this, everyone hurrying home to a boring dinner and a quick wank. I live among lackeys and opportunists. And I myself am one of them, too afraid to retire and write a novel that no one understands.

Terry placed his hands on the sides of his head and shouted into the river, "Stop!"

Embarrassed, he looked around to see if anyone had noticed, and someone had—two pockmarked skinheads, smoking thin cigars, laughed at him. One said, "That's it, boss. Have a word with the old river."

Laughing, the other said, "It's needed a good bollocking for centuries."

After they'd passed in swirls of cheap cigar smoke, Terry wished he'd laughed louder instead of producing nothing but a crazed grin; he wished he'd walked along with them, explaining himself so that they wouldn't think he was just another Waterloo nutter. But, like Vera always said, "No one cares, Terry." They were obviously Millwall fans. He imagined them punching and kicking him, and dumping him over the railings.

He walked to the middle of the bridge where he often took a minute to sing under his breath what he remembered of an old Kinks song, "Waterloo Sunset." This led him to another of their songs, "Lola." He thought to himself, ah, the surprising creative process. Observe the psyche at work, so simple. Lola. Boys will be girls and girls will be boys, it's a mixed up something; buggered up, bolloxed up world or something. How can I be a writer when I don't remember anything? Need to sharpen up. Echinacea. When Vera dies, there'll be enough insurance money on which to retire, and I will spend the rest of my days writing. Oh, what have I just thought? God forgive me! May dear Vera outlive the cad Langley. Please, for all my sins, let her outlive me.

11

He looked into the water and the rubbish had started moving down-stream.

* * *

Wet through and steaming, Terry closed the heavy door behind him, hung up his coat, and placed his briefcase on the umbrella-less umbrella stand. He smelled chicken roasting, vegetables steaming, and his stomach roiled with hunger. Vera called out from the kitchen, "You're late."

"I walked," he called.

She came fast out of the kitchen and along the little hallway to kiss him. "Bloody fool," she said, after pecking his lips. "You'll catch pneumonia and then we'll both be in shtuck street. You better change."

"You're a silly child."

"Sorry, darling. By the way, I broke down and bought Marty's novel. It's in my bag."

"Jolly good. I want to read that. It got a lovely review in the TLS."

Terry rolled his eyes and Vera patted him on the chest, laughing, and said, "Hurry up and get changed and I'll bring a pot of tea into the lounge."

Vera sped back to the kitchen. Terry went up the two flights of stairs and put on an old pair of jeans and a faded Arsenal shirt from the double year. He sat on the bed for a while and listened to the rain lash against the windows.

From the bottom of the stairs, Vera called, "Tea's on the table. What on earth are you doing?"

"Coming, coming, untwist those knickers."

He heard Vera laugh and go into the living room where she proceeded to clatter cutlery and condiments. Before putting his slippers on, he noticed his crooked toes with their dry, ruined nails, the victims of fungus, and thought back to when Nina Pym first seduced him. He'd been wandering around America and his arches hurt. She rescued him and he slept on the yellow hide-a-bed couch. Michael Pym was always at his bakery. On waking, Terry would find Nina Pym sitting on the coffee table, smiling at him, wearing a bosom-popping denim vest or some sort of Indian wrap-around thing. She gave him a foot massage, and then sucked his toes until his brain nearly burst. He had nicer toes back then.

* * *

12

He led in with: "Darling, remember I told you I went through a rather wild period…"

The fake coal fire warmed the living room with its pale gas flames, and his tea, grown cold now so that a milky film formed on it, had not been so much as sipped. Vera drank three cups whilst she listened.

In the narrow road outside their big bay window, rain bounced off the parked cars and dripped from the leafless sycamores lined up along the pavements. His explaining over, Terry looked outside to avoid Vera's eyes. The road seemed grayish under the streetlights, and it took him a moment or two to pick out colours: the red pillar-box on the corner with an old lady in a pink coat studying the collection times; people beyond the pillar-box, sauntering up the steps of the Catholic church in yellow and red raincoats; the bright blue MG, owned by a South African neighbour who had not moved it in three years. Closer, a pair of young Mormons, tipping a green and orange umbrella into the wind-driven rain, seemed to be advancing against the satanic forces of logic. Terry turned away, picked up his cold tea, swilled a mouthful, and then said, "Anyway, I have a son called Gilbert and he's in need of a dad right now."

The flesh of Vera's face looked young. She looked younger than him although she was six years older. Her pensive countenance made Terry smile. Her piled-up white hair, secured with a chopstick, and her light brown eyes left him speechless with love, but nevertheless anticipating a verbal assault.

"Say something," he said.

Vera reached across the table and tapped his wrist several times with her index finger. He felt like Zeus about to be humbled by Hera's respectable wrath. Then Vera said, "Are you willing to share him?"

Terry raised an eyebrow at her and asked, "Are you serious?"

"Yes."

"Of course. I should've had more faith. I was expecting a bollocking."

"I've loved you twenty years, Terry. You've always played fair with me, despite your naughtiness before we married. I always wondered if something wouldn't come back to haunt you. But I must say I don't see this as anything negative. I see it as an opportunity for you—perhaps for both of us."

"Always so wonderfully rational. Thank you, darling—so much."

"We need a purpose. I do at least—I know you have your never-ending novel…"

"Watch it."

"We're stagnating, and I don't know how long I've got…"

"Darling, no."

"We have to face reality, Terry. I'm pretty sure I'll get bad news on Wednesday and I can't think of anything better than having something to focus on other than myself."

"You're marvelous."

"Stop twinkling at me. I'll cry. Where does he live?"

"Well, Minnesota, but George tells me he'll be in New Orleans soon."

"Good, I'll be warm there."

"Unto us a child is born."

"Oh for heaven's sake, Terry." She jumped up and made for the kitchen. "You're so bloody histrionic!"

11

The freezing river flowed stiffly under Gilbert Pym as he looked down from the Hennepin Avenue Bridge into its dark eddies, imagining the brief drop and the shock of cold as he sank and tumbled underwater in the muscular current. With a clenching scrotum, he imagined scraping over the long series of saw-edged drops that terminated just beyond the Stone Arch Bridge.

The authorities would find a torso down by Hiawatha Dam and accompanying pieces of its main corpus would collect in the backwash with the flotsam and jetsam of the Mississippi. They'd re-assemble the essential parts of a man once known as Gilbert Langley Pym and his brother George would have to come out of hiding to identify him. Laura would have to look too. She'd be furious; she'd call him a stupid baby and slap his face, knocking his head to the floor. They'd eject her from the morgue.

The recurring vision of Laura in the missionary position with Ray, straining for orgasm, kept shocking Pym's consciousness. He couldn't keep it out, and with it came the attendant reasons—all his fault—that led to this situation. He preferred oblivion to this ceaseless viewing of his failures and their consequences.

The Friday night city hummed and steamed. Once, Friday night was magical, a time to kick back after a hard week, laugh with one of the girls, or George, eat a big dinner, guzzle beer. Now, a yellow leviathan of a post office building and three neon signs were the last things Pym would see if he chose to go the way of his father: Riverplace, Pillsbury Best Flour, Gold Medal Flour. Might he discover his father somewhere down the dark river amongst the shades of the dead? They could have a chat about jelly doughnuts and cheese kolaches. His father always smelled sweet, like cookies.

A wide safety lip beyond the railing on which he'd have to stand, and the act of climbing over it, separated him from the last great adventure. While he rested his forehead on the railing and felt the cold metal through the double knit of his hat, he wondered if his father's last thoughts were similar to this. What made his father, Michael Pym, choose this way? Pym easily conjured up less painful suicides; he was nothing if not inventive. Jumping into a freezing river was a hard act to follow, like watching Michael Pym walking around one day with a hammer on the steep roof of their home, pounding down shingles after a summer storm. The kind of nerve his father possessed would never be Gilbert Pym's to boast. It would be a clean symmetry—twenty years between the deaths of father and son. He pictured Michael waiting for him, saw for a second all our fathers waiting for us down there in the dark, and this image released another thunderbolt of grief.

To resist crying out and be noticed by the swarming eyes of nearby skyscrapers, he straightened himself and looked up to see the falls just ahead, all choked with crazy shaped icebergs, spooky in the diverse light; and his heart, for months nothing but a dried up fossil, stirred itself at the reality of suicide. A bus went by. He heard the city—the faint whoosh of the falls— and his bowels, too gutless for the death plunge, gurgling with gas.

A car full of youths crawled to a halt and a boy shouted, "Hey, fag! Waiting for your boyfriend?" Pym turned to stare at the boys. Their rusting Ford Taurus idled, and their young, bright-toothed faces grinned from the windows like mindless goblins. The impulse to go berserk, to pound the roof in, to pull teenagers from their safe arrogance, presented itself. But an ironic voice, one that often spoke inside him, asked: And will you run amok tonight? Break their bones and make them bleed? One way to worsen his despair would be to wake up in a cell tomorrow, charged with assault. It had been a long time since he had hurtled into enemies with fists and knees flying. The prospect of doing this presented itself as a way to wriggle free of the anguish, but he failed to summon up the necessary battle-wrath before his languid inner voice spoke again: Relax. What does it matter? Compared to all that's happened, who the hell cares? Let them think they're tough guys.

Pym turned back to the river and spat meaningfully like a man with a history. The voices continued a little longer, but then the boys moved on, hiding the truth of their soft youthfulness amidst derisive laughter and the stink of exhaust. Fifteen years before, Pym was much the same and he asked himself if he'd matured at all since then; indeed, had anyone of his acquaintance actually grown up? Laura perhaps, but now she behaved badly too, gorging herself on another man's semen.

People are stupid. Here's a lone man standing at the guardrail of a bridge late at night, and no one in the car has the smarts to say, "Leave that poor bastard alone, he doesn't look happy." And you, you stupid son of a bitch, remember how you spoke to George and the way you betrayed Laura. Asshole. Alone now—deservedly so.

Whipped, Pym abandoned death, turned, and plodded north across the bridge. Beyond De LaSalle High School, which he attended years ago on Peter Pan Island, stood his brother's recently remodeled house. It was near the dimly lit corner of West Island Avenue and Maple Place where the view of downtown resembled the cover of a science fiction novel. Pym looked over there and addressed George as he walked. "One minute you're the do-it-yourself George I've always known, coming over to fix my plumbing and drink beer. The next you leap out of the closet at me like Jabba the Hut with a lisp. Christ, how the hell was I supposed to react?"

Pym looked in at Nye's to see if Estelle waited there, but the chairs were turned onto the tables and an old man in an apron swept the floor. Earlier, around ten-thirty, Pym had started a quarrel with Estelle and then stormed away to drink alone over the river, first at the Monte Carlo and then at Runyan's, where the unattached women posed in mating plumage. The way they flicked their hair and wiggled their rears like preening parrots… it infuriated him. And the affected way they smoked their stupid cigarettes made him want to slap their phony, expectant faces. To think he used to dodge among them like a cunning piranha, probing for entry. Now he wouldn't want to fuck them with George's dick let alone his own. They had brought him to his knees; it was their fault; women with their beckoning facades, drawing fat dumb bozos like himself onto the deadly rocks of marriage, deception, and adultery.

And Mother.

Don't go there, the voice said… you're fucked up enough. Remember whose fault it is. It's your fault. All of it.

Yes.

Not even The Times remained open for a final attempt at inebriation, so Pym headed back along Second Street into his neighborhood. His face stiffened and the moisture inside his nose froze. The small, closely arranged houses looked cozy, bedded-in for the night, and a few, defying the gloom of late winter, still sported Christmas lights.

He tried to comfort himself by thinking of Estelle. He thought of how it felt to suck her taut nipples, to straddle her rib cage and slip his cock between her breasts while she held them just so and smiled, slightly cross-eyed; but nothing stirred; there came no distraction, only remorse and the copulating vision of Laura and Ray. An age ago, at Thanksgiving, he'd driven this same route, his heart filled with contentment. The stocks he owned at work were shooting through the roof, he had a great little wife who loved him, a mistress who couldn't get enough of him, a nice little house in which he'd been raised, and it was Thanksgiving, his favorite holiday. Everyone was coming to Laura and Gilbert Pym for a big turkey pig-out. Laura and George would cook, swigging sherry and laughing as they used the juices from the turkey to make gravy. His mother would be alone on the porch, wrapped in blankets, smoking. Estelle, with whom he'd been weight-training, would arrive via a different route. Laura's mother and sisters would be there; there'd be nieces and nephews—mostly from Estelle and Laura's families. Wonderful—it had been arranged for months.

Pym had let himself in the door and there was a hush, like the inside of a huge seashell. No people. No smell of roasting meat and pumpkin pie. No laughter, only the first stab of intuition, then damp, cold emptiness, and Laura's note: 'The banquet is canceled. You cooked your own goose, Gil. Whoever invented love deserves to be hanged. Don't even try to put this right.' A brick dropping through guts, numb legs—sorrow and embarrassment—not only are you busted but everyone in Christendom has the scoop. Not even Estelle arrived because George reached her on her cell phone and told her not to bother coming home either, so she headed to Wisconsin where her mom owned a trailer court. Thanksgiving was canceled and so was Christmas, New Year's, his birthday, everything. Now, just when there should be a hint of spring in the air, an Arctic front sat on the city like the Devil on a dead man's face.

As he approached the house he smacked his forehead. Why did you do it? What were you thinking? Unbelievable idiot. You sent it all to Hell! To add to Pym's woes, as if vengeful gods threw turds at him, the stock of the architectural dot-com into which he'd invested all his assets had gone belly up. And those gods had plenty more in store for him, bless their white marble asses.

Tonight, Pym opened the front door to the same emptiness and smelled gas. He switched on lights, checked the stove, and then went into the basement where he found someone had pushed in the window, knocking off the latch. A frozen wind blowing in had snuffed out the pilot light on the old furnace.

An odd smell, faint, like burned rubber or old boots mixing with body odor, baffled him. Pym shut the window, found duct tape to seal it and then re-ignited the furnace. Someone watched him. He spun, ready to fight, but confronted only the bare one-hundred-watt bulb, glaring off the white cinderblock walls.

Armed with a hammer, heart pounding, Pym searched the basement, then went up the steps to the kitchen and noticed the porch door ajar. A sharp knife from the utility drawer stuck up from the fissure of a cutting board on the countertop. The porch outside was dark. He closed the door, locked it, and slipped the chain into place.

Ready to lash out with the hammer, skin buzzing, he searched each room with no thought save a primitive longing to crush someone's forehead—whack one of those teenagers from the bridge—or that fuck, Ray! Ray, the right man for Laura. Mr. Maturity. Crack! Maxwell's Silver Hammer, yes. Coming in her mouth. Ahhh! Crack! God! Bury the hammer in the frontal lobe. Crack! Crack! Crack! Aaaagh!

Down on hands and knees, his fingers digging into the stair carpet, he watched tears sprinkle over the back of his hands. "Oh, no," he said. "Not you. Oh, no no no, not you."

A thud sounded in the basement.

Pym's skin leapt.

Only the furnace going on. Shit. He wasn't alone though, he felt sure of it. His inner voice said: Oh, this is nothing strange, just the family madness. He searched the rest of the house—even small places where no human could hide. Was George here, messing with his head? George was quite capable of such tomfoolery. Yes, only George knew the basement window could be easily forced.

"George!" Pym called. "Come talk to me. I'm sorry."

He wanted George in the house with him now. Like when he was a kid and George baby-sat because their mom was god-knows-where and the rotten fucker would hide because he knew how terrified Little Pym was of being left alone. What relief when he showed himself! Or George would read horror stories in the dark like Mother had done to him with a flashlight under the chin. Then, to make up for it, he would sleep on the rug next to Little Pym so Dracula wouldn't come out from under the bed in the night. That's when he held Pym's head on the yellow couch and farted in his ear.

He willed George to stand up behind the yellow couch and say, "All right, Gillie, sorry to scare you. Your brother's home to look after you." He wanted to take it all back—starting with the affair with Estelle, and all the arrogant things he had said to his brother to make him go away. It would be like George to teach him a lesson and then just turn up and everything would be all right again.

But George was too big to squeeze through a basement window.

And he had a key.

Pym found nothing missing. Not that he owned anything worth stealing. Laura had already hauled anything of value to her mother's place when she left—the iMac, the cell phone, the music center, the good television. The thought of Laura officiating over the movers, her Lutheran parents ferreting around like gray typifications of I-told-you-so, made Pym take another swing at the air with the hammer. Grinding them into dog meat was way too good for them.

Pym went to the antiquated answering machine on the table beside the yellow couch and pressed the flashing red light. One message only. Not Laura, not George, but Estelle:

"It's a cold night, Gil, and you left me alone. That was so embarrassing. But I forgive you. I figured you'd come back to Nye's but I guess you had to be stubborn. Please call me when you get in. It don't matter what time. I'm worried about you."

Pym sat on the couch, pulled off his boots, and put his feet on the coffee table. Arranged neatly at the table's center sat a pile of unopened mail. He went through it, setting the junk aside. Ultimately the only item he didn't set aside was a thick, rectangular envelope with his name and address scratched on the front in black ink as if the author were on his deathbed. The postmark over the stamp proved too obscure to read. He ripped open the envelope and pulled forth a stack of postcards—it looked like several dozen—bound by an elastic band. They smelled faintly of sweet perfume.

A yellow Post-it note on the top of the stack said, in red ballpoint ink, "Read this in order." It was his brother's printing, beautifully artistic, almost a new font design. Pym peeled the note off the top of the first postcard and was taken aback by the top image, a gloomy picture of a cave entrance. He turned the card over.

> *There is much to tell and you must listen deeply. Come closer, lift your eyebrows and think of nothing else but where the words take you. If you choose to listen and see, to interpret the story as you know you can, we will go to Hell together and bring back the ones we love. As an epic tale should, let this one begin late at night on bridges over dark rivers; and let us meet ourselves as we often are, alone, afraid, and looking into darkness.*

The message on the postcard was typical of George's poetic tastes, written in the rational neat cursive which won him praise and prizes in junior high; the scrawled, written-out address on the envelope belonged to someone else. He flicked through all the cards; they were all written in the same red ink.

The next postcard, a color photograph of some sort of megalithic monument, said only:

> *One foot in the womb tomb!*

In tiny Celtic lettering at the base of the card was printed: *New Grange, Co. Meath, Ireland.*

It would be a chore to plow through the entire stack of George's crap. The lazy bastard couldn't write a novel; no, he'd claim that a story told with postcards was an avant-garde response to American consumers with pitifully short attention spans.

George, who majored in Humanities and French, was a prolific reader, whereas Pym had taken a few classes in literature as general requirements then promptly forgotten everything in favor of books on architecture and business. The cave was an obvious reference to the entrance to the underworld. Or was it that thing from Kafka? The womb tomb reference was something George had lectured him about long ago, but he couldn't recall its significance, something about the recycling of life. This was the great flaw in George's plan for educating his kid brother: he assumed Pym had a memory—a deeply erroneous assumption; anything intellectual flew from Pym's brain like a flock of swallows.

Who was it went to the underworld? Orpheus, Theseus? Who else? He knew there were others. What was George driving at and who are we going to bring back from the dead? Dad? Our friendship? Is he forgiving me? Confusing—always trying to educate the jackass. Who the hell is it with one foot in the womb tomb?

He left the cards he'd read neatly turned on their faces with the remaining stack awaiting his eyes later. He felt too exhausted to deal with George's games tonight, but he couldn't help seeing the next one—a black and white picture of a grunge-dressed youth with cropped hair, dyed almost white, sitting on one of those suppository shaped pedestrian bollards. The boy's jeans were pulled down and his face displayed a theatrical expression of ecstasy. Pym groaned and turned the card over to read:

> *Gillie, my darling sibling, here begins our life in sound bites. One reason I have come to New Orleans is to escape all the information in Minneapolis. It's overwhelming; everyone's so well informed. I was being grilled like a fish on the fire of my own inadequacies. Here in Fat City nobody knows anything. As you would so eloquently render this situation: They're a dumb bunch of fucks. Love, Georgie.*

Pym rubbed his face in a frenzy and shouted, "What the hell? You're in New Orleans? You're kidding me! Crazy fat turkey!"

When George found out from Laura that his wife and brother were having an affair he deflated into depression. When George was upset he let everyone know it, but he got himself under control, moved in with his friend Mishawn, and told Estelle she would have to find her own way in life. Estelle liked to control George; controlling someone had a calming influence on her, and she was used to him. Surprised and hurt that George would dump her, pouting and expecting forgiveness, Estelle floundered for a while until it became clear that George wouldn't relent—he seldom did— and then she got over it. George continued to successfully team up with her at their prosperous little hair salon, but they were not to stay married. Estelle threw herself into her bodybuilding and aerobics. She maintained the self-improvement kick that George had started her on—foreign films and instant vocabulary books. Once she felt free of all obligation to George, she came after the moping Gilbert Pym like an Amazon in heat.

One Saturday morning George turned up at the house and put his arms around Pym. "Now listen, Gillie," George had said. "I have something important to tell you, and I think maybe you're the only one who doesn't know yet, because you're just such an ostrich."

Pym, rolling his eyes, said, "Let me have it before the media get involved."

"I'm gay, Gillie."

Pym could still hear the words. *I'm gay, Gillie.* And true to form, Pym screwed the whole thing up like the loser he'd always been. All his frustrations—his strangled ambition, the loss of Laura, his company's stock plummeting and the job dissolving—it all exploded in George's face and Pym ripped him a new asshole, called him a disgrace, a fuck-wad, a fat fucking faggot.

About the stupidest thing you can do in life is to be hosing your brother's old lady and then call him a fat fucking faggot on the same day he comes to forgive you and come out of the closet. Christ! *Fat fucking faggot.* What an asinine thing to say to the best brother a man could have. He looked after you from the start, he carried you on his back, he saved you from Ma. He raised you. Asshole! Motherfucker! You absolute worthless bag of rat shit.

Estelle, anticipating final victory, had rushed to spill all George's secrets, and Pym, to his shame, had listened.

The memory of Estelle, sitting in bed cross-legged with her vagina exposed like a lily, her big, rounded breasts perking up like something out of a Hindu temple and telling marital tales, set off a blood surge in Pym's loins. Even in the face of his agony over the loss of Laura, the thought of Estelle could send his emotions in a completely different direction. He knew this wasn't normal; something had gone wrong with him. Her breasts were like the opiate of the people! He couldn't remember who had said that. Groucho Marx? Love was one thing, but the allure of Estelle was quite another. No doubt it had much to do with her lovely face, shaped oddly like his mother's, with naturally elegant black eyebrows and irises as blue as morning glories—and those big lips made for kissing. Her powerful but sleek arms and slender wrists earned her the nickname *Wonder Woman* at the gym where they worked out. *Please call me when you get in. It don't matter what time. I'm worried about you.* The timbre of her voice sent a charge from the base of his skull to his prostate.

He should hate Estelle's guts—she ruined his life; hell, she helped ruin George's life. Her unfaithfulness to his brother, her contempt for anything to do with Laura—nothing put him off. He had zero resistance—he was a hopeless addict. He loved to just get her and hold her down and fuck her. It was never enough and he was always sore—he had to use a special cream. Then he'd suddenly dump her in the hope that Laura would hear of it and think he'd finally come to his senses and decide to return to him. But he couldn't sustain the separation and would let the image of Estelle take control of his mind and he'd soon be at her again like a frenzied chimp.

Then this guy Ray arrives on the scene and hell gushes into your basement. Pym shook his head. You should go back to the bridge… jump in the goddamn river why don't you?

The furnace thumped off.

Quiet.

He slipped out of his coat.

After a while Pym turned around and gazed at the door into the kitchen. He wiped tears out of his eyes and, frowning, looked around his dingy living room. It remained the way Laura had left it when she went to her mother's, yet tonight it looked different, a strange tinge he didn't like—a sort of menace. Something nasty that wasn't there before now inhabited the atmosphere of the house. He dialed Estelle's number. She answered immediately and said, "Oh, Gil. Jesus."

"You're a pain in the ass," he said.

"Yes, Master," she said.

"Cut that out, it won't work."

"Please, Master, I need you."

Pym laughed, said, "Man, what is it with you?"

With relief in her voice, Estelle said, "I'll be right over. Get the bed warmed up. I don't gotta go nowhere in the morning for once. I'll fix you breakfast."

Emotion rose in him. He closed his eyes.

"Are you there, Gil?"

"I'm here."

"You okay?"

"I don't get what you see in me. I'm a jerk."

"You been acting like a bit of a jerk. Don't mean you are one inside."

"Don't you agree that our actions define us?"

"Bit heavy for me, baby. All I know is you got great insides, you're the greatest guy, you just…"

"I feel like my brain's on fire."

"You know all this'll pass, and when it does I'll be there for you. Gotta gimme a chance, hon."

"It's not about you, Stella. I know I blame you when I get mad at myself and I'm sorry for that. Make sure you quote me next time. Shut me up. I feel like I'm becoming my mother. I'm just like her."

"Well, Nina don't look at herself like you're doing, that's for sure. She goes off and finds a new bar to cause trouble in... that's her answer."

"Maybe that's right though, just drift through life and make sure you don't get too wound up by it."

"Come on, you don't believe that."

"I dunno. Nothing seems to phase her."

"But she's horrible."

"Ah, Christ, she's just my excuse."

"Snap out of it now. You've had a good old tantrum."

"Tantrum?"

"You really let me have it in Nye's."

"I guess I should make it up to you."

"What are you going to do to me when I get there?"

"I'm going to fuck you and then kick you out in the snow."

"Yeah, right. Like you could, with your little pussy arms."

"Get here, you bimbo."

"Do you got bread and eggs and stuff?"

"Sure."

"There in ten."

"Hey?"

"Yes, hon."

"Has George contacted you?"

"No, hon."

"Shit."

"Be right there."

Pym went into the bathroom and lifted the toilet seat. He watched his clear urine foaming in the water. How many times had he pissed like this? How many times had he rammed his dick into Estelle? In just a few months it was now more than his entire marriage to Laura. He examined himself in the mirror of the medicine cabinet and hated the stupid face reflected there. What did Estelle see in him? He was a thinner model of his brother—the uncircumcised, blonde version. He flushed the toilet, and the swirling water represented all the tears he would shed if he could let himself.

A blue plastic safety razor rested in the sink; the casing had been stripped from the blade and the blade must have fallen down the plughole. A few tiny, red-brown hairs littered the porcelain. He usually put his razors back in the medicine cabinet but he must have been careless. He couldn't understand it. He opened the cabinet to get toothpaste and brush and, as the image of his own face moved, revealing other parts of the bathroom, he gave himself a fright by imagining his brother's face suddenly appearing beside his in the reflection. He wanted Estelle to arrive as soon as possible. He cleaned his teeth, then went and lay naked in the cold bed. His stomach pulsed and his armpits ached, but the anticipation of Estelle's arrival made his stomach flutter.

Pym was dreaming about George when a woman slipped into bed beside him. She felt refrigerated against his bed-heated skin, her nipples as hard as princess-peas. Until she gasped, "God, it's cold. Gotta get that heater fixed," he thought it was Laura coming home late from the hospital.

"How can you stand me?" she giggled, shivering against him.

"It feels good," he muttered, slipping back into the dream. George was in the basement with the tool bag, trying to replace the furnace. The furnace was ripped apart and the tools scattered, and he didn't know what the hell he was doing. Where the hell's Dad, Gillie? George kept asking him. Has someone been fucking with my tools? Pym's nose was being sucked, bringing him awake. He sniffed Estelle's breath—tonight she hadn't spoiled it by smoking. He kissed her, slid his tongue into her lovely mouth, felt her smooth teeth, felt her sucking back at him. She broke away, breathing heavily and bit his bottom lip while stroking his buttocks. He woke up a bit and tried to feign indifference. "You're deathly cold," he said, "like a corpse."

"Ish," she said.

"A very buxom corpse," he said, shifting position.

Estelle gently pulled Pym's foreskin forward with her cold fingers and nuzzled her knee between the pillow and the side of his face. She whispered, "How about a little necrophilia then—warm up the dead girl?"

His body, tumescent and lost in Estelle's beauty, suddenly teemed with vitality. He rolled onto her and she went with his movement, shifting weight so that he slid between her opening legs, her ankles quickly clasping behind his hamstrings, drawing him with a gasp into her tight warmth. She felt long and slim and cool.

She gazed big-eyed into his face, gritting her teeth, one hand lost in the hair on the back of his head, the other, like a child's, holding his bicep, and whispered, "You don't get it, do you? How much I love you." She shook his head like he was clueless, and then deep in his ear whispered, "I'm all yours, Gilbert Pym."

111

Estelle had waited at Nye's Polonaise room but Gil didn't come back. People had watched him go nuts on her; it didn't matter that they were just Nordeast barflies, she still felt like crawling under a rock. His arms flying everywhere—yelling and swearing. They sat near the door and all the singers standing around the piano went quiet and stared. And then to have to wait, scared to miss his return, and sitting alone like a loser. She left after an hour, drove home to the island, and changed out of her work clothes. They stank of bar and she threw them in the hamper. Then she called Gil's answering machine and left the best message she could muster. Boy, he was a hard man to love; he was in a big muddle. But he was better than anyone else. Gil's crazy shit was nothing compared to George's.

That mother of theirs. Jeez.

She felt a constant tingling inside her, which was pleasant but needed satisfying. It mightn't just mean she was horny for Gil; it could spell the onset of a bladder infection, which would be no fun at all. She felt a buzzing in the hips, only faint, and wanted to be wedged together with him, kissing. She wanted him to say, "Stella, I love you so much, baby. I know I'm mean sometimes, but I'm just in a muddle at the moment and I'll get over it and we'll settle down and everything will be okay. I love you, baby. I'm never gonna let you go."

She knew how funny this was but she wasn't going to give up hope. She went into the white bedroom and lay on the bed naked. The house felt warm. She loved looking at herself in the mirror above the bed. If she were Gil she wouldn't be able to resist herself. She wanted to make him say, "God, I'm so proud of you, baby. You work so hard at looking good. It ain't just good genes. I have to have you right now."

28

God, if he'd only call. And what the hell was he still so hung up with Laura for? She's a stick figure. Snap her like a dry twig! Laura liked clean sex, Gil had admitted—she couldn't sleep in the wet spot. And the way she'd gone off with that Ray as soon as she did. Bitch. There was revenge in that move—mean—not a thing Estelle would ever do. Laura knew how territorial Gil was; she knew what it did to him. Laura should have given them both a little time to settle things. It was nasty—how can Gil get over it now?

It was a horrible empty feeling with Gil out there all pissed off and damaged. Please God, let him calm down. Please let him call. She lowered the ringer a bit on the phone beside the bed in case he called and startled the hell out of her. Not that she'd be able to sleep. How could she sleep with him out there like that, wandering around like a bum?

She used the remote to turn on the television. It opened to Public TV—some depressing English soap with ugly actors and a dialect she couldn't understand. Why don't they have subtitles? CNN was all massacres and the burning of Hindu widows. The Weather Channel said it was just gonna get colder. So she put on the NASA Channel and watched through the eye of a satellite as it looked down on Madagascar. She practiced kegels as she alternately watched the television and herself in the mirror above the bed.

Resist, don't be bad, Gil may call when he's had enough of being grumpy.

She was good for ten seconds, then, with her middle finger, gave her clitoris a light tap, sending a shudder through her. The room's warmth and the big comforter made her feel luxurious. She didn't do it often, but sometimes she liked to just get into it on her own to let her mind run free. It was so much more fun with the mirror George had installed above the bed. Her nipples swelled; she wasn't going to be good; it would get her mind off old mister grumpy guts.

She imagined Gilbert nice like he was before the shit hit the fan. He'd lie between her legs kissing her, adoring her face, and she could come with hardly any movement at all if she thought about having his baby. What a baby it would be! She tried to feel it in her belly, the weight of it, its kicking. She imagined the moment when conception took place and a shudder went through her. She threaded her hands under her buttocks and pulled apart her thighs from behind. Her toes pirouetted, buttocks off the mattress, as her vagina opened in the mirror above the bed. With her fingers spread on either side of her petals she tugged them further open and imagined the dark cave that appeared there full of pushing scalp, the wet head of a new and holy child.

The phone rang and Estelle jumped half out of her skin—saw her own startled face in the mirror. George's voice said, "Don't be there in the morning, I'm coming over to get the last of my shit and I want to be alone."

"George. Hey, I had another fight with Gil."

"So what? It's not my problem."

"He needs you. Lighten up."

"You promised me you wouldn't tell him I was here. If you do…"

"I keep my promises."

"Don't make me laugh."

"Just the marriage vow. But it weren't no marriage, was it, hon? Stop being a prick."

"Don't tell him."

"I won't. But you should. Go see him, he's going crazy—I'm serious."

"You know I can't face him. He'll sit me down and he'll reason with me—after he's bludgeoned me with insults. I don't want anyone talking reason. Anyway, I was over there tonight. I needed some stuff."

"What stuff? I coulda gotten it for you. He might've walked in on you."

"You couldn't have gotten the stuff I needed. And he always goes out Fridays."

"Did you leave him a note or anything?"

"I left him something to ponder."

"Then he's gonna know you was there! So what's the point in all this secrecy? God, George, you are so goddamn stupid."

"Don't call me stupid. I had something sent by mail."

"But did you leave any trace of being in the house?"

"I may have."

"There, you see—stupid. He'll know you were there and he'll be even more depressed."

"I didn't think of that. I'm on all this medication. You can't always think straight."

"What have they done to you?"

"I'm a hell of a lot thinner for one thing, so don't be knocking it."

"How did that happen so fast?"

"Roux-en-y."

"Speak English."

"This is a full service outfit I'm hooked up with down there," George laughed. "Everything you need to become a sexy, middle-aged woman—toy boys, sex toys, counseling, and gastric by-passes. I have liposuction scheduled to get rid of my love handles."

"Life doesn't have to be about being thin, George. I've told you before…"

"Easy for you to say."

"I work out, George. It's a lot cheaper."

"Don't start. You know I'm allergic to my own sweat."

"Another of your excuses, babe."

"I gotta do what I gotta do."

"I know. There's no stopping you when you…"

"So don't tell him anything."

"Okay already."

"Leave the key under the geranium pot. I left my goddamn keys in New Orleans."

"How'd you get into Gil's place, then?"

"That loose basement window."

"My, you *have* lost weight."

"Don't be there in the morning."

"So I can't even see you?"

"No. I'll be in touch."

"Wait."

"What now?"

"Where can I get hold of you?"

"I'll get hold of you when I'm ready. I'm somewhere safe. I'm outta here tomorrow anyway."

"I mean down there."

"No way. If I tell you, he'll get it out of you. He has to find me himself. He has to use his brains, get his mind back, quit being a shallow little shit. He has to… hell… I gotta go, Estelle."

"Wait."

"Estelle, sweetheart, I have to go."

"What's it like down there?"

"It's the land of the dead, Stella."

"Don't sound too healthy to me."

"The grateful dead. You wouldn't understand."

31

"You have to help Gilbert. Somehow. You don't get it. He's really losing it—I ain't pissing you. Laura brought her new guy Ray over to fix the washer and Gil had to sit there while they were all lovey-dovey. She's such a bitch. He can't let go of her in his head."

"Then how come he's fucking you till your kidneys bleed?"

"I dunno. I'm not a psychiatrist. I know I'm his future, but I don't know how to make him let go of his past. You're supposed to be the clever one. You help him. I need you to do this, for him and me."

"You want him very badly, don't you?"

"I do, George. God, I really do."

"Your poor little heart. I hope it won't get broken. Gillie can be a tornado when he gets going."

"I know it, but he's so great underneath."

"It's true, he's always been like that. That's why I love him despite all the crap he's pulled on me. He's two-thirds god and one-third asshole. But the asshole part is going to receive its comeuppance."

Estelle began to cry. She pulled the comforter over herself. "I can't get enough of him. Please don't let anything bad happen."

"Is it love or sexual addiction?"

"It's love, you cynical—"

"All right, all right."

"Help him."

"I already have. I did something that will help."

"What?"

"I made a few calls. He's going to have to come down to New Orleans soon, and he's not going to like that. Make sure you encourage him. I have this big plan that'll end up in a party to end all parties. Laura's even in on it."

"Laura, but not me?"

"She's more trustworthy than you."

"You asshole."

"Anyway, you're in on it now."

"And you guarantee that this will help him settle down so's he'll be with me?"

"You know there are no guarantees in life, but by the time I'm done with Gillie he'll be in a different place."

"I love him so much."

"You're lucky, Estelle."

"How? His head's full of that stupid, zippy Olive Oyl bitch. And he's fretting over you disappearing. He's been talking a lot about your dad's suicide. And he hates drawing unemployment."

"I'll get it all back in balance, but right now I gotta stay low and keep moving. If he saw me right now he'd freak."

"Do you look different, hon?"

"A lot."

"Are you happy?"

"Not yet. But I'm planning on being happy."

"When's the big operation?"

"Real soon."

"Isn't it a lot all at once?"

"Yes, but I can take it. I want some time to enjoy it."

"I love you, George. Remember, you're not indestructible."

"Georgie."

"Okay—Georgie. I hope this works for you."

"I love you too, Stella. Good night now."

The satellite camera switched to the Outer Hebrides. Estelle went back to doing her kegels and then did some slow stretches, all the time watching the workings of her muscles in the mirror above her. She pulled out the Xandria catalogue and leafed through it, looking at all the fascinating sex toys she could no longer play with because Gil didn't approve of anything artificial. He made her promise to throw away all the sex toys she'd collected with George, but she'd hidden them in the attic.

When Gil finally called she was all hot in the face from stretching, and her heart started to pound at the sound of his voice. And when she replaced the receiver she didn't even know what she'd said, she was so happy—something about breakfast.

IV

Despite his body being in alarm at the roaring in his blood, Pym didn't want to wake up. The bed shook. What is this, a poltergeist, an earthquake, the house being crushed by an ice floe flushing down the Mississippi? Mother, in a mighty rage, slammed the walls of the basement with a sledgehammer. She came out of the dark at him with a big knife. Laura shook him out of his nightmare and her sweet friendly voice asked, "What's going on in that complicated head of yours, Mr. Pimstone? I'm not involved with Ray, George hasn't left you, your dad's still alive."

When Pym dragged himself fully awake, he understood that a jet liner had passed low over the house. Laura's voice remained in his ears and her face in the dark dissolved before his eyes. He pulled the curtain aside in time to see the plane skim over downtown, the lights of its undercarriage flashing. The plane was unusually low. You shouldn't fly so near skyscrapers these days. The noise had not woken Estelle.

"Stella, how could you sleep through that?"

Dead still.

"Hello?"

"A corpse," Pym whispered, expecting her to laugh. "The undead. Doesn't show up in mirrors." Estelle's face indeed looked livid in the sparse light. She looked like a woman in a coffin. He made sure of her breathing, and then he played with her nipples like they were the controls of a video game. He rolled them in the palms of his hands like the Karate Kid—wax on, wax off. He knew she wasn't faking because her nipples were soft. "God, you are one tired chick, what the hell have you been doing?"

He considered sexing her as she slept. Never once had he had such a thought about Laura; in fact, his body hardly reacted to Laura, but now that she belonged to Ray, he could barely function. He wondered if George had felt that way, or still did, about Estelle.

The flow of insight was like water torture.

He got up to pee and returned to bed with frozen feet. He wanted Estelle to wake up and fuck him long and hard so he wouldn't have to think. He'd willed himself to not be afraid of the dark. But the fear was always there, hovering beneath his rationality. He understood it was just insecurity—a caveman response to fear; attach imagery to the unknown—ghosts and vampires and zombies—like when he was a kid and George and his mother used to frighten the shit out of him. His childhood terror of the dark, of an implied spirit world, threatened to burst from the place he'd imprisoned it all these years. His mother's awful stories. He'd long ago given up the struggle with religion because if there was a supreme being controlling everything then there sure as hell could be malevolent spirits and god-knows-what-else accompanying such a deity. No, thanks.

As he warmed up he tried to fall asleep and not think, but the thoughts came anyway, delivering adrenaline and increased heart rate, then gut wrenching, like electric snakes inside him trying to push out through his navel. Sometimes the acid saliva of the snakes pushed up into his throat, but at last he fell into a fitful sleep where the snakes emerged and entangled both him and Estelle, slithering in and out of their orifices and securing them together like a package headed to Hell. Finally, he woke himself and chose the agony of self-seeing over the horrors lurking in dreamland.

Pym's worst betrayal was laughing with Estelle about George. Ignoring the increasing silence of his dad all those years ago was bad enough; being unfaithful to Laura had become such a habit that he could still only view it in terms of how it affected him; he probably could've kept his job too if he hadn't been running around telling everybody to fuck off. When he saw it all together in his mind it made him gag. But that wasn't the worst.

Before the shit hit the fan, Pym and Estelle were in George's bed at the house on Peter Pan Island in the middle of the river. It was a round white bed with a mirror affixed to the ceiling above it. Pym rested with his head sunk in the pillow, Estelle propped next to him. She'd pulled a big vanity mirror around because she liked to observe herself from all angles during sex. She touched the end of his nose and said, "I bet I know more about your anatomy than you do."

Pym grunted. Estelle tried to gently stick her red-nailed pinkie up his ass, and he laughed and squirmed away. She frowned, head to one side, and said, "Don't you like that?"

"Not particularly," he said. "But if it turns you on we can negotiate."

"Seriously. That ain't a turn on?"

"It's weird."

Estelle shrugged and said, "Your brother don't think so."

"Oh?"

"And others I know about—in my limited experience."

"Yeah, right."

She got in close to him and said, "I'm gonna stimulate your prostate and jump you again. It improves the turn-around time for a girl."

"Not with this puppy, you're not," laughed Pym.

"Your brother couldn't do without it."

"Explain."

She licked inside Pym's ear, moved her tongue around, and whispered, "I'm the one who does the penetrating in this family."

"No clue what you're talking about."

"Come on, Gil, don't make me give details."

Sitting up and laughing, Pym said, "That's exactly what I'm gonna make you give."

Estelle told Pym how over the years the sex between she and George went from unsatisfactory to nonexistent and then, after a month of couple's therapy, to the slightly abnormal and then to the wild and kinky, with her sometimes playing a sort of Bridget Nielsen role, strapping on an expensive, foreign-made dildo, purchased off the Internet. After a while George took to wearing her underwear to have sex in, and, as a result of this, could no longer accomplish the male role normally unless Estelle made him play a domineering dyke—her favorite game, of course.

Pym slid off the bed in a fit of laughter; there was nothing more grotesquely ridiculous than the picture in his mind's eye of his huge brother cavorting in stretched-to-the-limit lingerie.

Estelle swore she'd remained faithful to George throughout all these changes and she believed he'd been faithful to her too. It was safe—a slightly fucked-up heterosexual playing out fantasies—no harm in it. But after a while she wearied of the game and needed a rollicking good screw with a narrow-minded, testosterone-filled stud. Pym laughed and said, "So you chose me!"

"'Zactly," she said. "You're his brother—it seems less like adultery."

"I'm flattered."

Estelle glanced into the mirror and shrugged as though there was a television camera in there observing everything. "There," she said to the audience behind the mirror, turning her wrist over at the grinning Pym. "See?"

Pym grilled her on whether or not her obsessive bodybuilding had anything to do with wanting to be more like a man to counter George's nascent effeminacy, and she vigorously said no, of course not, it wasn't that serious. She just liked herself muscular, that's all, and she told him to get out of her face. Pym ignored her and laughed. "I wonder how you look with a big dick strapped on you."

She thought for a second, then said, "Good."

"Come on then, show me."

"No way. I'd never hear the end of it."

"You won't anyway."

"You are a bastard, you know."

"And you're a naive fool to let George talk you into all this sick shit."

"Naive maybe, but I could teach you a thing or two."

Pym got all mad at that because it implied she'd had more lovers than he, and that made him sick with a sort of loss of honor and it took them an hour to be friends again. When they finally made up, Estelle said, "I was just having fun. You're too sensitive, like George. You'll end up taking it in the rear."

"Is that right?" Pym mused, and then suddenly grabbed her and held her face down in the pillow and proceeded to get her in the rear. She squawked and squealed, laughing and bucking, calling him a pervert. When they were done, Estelle got up and fetched a warm, soapy towel and cleaned him up. As she did this, her hair hung over his belly and he thought of Mary Magdalene and her friend Jesus. Estelle nestled under his legs and licked his balls with closed eyes, and in a dreamy, distant voice said, "God, Gil, I love this with you. Never go away."

But go away he did, as always, back home to Laura who bounded up to him at the door, thinking he'd been off working out hard at Gold's Gym. He hated himself for betraying her at these moments—her innocent, rather plain face with no guile in it. How could he be doing this with a woman who was Laura's opposite? He coped with his guilt by simply not thinking about it; this was something he'd learned from his mother. When he asked her how she had handled all the fucked-up crap that had passed through her life, she growled in her smoky voice, "I put it aside, boy. The past is the past and I refuse to think on it. I think about what's up next and what's in the present moment. Your dad, Michael, he was a big dreamer—everything was a symbol. He drove us all crazy."

Pym had loved his dad; his mother knew this and sought opportunities to alter Pym's mind. This only made him more loyal to his father and finally he told his mother to stop doing it and they quarreled badly and she still wasn't over it. Nina would reincarnate as a skunk. She wasn't a nice person although she tried to look like one. She made a good living as a psychic and her clients thought she was wonderful and authentic, especially with the quarter Ojibwe blood she claimed. Pym was close to her when he was young; she opened him up very wide—same with George a decade earlier when she was much younger. She had that certain something and Estelle was very like her... big, athletic, raven hair, blue eyes—a sexiness so alluring it felt artificial, a gollum fashioned by infernal forces, a design so cunning that men would never suspect they were being drawn to destruction.

Pym knew this was nonsense, so it was easy for him to believe Estelle was only outwardly like his mother. Estelle wasn't truly promiscuous and he understood why a woman like her would need a man like him. And he understood why he needed a wife exactly the opposite: Laura—dependable, logical and steeped in integrity, which, once turned against him, was pretty final.

On the day George forgave him for having an affair with Estelle—which resulted in the big row, which was all Pym's fault, for which he would never forgive himself—George kept calling Pym a bastard. Everyone had been calling him that lately but for George to keep saying this was weird. "My righteous brother, the bastard," George would say, or, "My bastard little brother." Finally, Pym said, "Quit with this bastard shit already, you great fairy."

"You *are* a bastard, you know. Nobody's told you. Now you deserve to know."

"What are you babbling about?"

"She had you in wedlock, but you're not Dad's."

Pym took a swing at George but missed. George jumped away and screamed, "So now you're going to beat me up too!"

"I'm going to gut you, you damn pie wagon!"

Staying on the other side of the sofa, George asked, "What have you become?"

"Me? Christ, what in the fuck've you become? Jabba the Hut with a lisp?"

George's eyes became slits; Pym had never seen spite in his face. "I've always been like this, you bastard—it was only you and people like you with your hilarious put downs that stopped me admitting it. I thought, with the shit you've just pulled, that you'd cut me some slack when I admitted to you that I was gay. And always have been. Jesus fucking H Christ! You pig!"

Pym calmed down at the sight of his brother's flushed cheeks. He sat in the armchair. "Okay, then. I'll stay reasonable if you do. First tell me about this bastard stuff, but don't think I'm giving you a break on the faggot thing."

"I was here," George snarled, "when that Limey roadie fella lived with us for a summer. I was nine." George pounded the yellow sofa he was standing behind. "And he slept on this piece of yellow shit. Early every morning after Dad left for the bakery, Mom would come down and fuck him. I'd hear her having orgasms from my bedroom—she didn't care who heard. Dad knew, but he was cooler than all of us. Then you were on the way and she walked around as if she had some goddamn prince in her belly. But of course he never came back. He stayed over there in Limeyland with his own people. And after a while she shut up about it and realized what a mess she'd caused. I was sworn to secrecy forever. Fuck that now! And look how you're turning out—just like her and that dirty rat who slept on our couch for a summer at Dad's invitation. I never let it bother me and neither did Dad. You were one of us, but the truth is you're all her. You selfish little shit. Who needs you? Fuck you, Gillie, I'm outta here."

The easiest thing to get over in all of this was that he wasn't really his kind old father's son, but the offspring of some skinny rocker who got dumped in Minneapolis by his band while awaiting a court date on a drug charge. Pym knew the story, just not the affair part. But it didn't surprise him. He looked a bit different—blonde hair and a thin straight nose. He'd always been his own man, paddled his own canoe, as his dad would say. It didn't change anything. He wondered briefly about this new father and saw in his mind's eye a longhaired man with rotted teeth and sunken cheeks, begging on the London Underground like the homeless men he had seen during his London honeymoon with Laura. That nameless guy had nothing to do with Gilbert Langley Pym.

The losses were such now that the river seemed the best option—a few minutes of acute discomfort and then, after a struggle against his decision, oblivion; but, he reasoned, in the absence of any belief in divine judgment, he might as well stay alive in the warm bedclothes, if only to see what happens next. The only comfort was that he could lose himself between Estelle's muscular thighs; perhaps one day he would end by suffocating between them, drawn back to a womb like a grateful babe. The river would gradually freeze and the life in it would move slower and slower until it was forced to dig itself into the mud.

V

On Wednesday morning, after a fitful night, Terry pulled aside Vera's hair and stuck his tongue in her ear, making her shriek and slap at him under the duvet.

"Which is more unbearable," he asked, "the first or the second penetration of the tip of my tongue into your ear cavity?"

"There's no distinction," Vera grumbled. "They both mean sleep is over and that my role as tea-slave is about to begin."

"How about coffee this morning?"

"Oh, God. The America influence already?"

"Merely a whim, that's all."

"You're a bozo."

"I'm pure slime, darling, I know."

"One day you'll be exposed by the *News of the World*. Prominent psychologist takes brutal advantage of disfigured tea-slave."

"Oh, darling."

"I'm going to get your beverage now and then I'm going to make you earn your place in this nest."

"Yes, my dear, anything—even the hateful and beastly act of common copulation."

"I suppose you'll want the paper?"

"Unless you already know how Arsenal did last night."

Shaking her head, Vera slipped out of bed and opened the curtain, careful to keep her back to him. "Why would I know about Arsenal?" she asked. "Sod Arsenal, they're my greatest rival for your affection. I hate Arsenal."

You're wrong about that, Terry thought, as a vision of Nina Pym leapt ahead of Arsenal in the queue for his affections. He felt bad having such an impulse, and asked, "How's your arm feel this morning?"

"Like there's a wasp stinging my armpit."

"Dear me. When do we see Broughton?"

"Eleven-thirty. Now, coffee… black or white?"

"Black, please—two brown sugars."

As Vera pulled on her dressing gown, Terry held back a thunderclap of sorrow that threatened to leap out in a yell. Vera saved him by fleeing down the stairs, avoiding further talk of her illness.

Instead of breast reconstruction, Vera had opted for beautiful tattoos of exotic plants blended in with the silvery scales of her scarring, but Terry told her once that it was a bit like looking at an Edwardian curtain, which rather damaged her feelings. Fool! Thoughtless buffoon! Now, with the first indication that she had fallen out of remission facing her, they both knew that given how bad the treatments had been the first time, she would refuse any further treatment. Nevertheless, she was full of fight. "This bloody National Health, I don't know if I ever even had cancer. I was probably a guinea pig for their trainees."

He loved her attitude and told her that when she was angry the plant tattoos transformed into snakes, and she liked that. Snake woman, although she was really plant woman, rain forest plant woman, rain forest where all the plants that cured cancer are being cut down to make room for more bullshit.

But the National Health Service was not to blame.

Vera once had breasts to make a blind man see.

Before the relapse Vera had no doubt she was cured. She believed Terry would eventually adjust, love her the way she was. Her confidence shamed him. He didn't have the heart to say what he really wanted, which was for her to have as much reconstruction as possible, become a silicone goddess! But it wasn't her way, just as it wasn't her way to colour her hair or shave her armpits. She was a walking protest. Love me as I am! It was all perfectly reasonable in theory, but the sex part had become problematic.

Probably all moot now. Stop! Think positive!

But you make the best of it. He loved the way her back came down in a Y shape and then tightly rounded into her bottom and down to her strong legs. He used to be a big breast man but now he'd become a bum man. And what a bum she still had! *Fat bottom girls, you make the rockin' world go round.* He laid stiff and still for a minute, controlling his emotion lest she come up and see his raw eyes and know his sadness. One thing he could take off her shoulders was the burden of his own sorrow.

The bedroom needed tidying. No time for that these days. The master bedroom... the boudoir. He loved the sloping walls and spacious floors of the remodeled attic. Thick beige carpet, white walls, and deep window wells looked different from the other rooms in the late-period Georgian townhouse. Good windows and insulation shut out the city's noise. The neighborhood, splendid in its early days, then neglected, now enjoyed gentrification because of the housing squeeze in Central London. Terry and Vera moved in when it was cheap, back when they were still socialists. They volunteered for Amnesty International and went on marches with Tariq Ali in those days. Now, because of the house, they were rich—at least on paper. The house would sell for a million quid at current prices, but they loved it and had resisted opportunities to convert it into flats. It was packed with books and music and all the bumf they never threw away after trips to third world countries.

They remodeled only one room themselves, the kitchen—ultra modern, lots of double glazing, with an old-looking stone stairway down to the shaded little back garden with high walls. Terry listened to Vera down there now, crashing around, indulging her routine in her favourite room. It was the only room in the house that remained tidy. Vera simply would not tolerate an invasion of their mess. Terry was the same with the garden. They both had their tidy domains. The rest of the house was chaos. Best to tidy as you go, but... and then for her to have to leave her lovely kitchen. Her heart might be breaking down there. He wanted to run down to her and hold her, but she would know why he was coming. His footfalls on the stairs would give him away, and, just in case she wasn't thinking about death, his distraught intrusion would only set her off. Peace, leave her in peace.

Vera brought coffee and the newspaper; it baffled him how she did it so quickly. They read the paper as they had done for many years, with her propped up by a pillow against the bed's endboard and her cold toes nestled into his crotch, while they sipped their coffees. She read the serious news while he read the sports, then the books section, then the travel. He would read the serious news on the bus and leave the paper on the seat.

Today, caught between the excitement of having a son and the hollowness that had become present in him since Vera told him the prognosis of her checkup, Terry only went through the motions of reading the sports page. Arsenal's nil-nil draw in the Champion's League barely mattered. Vera had asked, "Are you willing to share him?" It made his heart ache. He didn't deserve her, couldn't bear the thought of life without her. Never to see her again? But there would be a son—and insurance money.

He slapped himself.

"What on earth are you doing?"

"Nothing."

"You just slapped yourself."

"I did not."

"Indeed you did."

"You're mistaken, my love."

"You bloody well did. You're losing it, mate."

He took her toes and kissed them under the blanket. *Losing it, mate.* Yes, that was it, wasn't it? Losing her and it. He sucked her toes and played between them with his tongue in the darkness under the duvet so she couldn't see his eyes, until he sensed her arousal. After a while, in a young breathless voice, Vera said, "Darling, if you're going to be that dedicated to my toes I do wish you'd move your nice face up to the other end of my legs."

Next on the morning's agenda would be a few minutes of vigorous inter-course. Since the removal of her breasts this had become harder to do. There had been embarrassing failures and his own ejaculations were more often than not devoid of intensity. To combat this, he invoked in his mind images of the women of his past. Always present, the hovering shadow of Nina Pym, a mag-nificent specimen of womanhood. Today she returned to him on that yellow couch in Minneapolis, on top of him, hair flying, breasts bouncing...

Fifteen minutes later, he was dozing with his head in the small of Vera's back, as she read the travel section propped up on her elbows.

"Gosh," she said.

"Hmmmmmm...?"

"Serendipity strikes!"

"What, darling...?"

"Reasonably good fares to American cities. Cheap time of year."

"What shall we do?"

"Well, I'm sure you've been to New Orleans—tom-catting in the sev-enties—but I haven't."

"This is quite unlike you."

She looked around at him, gazing over the top of her reading glasses.

He could only say, "George tells me Gilbert will be in New Orleans soon."

"I know. I was listening last night. I do listen."

"I could e-mail him."

"What are you waiting for?"

Gently, Terry bit her on the left buttock. Vera yelped and slapped his hairy old back. "Don't bloody well bite me, you bloody, bloody lunatic!"

* * *

The round Irish nurse with spectacles balanced on the slight upturn of her nose showed Terry and Vera into a windowless room with dingy yellow walls and sat them in wooden chairs with worn armrests. "Your doctor will be along shortly, Mrs. Langley," the nurse said. "We shan't forget you, so don't be panicking if it takes a while."

"This is the National Health after all," said Terry. Vera elbowed him.

The nurse smiled, her blue eyes sparkling, "And long may it remain so," she said.

"Right on!" said Terry raising his fist. Vera let out a sigh and turned away.

"Can I get you anything? A cup of tea?"

"A Guinness?" asked Terry.

"Ach, you're a devil," the nurse said to him. "No wonder your wife's poorly."

"That's right. It's all his fault," Vera said. "Actually, my dear, I could murder a cup of tea."

"'Tis the nerves, I expect. I'll see what I can sort out," said the nurse.

"Top of the mornin' to you," Terry said, to which the nurse frowned genially as one might at a half-wit.

Vera said, "You're such an idiot. You never stop your nonsense."

"I think you mean an eejit. Darling, I'm just being friendly. I like the Irish… they're too stupid to annoy me."

"What rubbish. You're half Irish yourself."

"And you just called me an idiot. I rest my case."

"You can't even be serious today of all days. What am I going to do with you?"

"Accompany me to New Orleans, dear heart."

"We'll see what today's outcome proves to be."

Terry frowned, slipped his hand over hers, and said, "Whatever the out-come, we have to get out of London for a while. You'll love New Orleans."

"I know I will. You'll make it fun—you always do. Pay no attention to my grumpiness. I'm just scared."

"Mustn't let apprehension get the better of you."

"Sod apprehension, Terry. I'm bloody terrified. Would you please give the polysyllabics a rest for a while."

"New Orleans will be grand. I'll work on my novel in the early mornings, like Hemingway, then we'll go and have breakfast in lovely clean bars and we'll get to know our new son."

Vera produced her strangled bird look.

"I will write," Terry insisted.

"Of course you will, darling."

"Cynical old cow."

"Don't you call me old."

"Well, I mean…"

"You've been writing this damn book for twenty years. A hundred others have written versions of it—even the hated Marty Kelso—while you fiddled around, perfecting everything. You should write Christmas cards or packaging copy for crisps."

"You've hurt me."

"Oh, balls, darling. Look, if you bring that smelly old folder with you, you can bloody well count me out. We can't carry it everywhere with us. It weighs a tonne and you never work on it. You don't write… you drink."

Pain sliced through him like white-hot scissor blades. Owl-like, Vera's eyes, full of have-you-got-it-now-buster, skewered the truth down his vision. "The truth hurts, doesn't it!"

Seeing Terry's embarrassment, Vera's eyes softened and she asked, "How about that offer of a cup of tea? It's very sweet of her. Please don't be a goon when she brings it."

"Yes, my equal."

Vera frowned at that, obviously not wanting to start on him again, and began reading a pamphlet on herpes. What she didn't know was that his book had changed yet again. She'd throw a massive wobbler if she found out, especially as now it was about her. On its profoundest level, it now became an attempt to create a world in which she could escape death. The only part of the original *The Tetropodic Recolonization of Mars* which had stayed the same since its inception as a puerile, bodice-ripping romp through the universe, with the voluptuous Nina Pym as the model for the fuck-princess,

Jessica the Sky Queen, was its subtext about humanity's fundamental need to escape the bounds of a planet locked into the specialization of its organisms, living in a few thousand feet of oxygen-rich atmosphere. Terry could no longer read the opening section *Jessica the Sky Queen,* because, quite simply, it was rubbish. He wanted to beat up the prat who wrote it. A sentimental empathy toward the lout he'd once been kept him from destroying the section, but he was tempted to do so every time he came across the yellowed, typewritten pages full of typos, clichés, and derivative scenes from Asimov or Herbert.

At the time of writing, in the late seventies, his support group, which met at a dirty muse flat in Crouch End, had loved it and praised him as the next J.G. Ballard. But other things kept encroaching—doctorates, careers, Vera, politics—until Marty the bus driver, a founder-member of that writers group, got nominated for the Booker. Terry considered hiring a psychotic client from Walthamstow to bottle the jumped up little shit, who remained all pompous and pleased with himself for insisting he'd still drive buses if he won. Little lefty bastard. If the Booker committee saw the Sword & Sorcery crap Marty Kelso used to write they'd all drink hemlock.

So obsessed was the young Marty with Tolkien that he dressed like a hobbit until he was forty-nine. Balding and nicotine-stained, he could no longer get women, so he finally found a pension-bearing job with London Transport. His book was about the angst of a lonely, balding, nicotine-addicted loser living in Chiswick, who drives buses all day and worries that the mother he buried in the back yard ten years ago will be discovered. What was that committee thinking? Terry would surely write a much better novel than that, but of course it would be ignored for being too idea-driven, too told instead of shown, too didactic. Does anyone read Cicero anymore, or Cervantes? Ayn Rand? Of course not—narrow-minded spunk bubbles, buggering up our literature with their Maoist mediocrity.

Calm yourself, calm yourself… think about the book.

The new focus on Mars was a more insightful treatise in fictional form about the perfectibility of humankind, and, recently, the defeat of death.

Vera, a rejecter of humanism, would immediately blow the premise. Everyone on Mars would die of leukemia within a year, she'd say. You're a child. You want a Star Trek future. Even thousands of years from now, if we don't destroy ourselves next week, we'll never get beyond the bounds of our own solar system—the distances are simply too great. There won't be any warp drive.

If the book had a flaw, it was that the characters existed mostly to provide a forum for ideas. His fictional model was Ayn Rand and his philosophical one was Miguel De Unumuno, both absurdly ignored by a polarized and shrinking intelligentsia. With the advent of Vera's illness, the book's emphasis had shifted to a love affair on the brave new planet between a brilliant psychologist and a brave Belgian countess who had come to Mars to escape the homogenized boredom of the European Community. She dies from radiation-induced breast cancer and, like all immigrants to Mars, is cryogenically frozen and housed in the resurrection caves of the Martian south pole. The Martians have defeated death by setting up the certainty, through absolute trust in the continued progression of science, in the ability to bring the dead back to life. The need for humans to populate the seeded planets of the near universe was so great that it was thought that nobody could be allowed to die.

Vera would be furious. "Everything dies!" She would fume. "Without death there's no life. Without death life would stagnate. Screw your head on straight."

He hadn't actually written any of this.

It was all planned out in his mind. The one time he did try and get something down on paper he became distraught at the thought of losing Vera with no cryogenic facility in place and had to go down to the pub.

He kept hearing her voice: "Write a short simple book about the here and now, you idiot. You'd finish it in a fortnight and earn thousands like little Marty."

Discovering himself as an untalented, pompous, insecure fool didn't really motivate fewer visits to The Lord Nelson. At least he was appreciated there as a character, a gentleman and scholar, who, despite having strong opinions, didn't take himself too seriously. Vera didn't concur with his self-assessment; no, she maintained that most of the patrons of the Nelson, young and old, thought he was a windbag. Kind, isn't she? Maybe he could just cryogenically freeze her tongue.

VI

Pym slept fitfully, his head full of horrors, and woke into morning to the clanging of a pan and the smell of fried bacon. He dozed until Estelle came into the bedroom with a tray of steaming food and mugs of coffee. To see her holding the tray with her hair piled up on her head, her powerful forearms, trying to blow a wisp of hair away from her eyes, made him smile. Pym sat up and she laid the tray across his legs.

"Eat," she said, "Mr. Insomniac."

"Big word for you."

"Don't start trying to break up with me this morning. I made you breakfast."

Pym laughed. Estelle concentrated on her food, eating ravenously, cross-legged, opposite him. She wore light blue panties that had a small wet patch in the crotch. She had fried him three eggs; he cut around the yoke of one, carefully laid it on a corner of toast, cut the corner off, laid a piece of bacon over the top of the disembodied yolk, shoveled this all onto his fork, and slid it into his mouth. After eating another of the eggs like this, he said, "This is good, Stella. What else you good at?"

"Feeding your new cat."

"What new cat?"

"The big calico in the kitchen."

"I don't know what you're talking about."

"Stop."

"Seriously."

"There was a big cat staring at me from the top of the fridge when I went down. I fed her tuna."

"It must've gotten in when the burglar left the door open."

"What burglar?" Estelle gazed out of the window. "What are you talking about?"

"Someone broke in last night. Nothing stolen though."

"You shoulda told me. I'da been scared shitless."

"I thought you'd snap their arms off."

"Real burglars carry guns."

"So you don't know anything about it?"

"What're you talking about? Why would I know anything? You're being a jerk again."

"That's it—you're dumped."

And away it went. Pym finished his breakfast during the argument, wasting the egg whites, which he knew would infuriate her, and she was history by the time he'd wiped up the bacon grease with the toast. Estelle didn't accept being history, of course, and insisted on a good-bye boink, which kept her around until she could say she had to leave and go to the salon.

"So it's your idea to leave," Pym said.

"Yes," she laughed, and ran out.

Pym went down to find the cat. Estelle had left the kitchen a mess. A can, licked clean of any trace of tuna, sat in the middle of the floor. "Hey, cat! Don't shit in the house, okay. I'm opening the door for you."

It was twenty below outside. With the door ajar he picked up after Estelle, jamming everything in the dishwasher, but the cat never appeared to him. Pym could use the dishwasher now, but the washer and dryer in the basement were still mysterious. He needed Laura's household skills. Now Ray enjoyed them.

Pym pulled open a beer and sat on the yellow couch with his feet on the coffee table. The furnace went on. He wanted music. There were no songs in his head. He owned a few books but nothing he could read without being reminded of his losses. He thought of the river and the St. Anthony Falls and how they were just cliffs under water; you could equally fling yourself off a cliff as be smashed to pieces on the rapids. He wanted the big cat that was somewhere in the house to come snuggle next to him. He tried not to think of Laura or George, and brought Estelle's image into his mind to keep them out. There came a cry of wind like a ghost passing through, and his hair stood up for a second before he realized it was the mailman. Then came full relief when this was confirmed by the plop of mail being dropped into the mailbox.

"Why am I so spooked all the time? What is this?"

He brought the small bundle of mail back to the yellow sofa and threw it all on the coffee table beside the stack of postcards. Bills, a *Hustler*, and a legal envelope from Hennepin County. The priority was to open the *Hustler* and look at the fake, airbrushed women. He wanted to call Estelle at the salon but resisted.

He reached for George's postcards.

On top lay a serene picture of Ann Rice's house in the Garden District. The message on the back, in George's gargantuan red cursive, said:

> *It's funny that as you get older, you get wiser, but you
> don't get any better at the things you're no good at.*

The tiny script on the next card, an overly colored shot of a café with a green awning, made Pym squint to read the text:

> *Café du Monde, Gillie. I come here every morning for
> coffee and beignets, and it became the center of my world.
> We're all just tourists here and it isn't open forever. Like
> that Eagles song, Hotel California. Paving stone floor. Fans
> on sloping ceiling. Green chairs and faux marble tables—
> round. They pull down a green screen against the cold. Ev-
> erything's green and white, and the balloon man, the trum-
> peter, and the wooden Indian are always here—Georgie.*

A picture of the ferry to Algiers up close with another ferry on the other side of the river; sunny day, packed with commuters:

> *Gillie Gillie Gillie: And the river runs through every-
> thing. Ok, not a river. A metaphor. The river that connects
> us—are we so unalike, you and I? Why should that be?
> When life gets like fustian jazz, and you're not intelligent
> enough to stay with it, if you're wise anyway, you know, or
> should know, to keep your goddamn mouth shut. Keeping
> your mouth shut has more to do with it than you think.*

A close-up of a spectacular pair of suntanned breasts:

> *Gillie, I know why you couldn't resist these. It's OK.
> The tour is too short for long-standing wrath. I love you,
> little brother, and all should be forgiven—Georgie.*

Pym laughed, wept a little, wiped his eyes. Next, a shot of the facade of an establishment for female impersonators, doing erotic dancing. Minuscule again:

You wouldn't know it but vampires live on Bourbon Street. Behind the gay cascades are derelict dwellings, courtyards piled with bricks and moldy banana trees, growing like devil weed. Rusty sixties lawn furniture on crumbling patios and ancient couples existing in dingy rooms behind yellow blinds, living on rats, waiting for a cure. You move here to escape reality. The thought of leaving terrifies you. You've become one of them, living off the tourists, waiting for a cure. Stay away, Gilbert Pym. No, come.

Pym took a few minutes to count the forty-two cards. George always wrote across the section meant for the address. The script spooked Pym with its square, almost cuneiform design.

A dazzling enchantress with cascading hair, leaning naked against a brick wall, featured on the next postcard; tall, slender, gracefully posed with her defined torso, big solid breasts, shapely limbs, and curvaceous hips, all served as a shocking contrast to the substantially wide penis nestled in her bush of pubic hair. Her countenance, with its dark, confrontational eyebrows, comely mouth, and direct gaze, collated all the features men desire in women.

"Holy Christ," Pym muttered as he turned it over and read:

> *Dear brother, mine. You are a stinking bastard, but I forgive you. I love you, Gillie, even though you've turned (partly with my help, I'm afraid) into a redneck motherfucker. Not that dear Mommy needed any more fucking. Suffice to say, I'm down here for a purpose that will change my life. Make me whole. I have been here on the front of this card. As you can see, she's not all she'd like to be. See how miserable she looks? I know the model.*

The cards, when shuffled through randomly, revealed seedy and provocative scenes from New Orleans and a surprising array of more cryptic depictions: a cracked flower pot, a beautiful little thumb-sucking Creole girl with blue eyes, assorted fish on a market stall; all accompanied backside by writing that at once revealed George's poetic gift and his mind's rambling, almost cultish resemblance to Nostrodamus or the Book of Revelation.

Pym wanted to write back and tell George he was full of shit but found no forwarding address or phone number. He turned to the last card in the pack, all glossy black, which said "New Orleans at night" in fuchsia cursive. On the back:

> *Gillie, I'm sorry, I haven't enough strength. I've sacri-*
> *ficed you and you'll never understand. To do this, you have*
> *to give up the one you love most. I'm so sorry.*

Pym sighed, walked over to the window, and looked out at the snow. Once again George engaged his mind with the faltering diction of obscurity—always trying to demonstrate his genius; although, this time some sort of life crisis threatened him and, typically, he couldn't come clean with the exact nature of it. The preposterous suggestion that George and he were alike struck Pym as an outrage designed to provoke him.

Overwhelmed by the prospect of examining all the remaining cards, Pym went outside and sat on the front stoop in the cold. He called to the unseen cat to come outside but it wouldn't show itself. Pym shivered as he looked at the top of the Hennepin Avenue Bridge and beyond to the sky-scrapers of Downtown. The twenty-below air crept inside his clothes. He should read a few more of those cards. Or should he call Estelle? He suspected her of holding back information. Pym knew George's *modus operandi*: the posted cards could be a ruse to hide his presence in town; something about the break-in smacked of Georgeness. Maybe call Laura. She'd say: "Stop trying to help George and take care of your own goddamn life. You're more of a loser every year I know you." Maybe call his mother? She'd be in a bar, smoking up a storm. He hated calling Estelle at the salon because all the staff knew the entire sordid story. What the hell. Pym went back inside and dialed.

Estelle answered immediately as if she'd been waiting. "Gil, honey," she said, "Just the stud I wanted to talk to."

"I'm glad you were at the front desk. I hate talking to that Mishawn guy."

"Lighten up. Mishawn's cool."

"So, what, are you the receptionist now? Those tits'll bring in some business."

Estelle laughed and said, "Not into this joint, they won't. I'm having to take a lot of George's clients, so I'm just now calling the last of them. I'll be here till at least ten tonight. Why don't I meet you somewheres?"

"Do you know where George is? Have you been holding out on me?"

"Mishawn knows more than anyone, but you're too sensitive to talk to him."

"I can't stand George's little butt buddies."

"Stop. That's nasty."

"Look, he was here. It wasn't a burglary, it was George. He sent me these enigmatic postcards, but I think it's just a ruse. It seems he's residing in New Orleans—the anus of America. His cards are pretty weird."

"Right, that's Georgie's deal. He sends them out to clients with all kinds of news and poems and stuff. They love it. Very cool."

"Stop saying cool."

"I can say *cool.* I can say *cool* whenever I like. You're not the boss of the world, Gil."

"Ask Mishawn what in the name of fuck my brother's doing down in that shit-hole."

"Ask him yourself."

The line went dead.

Pym sat with his hands on his head. He'd have to wait for her to call back now. Screw it. He dialed the salon and she answered. Pym said, "May I speak to Mishawn, please."

Estelle said, "Certainly, sir. One moment, please."

Bitch.

"This is Mishawn. How may I help you?"

"Gilbert Pym here, George's brother."

"Ah, yes… one moment…" and he partially covered the speaker and exchanged a joke with Estelle. When the hand came away, Mishawn said, "How you doin', buddy?"

"Look, Mishawn, cut the shit or I'll come there and cause a scene."

"Will you be coming by bus?"

Pym heard Estelle burst into laughter.

"Gimme a break, man."

"Then settle down and be nice—man."

"I got these postcards from George—from New Orleans."

"That'd be about right. Are they all from New Orleans?"

"I haven't looked at all of them yet."

"How diligent of you. What is it I can help you with?"

"I want to know what he's doing down there. I want him back. I want my brother back." Pym almost sobbed. After a pause, Mishawn's soft voice said, "Okay. We should talk. But I have a lady in the chair and I'm booked solid till six. I have to go to the Gay 90's tonight for a festival. I could meet you there about eight."

"The Gay 90's?"

"The same."

"Shit. Whatever."

"Is that a problem?"

"Is there a bar or something?"

"Right as you walk in. Stay there and I'll find you."

"At eight then, thanks. Can you put Estelle on?"

"Here she is."

"Yes, master."

"Is he gone?"

"Mishawn? Yes."

"He wants me to meet him at the Gay 90's tonight at eight. You have to come with me."

"No can do, bucko. I'm solid till ten. I'll come and save you after work—if you can hold on that long without turning into a flamer."

"Very funny. Forget it." He hung up the telephone, then pounded the side of the chair with his fist, kicking and shouting, "Goddamn you, George, you planned all this, you fucking fuck. Fucker! Fuck fuck fuck!"

Dust rose in a cloud like a jinni manifesting out of the chair where he'd thumped it. "And fuck you, too, dust! Fuck off!"

To distract his mind from the coming ordeal, Pym ripped into the mail and found himself pleasantly surprised that Laura had paid up all the bills. The Hennepin County envelope contained divorce papers. It was a way to get a no-fault, no-contest divorce within a month. Laura keeps the bits she took to her mother's place. He keeps the house and the mortgage. Despite his anger he admired Laura's fairness. She could make him sell the house; it had gained considerable equity over the three years since they'd bought it from his mother. Laura didn't want to damage his foothold, force him out of his childhood home—she'd said that before—but Ray MacGregor's wealth rather spoiled Laura's gesture; she'd moved into Ray's mansion on Mount Curve and could afford to be noble. Pym failed to hold off the image of Laura copulating with Ray; he experienced the peculiar sensation of megrim inside his skull, a sort of internal spinning. Now she's going to punish you. She's going to do all that you did. She knows how you'll feel about that. Imagine Ray coming in her face, fucking her in the ass. She'll do all that, you know. All the things you kept for Estelle.

"Why?" he cried.

George would have said, "Oh come on, you jackass, don't waste your breath whining. She's gone. You can save yourself some pain by letting her go now and getting straightened out."

Pym knew what his brother would say about almost anything, and it would always be reasonable unless the subject was George himself—then he had no clue.

"George, help me."

"Poor little Gillie."

"Pick yourself up, we're not going to wallow in this. We're going to fight. We're going for a run."

Pym put on two layers, two pair of gloves and ear muffs, and ran North to Boom Island and across the Eighth Avenue Bridge and then all the way down the West River Road to the Hiawatha Dam, and then back. He didn't think about Laura or George, he just ran. There remained a black channel in the middle of the river where the ice had not completely joined. It was like a fracture in a femur, or the skull of a newborn. The open water steamed. Pym's breath froze in the air and his eyelashes grew heavy with ice.

Completely dark when he finished his run, he drank a big bottle of water then stripped off, his body red and tingling, his legs aching, and left the pile of icy running gear on the kitchen floor. He went upstairs naked, turned on the shower, then looked at his red face in the medicine cabinet. "See!" He shouted. "They will not hold you down!"

In the shower, so as not to think of Laura, he thought of Estelle and the leg-spreaders in *Hustler.* Soon he had a big dong looking up at him with its eyeball-vacant slit like a blinded Cyclops; the foreskin rolled back of its own volition, making the turtle-like glans easier to lather. "How ya doing, good buddy? Did I freeze your balls off with that run?"

Pym wondered what his penis would say if it could talk.

As he dried himself he heard something run down the stairs. The cat. He put on clean jeans and T-shirt. As he searched for clean socks, he realized with a great heave of emotion that he was just as much of an emotional wreck as George. If he got George back, they could at the very least be two useless brothers together and maybe cooperate enough to get through to the end.

VII

The oncologist came into the little room and sat down, acknowledging their presence with a small nod. Terry's stomach sank. The doctor wore a track-suit under his light blue surgical scrubs and sweat lingered in the clavicle of his throat. He sat opposite Vera and opened the manila folder with her name on it, all the time avoiding her eyes and directing a single, rather furtive glance at Terry. His nametag said Edward Broughton and he was much older than he looked.

All his life Terry had loathed the English professional classes in their manner of situational sang-froid. Just look her in the eye and give her the worst, you bastard. If he had had the patience to become a doctor, he never would have been one of this type. He realized he was frowning and when the doctor looked at him again, the frown registered and the doctor blushed.

That's better, thought Terry… maybe there's life in you after all. During the early days of Vera's disease, when she felt desperate and vulnerable, she formed an odd bond with Broughton that Terry didn't like, even though he'd never met the bloke. Such a bond didn't appear to be in evidence now, but Terry felt the force of the grudge despite the tragic news Broughton was about to impart.

"Mrs. Langley. Vera." And Broughton looked suddenly at Terry, not at Vera. "As we suspected, all indicators show that you're out of remission and the disease is progressing aggressively. The PET scan confirms that the cancer has metastasized and migrated into some of your organs."

Vera squeezed the fingers of Terry's left hand. It hurt considerably, but he didn't withdraw them from her grip. Inside himself he felt nothing; there-fore, he welcomed the pain, the passion of her grip. He smelled fear; it waft-ed off her like salty humidity or a hot dishrag. Her face grew long and sharp

57

as she kept her eyes on the doctor. Terry's mind struggled with the guilt of not being the victim, not being able to be in Vera to share the fear. He pushed down the rejoicing in his soul that it wasn't him, that he could go on. Yet when he raised his right hand to his face he found it wet. How curious—to weep without knowing it. He couldn't wait to tell Vera.

They had been talking, something about why more chemotherapy would be useless, and now Terry tuned back in. "I can't say how long," Broughton said. As he spoke he leaned forward and pressed his finger-tips gently, opening and closing them in unconscious emphasis. "It's different with everybody within a time frame of about three to nine months. You haven't been sick for a while, so you may have some good reserves just now. But they will deplete and you'll start feeling increasingly unwell."

Vera said nothing.

Terry said, "So that's it, then."

Broughton frowned at him and stayed quiet.

"Are you having difficulty with this, doctor?"

"I am, Mr. Langley."

"Good."

"Darling, it's not his fault," said Vera, surprised.

"Of course it is. It's all their faults. They're scientists. They think they can improve humanity, but all they do is hasten our demise. Look at him... he jogs at lunch to stay heart-healthy. Don't you, Doc?"

"Well, yes. In fact, a little jogging wouldn't hurt you, Mr. Langley."

"Doctor Langley to you."

"Darling! Don't start. It's not his fault. Don't take pot-shots at the messenger." Vera stood up, pulling Terry up with her. They stood above the oncologist, who looked up at them with his blue, watery eyes.

"I'm so sorry," he said.

"I know you are, Doctor Broughton."

"I wish I could help more."

"Thank you," said Vera.

Terry said, "Bollocks."

Vera dragged him out of the little room. "God, Terry, even at a time like this you act like a football hooligan."

Terry pulled away from her and stood in the middle of the antiseptic smelling hallway, put his arms in the air and shouted, "Bollocks!"

A security guard with a youthful beard began edging nervously toward him. Terry looked at him and said, "Oh, yeah, right!"

He looked back into the little room and saw Broughton staring at his hands. Terry was about to let out a stream of invective, but Vera tugged his arm and said, "Come on, you're supposed to look after me. Let's get out of this place."

Outside St. Thomas' Hospital the traffic noise and wind-driven grime hit them like an emotional enema. They walked the few yards to the river wall and Vera allowed herself tears. "You're so naughty," she blubbered. "I can't take you anywhere."

"Well, we never did get our tea. Bloody Irish, promise you the world..."

Vera burst out crying and Terry knew why, not simply because she was soon to die but because she couldn't take him with her. The reality squatted on him—that he had limited time left with her and then he would never see her again. He held her tight. "Fucking hell," he said, "fucking bloody hell."

Big Ben chimed one o'clock. The sound drew their eyes to the ancient buildings opposite, buildings that had outlived generations of Londoners and would outlive generations more. Inside Whitehall, politicians with crooked teeth and ghastly hairstyles argued about how much more sin tax would be forced on the consumers of the United Kingdom. Terry noticed colours vividly in the river—Coke tins and McDonald's wrappers. "Look at that," he said, "American stuff floating in our river. Bastards."

"Oh, Terry dear, not now."

He shut it all out for a second, breathed hard, and finally said, "You should have lunch, darling. Anything you want."

Vera swallowed and calmed herself. Her eyes looked young, and Terry saw for a second how she must have looked in kindergarten. "Fish & chips," she said.

"I thought you'd want a curry."

"I'll have that tonight," she said. "I want fish & chips, the greasier the better. And I want pickled onions and bread and butter and cod roe with it."

"You'll be sick."

"So what?"

"Whatever pleases you, my epicurean."

"Just feed me and stop being clever. We have to go to the travel agent after lunch. I'm not spending my last days shivering through the end of a London winter."

"I'll resign immediately."

Vera laughed. "You're a funny old stick."

"Am I?"

"And thank you."

"What for?"

"In there. Making a fool of yourself so I wouldn't. I know what you were doing. You've done it before."

"You have no idea how much I love you. I will find a way…"

Vera pulled him down and kissed him and he knew why—he was about to utter heroic prose. She had a lovely mouth and lovely teeth, but he could taste the fear in her saliva, the same essence that came off her in the oncologist's office. When she finally released him, she said, "No more talk of it now till we have to."

He just looked at her.

"All right, Terry?"

He shook his head, looked across at Parliament, and said, "Right you are, darling. Now, where can we get me the freshest haddock in the city?"

VIII

Half an hour early, face stiff with wind-chill, and nowhere else convenient to hang out until eight, Pym plunged into the Gay 90's. A gaggle of security men in yellow sweatshirts clustered around the entrance and he had to produce ID to an obese, surly lout with greasy hair. Inside, the dim lighting and cheap seventies decor reminded him of Nye's Polanaise Room; he longed to be transported there. With ears burning, Pym checked his coat, strode to the bar and ordered a Heineken from a tiny barman. George often mentioned a client of his who had something to do with the 90's—Dashiell. A black blonde, Dashiell patronized George because of his reputation as an expert colorist. The tiny black barman wore blonde hair curled like a cherub.

When the barman put an open bottle of Heineken in front of him, Pym asked, "Who's Dashiell?"

The barman said, "She's not here yet."

"You wouldn't happen to know a big fella called George, would you?"

"Sure," said the barman. "Dashiell and Mishawn's friend." He rolled his eyes and added, "You mean Georgie."

"Georgie?"

"Sure. Georgie. Are you her brother or something?"

"Yes, I'm George's brother."

The barman shrugged, laughing, and said, "Sorry, hon."

Pym sipped his beer calmly. That rotten bitch—to let you squirm here alone like this—a sick motherfucking joke. I'll slaughter her, I'll chop her spine off! He didn't know what to do next. He was liable to lose it when he didn't know what to do next. Not knowing what to do next usually means that you're a loser. So he drank down the beer and asked for another.

The bar began to fill with men and Pym didn't like the way they looked at him and the way the stools next to him remained empty. He ordered a third beer, which prompted a sneer from the barman, like: stupid straight white boy, suckin' 'em down. Pym caught his eye, sighed and said, "Okay. So I'm learning. This is what it's like to not fit in."

"Uncomfortable?" asked the barman.

"I haven't been in here before."

The barman's eyes softened. He said, "It can get intense."

"I'd rather be over the bridge at Nye's."

The barman laughed and said, "Imagine how good I'd go down in there?"

"It must be hard," said Pym. "Being an outsider most of the time."

The barman leaned forward, put his hand under his chin in a sweet gesture of attention that women do, and said, "It's not so bad in this town. I had to leave Des Moines—kept getting my ass kicked."

"I'm sorry to hear that."

"Your brother's great, you know. You should be proud of her. She's overcome it all."

"Yeah, whatever. Say, is Mishawn coming in tonight?"

"Why do you wanna see her?"

Pym laughed and said, "I need his help with my car."

"She'll break her nails!"

"Look," said Pym, "George and I argued a while back, and he's offended. I want to explain, but I can't find him. I think he might be in town and avoiding me. I'm supposed to see Mishawn here at eight. Will she be helpful?"

The barman, floundering, looked around for help but had no escape route. Pym wanted to withdraw all he'd said. The barman backed away, saying, "You'll have to talk to her, hon."

"Sorry, man. I thought you might be in the know around here."

"I don't know nothin'. I stay out of domestic bullshit. Talk to Mishawn. They roommates or somethin'. Maybe talk to Dashiell. She a big friend of Georgie's. I'll point her out. Now you be slowin' down on them beers."

"I'm just looking for my brother."

"We get a lot of assholes in here. This isn't a place for assholes."

"I'm not an asshole."

"You don't seem like one."

"I'm not."

"All right. I'll send Dashiell when I see her. Chill out."

"All right. Gimme another."

"And don't get shitfaced."

"I won't."

"This is a family restaurant."

Loud, thumping music came from two different directions, creating an unpleasant discordancy in the smoke-polluted air. Pym took the barman's advice and slowed down on the beer. He watched the bar fill with boisterous friends for fifteen minutes. Unexpectedly, Pym felt a close presence behind him, followed by the smell of perfume.

A rich, throaty voice in his ear said, "You must be Gilbert—the Pym sibling."

Pym turned to find a new category of femininity. Dashiell. Black skin, most of it exposed, and copper-blonde, cropped hair; black party dress, tall as a Tutsi, science-fiction-sized implants. Pym said, "Yes. I'm looking for George."

"Don't you guys communicate?" asked Dashiell.

"Usually," Pym said. "There's been some tension. I want to put it to rest."

Dashiell laughed. "Tension's how you put it? That wasn't the way it came to me. Word is you weren't too understanding when she told you what she needed to tell you."

"It was a shock. I had a lot going on. I'm over it now and I just want to talk to him. I'm over it, see."

"I guess she didn't get to say all she wanted to say and I don't think she reckons you for a very good listener. I believe she doesn't want any contact with you."

"But... I love my brother. I have to talk to him."

Dashiell, smiling, slipped a long brown arm onto Pym's shoulder. "We all love Georgie. She the best, and God knows she need all the support she can get. That's why you ain't gonna get to talk to her for a while."

"So where the hell is he?"

"Safe in New Orleans," said Dashiell. "Wish we all were—where nobody fuck widju like here. Now, baby, I have to perform in ten minutes. I'll be around later, okay?"

"All right."

Dashiell burrowed down Pym's vision, discomforting him exceedingly, and said, "Come upstairs and sit out the show. Then you can buy me a drink and I'll spill the beans on your brother. She is such a scandal!"

Pym eyed the label on the green bottle. His stomach churned. In his heart Pym knew that if George were gay he couldn't help it—he wouldn't be able to just snap out of it. Pym also knew that he had to find the right vein in his mind, the one through which the truth displays itself; and he had to get right up close to the truth so that he could break out of his youthful fog. In lucid moments like this, he saw he had grown too long in the tooth to think like a teenager. He had always suppressed the smart, kind impulse that lingered below his insecurities, and acknowledged that he had always known George was different. When George married Estelle, that smart part of him had sensed an unreal air about the whole thing. With George's sexual preference now in the open Pym felt as though it had always been known, just as he had known he wasn't his father's son.

A beer bottle slammed on the bar in front of him. "What's this?" Pym asked.

The barman slid his eyes sideways and Pym followed them to a huge cowboy, smiling at him. Pym pointed at the beer and said, "Thanks for this. But just so's you know…"

"That's cool," laughed the cowboy. "Enjoy your beer." He sat next to Pym, and said, "So you're Georgie's brother, the Pym sibling?"

"Yep. I guess you wouldn't happen to know where he is?"

"New Orleans, I heard."

"Yes, I know that, but it's a big place."

The cowboy grinned and said, "Not so big. I reckon she wanted to start a new career. She was the greatest, you know. The kindest faggot I ever known."

Pym spilled beer from his mouth. There was something about the word 'faggot' that made him laugh. It was so high school. George called it Bi-school.

"So what's with this Pym-sibling thing?"

The cowboy shrugged and said, "It's your name. It's a small community. Everyone knows everything. These faggots are worse than women with their yammering."

The cowboy related how George always seemed to have money and gave it away to friends who needed it. Pym only half-listened; he'd heard this all his life. The cowboy, big and hard looking, reminded Pym of Ray MacDonald, and his mind jumped to Laura—her body under Ray's, her face smiling up at him as he bent to kiss her pretty mouth. Now she was having an orgasm, and the thought of that increased the cramping in Pym's stomach. His mother on top of the Englishman on the yellow couch came next— an image George put in him—Xena the Warrior Princess fucking the shit out of Aqualung, hair flying and boobs bouncing, that stupid cigarette sticking out of the side of her mouth...

"So she'll be okay down there, Georgie will..." the cowboy was saying. "People respond to her. They'll look after her as she looks after them. I wouldn't worry too much."

Pym shrugged. "We had a fight. I need to talk to him."

"Say sorry?"

"Sort of—and other stuff."

The cowboy frowned, then his face brightened. "Say, come upstairs with me. We'll watch the drag queens. They're something else."

Upstairs, the cavernous atmosphere of the smoke-filled cabaret room stung Pym's eyes. It was much smokier than rock concerts he'd attended; he found himself infuriated by the stupidity of the smoking and discomforted himself by breathing as shallowly as possible. In his thirty-odd years of Minneapolis residency, passing the Gay 90's almost daily, he never once attempted to envision the inside, thinking of it dismissively as a den of decadence. Faggot heaven, George called it before he came out. He should have remembered that when George threw it in his face how he had been out to everyone else for ages but couldn't tell his own brother—a jerk who had yet to grow out of high school. How did it all go down? "You still use the word 'fag' for chrissakes," George had said. "That went out years ago."

"But you ARE one! You fat freak."

"Who's the freak? You can't even hold onto that homely little prig of a wife."

"You've forgotten her name again."

"She's forgettable. Everything in your life is!"

"Dead right—that includes you. I can't believe you're doing this to me."

"To you? I'm the one coming out. And after pretending to be homophobic in your presence—for years—God, what am I doing to you?"

Pym had gone quiet then, and, as had always been the case between them during quarrels, Pym pulled the sincerity card. "Okay," he'd said, "I'll answer that truthfully."

"Oh jeez," said George, rolling his eyes, "prepare yourself."

"I'm embarrassed. Yes, embarrassed."

"Embarrassed of me?"

"Look at you! Like something out of the circus!"

"I've never pretended to be good looking—but you certainly know how to be truthful."

"All right. Fuck it. What can I do? Sorry, George. I didn't mean that."

"You did. You don't lie. Much. You get your brutal honesty from Dad."

"I don't know how. Look... All right, so now you're a faggot. Does that mean I have to show up on talk shows and support you?"

"I'm sure they'll have you on Jerry Springer."

Pym, putting on his pansy voice, said, "How could you?"

"Look," said George, "when you're mad, deal with me like your brother... otherwise just fuck off." His face white, George had stood up and left the house. The fizzing sensation in Pym's stomach had started then and continued increasing until now. He expected a conciliatory call from George, but none came, and now he found himself here, full of contrition, but among the enemy—the people who took his brother away.

The cowboy stood at a normal guy's distance from Pym and he felt okay with that. The cowboy drank beer and didn't lisp. He looked like he could kick some ass. Pym caught the barmaid's eye and said, "Two Heinekens."

"Hey. No, sir," said the cowboy. "You don't get to buy beer. I invited you." And then he grinned, teeth flashing. "You're on your first date." And then he roared a laugh which instantly transformed into a larynx-ripping cough. The barmaid, a sort of Joan Jett look-a-like, slid the beers across the bar and leaned forward to shout, "Roy, honey, you okay?"

"Yes," he replied. "I'm too funny for my own good. I'll kill myself one of these days."

"You already have," yelled the barmaid. As she did this, Pym understood that she was a man. All the women in the bar were men. The cowboy recovered and said, "No offense, Pym sibling, I can't resist shittin' you, you're so darn straight."

Pym said, "Just so's you're not disappointed..."

"Hey, I know, don't worry. George's bro' ain't buying no beer around me. George is a fine girl. Helped me out a few times. I just hope she gets what she wants down there."

"And what does my brother want down there?"

"Didn't you get the rundown?"

"I told you. We had a falling out."

"He was hitting you up for money, right?"

"No—I'm broke. Going through a divorce…"

"So you don't know why he's down South?"

"No. Today's the first I heard of it."

The announcer came out with a cordless microphone turned up loud and the music stopped. "Well, here you all are," she yelled. "My favorite people. Are you ready for the show?" The crowd roared back in a humorous interchange with her. The cowboy drew Pym's arm to him and spoke close to his ear. "You'd best watch the show for a spell. It'll explain a few things."

The music came on again with increased volume. The detail with which so many men tried to be women astounded Pym. It was one of those peculiar moments—they were coming thick and fast—when you discover something under your nose that you maybe should have known. The announcer, who wore a cheerleading uniform, introduced the first dancer.

There came an intake of breath from the crowd as the blonde woman with long legs and broad shoulders strutted onto the stage to a Gloria Gaynor number. Pym had to remind himself that she was a he. All the definitions had shifted in this place and he was suddenly no longer threatened. There was nothing here that attracted him. Although the skillfully disguised dancer was a fluid mimic of lewd female dance movements, she didn't possess that throat-drying quality that attractive women can. He checked his memory to the last floorshow he'd witnessed, which was his stag night at the Lamplighter Lounge in Saint Paul. Those girls had it; he had wanted them all. George, his best man and master-of-ceremonies at that stag night, pretended, as it turned out, to lust after one girl in particular, enough so that he had to be frog-marched to the limo. On Sunday mornings when they got together to watch the Vikings, George, in the early days of his marriage to Estelle (Pym was still in college), would hold a middle finger up to Pym's nose and announce, "Ah, vintage Stella. The aroma of Saturday night!"

It was funny at the time.

The whole room whooped it up for the blonde performer. Now he understood how Laura could only sit through one quarter of a Vikings game before disappearing—she had no connection with it. The cowboy pulled his arm, saying, "Ain't she something?"

Pym shrugged, sucked down the rest of his beer. "How does this relate to George?"

The cowboy stared at him, then looked away. Pym turned to buy a beer but one already waited. He looked at the barmaid, who winked at him.

The blonde finished and was replaced on stage by a tall, muscular black dancer, crammed into skimpy black leather; he was heavily made up and smoking a long cigarette. Dashiell. He strutted around a bit while the music started out quietly—a number Pym hadn't heard—and then flung his legs high when the main beat kicked in. As he danced he used the cigarette as a prop, and Pym understood once and for all that in this room cigarettes were sexy.

Dashiell held the cigarette too far down in his fingers, between the digits closest to the hand, like a sailor, not at all like a woman. Pressing his face against a mirror with ass proffered for the advance of an invisible lover and rubbing himself like a cat, Dashiell enthusiastically mimed the reception of rear entry. When the music shifted tempo he half-turned to the audience, still bent at the waist, and popped open the middle of the leather strap that served as a brassiere, and the large breasts, bulging tightly together, bounced around like brown water balloons.

It struck Pym that he loved to get Estelle this way and watch her breasts bounce in a mirror. He'd never done that with Laura—she didn't really have breasts. When he thought about it, girls show dents and bruises; they're luscious here, but sag there; they have stars of broken blood vessels on hamstrings, buttocks with dimples and pustules, fleets of freckles invading arms, skin tags and moles skulking under the flop of breasts or anchored precariously close to strong-smelling vaginas. Maybe that's what repulses homosexuals. Oh, well, all the more for me.

Pym nudged the cowboy, then shouted into his ear, "Dashiell's a big bastard. I'm glad I'm over here."

The cowboy laughed his hacking laugh and said, "Yep, me too. Wouldn't want her rolling on top of me in the sack. That first one though…"

Pym said, "It's a bit like a dream. Guys dressed as objects of desire as though the rest of us are a bunch of convicts."

The cowboy laughed. "It's a lot like that—being in prison, I mean. It's a life sentence. You can do your time in denial or you can embrace it."

"Really?"

"Look around you, there's every perversion known to humanity represented in this room. Boy, I could tell you a thing or two."

"That's okay."

"Ever heard of felching?"

"It sounds like something that would make me vomit."

The cowboy laughed and turned to watch the next dancer.

And on they went, one after another, and it seemed to Pym that they became increasingly unrealistic while he himself oddly became more comfortable with the whole scene. There wasn't any harm in it. What did it matter? They were just people having fun. Okay, George, come home, all is forgiven.

Then at last a very overweight dancer came on stage swathed in masses of silk. He danced slowly and elegantly and reminded Pym of the hippopotami in "Fantasia." He was about to laugh at the image when it struck him what the cowboy had been driving at all along. This was George; he was one of these. All Estelle's stories about the kinky cross-dressing flooded back.

You're a fucking idiot for not putting two and two together.

Pym turned to the cowboy. "Roy, is it?"

"Yes. Roy." The cowboy tipped his hat with a forefinger and grinned.

"So, Roy? Have you seen my brother do this?"

"Sure. She won the Over 35s at the Christmas pageant."

"There's a competition?"

"This is a competition. Tonight. You didn't know?"

"I didn't. I just came down to meet his roommate, Mishawn."

"Mishawn's on the way?" asked the cowboy.

"Supposed to be here at eight."

The cowboy's face became long. He had brown eyes like an old dog. "I gotta piss," he said, and went into the crowd. Behind Pym sat another Heineken.

An intermission started. Pym sipped the Heineken in the relative quiet, but the cowboy didn't return and he started to feel weird again, finding himself the recipient of ambiguous glances. He retreated downstairs to the street-level bar and with relief spotted Mishawn talking to the cherub-haired barman. Mishawn's thin shoulders and narrow chest gave way to an expanding stomach and wider hips; if not for the cropped magenta hair, multiple piercings, and delicate, trendy spectacles, Pym might have described Mishawn as hobbit-like. On seeing him approach, Mishawn's wrist rose and Pym felt chastened. His own watch said nine-thirty. "Sorry," he said. "I got hauled upstairs by a cowboy."

"Not Roy, I hope."

"It was Roy. What is it with you guys? He took off as soon as he knew I was meeting you."

"Roy has problems."

"What kind of problems?"

"Don't you know anything about Georgie's life? Jeez! Roy took advantage of your brother. He's not as nice as he seems."

"Is anybody?"

"I guess not."

"I didn't know anything about this life. He didn't tell me and I understand why. What about Dashiell? What's his connection to George?"

"Everybody asks about Dashiell." Mishawn smiled. "He has the look all the trannies want. And he's a capable organizer too. He runs a lot of things."

"What's a tranny?"

"A transvestite or a transsexual, Gilbert. Where have you been?"

A sensation like an electric shock ran through Pym at the finality of Mishawn's implications. Pym said, "My brother's not going to have a sex change, is he?"

Mishawn turned to the bar and looked directly at the barman, who raised his eyebrows and walked away. There was a light fuzz on the side of Mishawn's face and over the back of the ears. The neck was very thin and the throat smoothly elegant. Mishawn was a woman, at least originally.

Okay, Pym thought, okay.

"I think you mean gender reassignment," Mishawn said. "The simple answer is yes. But there's nothing simple about what Georgie has to go through."

Pym sat on a stool and placed his beer on the counter. Abba blared from the upstairs auditorium and the Rolling Stones pulsed from the adjoining bar. Dashiell, wearing a purple robe snugged tightly at the waist, descended the stairs like a pharaoh surrounded by sycophants. Watching Dashiell, but addressing Mishawn, Pym said, "I read somewhere that you had to live as a woman for a year and have psychological testing."

"Georgie was refused by all the major programs. That's the bottom line. It's too loud in here to talk details. She's taken matters into her own hands and is going to deal with it."

"In New Orleans?"

"Correct."

"So he's doing this illegally?"

"It's not uncommon, and not necessarily illegal. The hospitals are too rigid. People want what they want."

"And the free market's responding?"

"I guess. I never thought about it that way, but all power to people to invent themselves, is what I say. However…"

"I don't like this one bit. Is he in danger?"

"It's too loud to talk here."

Pym was about to suggest going into the restaurant area so that he could get the whole scoop on this when Dashiell stood beside him, very close, so that the rounded breasts were aligned with Pym's eyes. "I saw you watching with Roy," said Dashiell. "Did you like my performance?"

Mishawn leaned into the bar and sucked on her beer bottle. Pym said, "It was very artistic."

"Thank you."

"I was just talking with Mishawn about George's proposed sex change."

"I'd rather talk about me for a while."

Mishawn turned around and laughed. There were several men standing behind Dashiell and they laughed too. "After a performance," Mishawn said, "you should get to talk about yourself. How did it go Dashiell? I missed it."

"Good, I think, real good. I received deep applause."

"Excellent. Say, Dashiell, I have to go to the bathroom and the Pym sibling here has concerns about Georgie's safety down in New Orleans. Can you tell him why you encouraged Georgie to do what he's doing?"

Dashiell, exaggerating a stunned expression, said, "Okay." Mishawn returned a disgusted stare before slipping off her stool and pushing through Dashiell's friends. Dashiell asked the sycophants to get lost for a while because she needed to talk to the Pym sibling, then he slipped gracefully onto Mishawn's vacant stool. "Someone has a hot ass. She does my hair, you know, now that Georgie's gone. She's not as good with the color. And she's a counselor at the University, you know, where Georgie wanted to have it done. She doesn't agree with my advice. I told him, fuck it, go be what you wanna be. Fuck those assholes trying to control your life. I said go get it done with the Duvals in New Orleans. You'll have enough money left to take the riverboat up in the spring and we'll all be waiting at Boom Island to give you a triumphant welcome. I told him to book passage on the American Queen." Dashiell shrieked with laughter.

Pym forced a smile and said, "I see."

"That was a joke," Dashiell said. "American Queen?"

"Ah, yes. Isn't that expensive?"

"Sure is. But she'll have plenty left over from her savings if she gets it done with the Duvals—enough to have a real big party. She lucky—always got money."

"George works hard. Generally had two jobs until recently."

"Right. She be saving, you know what I'm saying?" As he said this, Dashiell leaned in very close to Pym, and Pym could read the eyes of seduction being rendered. The combined odor of cosmetics, strong perfume, leather, cigarette smoke, and metallic-smelling sweat made Pym gag.

He pulled away and reached for his beer, saying, "So it was you who advised him to do this?"

"Me and others. She'll be all right, man. Be cool when she gets home. She'll need you. Say, I got an idea…"

A pair of soft, cool hands slipped from behind over Pym's eyes. He knew the smell of the fingers and could feel Estelle's breasts pressing into his back; he put his hands over hers and drew them down, discovering a whole new definition of the word *relief.* Dashiell looked as though Estelle had put a turd under his nose. Estelle said, "I got off a little early so I could come and save you… Hello, Dashiell."

"Hello, Estelle."

Dashiell and Estelle held each other's eyes for uncomfortable seconds before Dashiell said, "I have to go and be with my fans now. Nice to meet you, Pym sibling."

"I might want to talk about this again at some time," said Pym.

"That would be more than okay," said Dashiell, and he slipped off the stool.

Estelle took Dahsiell's place and said, "Wow, that bitch has a hot ass." She wore a tight, black T-shirt that accentuated her breasts and shoulders. She'd fixed her hair in a big tangle of curls, wore way more make-up than usual and breathed pungent marijuana breath into his face.

Pym pulled a little away from her and said, "You're toking, you rat."

She laughed, took a big swig of his beer and said, "You'll get the benefit later, Mister Lillylungs. More to the point, how you holdin' up in here, dude?"

"Getting an education."

"Oh, well, now you got me to kick around."

"Don't you like Dashiell?"

"George listens to him over much. Dashiell does everything to serve himself. It's too loud to get into it in here... enough to say that he don't always steer George in directions that are good for George, only ones that make Dashiell feel good."

"Like go and get a big pair of implants, and have your dick snipped off?"

"Well, yeah, 'cept Dashiell still has his penis."

"How the hell would you know?"

"It's a long story."

"What story?"

"Dashiell's a big porn star. Emphasis on big."

"You're kidding me?"

"Nope."

"Level with me. Did you know George was doing this?"

Estelle looked at her big hands, turned them over, and then looked Pym in the eye. "I did. Yes."

"We're out of here."

IX

On Hennepin Avenue, pulling on his parka against a ripping, freezing wind, with Estelle walking backwards behind him in an attempt to close her long coat, Pym yelled, "Where did you park your fucking piss-can of a car?"

"Settle down. Don't walk so fast. Everything makes you mad."

"I asked you where George was and you said you didn't know."

"I didn't. I knew he wanted gender reassignment. I didn't know where."

"Gender reassignment? You mean dick-snipping, for chrissake. Why is this couched in bullshit?"

"So ignorant assholes like you can't as easily call it dick-snipping!"

"How can you, with your empty brain and your crappy grammar, have the balls to justify this shit by making me the bad guy?"

Estelle stopped, spread out her hands, and said, "Hey, college boy. Now it's clear—you need a girlfriend with a better vocabulary. Words get in the way, lover. All I heard was crappy brain."

Pym stopped and turned his face to the sky with his eyes tight shut, and shouted, "You fucking moron!"

"I get off work and come downtown early, looking like a million bucks, and you call me a moron. Thanks. I'm driving you home and then I'm going out alone and find a new boyfriend."

Pym got in the car and slammed the passenger door while she fiddled with the keys to open the driver's door. She couldn't get it open. Roaring, "Goddamn fucking idiot!" he leaned across and opened the driver's door.

"Silly me," she said.

"Silly you? I'm so angry I could tear your head off. You could've told me and saved me all this trouble, all this wondering. Hell, if you'd told me the whole stinking story months ago we could've headed off this entire thing. Goddamn it!"

She drove quietly, not reacting. Pym knew the ploy; keep quiet, don't shout back, let him blow off steam, then enter the conversation when we've all calmed down. As if the thought had been spoken he shouted, "And I'm not going to calm down. I won't. NO!"

Estelle burst out laughing.

"How can you laugh? You muscle-bound floozy!"

"When you have a temper tantrum it's like in a comedy. You're too nice of a guy to be dangerous. And whatever I do, you'll have forgiven me by tomorrow."

"You are SO manipulative."

"You wanna go to Stand Up Franks?"

"Fuck no. I wanna go home and murder you. I wanna cut your head off and kick it over the bridge, goddamn you."

"How about Nye's? It's closer."

Pym put his face in his hands and roared.

"The Times? Sofia's? Want some dinner?"

He sulked as she drove. They passed the railing on the Hennepin Avenue Bridge where Pym had stood the night before when the youths called him a fag. Nobody stood in that spot now but he remembered himself hunched in agony, a dark parody of a Minnesotan, wincing against the cold and the anticipation of a plunge. He turned to Estelle and said, "If you saw a guy standing at that railing, getting ready to jump, what would you do?"

The expression on Estelle's face didn't change. She looked ahead with pursed lips, holding the steering wheel, her posture upright so that her breasts looked Christ-defying. She was turning left at the end of the bridge when she answered, "I had to stop George once. From that."

"Jumping off a bridge? What, suicide?"

"That last. It's a mortal sin."

"Oh, yes, that's right, you're one of those when the chips are down. Poor old George."

"It is. There's a special place in hell for suicides."

"Okay, okay. We'll put it in your language. And what about people who slice off body parts because they disagree with the way God made them?"

"Don't duke it out with me. I didn't want him doing it. I like dicks... I mean... Jeez, listen to me. It was Dashiell and some of them down there.

But George was so miserable. He couldn't function—not even at work after a while. He wanted me to help him die. He couldn't stand himself—his body. He'd rip at the fat around his middle and run his head into a wall so that I'd have to take him to the ER and say he'd been in a fight."

"Why didn't you tell me about this?"

"He was so ashamed of everything."

"Go on."

"It was after Halloween."

"Oh, here we go."

"Yup. I caught him BJing that stupid cowboy that was always hanging around. It was at the Halloween party about two hours before you got there. I couldn't tell you all this. George was dressed up like some character from that old western rerun he liked, Gun Draw or something."

"Gunsmoke."

"That's it. And that stupid Roy fucker came as himself. I knew it would happen one day but I didn't expect it, not at all. I walk in the spare bedroom and there he is on his knees. Right under my nose. What do you do? I let him get on with it. At least the guy was wearing a condom—my eye picked that up pretty quick. Some part of George's brain was still working."

"I just met Roy tonight."

"He's on parole. Been in the joint twenty years for murder."

"Jeez."

"Yep."

"Then what happened?"

By now they were pulled up outside the house with the engine running and a tiny bit of heat trying to escape from the moribund blower. Pym's feet tingled. Staring, Estelle shook her head and said, "I just got on with it. I went and laughed with the others and drank a bottle of wine through a straw. It was a crazy party and I decided I'd put what I seen outta my mind. Then," and she turned to Pym and smiled, "you arrived. And without that bitch, Laura. You were all shiny-faced and blonde and too repressed to chance wearing a costume. You and me been running and working out together all these years and I never told you I wished I had a man with George's insides and your casing. I was pretty wasted so I decided to indulge in the casing side of things."

"You were pretty convincing as Xena."

"The Warrior Princess... right. I knew that would get you."

"Sounds planned."

"In a way. I always liked to tease you. You knew that?"

"Sure. You were impossible to resist that night. I guess I was ready to go."

"I took you in the garage and made you fuck me from behind. God."

"And you came like a cow giving birth."

"Pent up frustration. And he'd given me permission."

"This explains a lot."

"Next day I wake up on the sofa in a whirlwind of George's vacuuming. I got a headache to beat all hell and he's tidying like a maniac. He wouldn't look at me. I could've said it's okay, Georgie, we're even—I gotta cunt full of Gilbert. But I didn't."

Pym recoiled.

"Like a bitch I busted his balls and called him a cocksucker."

"Oh, man."

"You're right, I am a moron. Always will be."

Pym put his arms across her shoulders and shook her gently. "Let's go inside," he said.

"Can't we stop this and go somewhere? I hate this."

"No way, you got a bunch more to tell me."

She exhaled through her teeth, got out of the car, and slammed the door. She clattered around the hood in her heels with the wind tossing her hair. Pym turned off the engine for her because she'd zoned out and followed her inside.

As he took off his parka he threw her the keys.

"What the hell's the matter with me?" Estelle said.

"You're a moron."

"I'm gonna bust your pompous chops if you say that again."

"What happened next?"

"Don't you got nothing to drink?"

"Only Christmas Scotch."

"That'll work."

He rummaged in a cupboard and found three bottles of scotch dating back several years and brought one out that had its own glass attached to the packaging. He pulled it all open, letting the cardboard fall on the carpet, and poured her a big drink.

"What about you?" she asked.

He shrugged and said, "Maybe later. Right now I'm too mad."

"Fuckin-A, Gil. Gimme a break."

"Then what?"

"Then George wanted to die. He didn't want to be the way he was but he said he wasn't strong enough to put it all out of his head. I asked him what was in his head and he told me he was seeing everything through the eyes of a woman. What kind of things? I asked, and he turned on the vacuum cleaner. I come home from work that night and there's a goodbye note. You know the sort of thing he'd write. I look out the window and there he is, this little distant figure, walking on the bridge. I took the car up there and shouted for him to get in. He'd crossed the road when I got there and stood right where you pointed when you asked your question."

Pym rested his neck on the back of the couch.

"When he got in the car," Estelle continued, "he was bawling. 'I can't even leave this place,' he said. 'I'm a coward as well as a food addict and a closet fairy and an alcoholic and God knows what else.' It broke my heart to hear him. 'I'll help you,' I said. 'How?' he asked. 'I think I understand you,' I said. And he calmed down a bit. So then I helped him. Or I thought I did. I know it made him feel better for a while."

"Okay, what did you do to help him?"

Estelle took in a big breath and looked steadily at Pym. "You're gonna get pretty mad," she said. Pym, exasperated, said, "Just…"

"Okay, okay. When we were home, in private, we swapped roles. I told you some of that."

"You did."

"And you laughed."

"I did, jerk that I am."

"You are, totally."

"Call me that again…"

"It was more than just a little kinky stuff now and again. We got him his own wardrobe. He dressed like me. He had a black wig. After a while it was normal. It was like a new lease on life for him—we were like newly-weds, having sex and experimenting all the time. I'd started the thing with you and figured there was no reason to stop. When he wanted me to fuck him I'd pretend it was you fucking me. My head was all over the place, Gil. All I did was cut hair, work out, and service the sexual obsessions of the Brothers Pym."

"And your own needs, don't forget."

"With you, yes. I could've done without the cross-dressing thing any time. He needed it and some part of me thought he might get over it. I didn't even know how weird it was until Laura put a stop to it all. Then he was really hurt. Apart from his brief indiscretion with the cowboy, he said he'd been faithful. Now, I know you can't be sure when people are obsessed and addicted and all that, but when he learned I hadn't been faithful to him he sort of deflated. He dumped me—no second chances. I think he was glad of the excuse so's he could get to the next stage, which was to go with men and the rest of it. He was nice about it all—typical George. And he moved in with Mishawn, who'd been at the salon with us for a few years. I found out Mishawn knew all George's problems. They'd been talking for a long time and became very close. He's a counselor and social worker and stuff but also wants to keep cutting hair. So it all worked out. Somewhere in there George had a destructive little fling with Dashiell."

"So between you, Dashiell, and Mishawn you guys ruined him?"

"Stop. He did what he wanted. Besides, Mishawn took him in but she doesn't agree with the dick-snipping thing or all the weird, woo-woo stuff he got into before he left town. He went a bit crazy apparently with his new-found freedom."

Pym sat quietly while Estelle poured herself more scotch. After a while, she said, "Gil?"

"What, Estelle?"

"You asked for all this info. Don't turn around and tell me to go away because now you know too much about me and it's all ruined."

"It is all ruined, Estelle. And you are a moron. I can't believe you'd facilitate this crazy shit with my brother. You should've hauled him to a psychiatrist. Some other way was possible. This is your fault."

"God, you bozo, get with the program. You can't undo a lifetime of muddle by going to a goddamn psychiatrist. Thank your stupid mother for George's mess if you like, but don't blame me. I got him as he was, and if a three-hundred-pound guy says he wants to wear your bra and panties you say, 'Yes, sir, help yourself.' You're such a bastard sometimes."

"Yeah, that's right, blame Ma—she's an easy shot. Why don't you just get the fuck outta here. I'm sick of seeing your spotty face."

"I cannot believe what an asshole you are."

"I cannot believe what an asshole you have."

"Who taught you to be so abusive?"

"People like you. Maybe if you got off the steroids your ass would shrink and your brain would expand."

Estelle leapt out of the chair and stood over him, pointing at his nose. "I'll rip your nose off."

"Your breath stinks. Get out of here."

"You fucking piece of shit."

"You're the shit. You're not normal. You're all fake. Take a good look at yourself, all pumped up like some fucking freak."

Estelle's hands shot around his neck and squeezed. The tip of her nose almost touched his and her blotchy, flushed face swelled with blood like when she strained for orgasm. Her arms quivering with resistance, Pym gripped her wrists and dragged them down to her sides. She tried to bite and then head-butt him, so he turned her wrists inward so that her arms straightened out and she had to stand on tiptoe.

"Ow, Gil, you're hurting me. Ow, ow, come on."

"Are you going to stop?"

"Yes. Ow. Please."

He let her go.

"You motherfucker."

"Get your coat and leave."

"No."

"I mean it."

"I ain't leaving."

"I'll call the police."

She laughed.

"Okay." He picked up the telephone, and as he did so he noticed the message indicator flashing.

"You'd do it, wouldn't you?" Estelle shrieked. "You love embarrassing me. Make me as small as you can."

"I want you gone."

She put on her coat. "All right, but you'll be sorry."

"Just go."

He opened the front door and eased her outwards, but she swung around and slugged him in the jaw. She tried to hit him again, but he caught her hand and swung her around and pushed her away. It was a harder push than he intended and she was drunk, which caused her to stumble and sprawl into the snow pile beside the walkway. Her shoes came off and her legs went into the air and he noticed she was wearing no underwear. She'd had plans. He suddenly felt sorry for her and began moving forward to help her up, but she pointed at him, shouting, "I'm going to have you killed for that, you bastard, son of a bitch!"

"Oh, yes? And who will be your contractor? Someone from the salon?"

"I'll have a couple of boys from the gym do it. They'll snap your stupid neck."

"Maybe I'll snap theirs."

"Yeah, right. You pussy, I'll have them mangle you."

"How will you pay them? Suck their shrunken cocks? Let them fuck you in your fat whore's ass?"

Estelle got up and brushed the snow off herself and put on her shoes, saying, "If I have to, yes."

"Go home now."

"You're a dead man."

"Good, then I won't have to put up with you anymore."

"I don't got any keys."

"Of course you don't. Typical tactic."

"Fuck you."

He went in and found her keys down the side of the chair. As he turned to hand them to her she started slapping at his face. He caught her hands and dragged her to the door and pushed her out as gently as he could. He felt heartsick.

"Vern and Leo are going to kill you. They already hate you. I'm serious."

"Tell them I'll be packing."

"Oh, like in a gun? How would you work the safety? You can't even work your own goddamn washing machine without your ex-wife or, in a pinch, little old shit-for-brains here, coming over to help you. Gilbert Pym packing—that's a joke. You fucking loser! You are a dead man. Count on it."

"Why don't you head back to the trailer court and learn some more nice language."

Estelle stepped forward, trembling, but apparently couldn't think of anything to say. She spun around, got in her car and roared off, burning rubber. Sweat froze on Pym's forehead.

Inside, he locked the front and back doors and put the scotch bottle away. His legs ached and the skin on his jaw felt funny where Estelle punched him. With ears ringing from the row, he listened to his messages.

Mishawn, calling from a cell phone, classical music playing in the background: "Howdy, Pym sibling. I lost you somehow. The 90's can be over-stimulating. It must've been quite something for you to meet Roy and Dashiell in the same night. Anyway, just so you know, I share your concern about what Georgie's decided to do. I tried to stop it, but there's a compulsion working that I couldn't fight. You can call me at the salon in the morning and we'll discuss if there's an intervention possible. You're probably going to have to go down there, you know."

"No way," muttered Pym.

The recording continued: "You're obviously a good guy, Gil. Georgie thinks the world of you. He was devastated after quarreling with you so badly, and I know he'd be ecstatic over your willingness to understand now. But I'm afraid he doesn't want anyone talking him out of this, so it's going to be hard. We'll talk. Night, Pym sibling."

Next message, from the cowboy: "Hey man, Big Roy here. Where'd you go? Get a better offer? I found you in the phone book. I may be able to help you with Georgie. I'll call again, man. G'night."

The drunken, hokey cowboy voice, full of bullshit and manipulation, chilled Pym's heart, especially contrasted with the level-headed and warm voice of Mishawn. That's one scary guy, Pym thought. Just stay calm, he told himself... things are starting to spin. Within a few minutes he expected the phone to ring and it would be Estelle calling as soon as she got back onto the island. She'd be weeping and apologetic and would want to come back. He already felt lonely and afraid of the empty house, but he wanted her away. It was all spoiled.

Pym never had much reason to keep calm about things in the past, but he knew now that there was only one way to handle this situation—to find George and stall him on the dick-snipping, then talk it all out. He needed somewhere to call. He did well on the telephone with George; they spoke more rationally without body language and facial expressions interfering. He recalled a little about sex changes, but he'd never paid much attention. He knew that patients had to have counseling, long waiting periods, live as the opposite sex for a long time, and, he assumed that if an insurance company refused such an operation that it would be extremely expensive. He knew George had been working hard—all sorts of jobs outside his profession—including trying to be a stand-up comedian and a hand model, but he sure didn't have any great amount of savings. And he certainly hadn't been openly living as a woman for long.

Pym called Laura.

"It's me," he said, "Did I wake you?"

"Yeah, you know you did."

"Sorry, babe."

"No, you're not. But that's okay. I know you have to say that. Whassup? Not even you are inconsiderate enough to wake someone this time of night."

"It's more about George, I guess."

"You guess? Just a minute."

Pym heard her cover the phone. It clunked about a bit, then she asked, "Now what?"

"I miss you. Why does this have to be this way?"

"Because it must. I want it this way. Don't start now. What about George?"

"He's in New Orleans. I think he's going to have a sex change operation."

Laura laughed. He thought he could hear someone else laughing in the background.

"Is it that funny?"

She squealed again and it sounded as though she'd fallen out of bed. Now he could clearly hear a man's laughter in the background and Laura's muffled voice say, "It all makes sense now."

"Hey! What the fuck!" Pym yelled into the phone.

Laura came back and said, "It's just that… God, Gil, George as a woman… it just doesn't bear thinking about."

And she cracked up again.

"Hey. I need some help here. This is my brother you're laughing at. They're gonna snip his dick off. You know what I'm saying?"

Howls of laughter.

Pym hung up.

Laura called back.

"Sorry, don't hang up."

"I need your help."

"Yes, okay. Now, what are you going to do?"

"Have you got that fuck Ray in bed with you?"

"Stop it now. Hush."

"I'd like to…"

"Oh, come on, husssssh."

Pym went quiet.

"That's better. What's in New Orleans for him?"

"The Duvals, so I'm told. They do the surgery."

"Isn't that illegal?"

"Apparently not. I dunno. Fuck."

"Are you ready to go down?"

"Absolutely not. It's a shithole and I can get him back here if I can find him on the phone. Besides, there's a little matter of being broke."

"What else can you do? Has he had the counseling and stuff?"

"He was refused the program, so, no. He'll be handling it all himself."

"Good old George." She laughed. "He's an awesome organizer."

"Compulsive son of a bitch."

"I'm amazed he's doing this, but I bet he won't be that hard to find."

"I've got to talk with more of his friends."

"That'll be fun."

"Actually, they're nice. Some of them. Got nothing against them."

"There's a breakthrough. What happened to 'Goddamn fucking faggot fucks'?"

Pym laughed.

Laura continued. "You'll be next."

"Oh, fuck off."

She laughed and said, "You'd've been easier to live with."

"As a fruit?"

"They're kind and considerate. And tidy. You're a strange mixture—a pig with too much testosterone… and too many feelings. What's funny is that you learned it all from George."

"I can't talk about that right now. I'm worried about him."

"Shall I call the airline for you tomorrow?"

"I told you, I can't go down there. How would I even start?"

"Listen. You don't have anything else going on. It's worth using your credit card for this. George has been on the verge of a tailspin for years and now it's happened. He's saved you a few times in your life, and you did the dirty on him pretty bad last year. You owe it to him, Gilbert. Poor George."

"You don't understand. No money. None."

"I'll pay for you. It's worth it to me too. I love George. Besides, who'll do my hair if he doesn't come back?"

"Are you serious? I guess if I didn't have to worry about things back here..."

"Let's just do it. We're still married for a few weeks yet, and I can afford it. You need to be on the spot. You need to get off your ass for once."

"You can call for me if you like."

"Oh, thanks."

"Ah..."

"Just teasing."

"Call me Mister Pymstone."

"Can't. That was for a faithful man I once knew."

"I can still be that."

"He was the love of my life."

"Come back to me. I love you."

"No, never. But I'll get you to New Orleans."

Pym went to bed and stared at the ceiling. Too agitated to do anything else, he resorted to examining more cards. One drew him in immediately:

> *Gillie: The trouble is that most of our world is run by stupid people, and the trouble with stupid people is they usually think they're smart. They don't know they're stupid, but when you try to warn them they take it personally and, instead of thinking about what you've said and acting upon it, they get furious, and take revenge on you. My lucky thing is that I know I'm stupid. I'm just a dumb fuck of a human being with no self-control. Pray for me, little brother—I'm about to do something really stupid.*

Pym sighed and said, "Okay, dumbo, I'm coming to find you."

Pym looked through the other cards. It was like a new kind of novel—pictures one side, sound bites the other. You couldn't go back to reading ordinary books after reading this, because this one you read with your guts, not your eyes; this one was customized specially for you—each image, each text, could send you flying off to a story all your own. It wasn't language; it was intuition, interactive video—the kind of novel angels read. A coffin was being carried through a narrow, foreign-looking street, accompanied by a brass band made up of old musicians and women dressed in black. On the back George wrote only: *Oh Shit!*

Pym smiled. He could barely keep his eyes open. Estelle would soon call. He fell asleep. The coffin image remained in his mind, and he dreamt of meeting the George of old… embraced him on the street as the funeral procession passed. George wore a sports jacket and jeans, his hair was cut short, and he had moved the ubiquitous earring from the right to the left lobe.

This woke Pym up and he reached to turn out the light, noting as he did so that Estelle hadn't called. In the dark, he envisaged his brother's left earlobe again. As a little boy he would call earlobes 'ear-loaves' and George would hold Pym's little earlobes between thumb and forefinger and squeeze them gently, saying, "Gillie, you have beefy ear-loaves. When they're big enough we'll harvest them and fry them for breakfast."

"No, no!" little Pym would cry, running around the house, shrieking. "Don't cut off my ear-loaves."

X

Pym woke with a mouth full of blood. He sat up in bed, his heart pounding. It wasn't blood—it was only dream-blood in a dream that was already vanishing—something about waking up as a mummy. Was it a blazing angel standing at the bottom of his bed? No, that damn cat had slept on his feet all night but was gone now. He heard it run downstairs. He still hadn't seen the stupid thing.

He had one of those bladder-induced erections, but even with a full bladder surely you need something to stimulate it. What was sexy about waking up as a mummy? He couldn't lose the blood taste, or the fear. The dream refused to open further, but he guessed there was a witch in it somewhere. "Weird dreams. Man, this is bullshit!"

He got out of bed, put the postcards in the bedside drawer, and walked to the bathroom with his woody bobbing in front of him like the snout of a rocking horse. Urination could only be accomplished by using the sink. The more he pissed the more his erection deflated. It took forever and stank—urine the color of tequila. You're forgetting to drink, dude. You gotta keep liquids in you.

He thought about going for a run but blew it off and showered.

In the shower the erection came back and he realized he wanted Estelle. You jerk. Maybe she was hurt on the way home last night. She was plenty mad. Call her. No, you'd only be calling her so you can fuck her. As he dried himself he said aloud, "You need a new girlfriend, a normal one, a nice Suzy-cute blonde." He thrust his hips at the shower curtain.

As he dried his genitals the erection became insistent, as though he'd imbibed some chemical. In the mirror it looked a bit like a gnarled turnip. Deeply, he intoned, "Give me peace, unruly blackguard." All it needed was a nose and eyes like you do in e-mails. He stared at his penis in the mirror. Maybe that's a mouth—not a sightless eye viewed sideways, but a non-committal straight mouth.

"Ladies!" he said *sotto voce*, "Not you, Gentlemen. May I present you to... What did you say your name was, Baldy?"

"El Magnifico, who looks asleep even when he's not."

"El Magnifico—he who never sleeps."

The ladies applauded but started leaving when the thought of Estelle emerged and made his mouth go dry. He put on a flannel shirt and jeans and fastened the zipper carefully.

In the kitchen he drank water from the tap and then searched the fridge, finding it empty. He filled the empty tuna can with water and put it down for the unseen cat. No food, pussums... you'll have to catch a mouse. I'd better remember to make a place for it to defecate.

He went back upstairs, sat on the bed with wet hair and took the cards out of the drawer. Brother gone. Wife gone. Wife with Ray. Brother about to become sister. Dead dad, evil mother, no job, stocks trashed. No Estelle. He opened the blinds and looked across Peter Pan Island to downtown steaming in the cold. No Estelle. It wouldn't do any good to give way to grief. George had taught him that.

The phone rang.

Laura said, "I got you a ticket. Get pen and paper, otherwise you'll screw this up." He went downstairs to the kitchen phone and wrote details on the message board. The cat scratched in the basement.

"Two o'clock, change in Memphis," Laura said. "Pick it up at the Northwest ticket counter by twelve-thirty. You have to take a taxi into New Orleans from the airport, and I've got you a hotel. They had some kind of deal."

He wrote down the name of the hotel.

"How did you choose this place?"

"Mishawn told me it was the one George stayed at when he first went down there."

"How do you know Mishawn?"

"He does my hair when I can't get in with George."

"Two o'clock today, you say?"

"Exactly then, Gilbert Pym."

"That's gonna be tight."

"Get to it, then, buddy."

"Come back to me."

"No."

"How much did this all cost?"

"It's covered."

"Thanks, babe."

"Sure. Now go and find that windbag and bring him home with all his parts. And by the way, don't call me 'babe.' It sounds ridiculous."

* * *

Pym only owned a big sports bag and a small holdall in which to pack clothes. Laura had taken the good cases, the ones they'd used on their London honeymoon. Why so nice now? Guilt, that's why. She was fucking Ray and she was feeling guilty; he should tell her to stick her money where the sun don't shine. He secured the postcards with an elastic band, the over-colored picture of the Café du Monde on top. The telephone rang again. He looked at his watch as he answered to see if there was time to nail Estelle once before he left town.

"Hi," the voice said. "This is Mishawn."

"You caught me just in time."

"Where you headed?"

"New Orleans to find George."

"You're doing the right thing."

"You sure?"

Mishawn laughed. "How can anyone be sure of anything with this crazy stuff? You just have to pick a course of action, then go do it."

"I have no clue what I'm doing but I gotta do something."

"I can't say I'm at all comfortable with what's going on. I haven't heard from Georgie. He didn't want you knowing anything, but he promised to stay in touch with me. That hasn't happened."

"I guess I can see why he's kept me out of the loop. I've been an asshole."

"George just wanted out of being a man. He didn't want you adulterating his decision. He said you were amazingly honest and sensible and that you'd talk him out of it."

"I'll have to see what the situation is. He should do the therapy first, shouldn't he?"

"For sure. But he knows that already. He told me he'd designed his own therapy. He was on some kind of diet and when his weight's down to a certain level he's planning on having liposuction. He's got it all planned out."

Pym laughed. "Yup, that's George."

"Just like him—bargains."

Mishawn laughed.

"What else?"

"He's told me so much about you. He keeps photographs—one in particular. You and him as kids, both with flattops. He's fifteen, you're five. You have big ears."

Pym laughed. Mishawn continued, "When he came out to you, he needed your approval. I told him you wouldn't understand. He thought you might."

"Sounds like he has a plan and means to return at some point."

Mishawn laughed and said, "As your sister."

"Oh, jeez."

"Look, I've heard some stuff about this outfit that will do the operation on George."

"Spill."

"I hope it won't put you off going down, but they're kinda bizarre, scary even—enough to give me the creeps. There's an old French surgeon that handles the work, and his wife's said to be a witch."

The word 'witch' opened a thousand curtains. From a shocked, animal paralysis, Pym could only say, "Who told you this shit?"

"Dashiell."

"Of course."

"Dashiell knows everything. The witch promises this thing called a 'glamouring,' which helps a person look, or think they look, better than they do. All the trannies are talking about it."

The word 'witch' was freaking him out.

"Look," said Mishawn. "You wanna ride to the airport?"

* * *

Mishawn's ten-year-old Accord had a fender hanging off, but the heater worked. Pym wanted Mishawn to swing by the salon to make sure Estelle was okay and, while they drove, he explained about their fight the previous evening. The salon was north on Broadway, and from the street they saw Estelle checking in a client. So friendly and warm, he couldn't stop looking at her. He noticed a pink bandage on her right hand; his eyes watered. Mishawn smiled... blushed a little.

Pym laughed and said, "She's magnificent, isn't she?"

"A work in progress," said Mishawn.

They got onto University, then 35W, and headed south to the airport. Mishawn's yellow hair laid flat against his head. He had a broad, well-fed, Danish-looking face. After a few minutes he said, "I'm sure you've guessed I was George's lover."

Pym rubbed his hands vigorously over his face. "You're not now, then?"

"No. We broke up. I didn't want him to do this thing. It's ridiculous. He's too old and he'll look a fright. Hell, he already looks a fright. I took him the way he was but that wasn't good enough."

"Tell me everything I need to know."

Mishawn's eyes fluttered. Quietly, she said, "When he did call he was weird, and secretive. He seemed paranoid. Now, no calls—for a long time. That's unlike him. You should know that all the big facilities turned him down for the operation, and the surgeons that would simply do it without all the hoopla were charging fifty grand. George found an outfit, a pretty scary one in my opinion, that'll do it for ten."

"What do you mean by this glamour thing?"

"I can only think it's a scam. In reality it's probably just coaching in how to hold one's bearing and stay out of direct light, that sort of thing. But it feels weird to me. I don't know how legal they are. I don't like George being mixed up in it. I could kill Dashiell—she's such a selfish shit—she sent George off to check the whole thing out."

While Pym watched a jet take off as they drove over Highway 77 on the Crosstown, he tried to imagine a spell that could make you better looking than you were. Implausible. But how do jets fly? He couldn't build one. He could design buildings, compete in triathlons, give women orgasms, but he couldn't make anything fly and he'd probably fail at making fire. The idea of a witch was ludicrous, yet he fully intended to get into this mysterious tube of flying tin and zoom at supersonic speed to the anus of America. It's all in what you choose to put your faith in. The idea of a witch, though—that word conjured hair-whitening fear from his childhood.

Outside the terminal, Mishawn gave Pym an envelope and said, "Call me if you need help. There's the brochure in there that George responded to. You'll notice it has no contact information on it. I couldn't find a website or anything and I find that very scary."

They both got out and went back to the trunk. While Pym pulled out his bag, he asked, "Can we get some more information out of Dashiell?"

Mishawn thought for a moment, then said, "My feeling is that Dashiell has some very nasty connections in New Orleans. She's twisted, manipulative. You must stay well away from her."

"What the fuck am I getting myself into?"

"I guess I should come with you, but I'm not the adventurous type. If I can help you from this end I will."

"You already have," Pym said, "You recommended that hotel."

"What hotel?"

"The one Laura booked for me."

"I don't know anything about any hotel in New Orleans."

"Why would Laura lie about that?"

"She's mixing me up with someone else."

"Probably. It's strange, but I guess I shouldn't look a gift horse in the mouth."

"What the hell's a gift horse?"

"No idea."

They laughed, and Mishawn put his little arms around Pym's torso and squeezed, knocking his glasses askew, and said, "Good luck, Pym sibling. Be careful."

* * *

Pym sat by the window. No one claimed the seat beside him. Surrounded by strangers, he wondered if their blank faces held in check the same nervousness he experienced before takeoffs. He pulled out his brother's cards, soon becoming so engrossed that he barely noticed the great heavy contraption in which he put all his trust lift into the air amid the usual roar. The aircraft banked over the Twin Cities and Pym took notice, looking out of the window. Below, the mostly frozen Mississippi, splitting the metropolis, Minneapolis on the west side, Saint Paul on the east, shone

in the sun like frosted ivory. Huge fissures of open water, black and jag-
ged, unseen during his runs along the River Road, startled him. Grateful to the cards for a moment, Pym looked for meaning in the order of the
pictures. When the aircraft leveled out he saw how small, flat, and mean
everything appeared on the earth's surface; being so far above it put humanity in perspective—puny and defenseless, like Neolithic clans with little
imagination other than to make squares and circles. That feeling vanished
as the plane flew through the clouds and then above them into the blue
curve of the planet.

Below, the billowy tops of clouds never seen from the ground,
and above, endless space and nothingness. No matter if you die. Why did
it matter so much that George be a female instead of a male? We are
small and temporary... what's the point in fucking around?

The answer came back—because it does matter—pull yourself together.

Why only forty-two cards? An anecdote for each year of George's
life? Coincidence? The act of forced cogitation created a sort of blur-
ring in the synapses, stiffness through lack of use—in other words, stupidity. Pym hadn't had any interest in thinking since college, but suddenly the
situation required it. His intellect felt sluggish—a slack, rusted mechanism
with no dynamic ghost activity in the machine.

The other part of his brain, the under part, the ape-man part as George
used to call it—that was working just fine. Rescue your brother from a fate
worse than death. Instinct, yes. But you can't rely on instinct. You have to
bring the whole thing alive; the intellect is the great interpreter, the great
seer, that which hauls understanding from the ocean of impression and half-
truth that resides in the unconscious. In this regard, Pym realized, his brain
had atrophied in a brine of puerile imagery. He popped the side of his head
with the flat of his hand and said, "Wake up, dude."

An oldster, sitting at the opposite window, put down her magazine and
frowned at him. He smiled and shrugged, looked down at the postcards.
The next one depicted a woman in a suit helping a young man through
a revolving door by placing her hand on his left buttock. The hand,
bare of rings but festooned with long, painted nails and a mass of bracelets
at the wrist, immediately stirred Pym. It was a faceless picture as the tall
blonde woman, perhaps in her late forties, seemed to have dominion
over the young man. Pym flipped the card and read:

> *Gillie: One day we must talk about the time when I threw Mom out of the house and Dad had to know why. When will we be ready for that conversation, eh?*

Never, I suspect. Your call, Bro.

Pym's face went red and his scalp cringed.

A recurrent dream broke open: his mother. He always dreamt this and always set it aside. Her chasing him upstairs with everyone watching. What she intended in her pursuit terrified and excited him. He eased his seat back as far as it could go and looked out the window.

George's card referred to an incident twenty years ago when Pym was twelve and George twenty-two. It happened to someone else, or was it fiction, something made up? It was about a college boy, George, who comes home to discover his mother, Nina Pym, very stoned, laughing, red in the face; and she has little Pym sitting on the armrest of the yellow couch with his jeans around his ankles. His twelve-year-old dick sticks up like a thumb as she squeezes its base with one hand and wrenches down her underwear with her other.

George stands stunned in the kitchen doorway. Nina sees him but doesn't stop. Does little Pym see him? Don't know. The room smells of weed and whiskey; Nina smells of perfume and silk. She's all undone in front and her big breasts, the nipples standing up like buttes, wobble in front of little Pym's eyes. He wants her to do it; he doesn't want her to do it. Which is it? She's lowering herself onto him—he can smell her sex, and then she suddenly flies sideways, lands on the couch and bounces onto the floor. George has veins sticking out in his neck as he shouts, "You pig!"

None of this is real. Your brother stands you up and pulls up your jeans. "Get the fuck out of here. Don't ever let her touch you like that."

Are you relieved or disappointed? You go sit on the stairs, watch, listen.

Nina looks around, dazed, and starts tidying herself. She looks for her cigarette, fails to see it resting in an ashtray under a lamp, and goes to light another one. George knocks it out of her hand. Nina says, "Are you gonna beat the shit out of me now, big man?"

"You piece of crap. Are you going to try and turn Gillie into a dwarf too?"

Nina stands, steps into her panties and pulls them up, nearly falling, then says, "You've insulted me."

"You insult all of us. You're a whore and you bring your whoring home. You make dwarves of us all."

"Ungrateful fat loser."

"I should cut your head off and mount it on the wall."

"You mounted me already, Georgie boy, remember?"

"Yeah, you thought you could cure me, make a man of me, you fucking mad bitch. You shrank me down inside so that I can't be me. You're not gonna do that to Gillie—no fucking way."

"I gave you your life. Now I'll take it back, however long it takes. I won't forget this insult."

"Just so long as you leave Gillie alone."

"I was only fooling around… I wasn't going to do anything."

"Right, like you just fooled around with me."

"I was just going to do what the nigger mothers do to make sure their sons have nice big dicks."

"You drunken lunatic, that's nothing but folklore. And another thing…"

"Oh, another thing, is there?"

"Yes, don't be infecting my brother with your racist shit. I hate it. We all hate it. It's embarrassing—you're like some throwback."

"Shall I put you over my knee and spank you, Georgie?"

"Get the fuck out of this house," says George.

Nina spits in George's face. "You get out. This is my place."

Little Pym jumps as George slaps the side of her head, sending her sprawling on the couch, her hair flying. Whose side is he on?

"It's Dad's house and you're a whore."

Nina crouches, looks up at him with her eyebrows meeting. She's like an animal, one that eats meat. She leaps up and starts slashing with her nails, zipping open a line on George's cheek. He holds her, turns her, walks her to the door, and throws her out. She stands outside, roaring, banging on the windows. George goes to the window and shouts, "I'm calling the cops and I'm going to tell them what you did."

Banging banging banging. Little Pym covers his ears. Finally, it stops. George comes up the stairs, takes Little Pym's hand, brings him back down, and sits him on the yellow couch. George's cheek seeps blood from a deep scratch. He says, "That's not supposed to happen to kids. She's finally flipped. It was always in the cards. She has to go away. She did it to me and it fucked me up and I'm still fucked up."

"How?"

"Never you mind. You just forget this happened and be normal. When the time comes, and I'm here to tell you there isn't any hurry, you find a nice girl and forget all about your old bitch of a mother."

Little Pym wanted his mommy. Whose side was he on? He could only say, "Where will she go?"

"Don't worry about her, Beefy Loaves... she's a bottom feeder. She'll survive in any environment."

The image resulting from his mother being called a bottom feeder remained in Pym's mind—a beautiful, middle-aged woman crawling along the riverbed of the Mississippi, sucking in mud. The thought of her still both repelled him and set him on.

George called the police and they took her away and she spent the night in a detox unit. Later, a butch-looking social worker came around to interview little Pym, but she refused to believe that anything serious had happened. "Mothers don't do that to their sons," she said. "It's only fathers."

"Only fathers get reported," their father, Michael Pym, said bitterly. She gave him a foul glance and wrote something in her notebook. "Usually," she said, "there's a lot more than one culprit in a dysfunctional family. What else goes on with you guys?"

"Dad's never harmed us," said George. "It's her—she's out of her mind. She did it to me..."

"Oh, for god's sake," spat the social worker, "you must think I was born yesterday."

Nina never lived with them again. After putting everything in George's name, Michael took his leap into the river, and George looked after Little Pym because the authorities didn't know there was no mother at home. They owned the house, and insurance money, plenty of it, paid for college. George eventually let Nina have some contact and hired her to run the bakery for a while before he decided to sell it and buy a hair salon.

Gazing into the clouds, Pym was so deep in reverie that the cabin attendant had to reach across the empty seat and touch his arm so that she could give him peanuts. The past snapped shut as his eyes registered the pretty face. Something George would say jumped out of his mouth at her: "Thanks. You know if you feed us peanuts, we'll act like monkeys."

She leant in conspiratorially and said, "It's a zoo in here already. I should pass out Zoloft." Then she left, laughing. She was in her forties. Pym thought: Older woman, she'd have no inhibitions. Then he wondered why he had such an automatic thought. Was it the curve of her breasts inside the uniform blazer? The peanuts stuck in his teeth. Breasts will get your attention like nothing else, you dirty little bastard. *You pay peanuts, you get monkeys* was something George had gotten from that Limey by whom Pym was allegedly fathered. Me, monkey boy... ooh ooh.

The cabin attendant returned; she smiled down at him and asked if he'd like anything. He grinned and said, "Your number."

"I mean beverages," she said.

"You've seen it all before—been the world over, serving monkeys like me, haven't you? I'll have a red wine."

She handed him two bottles, took money for one, and said, "Now you be a good boy."

Pym sipped the wine and lost himself in a fantasy of how he could get the flight attendant in the toilet. He'd done that with Laura on their honeymoon during the flight to London. Laura wore this crazy little summer dress and he had fooled her into coming to the john with him to clean their teeth while the movie played in the dark cabin. The dress had a musical theme. They wedged together into the cramped toilet and he pulled up the dress and sat her on the basin with her legs splayed. She kept slapping his back saying, "I can't believe this. You're an animal." He could see her narrow back in the mirror. She was a good sport—trying to be, at least—but she couldn't come; so he did—very quietly—not his usual roaring. He told her she was now a member of the mile-high club. "I don't care," she said, "and if you tell anyone, I'll leave you. Now I'll be sticky all the way to London."

He only told George. George told him he did it like that with Estelle all the time. Estelle didn't exactly verify George's claim. "Right," she said. "In his dreams."

He could let Ray know though. She's already fucking left. "Ray, you motherfucker, did you know..." No. You would never do that. More's the pity.

The cabin attendant brought Pym water. He liked her hips and legs in the tight uniform. Very straight teeth. He felt wadded and heavy in his nether regions; he was used to ejaculating a lot and it had now been about twenty hours. She—her nametag said *Shari*—made pleasant with all the travelers, not just him. The voice, very loud between his ears: Why are you such a prick?

* * *

Pym had to change planes at Memphis. He loitered to see if Shari would de-plane, pulling one of those little cases, but he had to catch the connec-tion to New Orleans. Airports, Pym thought, are the same everywhere—people rushing, Macdonald's, cheap crap sold dear; George called them consumer microcosms. Pym found his gate just in time and continued on with the journey. He felt defeat at not seeing the cabin attendant again.

He had a window seat, slept almost immediately, and was barely aware of the takeoff. He woke to see the Mississippi below, meandering and mud-dy, crescent and oxbow lakes formed where the old flow was, steamy vegetation, river geology everywhere—the sump of America.

On the ground, he was surprised by all the black people; he half-expected to have to go through customs. A cab into town cost twen-ty-five dollars. The driver, a nice man who knew a lot about the Minnesota Vikings and wore a colorful Rasta cap over his dreadlocks, agreed to drive him by the Café Du Monde on the way to the hotel. "Everyfin' close here, mon," the cabby said. "Dis a small town wit a big heart. You gonna love my town."

With the cab's windows rolled down, the humid air felt like a woman's breath on Pym's winter-dried skin. He passed an ornate graveyard that looked like a city built for dwarves. He passed through a real slum for the first time in his life and knew immediately that the way he looked at the world was going to alter. Strange looking moss hung from unfa-miliar trees. He saw palms. And on Canal Street paper flew around in the wind. Trams, stupidly done away with half a century before in his own city, moved the people around. It was overwhelming... too exotic. It made him sleepy.

On Decatur, the taxi slid up to the stoplight beside the Café Du Monde. It was a very ordinary establishment, crammed with tourists; nev-ertheless, seeing it lifted his spirits and made him anticipate being face-to-face with George again. "So that's it, right there?" he said to the driver. The driver nodded and just stared at it for a minute without saying anything. Then he shook his head and said, "It's in all the tourist guides, but there's better places to hang out."

"Not a good place to find chicks, then?" Pym laughed.

"Ones big as barrels from Nebraska, maybe." The driver laughed, moved the car forward, and then turned left into the narrow streets of the French Quarter. The warmth made Pym yawn; his brain felt fuzzy. He decided to get cleaned up at the hotel before looking for George.

The cabby dropped him off outside the hotel, and, as he pocketed banknotes, said, "Enjoy my city, mon."

"I'll try," said Pym.

Everything was ready for him. A young black man, elegant and polite, with a long clean face, nametag saying *Tibone*, showed him to his room and waited for Pym to get settled in before leaving.

Go slow, Pym told himself. Get your bearings—this place is like a third-world capital. To his annoyance he badly needed another nap—maybe he wasn't used to red wine. He stretched out on the bed and closed his eyes and saw in his mind's eye the flight attendant, whose name he'd already forgotten.

XI

The burlap sack containing the bones of Nadine Duval's mother watched from the shadows at the far end of the attic. Nadine stood before the cracked mirror, and, with the middle finger of her right hand, drew a circle around her navel with menstrual blood. The tiny gap she left in the circle faced the center of the earth, and she wore nothing but a chain belt from which hung a large cluster of keys. She knew whom she wanted, but out of respect whispered, "Which of you will come forth?

"Turn your lights on.

"Protect me, fearsome Nephilim, as I have protected you. Surround this Djevo and protect it from Baka, Matebo and the avenging Nkita. Keep the Zandor at bay until I need them.

"Come forth, my woman. Come forth, my love."

Alone Nadine did this—as always. Not like the twitching fools who went before her with their ridiculous chickens and infantile mumbo-jumbo. Through the fusion of the bygone ones, the inspirations of Mawa had brought Nadine here to the place of wisdom and spiritual evolution. Her inhabitants lived in the dark pyramid, the eternal city, every one of them grateful for life, the life given by Mawa who overlooks the city from its pinnacle.

Warm with buttery candlelight and the reflection of a hundred small mirrors, the sanctum, an attic section of the Spanish house, drummed with rain on its roof. Nadine smiled at the gift of rain; yes, a million distant drumbeats from time far off and lands distant.

The cracked French mirror resisted her, threw back her eyes. It rested against the abandoned poteau-mitan. In the mirror slept her ancestor, the original possessor, Mademoiselle Charlotte, a woman who owned slaves and was now one herself. The crack resulted from Charlotte's head hitting the glass during the Port-au-Prince revenge and that aristocrat's blood still stained the mirror's backboard as a reminder to all those who rule weakly. A stickler for detail was Miss Charlotte. How she hated the great fusion. The lesser mirrors around the room reflected parts of Nadine, exposing her at all angles to the cracked mirror so that she lived, fragmented, within it.

Everything depended on defeating the will of the mirror; there would be no sight without penetration into its depths. Eyes narrowed, Nadine uncoiled the python of her souls and sought traction with the earth's still center. Difficult work tonight, but not impossible, like drawing life into the dead; no, drawing life into life was the trick—the doubling and layering and believing, the stacking and packing.

The voice began, small at first, in the distant palace beyond the mansions and suburbs of the corpus, distinguishing itself from the abiding multitude but waking them in every dormant cell as it rushed to the gates of consciousness. Tingling in her spine and the approaching high-pitched tone of the voice signaled a successful beginning. At last, the voice merged with the corporeal senses and became dawn light inundating her as she stood before the candle-glow. She ran her middle finger through the slit of her vulva until smegma and heating gel ran down the inside of her thighs, mixing with the thin blood already there. Her vagina wrapped around backtime, squeezed it, turned it inside out so that her muscular concentration brought forward the work, and the voice spoke behind her eyes in one of the old tongues: *Deus Factus Sum. I am in the East and in the West, I am below and above, I am the whole of this world.*

Light dimmed, her body dripped, and the keys bunched cold against her pelvis. *Bring forth dark matter, shadow-matter, invisible matter. Be.* The awoken amalgam of deities clamored for release, but, on the point of exit, amid the shrieking and heaving lungs, it was Ishtar's feline eyes that shone back from the mirror—it was her eyes that merged with owl-eyed Marinette Pie-Cheche.

She shook in union with the merged entity, her spine electrified, and danced to the drumbeats of the rain as the spirit rode her in its pent-up lust. When she gained control of it, her uterus squeezed and her nostrils flared with the iron scent of long-kept blood streaming down her legs. Blood pooled around her feet.

"Find my golden object of desire.

"Control the magic, keep it tight.

"Bring to me the father of the One.
"Control the magic, keep it tight.
"Deliver the seed of your protection.
"Control the magic, keep it tight.
"Enter the snake-hole to other time.
"Control the magic, keep it tight.
"For this body will die, its bones in the sack.
"Control the magic, keep it tight.
"We must make the One from gold and black.
"Control the magic, keep it tight."

The goddess dropped heavily to the boards, padded to a door in the corner of the mirror, rotated her cat's head with owl eyes for a last look back at the host, then slinked around the door-jamb, and tore free.

The commerce of Hell converted in her hearing to the muffled noise of Algiers, and the forest moonlight gave way to that of the candles in the old Spanish attic. She was there and here. She trembled in oblivion until the work descended from the big to the small, and she had it—the groundwork laid; the despoiled one, the adulterer, would come—he who her protectors had revealed through the twisted longings of his fat sibling, George. Shining, Golden Pym! How she loved him! Oh, put his cock in your mouth, milk him, have his baby! The chosen one!

No! Outrageous and weak to desire so much for the body! She would gorge on him, tear him to pieces! How dare he make Nadine feel!

Fill him full of bad stomach, wet shit, and smelly farts. She would heal him and steal him, and the fat one would give up the body he hates. They must give up each other. Only then could she let the Zandor swallow them.

The fat bossal, George, came into view and his eyes hungered to see his new form. He was yet in the world but would soon have to hide in her with the others until her plan for him ripened. She saw the soft-brained giantess, Estelle, a body big enough for the fat bossal. He would be trouble, though, the fat one. He was part of people who cared... strong people; the brother Gilbert and the old mother, Nina, smelling suspiciously like Erzuli, one who has seen to the lower depth and understands the threat of nothingness. They would fight. A unanimity of mutilated ones loved Fatso for his generosity and wisdom. But, as is usual, their vanity would aid the goddess in her triumph.

She already prepared a mansion of love for the distracted Gilbert and filled it with his obsessions. He would be alone there often and would need them. His scent for sex was her weapon and she would pluck him with it. He floated soft and pointless in a world he made no effort to understand. After her there would be an end to his roving; he would follow like a dog, wild-eyed and panting.

She would keep him at least until the girl-child came, the One, to replace the unfortunate Fortuna, Nadine's first attempt to ensure the future of her multitude as her mother did by birthing her. Poor little Fortuna, the first child of her womb, spoiled by Nzambi because she was made from too much like material—the material of the once-beautiful plantation owner and the aging Duval. A shame. She would make a better one with the seed of Gilbert Pym.

Step softly, though—there resides good in him despite his being ruled by the traumatized and tantruming boy of his past, greedy for the incongruities of adventure and security. He is as one lost in the darkness of childhood, but inside him beats the potential of a stalwart heart of which wise old Baron Samedi had warned: "Beware of a sharp-weaponed hero lurking at the cave door."

Fury at goodness shortened her breath. The blindness and hypocrisy it engendered—the cringing, cowardly People of the Book with their frigid mono-god! But experience proved that destroying goodness too thoughtlessly brought anger to the spirits. Images of destruction flew from the mirror; a great flood, a great sky full of deluge, a brown river pouring over the levees, drowning the multitude inside her, damning them to the house of nothing, so that their identities floated gap-mouthed in oblivion and moths fluttered where tongues once spoke.

These Pyms could be her downfall if she wasn't artful; their skulls too thick for magic, they need nothing in their health. Crows fly from their mouths, they can live alone, they need less than the mice and starlings we feed on… her friend Huwawa would die, and the bull of her heart would be ripped limb from limb.

"Stop! Cowardly, mambo bitch, get control!"

Without this, no future. What pleasure in life without the earned right to its existence? Let's revel in the challenge and be flung to oblivion if we fail! I will stir so much death that the river will turn red.

She stood up from the pool of her blood.

The woman she was stood taller in the mirror and smiled. Before her stood the future, the prize made from her and the golden Pym: light brown flesh and Negro lips and Gaulic nose and Irish eyes and Indian cheekbones

103

and cascading soft curls the color of wet sand—a beauty so ascending that even the gods would rush into orbit around it. She felt the girl's soul already waiting in her womb.

The fat one had gone home and collected the items needed for his payment. She thought with disgust of the work at hand. A paltry fee for the Glamour that the fat one desired. What prices these fools will pay for trifles, mere fleeting visions. I gain the brother, the shining one, golden and white, my opposite. I will install his light inside me, the dark-matter on the outside, and keep him forever to build and expand the walls of the eternal city. I do the world a favor to corral this mad lion, to excite him inside me, his gold to my ebony. Come forth to my aid, dark gods of Africa, and the distant Sumer, Egypt, northern Forest, southern jungle, all you tired, forgotten ones, thirsting for nourishment. Receive this gift.

The dedication was set.

Breath returned.

Time to let the obedient ones see.

She watched, fascinated, as the spirits, woken from their dreams, looked through her eyes at the face of their host and were reminded that they lived. They clamored inside her, each one so near and dear, so rapid in passing, some angry, some sad, all captives and crying out against the walls of the city while the Mother's final answer remained the same: "Isn't Hell preferable to oblivion? Shall we cast you out like scorpions from a shoe?" They quaked at this and fell silent, eclipsed.

She convulsed one last time as the multitude receded and lay still, while the lights of the eternal city dimmed to black. She vomited yellow bile, spat it into the blood on the floor, and stood, trembling. The keys at her waist rattled as the mirror folded back to reflection.

"You're just a mirror," Nadine hissed. "Don't forget that."

The keys had rattled—not a good omen—but only forward existed. A ship's horn bellowed on the river and a car passed below the balcony on Atlantic, playing Zydeco—old Duval's romantic taste. His Mercedes turned into the gate and halted in the courtyard. She remembered him—long ago, when she was her mother, his big cock in all her places. And now he's a listing galleon, drifting without sails, inhabited by rats, and her mother a sack of bones, trapped in the dark. Don't touch them lest they rattle.

Her body excreted multiple odors and the stillness of the attic allowed her to hear the distant hiss of traffic on the Crescent City Connection. Dead

Marie and dying Duval—soon she'll unite them. This flesh is made of them. She must wash. Back to the world, and the sound of Highway 90 a few blocks away, disturbing the night like the voice of an eternal python.

XII

Pym woke in darkness to the clip-clopping of an iron-shod horse in the street. His neck ached, and the tail of a dream, something alarming and significant, slipped out of reach. He wondered if something was wrong with his brain since he could no longer recall dreams. His stomach fluttered and he felt relief at being awake. But his inability to recover the dream disturbed him, as though it continued independently, out of his control, in the parallel universe of his subconscious.

Irritated by the fact that he wouldn't sleep well later because of the rather long nap, he swung off the bed and turned on the bedside lamp. Rotating his neck so that it crunched and squeezed sinus juice into the back of his throat, he stepped through the French windows onto the balcony. A warm, misty rain fell and the humid air immediately enlivened his skin. He wore a soft pair of baggy cotton shorts; if a woman walked underneath she would be able to look up and see the eye of El Magnifico looking down at her. This thought made him laugh.

A horse and buggy, driven by an old man in a top hat, holding a whip, with several passengers huddled beneath black umbrellas, waited at the end of the street for a group of people to cross the junction. When the junction cleared, the buggy turned right and the footfalls of the horse mingled with multiple strains of music coming from several directions. Neon light and streetlight reflected in puddles, shop windows, and the chrome of parked cars. The buggy stopped in front of the hotel; he could just make out its rear wheel.

From the neighboring French windows, a few paces along the balcony, came canned laughter from a televised game show. His father, Michael Pym, hated phony laughter—he'd leave a room. Pym smelled perfume. Below

106

the volume of the television a man spoke in deep, gloomy tones about hurrying to make a reservation. His neighbors liked their French windows fully open so that the long net curtains billowed outward slightly.

Across the road on the corner, just to the right, stood a dimly lit restaurant; the people from the buggy, two men and two women, walked across to it, their laughter echoing around the street. From next door the voice of a woman, speaking from what sounded like the inside of a bathroom, said, "Eddie, for crying out loud, honey, relax."

The building opposite, an old warehouse, of which the restaurant was a part, rose two stories higher than where Pym stood on his balcony. The timbre of the woman's voice next door caused a leaping sensation in El Magnifico. Pym laughed. Some of the windows in the building opposite were broken, and all were dark. Just above the restaurant, though, two black cats, detectable only because of their yellow eyes, looked out onto the street. What about that unseen cat back at his house? He'd have to call Estelle and ask her to feed it and take care of its defecations. Calling her about a cat would be a good excuse to bury the hatchet.

His neighbors turned off their television and shut the French windows firmly enough to send a tiny shock through Pym's legs. The moist air made his skin tingle, and a song, an old Steve Winwood favorite of his mother's, started somewhere. The muffled sound of a door closing, accompanied by a vibration in his feet and their lights going off told him his neighbors had left. They were going to dinner; out for the night in New Orleans. Pym's heart suddenly and inexplicably squeezed with joy. The song, one with which he'd always identified, "Back in the High Life Again," stood out from the jazz and blues rivaling it. He surveyed the street to make sure he couldn't be seen by anyone but the yellow-eyed cats, and then he danced.

* * *

Curtains of rain swept the street and an old black bellhop with hazel eyes loaned Pym an umbrella. They stood in the hotel's cramped entryway and Pym eagerly anticipated springing into the strange, foreign night as soon as the downpour abated. The umbrella, the bellhop said, was one he had been holding for a former guest who had forgotten it but who had promised to return and give him a substantial tip for looking after it. The bellhop had wiry white hair and a cropped white beard;

when he spoke, his hands moved delicately as though reluctant to disturb the air. The owner of the valuable umbrella apparently hailed from Port-au-Prince, he told Pym, and his rooms were already booked for Mardi Gras. "Yes, sir-ee, I got me a big tip coming from that gentleman, but you can use his umbrella seeing as the rain be coming down like rats and cats."

"That's cool," said Pym, taking the umbrella. "Thanks. I've never used one of these before."

"You need anything you just ask for Sammy. That me—Sammy."

Pym smiled rigidly, waiting for the old man to release him.

Pym anticipated exploring the streets without the layers of clothing that restricted his movements all winter in Minnesota. He wore jeans and loafers and a plain black jacket. The old man produced a small map. "The Quarter's kinda small but this'll come in handy," he said.

"Thank you. I'll be looking for my brother," Pym said, and then felt goofy for relaying this information to a stranger.

Pym marked that the old man looked at him strangely, the hazel eyes cast both close and distant, before, with flagging enthusiasm, he said, "Dis hep ya find him."

The downpour stepped up another notch and Pym waited. The old man started in again about the wonderful gentleman from Port-au-Prince and the spectacular umbrella and the fact that if it kept raining like this there wouldn't be no more New Orleans for gentlemans to return to. "One day we all gonna drownd." He laughed.

After some moments, Pym looked at his watch and said, "Excuse me, but how's that restaurant across the road? Would it be a good place for my first meal in New Orleans?"

"Yes, sir, indeed it would. I personally ga-ron-tee you'll eat like a duke at the Maison de Veau. Order the veal. Everybody eat the veal there and say it good. I don't be eating there myself, mind, on account of the price."

"It's kinda pricey?" asked Pym, backing away slightly.

The old man stared at him for a moment, then shrugged; he reformed his smile and said, "You eat there, young man, never mind the price. This is my town—you only live in that body once. Enjoy."

"All right, I will," said Pym and stepped off the curb into the wet street. "See you later." He opened the umbrella and felt the rain hammering down on it as he fled from the old man's gravity into the warm rain. But only for a few yards. He stopped outside the restaurant and read the menu. Veal, his favorite meat but seldom indulged in because of its expense, was definitely the house specialty. He decided to treat himself this first night, then stay frugal.

He joined a line for unreserved seating. The line started inside the restaurant but he joined it outside, under an awning with rain streaming off it. He closed the umbrella, shook it out, buttoned it closed, then leaned on it like Charlie Chaplin.

In the left hand pocket of his jacket, his hand fingered George's postcards. Zydeco music played—incomprehensible French lyrics, which nevertheless made him think of loss—faithless women in the arms of other men. The quiver returned to his belly and the inner voice responded: You're feeling sorry for yourself again, asshole. Just quit it.

The line moved suddenly and Pym entered an uncomfortably warm foyer. Ahead of him, several couples waited; the men had their arms around the women. The women looked up at the men. The couple nearest him, quite drunk, kept kissing and pulling at each other. Another couple in the front stood by a small, dark-haired girl with long eyelashes and a bare midriff. Pym moved up a step, meaning to catch the girl's eye as a group of people pushed in the door behind him. The drunk couple looked as though they might copulate where they stood. The man put his face at the woman's ear and whispered too loudly, "I'm gonna suck your pussy till you pop a gasket."

The woman gasped, and said, "And then you'll nail me. Fuck me till I'm dead." They smashed their lips together but everyone ignored them. Pym closed his eyes, shook his head, and stepped past them into an open space, an arm's length from the seated girl. As he did this, a yell rang out. He gazed around the restaurant wondering what new crime he'd committed.

A man stood pointing at him.

"There he is!" The man announced to the restaurant. "The Secret Dancer."

The man, tall, oldish and bespectacled, with a barrel chest, stood by the window. A white-haired woman smiled up at him. Patrons seated at tables adjacent to the window looked in Pym's direction and laughed. He realized that from the window, through the shaded blinds, anyone sitting there could see his balcony. His face stiffened with hot embarrassment; to make it worse, they clapped—the people at the tables, the waitresses, the barman, and the others waiting in line.

The big oldster came over, dodging, agile as a skater, between the tables, and held out his hand for Pym to shake, saying, "Sorry, old chap. Didn't mean to embarrass you." He looked at the other people in line and laughed. "Look at his face—priceless." The man's thick glasses, like the big ends of binoculars, magnified his blue eyes to ludicrous effect. "Please join us at our table," the man urged.

Pym, somnolent with shame, let himself be bustled through the tables, the amused patrons smiling at him, one woman reaching out to touch his hand as he passed, while his tormentor, old google-eyes, shoved him from behind toward the smiling white-haired woman. "You don't mind, do you, darling?" The man said to her. "We can't let this astounding dancer stand there all night."

"Of course not," the woman said, then, turning to Pym, added, "but it wouldn't make much difference if I did, would it? Please sit."

Pym thought: who in the name of fuck are these crazy old bastards? He hooked Sammy's umbrella over the back of a chair and sat down.

"This is Vera," said the man. "And I'm Terry."

"I'm afraid we're English," said Vera.

Announcing loudly in a theatrical baritone, "Indeed we are English," Terry turned to the restaurant and bowed.

A fat-faced man in a blue suit two tables away laughed and broke into song:

"In 1814 we took a little trip..."

"Terry!" warned Vera.

Terry, laughing, was already walking over to the singing man, ignoring Pym altogether.

"He's quite mad," said Vera. "Uncontrollable when he's in his cups, but mad all the time. Never mind him. Look, we loved your dancing."

Pym understood that he had only been a temporary celebrity. Terry shook the suit's hand and then began singing with him: *We fired our guns and the British kept a-coming, but there weren't quite as many as there were a while ago. We fired once more and they began a-running', down the Mississippi to the Gulf of Mexico.* They sang a second verse, with Terry conducting and many of the patrons joined in. When they were finished, Terry said, "Ladies and gentleman, much as you must love that little ditty you are probably unaware that the United States essentially did not meet her main objectives in the British-American War of 1812 and can basically put that war in the loss column."

The crowd booed.

Terry said, "Thank you thank you thank you." He bowed grandly.

Vera turned over a glass at the table originally set for four and poured Pym a hefty shot of full-bodied Merlot. "Terry will educate that fat man on the finer points of American history. He'll return when he's intellectually bludgeoned the poor devil into oblivion. And if the fellow happens to be an academic we'll have lost Terry for the remainder of the evening. Your dancing was lovely... what were you listening to?"

"Vera, is it?" Pym said through the wine.

"Yes," she smiled. "That's it."

"Well, Vera. This is moving too fast."

Vera threw her head back and laughed. "You've hit New Orleans," she said.

The Zydeco kicked in and the drunken couple standing in line began to dance. Another couple stood and danced with them. The barman grabbed the waitress and forced her into a dance. "New Orleans," said Pym and raised his glass. "This sure as hell wouldn't happen back in Minneapolis." Vera picked her glass up and clinked it with Pym's.

"It's pretty obvious that you just got here," Vera said.

"Yep," Pym said.

"Come on then," said Vera. "Entertain me... since we both seem to have been abandoned."

Pym looked at her and laughed. Terry dodged back through the tables, a lunatic's toothy grin on his face, and hand held out again for another bone-crushing, joint-jolting shake.

"So, that gormless fat blob of a Texan is dealt with, dear. And Mr. Dancer! Sorry to leave you... Welcome to my town."

Vera said, "Stop it, you fool."

Terry said, "All right, darling." Terry took off his glasses and wiped them on the napkin, his eyes squinting. "Now, sir. What's your name?"

"Gilbert L. Pym."

Terry exploded, "Ah! We've hit the jackpot."

"Terry, dear, do calm down," said Vera.

"But Vera! *Gilbert L. Pym.* It's so literary, so American—like a character from Melville or Poe. Splendid."

"Stop it, Terry. He was just about to entertain me."

"Really? Was he going to dance?"

Pym felt embarrassment turning to anger.

"Terry," said Vera, "you're going to get punched again."

"Oh, dear. You Americans have no sense of humor. Have some more wine. How do you say it? Chill out? Ridiculous expression, but never mind. Order some veal! Waitress!"

Vera leaned in to Pym and said, "You see—quite mad."

"Yes," agreed Pym, unwinding a little. Terry looked at them, laughing. "Would you like me to kill him?" asked Pym.

"Dear me, no!" said Vera. "He's far too valuable. He's loyal and he tells the truth, and he's a laugh a minute. Couldn't do without him."

"I sure could," said Pym.

"This is an absurd conversation," said Terry. "Let's change the subject. Tell me why you were dancing on your balcony. You looked happy. Are you?"

"Not at all. In fact, quite the opposite. It was just a moment."

"A moment?" asked Vera.

"Being here. All set up. Free for a week or two. Then there was this old Steve Winwood song that my ma likes, playing up the street. I didn't reckon on having an audience."

"Men should dance," said Terry.

"Don't start," said Vera. "Not tonight, darling, please."

"Why ever not?"

"Because it's a nuisance. Not everyone wants to hear your theories on modern masculinity."

"I bet Mr. Pym does. Or should we call you Gilbert. No! We'll call you *Dancer*."

"Call me Gil. What theories?"

"Ahhhhhhhhh no," said Vera. "For heaven's sake, stick to discussing the menu. There'll be talk and talk and talk, and serviettes covered in book references, which he'll insist you find tomorrow—and masses of articles, and films. He'll get you learning martial arts and mountain climbing. He wants everybody to be nice. There'll be hugging and weeping and men's groups and grief counseling. Oh, I do so loathe it all."

"Ignore her, dear boy, she's menopausal."

"Well, at least order me another bloody drink before you launch in. You know he's a psychologist, don't you, Mr. Pym? I mean, be warned. He can't even turn off on holiday. Bloody old fool."

"A shrink!" laughed Pym. "I heard most shrinks are nuts themselves." He let that sit while he drained his wine. Above, a bumping and running on the ceiling made everyone near the windows look up.

"It's okay, y'all," said the waitress, "it's just Romano's cats, playing."

"So you don't keep the veal up there?" asked Terry.

Mystified, the little waitress said, "Sir?"

"Never mind. Now, Gilbert. Did you know we're staying at the same hotel? Did she tell you, this beastly wife of mine?"

"I did not tell him yet, Terry. There wasn't time."

"Well, we are. There. That's that."

"Ridiculous man."

"Is it true, then?" Pym persisted, "that people become psychologists because they're a bit nuts?"

Vera and Terry said *yes* in unison, then burst out laughing.

The waitress brought more wine. Terry reached across and touched his wife's wrist and said, "But we're happy, aren't we? Two little nut cases."

"Yes, we are, darling. We are indeed."

"So you're both shrinks?"

"He's catching on," said Terry, pouring more wine.

"He's the therapist," said Vera. "I'm actually a social worker but I have a license to counsel people."

Terry shook his head and said, "A license to kill—it's terry-fying, isn't it?"

"Oh, you sod! Shut up, or I'll wank you... I mean whack you."

They laughed hard into each other's faces and Pym felt sad to be left out, to be without a companion to laugh so intimately with, no one to match him, throw an arm around after clever teasing. He said, "I'm out of my depth with you two. I barely made it through college."

"Same with Terry," said Vera, "he went barely through his twenties."

"She means nakedly. Your wry wit is stunning, my angel, my little Open University seductress!"

"We both came to our professions late in life, Mr. Pym. We met at what's called the Open University in the UK. If you get a degree through there and you have some talent and drive you can go on to better things. That's what we did. Instead of having kids, me anyway—he has one. We were a pair of late developers."

"That's what I am."

"I thought you might be," said Terry. "I said that, didn't I? As he was dancing so beautifully on the balcony."

"Actually, Terry, you said nothing of the kind. To quote, you said, 'Look at that sappy cunt, prancing around on the balcony like a fairy.'"

"Well, close enough. That's what I meant."

"I see. Now it's clear."

"Cynical harridan."

"He invents everything as he goes along. He's very good with his patients though."

"I'm very patient till they pay."

"You two are a trip," laughed Pym.

"We're *on* a trip, yes, always tripping."

The waitress brought steaming plates of veal in succulent sauces. She set a dish in front of Pym that he hadn't ordered but it looked appetizing, so he shrugged and cut into it while Vera and Terry continued to banter, ignoring the plates set in front of them. Laura would throw a fit if she caught him eating veal. He noticed Vera yawning and slurring her words. The food sent his mouth into salivary overdrive. As he ate, that feeling of happiness that he'd experienced on the balcony returned. Eating veal in New Orleans was like dancing.

"Look at old Gil, tucking into that," said Terry, pointing his fork. "Come on then, mate. What in hell is a nice Minnesota lad like you doing in the new Babylon of the Americas?"

Pym, surprised at his own candor among strangers, told them most of it—his quest for a vanished George, the plummeting stock of the start-up, being laid off, the loss of Laura, the bizarre childhood. He felt encouraged by Terry's extroversion and was pleased that his self-deprecating stories created laughter. He omitted the sexual obsession with his brother's wife and that all he had left in the world was a fat fuck of a brother who was about to have a dick-snipping.

Despite their laughter, the English couple attended to his story as though they wanted to capture every word. Finally, Terry reached across and tapped Pym's wrist. "Poor old chap," he said. "I suppose it's no consolation to know that there are millions of people, just like you, trying to find a purpose and who manage to get from one day to the next."

"You're right—it's no consolation."

"Of course, of course. Now take that couple over there. Look at their body language. What's going on there?"

Pym turned to look over his left shoulder. Three tables away sat a distinguished looking man in his forties with a fine-featured young woman whose thick, red hair tumbled around her face. The man's eyes looked big and haunted—sort of how Pym felt most of the time—staring off into space as the pretty woman spoke soothingly into his ear.

"I see what you mean," Pym said to Terry. "He seems to be contorted in agony. She's trying to manage him. Been there, done that."

"They're at our hotel too, you know."

"Oh, really?"

"A very odd couple, aren't they, dear? I bet they're having an affair and there's some sort of horrible mess unfolding. Poor devils."

Vera looked at Pym and said sleepily, "This means they'll be our friends by tomorrow. Terry will have to check this affair theory. He doesn't believe in privacy."

"Privacy sucks," said Terry.

"Affairs suck," said Pym.

"Hear, hear," said Vera. "They're very dangerous. No more affairs, eh, Terry?"

"Oh, darling."

"He's good now, Mr. Pym. But he was a very naughty boy when he went through his mid-life crisis. He didn't need red cars—he needed red heads. Notice how they're still on his radar?"

"That's harsh," Pym said, laughing at a suddenly subdued Terry, who sat with his big magnified eyes focused on the table. Vera felt under the table while Terry put his head back and rolled his eyes. Vera said, "There's only one owner of Jumping Jack now, eh Tel?"

"He's exclusively at your ravenous beck and call, old luv."

"You two are bizarre."

"I'm losing my bizarreness though," Vera said, yawning. "I have to hit the hay soon."

"Right you are, my darling."

"You should go and talk to our intense couple over there," said Vera as she got up to use the restroom. "Tell them to stop it. And, what is it you Yanks say? Shape up!"

Pym and Terry laughed. With Vera moving out of earshot through the tables, and the zest purged from his voice, Terry said, "Sorry if I'm a bit of a pill at times. Lot of stress at the moment."

Pym offered, "I would think Vera would be a pretty good stress reliever."

"Oh, definitely. My God, yes. I'm so lucky. So, where will you begin your search for your brother?"

"The Café Du Monde."

"Where else but the Café of the World? Beside the greatest river in the world? You're entering into metaphor, young man." Terry tapped Pym's sleeve with his index finger. "How I envy you."

"And you? Why are you here?"

Terry gazed directly at Pym, a sort of magnified, blue-eyed, English-actor look. "My son's here."

"Oh, cool."

"And also... Ah, why shouldn't you know... my wife's dying. I want her to see everything before she leaves me."

"Shit."

Terry said, "Exactly. But, that's life, isn't it? We do our best, or try to, or should try to. Most of us don't bother. I didn't used to bother till I met Vera. Now I do my best... which is pathetic. What else could it be? The main thing I find is to not sweat the small stuff. Life's too short."

"You're right. And look—I'm real sorry to hear this."

"Of course you are—you're a nice lad. No more talk of it now, all right?"

"Okay."

"When she returns, empty-bladdered, I'm going to take her back to the hotel. Then I'll be off for a wander until I'm sleepy. We'll probably see you tomorrow."

"I hope so."

"It's guaranteed, young man. Absolutely guaranteed."

* * *

Vera linked her arm through Terry's as they walked across the road from the Maison de Veau to the hotel's entrance. Terry's nerves, his entire corpus, shivered with concentrated anguish. Gilbert Langley Pym, the child he'd sired on the love of his life, the goddess tattooed on his libido, had dined with him for an hour, ignorant of Terry's paternity. Mindful of the boy's thirty-two years without his real father, and seeing clearly the mixed genes of Nina and himself emblazoned in the boy's eyes, cheek-bones, hair and lips—hell, he even sported Terry's plump earlobes—Terry felt it wasn't the right time to lay a thunderbolt on the young man.

He should have always been with this lovely boy, this shining knave. He should have let Nina join him in England. The spell of Michael Pym's fatherly friendship told him no, she's a married woman. Stay with your husband. But he could have married her, nuts as she was then... sorted her out. The boy could have played for Arsenal, England even. He looked a bit like Alan Shearer but with the hair of Dennis Law. Shear-er should play for the Gunners instead of those pimply Geordies. We need more Englishmen in the team.

In front of the hotel's entrance, Vera gave Terry's arm a series of violent tugs. He looked at her stupidly, as if he didn't know her. "I know what's going through your mind," she said. "You stupid old fool."

"I'm sorry," he blubbered. "Of course you know."

"We better have a drink at the bar," Vera said. "Otherwise you'll start crying and banging on in our room about mortality and lost chances for attaining existential grace, and I'll never get any bloody rest."

Terry laughed, turned, and kissed her forehead. "You're wonderful," he said. "What would I do without you to keep my feet on the ground?"

Vera tried to hide it, but Terry could feel the shame, the feeling of being second best beneath her countenance. It was all his fault, as were most things, and for all the honesty that existed between them he wished he'd never told her about Nina Pym as part of an explanation for the affairs he indulged in through his thirties. Honesty is not the right pol-icy when you try to explain to a mere mortal that you've been in love with a goddess nearly all your life.

"Actually," he said, "I was thinking about Arsenal."

Vera halted abruptly and looked at the sky. "Take me now," she said.

Terry laughed, relieved that he had something else to think about, and said, "Come on inside. Let your old stick treat you."

"I'm tired," Vera said. "I have to sleep, otherwise I'll be shot for to-morrow. But let's sit at the bar and talk sensibly about this new son of yours and how we're going to proceed. You mustn't be thinking of Arsenal in situations like this, Terry dear, it isn't healthy."

"Yes, darling. You're marvelous."

"No more compliments, no more deflecting..."

"Yes, my angel."

"Terry!"

"Sorry."

Being close to Nina Pym made sperm go into party mode. It was Nina, all those years ago, reveling in Terry's rolling stone, fake bad-boy persona, who had named his dick Jumping Jack Flash.

Over thirty years ago, Terry had alighted the Greyhound at the Min-neapolis bus terminal and saw Wonder Woman kissing a man much older than she, while a large overweight boy stood beside her. The man had short hair and it took a while for Terry to understand that the man being kissed goodbye was in the military and was maybe going to the war. As Terry waited for the driver to pull his pack from the underbelly of the bus, he watched the shorthaired man get on the bus in the opposite bay. He watched the bus back out of the bay, and then he followed the beautiful woman and the heavy boy out of the bus terminal.

"Excuse me," he said, "I wonder if you'd mind giving me some direc-tions."

She swung around, already smiling. The full mouth, the dense dark hair moving like sea-grass in the mild breeze. More than an actress, more than a model, more than something made of marble that some desperate god had breathed life into. I'm in love, he thought.

"English!" said the goddess.

"Correct," he said. "You have a good ear."

"Where you headed?"

"The Y."

"Ish. You don't wanna stay there."

He shrugged, kept looking at her. She smiled, slipped on a pair of sunglasses, and looked not at him, but at the fat boy, as she said, "Well, we gotta spare sofa. He may as well give me the money as the stinking Y. Whaddya say, buddy?"

The boy shrugged, looked at his shoes.

"Whaddya say, Mr. Brit? I could sure use the extra bread."

Nina made love to him twenty times before they talked about her husband. It was a certain kind of orgasm that got her talking, a deep cavernous one that came after several lesser ones and then had her rolling around on the bed with an excruciating uteral cramp. She was like a bomb gone off. "No way," she kept saying, "No way," as she rolled around, laughing and crying.

Then when the cramp finally relaxed, she said, "That's it. I reached the limit. No one could come harder than that. I'm still dizzy. Stop looking so goddamned cocky—you didn't make that thing, God did!"

He pulled her toward him and mimicking her accent, said, "Stap looking so gaddamn cacky, you didn't make that thing, Gad did."

She pointed her finger almost up his nose. "I'm not the one with the weird accent, you are. This is America."

"I love you," he said.

She sat back and looked at him; her eyes filled with tears. "Michael's coming home," she said.

An army reservist, Michael Pym baked cakes for a living and had his own little business. Nina had come to work at the bakery right after high school, intending to make big money for college by working nights. She worked nights all right and soon she was pregnant with George.

As a young man, Michael had fought in Korea and went back in the reserves after George was born so that there'd be a little extra cash. He'd risen to the rank of catering officer—Lieutenant. Five days into his annual month's tour his back went out lifting a sack of flour off a skinny private who had fallen over with it—a severe enough strain to be sent home. It was a relief because there had been rumors that his unit was going to be called up and sent to Vietnam.

When Michael got back, he lay in bed a few days and then went to the Veterans Hospital for an operation. On his return, Terry was still there and the story was that he was a roadie with The Kinks and was awaiting a court date for a drug charge. It was an elaborate and exhilarating lie, formulated by Nina. "I love Mike," Nina said, "and my Georgie, but I can't let you go… you're my prince. You're the only one who can fuck me properly. Never go away."

Terry painted the house, mowed the lawn, played with George, and helped at the bakery while Michael Pym convalesced on the yellow couch, watching television. Often, with a Twins game on, Nina would make Terry come in her mouth in the kitchen. She was desperate because there was no time to fuck properly. She had grown accustomed to those big orgasms and they'd gone away since Michael came home. The first morning Michael went back to work, easing himself out of the house at four-thirty in the morning, Nina came straight downstairs and got on top of Terry and rode him like a mad woman on the yellow couch. When she was done screaming, doubled up with the usual cramps, a voice called down the stairs.

"Momma?"

"Go back to bed, Georgie."

"Momma, come up here."

"I can't, Georgie. Momma's busy. Go back to bed."

When Michael got home he took Terry aside and thanked him for the work he'd done at the bakery. He said he liked his style and that everything had been arranged just so. "You got class, you Limey asshole." He took him fishing for walleye that afternoon, shared how much he loved Nina, how she was the apple of his eye, how he wanted a little brother or sister for poor Georgie, who was a queer sort of kid and too much alone.

They had a beer afterwards because it was hot. They got in late. Nina, furious, waited in the kitchen. The boy was in bed. "What bullshit has old Pym been feeding you?" She asked of Terry. He couldn't look at her and he saw in her face that she knew immediately what was going to happen next.

In the morning, when she came down to fuck him, he couldn't get an erection. He was full of guilt. "Don't you love me anymore?" she asked.

"More than you'll ever know. But Mike's a great guy. I feel terrible. It was okay when I didn't know him. Now I caught fish with him."

"Christ, men are such assholes."

"I gotta get back to Blighty. There's a course I'm enrolled in starting in September." It was a lie—he was learning from her. It was from a song by Rod Stewart, just plucked out of the air like magic.

"I'll come with you," Nina said. "Mike won't oppose me. We can get married there. I wanna see Carnaby Street." She started to suck on him and he couldn't help himself and away she went again, jamming on him, wailing and shrieking, so the kid came to the top of the stairs, crying again.

When Nina went shopping with Georgie, Terry stuffed his belongings in his backpack and called a taxi. While he waited, he sat on the yellow couch and wrote a note to the effect that he was grateful to the Pyms for their hospitality but that he had over-stayed his welcome, was feeling home-sick, and didn't want to face the pain of tearful goodbyes. Please forgive… *et cetera et cetera.*

That afternoon he boarded a Greyhound for Los Angeles.

* * *

Now, sitting at the hotel bar with Vera, his mate of twenty-odd years, Terry felt cowardly to have disowned the love of his life so easily, his loyalties scrambled by the wily manipulations of Michael Pym. Gilbert's revelation that Michael committed suicide around the time Terry settled down with Vera clanged away in him like cracked bells. Michael would be approaching his eighties now, and his sagacity would have come in handy. What a waste.

"You know," Terry said to Vera, "the second Gilbert walked in the restaurant I knew who it was."

"Yes, it was shocking—your spooky eyes and sprouty hair."

"Spooky? How faddish, darling."

"'Cept his are green, I noticed."

"My mother's—like liquid emeralds."

"No wonder she was a floozy."

Terry laughed. "Yes, well, she certainly got plenty of attention, bless her heart."

"Are you going to tell him?"

"I don't see how I can at the moment. How does one approach it? And wouldn't it be rather egocentric?"

"I suppose it would."

"What if I can just be his supportive English uncle and leave it at that? He has a dad, albeit a dead one."

"Terry, that's badly put."

"I put everything badly. I'm a brute."

"A beast."

"What do you think? Should I tell him? George gave me no indication of what I should do in that regard, and now he's vanished. I'm quite cross. He orchestrates all this and then buggers off."

"It's worrying. I hope he's okay."

"Well, of course."

"I don't think you should be hasty. Let's get to know Gilbert for a day or two and see how the psychological land lies. You don't want to muddle him any further. You also risk his anger."

"I hadn't imagined that."

"Really?"

"No. I can only imagine fascination. I suppose because that's how I'd feel. I'd love it, but there again I didn't have a father, and I've only survived in the world because I found you."

"Don't be silly."

"I love you, my angel, my saviour."

"Oh, put a sock in it. Your mum may have been loopy, but you have your wonderful extended family. You did all right."

"I didn't, you know. I really didn't. I believe firmly that had I enjoyed the presence of a father I would have been a much finer person for a larger percentage of my life. At this stage a certain amount of wisdom kicks in, or should, and you can begin sorting things out for yourself, but I wish I'd had a dad to go and watch Arsenal with."

Vera laughed, "Oh, Christ, you see, everything comes down to football."

"Well... or... fishing in the Highlands, hunting in Kerry, hikes in Snowdonia."

"It's funny, we've never talked about this. Sounds like you wanted a father from the aristocracy rather than Islington."

Terry laughed. "Yes, I expect my pretensions are running way ahead of my breeding. But isn't that always the way? Look at Hitler."

"You're mad, Terry."

"I don't know what to think about any of this, to tell you the truth. I'm just a man of flesh and bone, not long on this strange planet. All I know is that I live from day to day, vaguely conscious, dependent on placing food and drink in a hole in my face which comes out the next day from another hole where the sun seldom shines, and that in between those actions I'm bothered by these idiotic questions about existence. Then I find I have a son, and worse, one that looks like me, and suddenly all else fades and I want to protect him and give him a life without all the pain I had. It's a sudden travail for the like of which I'm ill prepared."

"Poor old sod. You should've kept it zipped, shouldn't you?"

"Easier said than done."

"Is *she* going to turn up on the scene?"

"Nina Pym? I don't know."

"I'm not sure how I'll feel about that. Will she be a threat to my dominion over you?"

"Your sovereignty?"

"My ownership, yes."

"Darling, that was years ago. There's nothing of that left in me now. When I nearly lost you at our beginning, that was all burned out of me."

"You're referring to your confusing dalliance with Nurse Buxom before you'd thoroughly convinced me that I wasn't just another of your collectibles. I was serious in the restaurant—you still get this wistful, far-away look in the presence of redheads."

"Oh, please, darling—that's all long gone."

"I hope that's true."

"It is."

"Good. I'm going to bed, then. You finish your drink and then go and see the night life so you'll have something to put in your never-ending book."

"Darling, you're cruel."

"Good night, old prince."

"Good night, my angel."

Vera left and Terry's conscience spilled over hot and caustic. You're such a bloody liar! You damn yourself with your lies. When will you stop it? He somehow refrained from slapping himself.

In a section of Terry's huge novel portfolio reserved for notes, Terry kept a few mementos of his past. Vera, right as usual, would be annoyed to find the last love letter he received from Nurse Buxom, a girl whose name he couldn't quite remember without Vera's help. It was all subtext:

> *Here's the daily maintenance for lions over 40:*
> *1 aspirin 81 milligrams (get the chewable baby aspirin, because if you ever are having chest pain, you'll want one that you can absorb into your system as quickly as possible).*
> *1 vitamin E capsule 400 I.U.*

If you are ever feeling chest pressure/pain that radiates down your arm or up into your jaw (especially on the left side), ring emergency services and then lie down until they get there. People also feel nausea or perspire heavily unrelated to exertion sometimes.

The worst thing that you can do is try to drive yourself to Emergency, and we've had people being driven in by friends or family members that had a full-blown arrest in the car. In the ambulance they can give you nitroglycerin, morphine, oxygen, etc., plus, most importantly, they can defibrillate you right away if you arrest en route.

This is all stuff that I hope you never have cause to need to know. Perhaps you'll be around someone who IS having an MI though, so it helps to know what to do. When you're having your next physical, explain to your doc that you have a family history of early MI (your mum)—that will usually lead to them checking things out a little more thoroughly diagnostically than they might otherwise do.

The letter was the result of chest pain he'd felt after strenuous intercourse with the authoress in the toilet of a commuter train headed for East Grinstead. They later determined it was the sausage sandwich he'd gobbled down on the platform at Victoria. What a lovely girl she was— extremely intelligent—be forty-five now. The lovey-dovey part of the letter was gone, only the heart health instructions remained.

Terry ordered another Manhattan from Tibone and pulled from his jacket pocket and unfolded the crisp print-outs of George Pym's e-mails. He read through them again, searching for some clue as to why George failed to show.

Dear Terry:

Great talking to you on the phone but I can't afford it anymore, so I hope you don't mind if we continue this with e-mail.

It's best if we all meet up on neutral ground if it's all the same to you. I'll be in New Orleans, as you know, and I have friends there who'll help us do this. Can you get to NO? I'll do the rest at massive discounts.

Thanks, Georgie

Terry:

Glad you can pull this off. But I'm real sorry to hear the bad news about your wife. I'm glad you're bringing her. I guess we'll all have lots to talk about. Not the least of which will be my ma, Nina, who will not be invited to this weird little reunion, she would create havoc.

I'm working on your accommodation.

Terry:

No, it wouldn't be a good idea for us to have my mother in on this. I'm afraid you have no idea how self-centered, narcissistic, and histrionic she can get. She knows something's up, but as long as Laura and Estelle don't blow it, Nina will be kept out of the loop. I know this sounds mean—just trust me for old time's sake. Glad you understand.

Terry:

I know you handle all sorts in your profession, but my ma is the mother of all toxic parents. You won't regret her absence.

Here's the agenda. I'll meet you at the airport and take you to your hotel. It's owned by an acquaintance and you can stay as long as you like as it's the off-season right now.

We'll get Gilbert down from Mpls by midweek and start work on him. We have to get him over this ruined marriage thing and into some sort of serious commitment to my ex, Estelle, who is perfectly suited to him. He has to shit or get off the pot as far as Estelle is concerned. He's fucked us all up enough as it is, the little bastard (oops).

Then we have to explain who you are.

Then my gender reassignment.

You're the expert. I hope you can handle it all.

> *Terry:*
> *Thanks for asking.*
> *I'm having surgery any day. I've done all the thinking, this is what I want, and, as you say, a person like me has indeed covered all the bases, so don't worry. I'm scared and excited. I've given up everything to get this, even my brother. He deserves what's up ahead, he's been a bastard. It's up to you to save him now. I'd like to kill him and bring him alive again as a toad. You have to stop me!*
> *Attached find booking arrangements in case of mix-ups. I'm so fucked up, forgive me.*

With no new insights, Terry refolded the e-mails and put them in his pocket. He finished his drink and then went upstairs to kiss Vera goodnight and tuck her in.

* * *

Pym stood outside the Café Du Monde, debating whether to enter. Jackson Square, all lit up opposite with the illuminated Cathedral at its farther end, and horse-drawn carriages drawn up on Decatur, created the impression of a festival waiting to happen, but, with the damp air turning chilly, few people walked the streets. Pym didn't feel cold. In fact, the walk down Chartres heated him up. Packed with food and the glow from Terry and Vera's wine, he felt content for the moment and even admired the peculiarly shaped man-hole covers.

He entered the café and found a table at the far end where he could see out to the horse-drawn carriages. Pym's heart pounded and his thoughts all went to cover the knowledge that he was quite alone. There were more servers in the Café Du Monde than customers. And the servers were mostly Asian. He felt a powerful urge to retreat back to Minneapolis now. A few hours in this city and he may as well be in some ethnically confused corner of Brazil. Like the messages of meaninglessness he'd read about in college, and failed to comprehend, liberal arts electives— now he got it. The empty pointless streets of Sin City—his bowels contracted and he felt emotion flooding up through him. An hour or two ago he was dancing on his balcony. Now, suddenly, he wanted to fling himself into the river. He'd been alone at Thanksgiving, alone at Christmas; drunk at Nye's on New Year's Eve, no memory of New Year's Day. He wanted his wife, he wanted his brother, he wanted his job. He wanted children—maybe a reason to be in the world. A rush of anger welled up against his parents, weakling and bitch, brought him to the world and then set him loose like a seed in a storm drain.

A tiny waitress had crept up on him and stood, slightly at his shoulder. His eyes were tearful and he used a gaze into the menu to cover himself, but he couldn't say anything.

"I Lulu."

"Hello, Lulu."

"You already eat supper?" the girl asked.

Pym nodded.

"Jus' wan' coffee, den?"

"Sure. Café au lait," he said, pointing.

"You wan' beignet wiv' coffee?"

"No, thanks."

"Be right back."

"Okay."

Pym watched her tiny back dodging through the empty tables. She was nothing to do with him except that she was so clearly from somewhere very far away. And the sorrow welled up in him like a blocked toilet. All the mistakes from childhood, all the games he'd played trying to protect something that didn't really need protecting. Laziness, lethargy, silence—all manner of failures. The failure to make good on his promise to Laura—to make every morning they woke together like Christmas. He could've done this. Pride was in the way. A boy's pride. If there had been someone to tell him—what then? To teach him to avoid stubbornness. Idiot. Now alone. He took out his own postcard, wanting to write a succinct truth to Laura like George had done forty-two times for him. He stared at the blank card.

Go back to college and start again, loser.

The waitress came back, holding his coffee. She frowned when she saw the postcard in front of him. He'd not imagined for a second that this might be the waitress that George had made reference to. She wore almond shaped spectacles. She set the cup beside his clean postcard and said, "You're welcome," before he'd thought to thank her. Even in his sitting position, his eyes were almost level with hers. It just came out. "Were you the one who was kind to my brother, George?"

"Yes," she said.

"Thank you."

"He the one kind to me."

"Where is he?"

Her eyes looked big and grainy through the almond-shaped lenses. "Not know. He no come back. I worry, den fink he find other café, other fren."

She looked back toward the kitchen, then sat down. "You come to look for him?"

"Yes. He sent me these cards." He took the pack out of his pocket and turned them. She smiled. "I know these. He sit over dere. Near kitchen."

"He would."

"You find Georgie. Dat good. Good person, but mixed up."

"How can you help me?"

"He dress funny. Like bag lady from eighties. Only not look like woman."

Pym laughed. "Looked hideous?"

"Yes. Scary. You find. Take Georgie home. New Orleans no place for him. Y'all go back Minneapolis, yes?"

"Maybe. I just want to find him. Talk to him."

"He sometimes go to House of Large Sizes over dat way. I show you later if you want. Pretty lady dere. His fren. Fren of all like him."

"We have to improve your English."

She laughed. "Georgie say same. No good—I not smart. Speak shit French too."

"I can't speak any French. I'm a total dolt. You're very brave. You try to speak."

"I walk wiv you to House of Large Sizes later."

"Won't it be closed?"

"No. Open late." Then she left. He put the cards away and reached for the *Times Picayune* spread lavishly on the next table. The headline boasted a murder rate two ahead of Detroit. People, tourists mostly, were being attacked in the graveyards. A woman had died of a heart attack after discovering a corpse attached to the propeller of a river cruiser. The body was not yet identified. Pym stared at this little story. His mother and George.

Ma finding a dead George in a dress; she'd take it in her stride though. He laughed, saw her rheumy eyes and smelled her dragon's breath. Her throaty voice said, "George is around somewhere, he'll be fine." As a child, Pym would sleep against her; the smell of her silk nightgown, his little face pillowed between her breasts—she smelled okay then.

He wondered what it would be like to make love to a homely little Asian.

* * *

Vera draped her underwear over the end of the four-poster bed while Terry turned down the bedclothes. "Come on, lass," he said, "in you hop." He was quite drunk and seeing slightly double, so he wasn't quick enough to avert his gaze from the snakes and vines of her chest. His heart started to pound. Vera pulled the bedcovers up to her chin and said, "You forgot to make me brush my teeth."

"You can do it first thing. Did you take all your medications?"

"Yes, Terry."

"Are you lying?"

"No, Terry."

"I'll believe you… thousands wouldn't. Look, I'm a bit wound up," he said. "I want to prowl around a bit."

"See if you can find that boy of yours?"

"Do some spying."

"How do you feel about meeting him, darling?"

"Peculiar."

Vera lifted her hand to his cheek and said, "I can't believe this George fellow didn't follow through with your plan. It all seemed water-tight after all those e-mails."

"It's an appalling balls up. He deserves a kick in the kyber."

Vera laughed and said, "You should've seen your face when Gilbert danced on the balcony. You had no idea it was him."

"I'm an idiot. That's exactly the sort of thing I do when I'm alone."

"As I suspected."

"But weren't you clever, darling? You twigged immediately."

"Nothing clever about it," Vera laughed. "It's just sod's law—the first lunatic to turn up in our hotel was bound to be your son."

"I see."

"Were we right to stay shtumm about your paternity?"

"My paternity?"

"Isn't it a lovely word?"

"I wanted George to break the ice. It would've been a rotten shock to do it over the veal."

"Having you as a father? You did your best to make him want to hang himself just meeting you as a stranger!"

"Thank you, darling."

"You are who you are—mad as a hatter—so you may as well get him used to it. He probably has similar traits if I know anything about genetics."

"Which you don't. Shall I bring your meds now?"

"I'll take them in the morning."

"You just said you took them."

"You tricked me."

"I'm getting your meds and you're taking them."

"They make me feel tired and ill. Besides, what's the point?"

Terry just stared at her.

Vera said, "Don't twinkle at me, Langley. You're so bloody righteous, like an old matron."

"You need them."

"Oh, all right. Christ. You just want me doped up so you can stay out late and then sleep late in the morning. Don't stay out till sparrow-fart, please, darling."

"Will you be afraid?"

"It's a strange place."

"You're safe."

"Supposing I die in the night? Imagine the fuss, to end… down here in the anonymous tropics."

"Darling, come on now."

"I'm sorry."

"Plenty of life in you yet."

"We'll see, won't we? At least you won't be alone… you'll have your American thing back."

"What on earth are you talking about?"

"This wonderful son. He's like a prince. You're so lucky, aren't you? You've been lucky all your life… you fall on your feet like a cat. You'll have a full-grown prince to impart all your wisdom to."

"If he doesn't hang himself."

Vera laughed and said, "No, darling, you're very wise. My clever, clever old goat. And I'm lucky—to have lived these years with you."

"Darling, this is not the end of a David Lean film."

"You swine!"

"You thespian!"

"Wake me up when you get in."

"Dirty cow. You have sex on the brain."

She held him by his chin, and said, "Always. Anyway, wake me up—so I know I'm still here."

"Darling, please..."

"Now bugger off and have a drink, but don't get mugged."

* * *

Pym waited for Lulu under an awning while rain fell. Water rose quickly in the drains and Decatur street flooded quickly. Then the rain stopped. Pym kept the *Times Picayune* rolled up in his jacket pocket. He strolled a few feet toward Jackson Square and looked at the soaked horses and dripping carriages standing untended. The levee of the river rose up to his left and he was startled to see the masts and funnels of a huge ship passing south with scores of small lights. He looked back and there stood Lulu, shivering under the awning.

She seemed even smaller in a heavy black motorcycle jacket, jeans, and black shoes with blocky, Cuban-style heels. Pym went to her, and, as he approached, she smiled. In an attempt to look pretty, she'd let her hair down and replaced her little glasses with contact lenses. Pym laughed. "All right, lead on, Lulu."

The map of the Quarter, laid out on the very rational looking tourist map that Sammy had given him earlier, wasn't as easy to navigate as it looked. He had studied it in the café, but he didn't want to insult Lulu by using it as she walked fast away from the river, taking him down alleys and through buildings. The streets became more crowded now that the rain had stopped and he had lost his orientation to the hotel. Pym felt out of his depth again and disliked being led around by a stranger. Lulu clopped along in her huge shoes and leather jacket without speaking. She had beautiful hair. On some level though, the thought he had indulged in earlier—of having sex with her—disturbed him. She caused no point of arousal in him at all save perhaps one born of curiosity. But he told himself he loved Laura, and she'd left him for Ray—and this was fucking with his libido. He missed Laura's sanctity. Then Estelle crowded Laura out and a zing of lust sprang up his spine. It was the image of Estelle that always caught him. Ridiculous!

In a stand-up open bar they passed, Pym saw the crazy Englishman, Terry, beer in hand, glasses blazing, chin jutting forwards, causing two well-dressed black men to crack up, bend double, slap their knees. God, George, Pym thought, what the hell have you gotten me into?

Pym pretended not to see Terry and kept moving.

Lulu turned into a street and the atmosphere changed. Pym couldn't see the street sign. He saw only men around, and anyone wearing womens' clothes was a man underneath. He knew the look from his baptism of fire at the Gay 90's in Minneapolis. He passed a bar with music blaring; inside, women with long legs danced erotically. He stopped for a second to look and Lulu stopped too. Her expression remained blank. Pym looked at her, pointing with his thumb. "Boys, right?"

"Right," she said.

"Is this what George is trying to achieve?"

Lulu put her head to one side and thought. "No. He just wanna be happy. Come on. You see."

After a few blocks they reached a small storefront with big red capitals across its facia: HOUSE OF LARGE SIZES. The dimmed lights inside made it look closed. "Here it is," said Lulu. "Another be here. Sasha. She help you. I stay, or I go?"

"Stay. We'll have a drink after."

Lulu laughed and then tried the door, unsuccessfully. Pym gave it a shove and it flew open and banged back against the doorframe, causing Lulu to let out a little scream. A woman appeared out of the gloom and turned on a light; she was tall and dark and strode toward the open door. "I'm sorry," she said. "We're closed." Silhouetted against the light at the back of the store, the woman's shape was extraordinary, almost too good to be true— like Jessica Rabbit.

"I pushed the door kinda hard," said Pym. "I didn't mean to be breaking in or anything."

"That's okay, honey. That door ought to lock better, and I was going out soon, so didn't turn the bolt. I apologize for being inhospitable, but I'm late for an appointment and have to be out of here."

"I understand you know my brother, George Pym?"

"Oh yes, sure."

"I'm trying to find him."

"I don't know his address, hon. But maybe if you can drop by tomorrow during business hours I'll do all I can for you. Are you sure she wants to be contacted?"

"Sure he does. I'm not like trying to deprogram him and shit. He's my brother."

"All right. We open at ten tomorrow. I'll be here. Come find me. I'm Sasha. How you doing, Lulu?"

Her face expressionless, Lulu said, "I wanna fine Georgie too. He fren."

"Has he not been contacting y'all?"

"It's no big deal, Sasha," said Pym. "We've just missed each other, I expect. But something's come up and I haven't got time to wait a month for him to get his shit together and call me."

"I'll ask around tonight. Maybe someone will know something. I ain't seen him neither for a while. Hey, I gotta run, kids."

On the sidewalk, headed back toward the neon lights of what he now understood to be the famous Bourbon Street, Pym felt a sinking sensation in his gut. Sasha gave something away. Pym couldn't say exactly what it was, but he didn't quite believe her. He was amazed to be drawing on an intuition he seldom needed to use. The last time was with Laura when he was asking her on the telephone if she was seeing someone else and she said no and Pym knew she meant yes.

Lulu wasn't saying much. She clomped along in her big shoes. Pym looked down at her and said, "You know I hardly looked around that store. What was there? Big clothes for fat cross-dressers like my bro?"

Lulu stopped and looked at Pym and said, "Dat mean! You be nice. Or Lulu not help, say fuck you."

"I get insensitive during bouts of frustration. Sorry."

"You be nice."

"I am nice."

"Mean man get no girlfren."

"Depends. Some women only like mean men. My mom was one of them. And my wife just left me for one."

"Maybe wife go to nicer mean man than you. Less of two bads."

"I hadn't thought of that."

"Better start finking. Maybe Georgie gone 'cus you stupid and brutal."

"Okay, okay, I'm sorry."

"You buy Lulu drink at good bar. Lulu got no money."

"Lead the way."

Lulu headed straight for the bar where Pym had just seen the crazy Englishman.

"Must we go here? It's loud."

"They all loud."

Pym couldn't see Terry as they entered. A man reached out and grabbed at Lulu. She threw his arm up in the air and he laughed. "Pig," she said. "Hey, Lulu," said the man as they walked deeper into the bar. "No BJ for Billy-Bob?" Several other men laughed.

When they sat down, Pym asked Lulu what that was all about. She looked at him as if he was an idiot, then asked, "What Georgie tell you about me?"

"That you were kind. That you let him sit for hours in your section. That he had run out of money and you fed him."

Lulu opened her bag and took out a very long cigarette and lit it. She had a peculiar way of smoking. She offered him one but he refused with a slight grimace. "George not tell you I boy?"

The information passed through Pym like a mild electric shock. This one had fooled him. The ones at the Gay 90's, the ones just now in the street nearby had this peculiar puffy maleness to them, reminding him slightly of aliens masquerading as humans. He couldn't help it. He wanted to be sympathetic but he found himself repulsed by looking at them—particularly because so many of them appeared to be taking themselves so seriously. But this one had fooled him. Finally, he said, "No. He..."

"You have disappointed in me?"

"No. It doesn't matter."

"No?"

"I mean, why should it?"

"You need something from me?"

"Only help in finding George."

"Ah. You no want BJ?"

Pym laughed. "No, I don't want a BJ, especially from a man. Anyway, I still have a wife. Sort of."

Lulu smoked and looked around the bar. "Okay. Dat fine. I still help you. But Lulu very low on money."

"I am too. But I can help you out a bit."

A waitress came and took their drinks order. Pym found himself look-ing at her carefully—how did he tell the difference before? He looked at their waitress, dressed in jeans and a tight T-shirt, which complimented her breasts. It was not as cut and dried as he thought. But yes, he'd bet money the waitress was really a female.

The bar, walled with mirrors and white marble, reflected himself and Lulu reducing into infinity, and others, too, all these patrons collected to-gether in this little bar and sort of being spun off. The thought boggled Pym's mind. "So," he said to Lulu, who was herself lost in thought, "were you expecting some business from me?"

She shrugged, saying, "Maybe. Don't matter none."

"Good. Because that stuff's not my scene. Doesn't work for me, you know what I'm saying? My brother maybe, but not me."

Lulu laughed, and said in a funny American accent, "Not me, buddy," and then got caught with a fit of coughing. When she'd recovered herself, she said, "Sorry. Yes, yes, no problem. We laugh a lot at you guys."

"Us guys?"

"Yes. Never mind. Not important." Then she burst out laughing again. Pym found this infectious and laughed too. He used this as an opening to say, "Explain some of this to me. I'm clueless."

"Yes. Hahaha. You clueless."

"Are you a cross-dresser, or have you had an operation?"

"The second."

"That's why you befriended George."

"A little bit. Georgie very kind too. She confused though. Living in dream. Me, I do this for money. Made a lot of money for a while. Now, money gone, but I have condo and pension plan."

Pym laughed. "That's good. What happened? Why no money now?"

"Got busted. Went to jail. They don't know what to do with Lulu. So I'm protected and in solitary twenty-three hours a day. No hormone treat-ments. Best asset shrinks away. Gotta start over. Hormones expensive. When breasts come back, it party time again. For now, Café Du Monde. Work with stupid Gooks." Lulu laughed at this as the waitress, also picking up Lulu's infectious laugh, placed the drinks on the table. "Y'all're having fun here, I see," she said, smiling at Pym.

"We are indeed," said Pym copying her accent as she left. He was about to launch into a flurry of questions when Terry, the Englishman, slid into the booth beside him and just looked at him, smiling. Pym said, "I suppose this was inevitable?"

"A small section of town," Terry said. "I've noticed that you see everyone at least three times a night here. Who's your little friend?"

"Lulu."

"How do you do, Lulu. Are you from New Orleans?"

"Yes, before from Saigon."

"Ah yes. A great city. I know it well."

Lulu's eyes got shifty. "You know Saigon?"

"Yes, I do. It's a cheap place to vacation these days. I expect your parents left there a few years ago, yes?"

"Yes."

"Lulu's a friend of my brother."

"You're quite the sleuth."

"He mentioned her in a postcard he'd written from the Café Du Monde. She works there. After I left you tonight I went there for coffee. And there she was."

"I deduced all that, dear boy. Now, did you notice that lovely waitress? Priceless speech patterns. She has the most unlikely name for a southern belle—Doris. I associate that name with char ladies from Manchester. Have you any idea what I'm talking about? None at all? Okay, onto the next topic. Let's see..."

"If Vera was here," laughed Pym, "she'd tell you to settle down."

Terry mimicked Vera's voice. "Terry, take a breath, darling, and shut your bleedin' cakehole."

Lulu looked alarmed. "It's okay," Pym said to her, "It's a crazy Limey from my hotel."

"I do not dance on balconies, old chap."

"Not now, but I'll bet you used to."

"Yes, I did, actually. Quite a bit. Especially during my days in Rio. This place is not unlike Rio, now I come to think of it."

"What he say?" asked Lulu. "He foreigner?"

"That's it, Lulu—a foreigner. I'll translate for you if you like."

"You tink he be wantin' BJ?"

Pym laughed. Another drink appeared in front of him. One of the two black men Terry had been talking to earlier bought a round and sent it over with Doris the southern belle waitress with priceless speech patterns. Terry took his and joined the two black men at the bar. They had left earlier and then returned because nowhere served better stand-up drinks than here.

Lulu fidgeted. "I leave now," she said, but the two men, followed by two very beautiful African-looking women, came over to the table to meet Pym. One of the men looked at Lulu and said, "Miss Ho! You're back in town, girl." He put his hand out to shake hers and she demurely responded. "This is Lulu Ho," he told his companions. "And you must be the dancer?" he said to Pym.

"This is Rick," laughed Terry. "He's a cop."

"We better be good, then."

"Not on my account," laughed Rick.

"I told him about our early evening encounter," said Terry.

"Do you know everyone in New Orleans, Terry?" laughed Pym.

"Not yet. But the night is young."

"Welcome to my town, Mr. Pym," said Rick.

Everybody shook hands. Pym failed to catch the foreign-sounding names of the other man and the two women, but their warm, gentle handshakes made him like them. Rick's woman wore ropey dreadlocks, big silver earrings and bracelets, and the big fleshy lips of her mouth were painted red. Pym watched her interact with the others and move her tightly clad bottom to the music. He saw her at all angles and in multiple images through the mirrors lining the bar. That naughty little breeding spark shot through his nervous system.

The mirrors also revealed a pissed-off-looking Lulu, an observant Terry, and the alertness of the second woman, not quite as attractive, who swept on Pym like a curious stingray. She had to step in front of Rick and Terry to block out the view of Rick's woman.

"You look like that film star," she said, looking up into his face and tapping the middle of his chest. This one had more flesh and more silver on her, but the same lips, and her bead-braided hair fell about her shoulders. "I don't know who you mean," Pym smiled. "Eddie Murphy?"

She laughed and gave him a sexy, friendly shove. "No, mon. You know, dat pretty white boy..."

"You have a nice accent."

"Jamaica," she shouted above the music.

"Are you all from there?"

"No, no. Ricardo and TJ are from here, but they still very Haitian. And Matilde, Ricky's wife, she his second cousin from Port-au-Prince. She royalty."

"Wow..." The music crested and they both shrugged, unable to hear themselves speak.

A huge, elderly man entered the establishment followed by a tall woman who shook out an umbrella as they settled around a stand-up table. Lulu stared at the man. His expression was one of arrogance and he kept his eyes cast down and his nose flared. The woman sat on the high stool beside him and smiled at the waitress. The peculiar couple sped off into infinity in the mirrors and Pym suddenly understood that this was the shadowy woman he'd just met at the House of Large Sizes—Sasha. She looked at the police officers and looked at the man she was with, and then gave Pym a little wave that could have been interpreted as furtive.

The police officer, Rick, didn't notice who had entered and tapped Lulu on the shoulder, saying, "You gonna be good girl, Lulu?"

"I have rights."

"I'm not hassling you, honey. Just don't be fucking around, okay?"

"She's a friend of my brother's," said Pym. "She's okay."

Rick's friend, the other police officer, said, "Hey, Rickie—you off duty, man. Chill out."

Matilde put her arm across Rick's shoulder and said, "He's never off duty. Are you, baby? Gonna die of a heart attack just like his daddy."

Terry looked from one to the other with his huge eyes, making Pym laugh. There was too much happening. He wanted to look at Sasha and the big man. He wanted to look at the waitress and the exotic Matilde. He wanted to be alone with Lulu and find out more about George, but he decided to relax and start fresh tomorrow.

More drinks came. People sent drinks over, the table crammed with glasses. Pym, drunk now, sweating a little and full of good humor, took stock of the fact that less than twelve hours ago he was freezing his ass off in frigid Minneapolis, and now he languished in the friendly company of two New Orleans police officers and their wives, an extroverted Limey, and an increasingly inebriated transsexual. After a while Terry danced with Matilde, Lulu got into a heated conversation with TJ's wife, and Rick and TJ stood on either side of Pym and told him Lulu's deal. In turn he told them the story of how Lulu had helped George.

"You know, man," said Rick, "I'm too fucked up to say much about this thing with your brother tonight. But if you ain't located him within a couple of days, and we already almost through the first day, you give me a call, okay?" And he handed Pym his card, looked at TJ and said, "I don't like the sound of this story."

"Me, either," said TJ, "but I'm off duty, so fuck you and your goddamn inquiring mind."

Rick shrugged, looked at Lulu, and shook his head. "Okay, buddy. But this place is a fucking cesspool. It's shameful—human being oughtn't to live this way."

"You and your momma woulda been on the Spillville committee, man."

"Damn right."

"You be an unpopular brother till the end of yo days."

"Wouldn't bother me none. Nor my momma. Wanna live in a clean town and be proud to have the English visit and be impressed. And the cold-ass Minnesotan—and not have to be mugged and ripped off and hassled by pimps and whores and other trash."

TJ laughed and put his arm around Rick. "Man you are a heavy motherfucker tonight. Drink a lot, please—and ree-lax your royal ass."

What Rick was being asked to do was something that came second nature to Pym—drink. He drank them all under the table. Even Terry. He had to put Terry in a taxi and send him back to the hotel although it was only a few blocks away. The two cops and their elegant wives were reduced to slurring, rumpled zombies who waited glassy-eyed outside the bar for available cabs. Lulu fell asleep, curled up on a bench. Pym wondered, in his altered state, what it would be like to have sex with a transsexual. He wondered about the scarring, if they could have orgasms, if they still preferred it up the rear rather than in an artificial doo-dat. He kept looking for the Sasha woman but she'd disappeared. The waitress became businesslike and unavailable—wanting the drunks gone. He woke Lulu and they went outside.

"You walk me home," Lulu said.

"Yes. And tomorrow we find George," Pym replied. "Okay?"

She shrugged.

Lulu lived just outside the Quarter, a block beyond Esplanade. At the door she said, "You come in. Dangerous walk back to hotel. Stay." And she put her arms around Pym's torso and tucked her head in against his ribs. If anything wild was going to happen it would've happened then. But it didn't. Her cells were male. That was enough, and Pym's reptile brain said no fucking way am I letting you try this—no experimentation for you tonight, Gilbert Pym! "I don't think so, Lulu," he said. "I need to clear my head. I'll find you tomorrow at the Café."

Lulu turned and went inside without speaking.

For a place with such a dangerous reputation, Pym was surprised at the uneventful walk he had back to the hotel. There were worse places in North Minneapolis. He passed some women lurking in doorways who hissed at him and some terrifying dives where the eyes of men in baseball caps followed him like wolves, but he arrived at the hotel safely, found his room, and went out onto the balcony. The restaurant across the road was in darkness, but he could hear music coming from somewhere—jazz. Django Reinhardt. He didn't dance this time. Then he heard the sound of lovemaking. It came from the room next door. A woman cried out. And then a man did the same.

Pym went inside, closed the French doors behind him and, head spinning, sat on the small desk chair in front of the mirror. No music came from the room next door and the only sounds he heard came from minute movements of his own body and the voices, old Terry's mostly, echoing in his mind. He dragged himself up, piling his smoky-smelling clothes under the door of the wardrobe, cleaned his teeth, and rolled into bed. The smell of bar on his skin disgusted him, but he'd shower in the morning. He turned off the bedside light and fell immediately into a jerking slumber and became the heavy front end of a big old Chevy as it broke through ice and slid through black water to the bottom of a lake. The dream woke him. He lay looking into darkness, the sleep re-gathering around him, and for some reason suddenly remembered that he hadn't returned with the umbrella old Sammy loaned him. "Where the hell did I leave that? I'm such a fuck-up." And he started beating on himself again in the unforgiving dark so that the impulse to sleep vanished. He turned on the light lest the list of self-recriminations overwhelm him. He reached for George's cards, rolled off the rubber binding, and read the next one:

> *I dreamed that death enters through the anus. It penetrates our most unholy hole and gradually freezes us. I think of those Minnesota twenty-below nights when you wonder how animals survive. That's what death is if you don't do something about it—unimaginable cold. So, in my terror, I sought out a warm place of survival. Through ars moriendi I found that place. It's not an outside, but an*

inside; the last place you'd look, but it's right before our eyes—escape, salvation in the mind, like flesh on the bones of the forever dead.

Frowning, uncomprehending, Pym slipped the card to the bottom of the pile and read another:

What if I loved my brother with all my heart? What lengths would I go to keep my brother safe and beside me forever? A soft mechanism, a blasphemy so sweet that even angels weep when humans find it is available to us—hidden by that skinflint, God. A time will come when you will thank me, but for now, please just forgive me.

I remember you sitting in front of the TV with your thumb in your mouth watching Mr. Rogers when Ma staggered in from one of her all-nighters. I had to skip school to look after you. You ran and greeted the bitch like she just got off work. Such an open-hearted little boy. What happened? How come your heart wasn't open to me when I needed you?

Pym felt sick.

XIII

Nadine Duval watched George Pym walk up the squeaking, shadowy stairs, swinging his silk-stretched ass. Brought-forward inhabitants, a great multitude, bore witness through Nadine's eyes. Circus Day for them, she decided, as they fought like hogs for the choicest position, light being their only fodder—the fuse that drives the spark of cognition and thus the error of individuality.

Cogito, ergo sum.

Idiot—he's within, too—amongst him other delusionals inherited from Mother.

Pascal and Puju stood, watching, both expressionless and professional. Lulu, Nadine's technician, ran the hidden camcorders from the office, controlling the lights and the soft Caribbean music. George would know nothing of Lulu's presence.

Nadine needed the Baron but he had chosen conventionality, remained loyal to the local hougan, and avoided her. The Mother in her burned with fury at the cowardice and ignorance of the old leadership. She would destroy them all when this work was complete.

Near the top of the stairs George Pym began to wheeze, and with the wheezing his swagger lessened. To help, Nadine had lodged him in a room near the attic portal, but still his progress was labored. Nadine whispered, "Slower than that, sugar."

She rented a place inside him; saw everything, shared his humanity, could predict each synaptic anomaly. So fucked up. George would have to get rid of that waddle, a feature of years spent as a fatso. Much of his extra weight had dissolved through the gut-cutting and subsequent illness. Its soul, though, the soul of his fat, clung to him like an aura.

Nadine brought forth her bright friendly smile and encouraged George to the top as his eyes rose to her. The face wasn't so grotesque; the collagen helped, as did the eye tucks, and the skillful use of cosmetics, learned from Sasha, would serve him well in the short term.

He knew now how to seek out shadow and avoid direct light. But he wore the attire that drove his libido, that of an aging mother's boudoir from 1970. But the thin scar down his cheek, a gift from a wrathful mother, would always lend him an air of dockside menace, however daintily he minced.

"As you ascend," Nadine said gently, "let the Glamour descend over you."

George nodded, blinked, de-bulked but still bovine.

"Be it, Georgie," Nadine said. "If you don't be it, it won't be. You won't be. Work, Georgie, work!"

George halted.

"You are the She."

George gasped.

"Close your eyes and see."

George closed his eyes.

Nadine sprinkled the dust on him. It floated about his head like ash after a fire. He sniffed it first, then lifted his face to it, and extended his tongue like a child catching snowflakes. The burning snow.

"You are that shape your soul desires."

As he inhaled the dust, George's head fell back, exposing his thick throat, and his face, a display of ecstasy and relief, almost caused Nadine to betray herself with laughter. Amazing how a talc pounded from bitterroot could work such wonders on one determined to believe.

"Your eyes will water and you'll sneeze. That'll be the ugliness leaving you."

George sneezed repeatedly. His body heaved with the sneezing so that he leaned forward and steadied himself on the stairs with his big, red-nailed hands. When the sneezing ceased he hiccoughed and burped. Nadine sneered and inside herself said, "Like a hippopotamus at ablutions," which sent the multitude into delighted uproar. Nadine sprinkled a vial of chicken blood on him and he raised his face again, catching a taste of the blood on his tongue.

He went into convulsions.

The Loa rode him while Puju and Pascal watched.

Nadine became the Loa, ravaging every cell.

George slowed, stopped, a string of saliva attaching him to a step.

"Welcome, Georgie," whispered Nadine, "Welcome to your new family."

He looked around, dazed. Nadine said, "All the way up now, sugar. Your friends are waiting on you."

Pascal and Puju readied themselves behind her. She knew how they longed to thrust into her ass. To render themselves potent they imagined mastering her. She possessed them like panting, wall-eyed dogs, tantalized by the prospect of someday gaining entry to her guts.

The soft yellow candlelight, reflected in the multitude of mirrors; the rich rolled-out Persian carpet, so complicated in pattern; the draped white fabric hiding the rafters; the strewn pillows of silk and Arabian wool; the low mahogany table set with wine goblets; and the dishes of dates and figs to dip in sweet, honeyed yogurt, resembled the inside of a desert tent, the sort of place humans had taken joy in since Sumerians invented luxury.

George stopped a few steps from the top, contained himself with closed eyes. When his eyes opened they smoldered. His buttocks rolled, and breasts built mostly of aura bounced together.

Nadine smiled.

Inside her, the crowd fell about laughing. Such scum! They loved this as they had loved superficial, stupid spectacles all through their worthless lives. What would it be like for George when he resided temporarily among them, poor bossal? Nadine stood at the center of the Coliseum, the empress of ceremonies, pointing all eyes on the performance. There is no death, the multitude chanted. Do as thou wilt shall be the whole of the law.

"Thank you, Mistress," said George.

The crowd settled in for the show as George reached the top of the stairs. Mistress, he had called her. She liked that, she would incorporate that—Mistress, yes—Miss Stress, it would be the name of her spirit when she passed on into the big world, one to rival Mademoiselle Charlotte, she would ride the adepts and bring to their brains complication, twisted anxiety, horrific foresight. Thanks, Boy George—Georgie Girl—Georgie Porgy. The crowd fell about at her comedy—if they didn't, she'd kill them.

Nadine said, "Here be Pascal and Puju. They're going to party with you this evening."

George shook hands like a courtesan, batting his eyelids.

The crowd, outraged at such grotesque mummery, fell about choking with mirth. They beat their breasts, they coughed, they collapsed in heaps.

Pascal said, "We like a big girl. We can be a little rough. You okay with that, Georgie?"

George smiled, nodded. His eyes dropped to Puju's readied crotch, his head turned slightly—his dreams come true. Pascal, the more ironic and literary of the pair, turned away and laughed, then took George's arm and moved him to the thick carpet with the pillows. The crowd roared, "Don't do it, Puju."

In his mother's voice, George asked, "Are you Romanian, Puju?"

So sharp, so clever, thought Nadine, he could be so much more than this.

Puju stepped forward like a trapeze artist and said, "Surely it is not my accent you identify me by, but this battering ram that will soon smooth out and whitewash your insides."

"Oh, my," breathed George like Blanche Dubois. "And you, Pascal? Are you...?"

"Yes, and I'm going to..."

Nadine settled herself in some pillows with a goblet of sweet wine. She didn't always watch this muck, but if she didn't on this occasion her inhabitants would riot and ransack the city, which once before had resulted in a month's stay in the psych ward, downtown.

She could let the light in through her eyes while she conjured the young god, Gilbert Pym. Soon she would start the work on him and there would be yes yes yes instead of no no no.

Her yoni, like a spiked blowfish inflating in her, ached at the thought of Gilbert Pym. Her mother came forward and got control of her—not now, not yet, got her focused back on the Glamouring of George.

Kissing and stroking and sex oil and vibrators and George begging "Fuck me, fuck me," to the howls of Forum delight, and the two performers went into him back and mouth, his ultimate dream, while Nadine sprayed perfume around against the great array of male bodily fluids pervading the attic air.

All her trannies desired this humdrum conventionality. That a person would give up a soul to experience this was beyond her, but she understood the need of some men to witness the outer boundaries of femininity. In disdaining their quest, she helped kill them. Kill as many as you can, the

Goddess taught. They are like weeds, they always return; spare the killing and they choke the planet. Let their blood at least fertilize it, like the blood of swine in a field of shit.

The squeaks and squeals emanating from the ecstatic George were indeed like those of a pig in a trough but Nadine had coached him well in the perceptive shift to another reality where the ring of his voice, so young, high and arousing, was that of his mother. Reality is such a many-splendored thing. He longed for possession, poor bossal, to not be his gross self.

She recalled her first interview with him. Panting after an altered state, George surrendered every detail of his life, rolled it out right there among the candles and mirrors that he had yet to understand. He revealed his conundrum, the secret clash of adoration and loathing of his bastard brother, Gilbert, the boy who was everything George wasn't—golden haired and green-eyed, lean and mesomorphic, mindlessly heterosexual and vigorous from the moment of conception—and beyond doubt the old mother's favorite. George stood by and said nothing as his mother betrayed his beloved father with a wild Englishman, and Gilbert was the outcome of a towering love, which the mother continued to harbor. As Gilbert grew, George saw the Englishman in his appearance and everything he did, including a penchant for teasing. He'd never forgotten a quip of the Englishman that went: *Georgie Porgy pudding and pie, kissed the girls and made them cry.* And as Gilbert grew to manhood he displayed the same easy style of brotherly love, which was all roughness and ridicule for a soft fat sibling. And this drove George to develop his intellect and stay ahead of the shock-headed Gilbert, and then marry a woman equally as beautiful as his mother, even though in his heart he knew he couldn't hold her, for the one he really loved was indeed his brother. His great fantasy was to be his wife, the beautiful Estelle, and to live forever with his beautiful brother Gilbert. When the inevitable occurred and his wife betrayed him with his brother, he was furious beyond words. Revenge would be his, and for this reason George offered up his brother in exchange for the magic Nadine promised to provide, the *ars moriendi.*

Thus, Nadine learned of Gilbert Pym, saw his photograph, heard of his exploits and felt like an ancient queen in love with a prince she'd never met, the love heightened by the sweet songs of an ugly minstrel. The silly young hero would temper with age into a warrior king who would be worthy of her, worthy to mate with, perfect for her and the perpetuation of salvation.

She told the Baron of this, and at first he helped her, after warning that love is like the tiger's tooth, but now the Baron is gone and she must forge ahead alone.

The attic of the Spanish House was a classroom the night she parlayed the treaty with George Michael Pym, the fragments of possibility visible from every angle, and it became clear to her that George's overriding drive in all things was to be this—his mother in the throes of ecstasy. A frightening, powerful mother, to be sure, though one who didn't comprehend her own potency. A perverted and corrupt mother, although she had no true sense of her own corruption, having been left without boundaries by the silly nonsense of the sixties and the fatuous platitudes of the New Age movement. But a self-professed witch nonetheless, one with magnificent genes, which would help cocoon the next incarnation of the goddess.

The stories of these wretches fascinated her. If they could see her own story, how paltry and insignificant they would feel. And how pathetically predictable are these mortals. George had seen his mother dressed in the black silk gown he himself favored and watched her go downstairs to her lover, the silk clinging to her slim but voluptuous figure. He followed like a rat and hid himself, watched up close to see the penis plunging frantically, the straining and reaching for orgasm. The cataclysmic shrieks of a powerful woman orgasming with a strong man.

It frightened poor Georgie, made him cry. Poor little mite.

He loved his father. Mother betrayed father. Father committed suicide. Mean bastard brother, whom Georgie loved, called him a fat fucking faggot. Poor Georgie only trusted Nadine now. Sign over insurance in Last Will and Testament to Nice Nadine, the savior of all humankind.

She sent George to Minneapolis, where she'd engaged the aid of a bossal, Dashiell, and George successfully brought back the items she needed for the gris-gris bag, which would shortly be in production. In the second interview, she smiled. "Georgie," she whispered, "you done good, sugar."

"Is it complete?"

"Yes."

"Do I get what I want now?"

"I have the items. I keep my word. In a few days Doctor Duval will transform you..."

Nadine felt Gilbert Pym coming through again. He was snarling, he threw her mother aside, so that the old woman clattered into the sack in the corner. "What are you fucking doing to my brother?" The hero bellowed. "Give him back to me!"

The crowd turned away from the fucking to watch a hero's rage.

Bring forth Miss Charlotte.

The crowd turned back to the sex.

Charlotte went to Georgie, touched his sweating forehead. He turned his eyes to her, his mouth full of Puju. The touch was electric and Charlotte zoomed into him, rode him, so that he jolted. His passion went into a frenzy. Pascal laughed, holding him in place and shouted, "Whoa, Nelly!"

The unwatched hero saw it all for himself as the adept sank deeper into imagination, became lost in the ecstasy of the cocks going in and out of him. He is his mother being fucked by his brother. It's completely worth giving up his brother for this.

It's completely worth killing Estelle.

Nadine couldn't stay for long; it was like hell in there.

She stood, hands on hips, disgusted, the stink of shit in her nose as Georgie made her ears ring with the first full-fledged, all-pelvis, all-woman orgasm of his life.

The crowd loved it.

"Okay, show's over," Nadine told them. They slunk away, besotten and smug, to their slots.

Georgie reclined between Pascal and Puju, breathing hard. Nadine felt sick of it all. She wanted to get him scrubbed up and down to Duval. Miss Charlotte walked back into her, looking humiliated, and told her to at least have the decency to let the poor fool enjoy the afterglow.

Such a bitch.

The bones of Nadine's mother rattled in the sack by the wall.

It's not enough, said Mother, and flew into her so that she jerked like one electrified.

She heard the drums. They came closer.

She danced forward with the drums, her keys jangling, and stepped over Georgie, a giantess overstepping a mountain, so that he gazed up into her crotch. Grimacing, she opened over him and pressed down. The men stood away, deflating as Georgie disappeared beneath her skirts. They were simple and would see the personification of the white python absorbing a soul and birthing a zombie.

She squeezed and sucked with her thighs, drew his aura up into her, and came on his head, leaving him soaked. The bossals steadied her, helped her off. Georgie crouched, whimpering.

Her mother left and Nadine finished her wine, watched Pascal and Puju bathe Georgie in warm soapy water. She felt like cutting his throat and watching the blood fly everywhere. She should just kill them all, but no, she is love, life… no killing today.

Puju and Pascal fed Georgie dates dipped in the honeyed yogurt. He ate a few and then began weeping.

"What is it, Georgie?"

"I'm so happy," he said.

"There's a long way to go."

"I know. I'm ready."

"We have to go downstairs now and prepare you for Doctor Duval."

XIV

Pym woke into late morning with a dry palate and headache behind his eyes. The bedside light still burned and George's postcards rested in his hands, meaning he hadn't moved all night. He remembered no dreams.

He replaced the rubber band around the cards, turned off the light, and rolled out of bed. In the bathroom he pissed like a horse, and, as the water yellowed and foamed under his stream he thought of Lulu and the House of Large Sizes with its intriguing proprietress, Sasha. Then Laura found her groove in his mind, engaged in her perpetual orgasm with Ray. He shut his eyes, trying to pull something else forward. The previous evening's carousing came back to him.

"I had fun," he said to himself in the mirror. "Good boy. You didn't do anything dumb." He remembered the sound of the people making love next door and thought of Laura again, but then Estelle nudged into the thought and saved him from the pain. He wanted to smell Estelle's hair. Then Laura with Ray broke in again and the bile rose in him. "Don't think," he told himself. He thought about calling Laura, but the lump in his throat meant it wouldn't be a good time to talk to her—he'd end up begging. He shouldn't call Estelle either.

Pym pulled on jeans and a plain white T-shirt and went out onto his balcony. The woman from the restaurant, the redheaded one with the hollow-eyed man whom Terry had pointed out, sat sunning her legs outside open French doors. It was they, then, who had been making love last night. Beside her lay the remains of a continental breakfast on a round, pewter tray. She looked slowly at him, sunglasses on, and nodded.

"Good morning," Pym said. He pointed at the tray, "Do they deliver that to the room?"

She thought for a moment, and then said, "A tray should be outside your door."

"Oh, really? Thanks."

She smiled and looked back up at the sun.

Sure enough, a tray waited outside his door, the coffee pot still warm. He brought the tray back out onto the balcony. Only the woman's tray remained but her doors were open, the curtains blowing outside the French doors in the mild breeze. Pym sat, poured black coffee, and ate a croissant and a muffin.

The woman came back out, this time without her sunglasses. Pym loved her eyes, wide yellow-green ones. She wore a silky, floral patterned dressing gown and her damp hair fell across her shoulders. Nervously, Pym said, "As you can see, you were right."

"I'm glad," she said, and sat, brushing her hair.

"I hope I'm not disturbing your privacy," Pym said. He realized almost before the utterance departed his mouth that he was producing a version of old Terry's crisp and polite habit of discourse, and, to Pym's immense pleasure, the woman said, "You would be if you weren't a gentleman, but you obviously are—so it's all right."

Pym smiled and lifted his cup. "That's very kind of you. This place brings out the best in me."

"Oh dear," she laughed. "It does the opposite for me."

Pym laughed and said, "I expect that's the more normal reaction."

"Is it?"

"I guess. I'm just a naive Minneapolis boy. What do I know?"

"That's a cool town. The Mini Apple. The Twins and the Vikings, right? Cool. I'm from Chicago."

"Chi-town. The Bulls."

She laughed, looked down at her knees for a moment, then said, "Well neighbor, I'd best leave you to your breakfast and go get changed. I gotta shop." She cleared away her things and retreated inside, closing the French doors. Her scent remained in the air—all around him. "George," he said under his breath. "What've you gotten me into? This place is gonna kill me."

An urge to connect with someone swept over him—to not be alone. He couldn't call home yet, but he called reception and asked Sammy for a connection to the Limeys' room.

Vera answered.

"Hi, Vera, this is your friend the dancer. How's Terry doing?" Pym asked. "He was pretty looped last night."

"Hello, Sonny-Jim. I'm afraid he's still looped," she said. "I'm looking at him as we speak. He resembles a pharaoh—the mummified version—aside from a slight movement of the chest cavity. But you're a sweet boy for ringing. I'm sure he'll be infuriating the locals again by mid-afternoon."

"I'll catch you later, then."

"I expect you will. Cheerio."

"Bye."

Pym stood in the middle of his room. He'd never done that before, called complete strangers. "Bizarre. This whole thing's bizarre."

Pym threw on his jacket and went to the Café Du Monde to see Lulu but she wasn't there, so he found his way to the House of Large Sizes on his own. He stood outside and looked at the mannequin in the window which, in daylight, presented a shabby, dusty aggressiveness with its pale, exaggerated female features and size twelve feet. The red lingerie, studded leather fetish-wear and sex toys strewn under the huge spiked heels made Pym think of Attila the Hun. Dashiell's dancing at the Gay 90's in Minneapolis sprang into his mind—ultra masculinity transformed into twisted femininity by some inexplicable design of nature; barbarians in drag, burning down the gates of the Western Empire.

Lights shone inside the shop.

The tall woman, Sasha, checked merchandise on a rack. Inside, in the window well, a man with a shaved head sat next to a small magazine and bookrack, reading, his back pressed against the glass so that vertebrae showed through his faded, pink T-shirt.

In his jacket pocket Pym fingered the postcards; he remembered one that mentioned the House of Large Sizes or Sasha, he couldn't recall which. He pulled out the cards and sorted through them. In a Victorian style, vivid blues and greys, he found the sketch of a slim man with breasts and long hair, naked but for a see-through shawl, bending slightly over a pool and gazing at his reflection. Reflected in the pool, rather than the man's rather prominent penis, was the subtly drawn suggestion of a vaginal slit behind a fuzz of pubic hair. In other words, the man in the picture saw what he wished was there but what in fact was not. It was fascinating—to see yourself as you were not. Maybe Pym could find himself one of those pools—get a bigger dick!

In miniscule cursive lettering, George had written on the back of the card:

> *Well, brother, as you can see from this picture, I'm*
> *coming to terms with my condition. If it wasn't for my new*
> *friends I would be at the end of my tether—literally. There's*
> *a community for me here. I'm home. My soul is like her*
> *on the front. She has a figure to die for, doesn't she? She's*
> *drawn by a local artist who used my friend Sasha as a mod-*
> *el. Sasha's wonderful—saved my life. Her shop supplies all*
> *my needs. I'm going to get changed all around so I can be*
> *like her, like I've always been inside. You're lucky being so*
> *sure of yourself. I must of brought you up right. -Georgie.*

So, thought Pym, Sasha's one of them. Or maybe she just modeled and the artist drew in a penis. In the window bay, where the man with the prominent vertebrae read, Pym noticed a rack of similar postcards. He walked in, the door swinging open easily this time. He stood behind Sasha who was crouching, untangling some dresses. Her hair fell straight like an Indian's and she wore a light, leopard-print skirt and black leotard top. Her feet were bare and she wore silver rings on her toes and fingers, a mass of bracelets on both wrists. She smelled of a light citrus perfume. The small of her back was very slim.

"Sasha," Pym said. She looked around at him, smiled with her mouth but not her eyes. The eyes looked alarmed. Pym liked her lips and white teeth. A voice went off in his head that said please don't be a boy.

"Georgie's brother, right?" she said.

"That's it."

Sasha stood, her breasts large and round, her shoulders square. She held her hand out and shook his. It was warm and soft and gentle. "Darryl," she said gently, "Can you watch the place while I go upstairs for a while with Mr. Pym?"

The man reading in the window stirred himself and said, "Sure thing."

"Walk this way, Mr. Pym."

The stairs were old, narrow, and steep. Sasha walked up sideways slightly, her bottom revolving almost in Pym's face. Her calves bulged and the sinew holding heel and calf together flexed as she moved upward.

Pym consciously resisted his attraction to Sasha. He felt wrong resisting. It wasn't fair to George somehow. It insulted him. The night before, seeing Sasha briefly in the bar in her black party dress and high heels and brown coat draped across her shoulders had sent Pym into a brief inquiry concerning attraction itself.

At that point, of course, he wasn't thinking that Sasha was really a he. He knew booze increased attraction, even in some cases to items of nature considered hideous to the sober sensibility. But the range of what was attractive was expanded in New Orleans because the boundaries of what beauty should be were drawn wider. Something from a Humanities class he'd liked in college returned to him during all the hubab of the bar—Thomas Mann… *Tonio Kruger,* or *Death in Venice*—something about the order and safety of the North contrasted with the disorder and flexiblity of the South—and here it was, all in one country called the United States of America.

It was rare that Pym would remember a mere thought he'd had a night before. But walking up rickety stairs behind a pair of buttocks he wanted to squeeze himself between was completely new. He felt quite proud of this explosion of stimuli, which brought long-dormant learning into play from his college years. George would be ecstatic—Gillie, you're remembering.

And at the thought of remembering he felt a flutter of a mood change and shifted away from that direction lest he remember too much.

At the top of the stairs, Sasha turned to him and said, "I apologize for my stairs. I call them the cardiac squeeze. Can I offer you some tea?"

"Sure, whatever." Looking at the layout, the book-lined walls and exotic plants, Pym said, "This is quite something up here."

The apartment lay open around a blocked-in kitchen at its center, the varnished plank floor leading to a mirror-lined bedroom at the back and a huge verdant balcony at the front. The walls of the sitting area were crammed with neatly organized books and CDs on glass shelves with stainless steel struts, and soft white leather furniture surrounded a glass coffee table and a state-of-the-art television. Net curtains over the French windows blew gently inward so that, from the top of the stairs, Pym could see an old fat man with cigar reading a newspaper on the balcony opposite.

"This is the nicest apartment I've ever seen."

"You're very charming, Mr. Pym. Georgie said the same. Though you and she don't look too alike. She loved it here. But she only came up once—the stairs were a bit much for her. "Come and talk to me in the kitchen."

Pym laughed, then felt cruel, disloyal. From the kitchen he could see into the bedroom, where mirror-lined walls reflected a round, raised bed at the center of the room. Pym smiled, thinking of Estelle and George's bed-room on Peter Pan Island. To cover his amusement, he said, "George has a bedroom in Minneapolis similar to yours."

Sasha just looked at him with moist eyes. She was about to say one thing, but then said something else. "Last time I saw Georgie was months ago, it seems. She was living cheap over the river—in Algiers last I knew."

"You know the address?"

"No, honey."

Sasha moved around the kitchen quietly in her bare feet and her brace-lets tinkled as she dropped teabags in a pot and set white enamel cups on the cream-colored countertop.

"George seems to consider you a close friend. I thought you might know where he lives."

"Ha. A lot of them come here. They need the big sizes until they slim down properly. I feel sorry for them. They fall in love with me and the whole scene. But there's a lot like Georgie. I can't keep track of them all. Georgie's hard to forget. And funny. God, she's funny. She did a great impression of a heart attack at the top of those stairs."

"George always wanted to be a comedian."

"Yes. She's making some progress toward that, I heard. I think she's done some improv around town and gotten some engagements. I never went to see her yet. Find out for me where she's playing. I'll go with you."

As she said this she gently pressed two fingers, index and pinky, the middle ones curled under, against Pym's wrist, then withdrew them.

"Forgive me for asking, but..."

"Am I transgender? Yes."

"Good." Pym felt his face getting hot, like he'd been caught in a lie in school. "I just wanted to be sure."

Sasha laughed. "Confusing, isn't it?"

"How do you mean?"

"Well, this is my life, Mr. Pym. It's a rather narrow one, but I like it. I know human nature quite well, especially the male side of it. I've seen ev-erything. I know for example that you're heterosexual, but I also know you like me. Aren't I clever?"

"You certainly are easy to talk to."

"What's the point in being closed off to people? You're dead a long time.

"Most men have your reaction but I respond to very few. I have to keep my energy centered. This," and she swept her hand gracefully the length of her body, "all takes a lot of attention."

The kettle boiled and Sasha poured the hot water into a silver pot wherein she had placed tea bags. She put honey in the cups. On the exposed brick above the stairs were nude photos of her, black and white ones. She caught him staring at them. "Yes, that's me last year. It was during my little crusade to prove that it can be done successfully. Although I say it myself, I'm quite impressed with how it all turned out. God didn't make me, I made myself."

Pym winced playfully, thinking how Terry would do this, and held his hand over his head, saying, "You're not a good person to stand next to in a storm. Perhaps you should modify that statement to something like God got me started, but I finished the job."

Sasha laughed and held his shoulder. "God's one of my customers," she said.

Pym covered his shock at this statement with a Terryesque question. "And what, may I ask, is the currency of his patronage?"

Sasha's face broke open with delight. "You can banter!" she exclaimed. "How refreshing to meet a Midwesterner who can banter. The answer, I think, is flexible genes. He gave me something not many people have. I'm able to make myself look the way I want."

"You're very beautiful," Pym croaked. "Most of them aren't though—"

"Them?" Sasha laughed. "I'll forgive you for that. It's true that most men who try to change gender look pretty hideous. I'm one of the lucky ones who really can pass instead of just thinking she can."

Sasha picked up the cups and placed them on top of the range beside the kettle. She poured the tea out of the tea pot, picked up the cups, and walked through the living room and out onto the balcony, jangling as she went. Her bottom rolled exaggeratedly as Pym walked behind her. Everything about her was slightly better than a real woman could hope to be—bigger breasts with no sag, tight shapely buttocks, strong but slim legs, small ankles, slender yet muscular arms, a wasp's waist, thick, straight hair, high cheekbones, big chocolate brown eyes, big lips. She placed the cups on a little table and turning, said, "Sit and relax and I'll be right back." As Sasha said this she looked up at him and gently pressed her hand against his chest.

Pym sat and leaned back in the chair, crossing his ankles. The sun was out and quite warm but the balcony had a roof over it, which he found charming. Warm, moist air made him sigh with pleasure. He sipped his tea. He seldom bothered with tea, but this was good—fruity. "George," he muttered, as if his brother were a secret presence beside him, "I love this fucking place."

He took off his jacket and placed it over the back of his chair. Who would care if he had a girlfriend that used to be a man? Who would ever know? He could sell the place in Minneapolis and move down here. He could get something going with Sasha. Move in here. Be looked after. Lift weights all day. Run. Protect her. Very cool. He imagined himself fucking her on that big round bed. Would it be different—the surgical pussy? Probably like someone had twisted it like a tea towel. But it wouldn't lubricate normally. You'd have to use KY Jelly. And a man would be stronger; Sasha would be able to hold there while he did it doggy fashion, whereas Laura couldn't hold there for long; she'd nearly go through the wall. Then he noticed that for all the erotic imagery being produced in his brain, there was no erection. Body saying 'no.' Typical. All those years of calling them faggots. And often, in the past when he intuited that he was on to a sure thing with a girl there was a period of stillness in him until the action started.

But no, it wasn't that old stillness. It was a little core of outrage. *How can you be considering this, you traitor.* Or was it: *She's dangerous, she's some sort of vampire; proceed no further.* This last thought brought a tingle to his scalp, and his scrotum tightened. The word vampire echoed around in his mind—something George had written in the postcards. Ridiculous. Still, when he heard the toilet flush and her soft footsteps, and he looked up to watch her come onto the balcony, he had a close look at her teeth.

"How's your tea, baby?" she asked.

"Excellent. Never had it like this."

"Lots of new experiences down here, I'll bet," she said as she settled into a chair facing him and sipped her tea. "You gotta girlfriend up north?"

"Separated."

"Kids?"

"No. How old are you?"

"Twenty-nine. You?"

"Thirty-two."

"Been tested lately?"

"Tested?"

"Yeah, tested. Don't you get tested?"

"Tested for what?"

Sasha rolled her eyes and smiled. "HIV, sweetie, whadya think?"

"No. Like... no... I've been with Laura... for years... no one else. Well, there's Estelle, but that's another story."

Sasha stared at him. It was a stare that he interpreted as: You're way out of your league, pal, but I'm going to bring you up to speed. A shiver went through him. Her gaze unnerved him. "What?" he asked.

"You're kinda like a virgin," she said. "You're a prize."

"You're the prize. I bet the whole town worships you."

She shrugged, stared at him with a peculiar half-smile that created embarrassment in him, enough so that he couldn't look into her eyes, and shiftily asked, "So who was the old guy you were with last night?"

"I wondered when you'd get around to that. It's sordid and I don't want to tell you about it. It could spoil our new friendship. We do have a new friendship starting, or am I mistaken? Is that a pistol in your pocket or do you like me?"

Pym laughed and said, "You're not mistaken about a friendship."

But she was losing him. She was hitting on him sort of the way a man would, not the way an aggressive woman would; and there was no pistol in his pocket, no erection; in fact, he felt as he imagined a woman might when being talked to a certain way by a man. The alarm still sounded in him about something he couldn't quite identify. "But," he said, uncrossing his legs, "we do have to talk about George a bit more. That's why I'm down here. Is he okay? Tell me what you know."

"All right. If you'd rather spend your allotted time with the Queen of the Quarter talking about Georgie, who, by the way, will undoubtedly turn up any day, then that's your loss." She smiled and winked as she said this. "I can't leave Darryl alone down there much longer. Poor thing. She's useless with making change."

Pym laughed and said, "Maybe you'll invite me back?"

"Yes. Take me out tonight. I'll show you around a bit. Nice big strong man on my arm at the Heart of Babylon."

"Okay. You close at ten? Shall I be here then?"

"Yes. Now, what else about Georgie? Quick."

"Will he have had this operation by now?"

"Was she having one? Was it scheduled? I thought she had to go through the counseling first. No, I remember now—private deal, wasn't it. Yes, I'd expect he's had it done and is recovering somewhere quiet and taking medications like a good girl."

"That's the first time you've referred to George as 'he.'"

"Can you beat that? You are one sharp cat. I'm relaxing with you, I guess. Look. George'll always be a he. With all the surgery and hormones money can buy, George'll always look like a football coach in drag. It's sad. Our affliction—and some will tell you it's no affliction at all—is one firstly of the mind, not the chromosomes or accidents of birth. That's a lot of nonsense most of the time. We're narcissists is what we are. We're lost within our own little fantasy worlds. We create these fantasy worlds early in life, as little boys because in most cases it's boring or too much of a challenge being manly. It's rude and loud and unfulfilling, not to mention painful. Women have it much easier if they're attractive. Can you imagine what those silly feminists would be doing with this speech if they overheard me? It's true. And sex, well, what a challenge, poor old men. But you gotta love 'em—all fucked up in their heads but what would little girls do without you? He just wasn't cut out for it. This is what I'm cut out for... I'm lucky. I was half-way there already. Someone like George, no, they should see themselves more clearly. They should stay as cross dressers, not try to change gender. But what can you do? This is, after all, the land of the free."

"Wow."

"More than you needed?"

"Yes. But it's right. I can't imagine what he thinks he's doing. He's worked all his life for a pretty ordinary income. He can't afford this. When he wants something, he wants it now. Including food. He wrote me a card with a drawing of you on it. The one looking in the pool."

"Oh yes. Darryl—downstairs—does those for me. Aren't they good?"

"Yes. They're clever. But, George, he indicated he could somehow have a chance of attaining that. Impossible. Why are you all so obsessed with this seeing, this peculiar seeing the self? It's spooky."

Sasha raised her eyebrows and said, "You're very observant, Mr. Pym. That's exactly how it works for most of us. Not all, of course. Me, I'm in love with the reality of my own very expensive body. It's a work of art that I've directed. I won't have it long, so I'm going to enjoy it. When it goes, I'll stop entertaining myself with images of myself and the attention of others, and grow into a broader person. Not yet. Georgie, she'll have to look in the mirror and not see her real self. She'll need a powerful spell to keep seeing what she wants to see rather than what's there. Some of them can do it with simple imagination but Georgie's reality is too big."

There was a sneer in Sasha's voice, a cruelty that sent a little jolt of fear through Pym's spine, but he ignored it and said, "I knew all this on some level."

"Of course you did. That's why you'd try to stop him. That's why there's counseling and waiting periods. But the conventional wisdom is that if someone wants to do this, then they must be right. Bullshit. They need counseling all right. They need to be in the nut house."

"But it's too late—you're sure?"

"He's healing up quietly somewhere. Relax, Mr. Pym and enjoy my town."

"I'll try."

"Y'all gotta leave now. I need to work. Can I count on you for tonight?"

"Of course. But... I'm not rich."

"I am."

Pym stood and put on his jacket. He knew she was going to come at him, but he was ready and cleverly got himself through the French doors and to the stairs. Sasha followed him down. The shop was full of customers. Pym was used to them now; he didn't even think about it. All men—some in drag. Sasha saw him to the shop's entrance and hugged him. She stood in her bare feet a little over a head shorter, so he was able to avoid her available mouth.

* * *

The pleasure Terry took in writing freely, whilst sitting like the great Don Miguel himself on the balcony, with the lovely Spanish fountain splashing and gurgling in the courtyard below, gradually eroded when he realised how unusually hushed the room behind him had become. He coughed a few times which would usually prompt a birdcall of some kind from Vera. Her quiescence unfocused his mind and the writing rhythm flew away. Did she have the hump because he started the day with a hangover? Or did she think that his taking time to indulge in his stupid scribbling was an insult, given the paucity of time they had left together? And what he feared most, though she never mentioned it, was that she obsessed about death, like anyone would, and looked, as the condemned must, into a future of black nothingness. He wished she at least had the disgusting duality in her that he possessed—a disdain for religion but an incongruent faith in the soul's immortality. Of course, Vera was far more honest than he, and her courage in the face of death only served to frighten him.

In the taxi to the airport a few days ago he had tried to broach the subject of what she wanted done—of funerals and appropriate things to be said by loved ones and the like. They were jammed in traffic and the red flank of a bus throbbed beside them. She stared for a long time at the red metal of the London bus before at last saying, "I suppose I must respond sensibly."

"It would be helpful," he'd replied, gently.

Vera looked at him, her eyes big and dry, and said, "Tell them I couldn't bear the thought of never seeing the colour red again. Tell them that my fear was so unspeakable that not even you could articulate it. Tell them I wouldn't give in and hoodwink myself at the last like some deranged Joan of Arc. Tell them I refused to let this fear panic me into a belief in belief itself, to some muddled return to infantile thought. Please lie to them, Terry, and tell them this was my finest hour." And she thrust her hind-head against the seat's headrest, her lovely throat pulsing with rapid swallows. The cabby's eyes watched her in the rearview mirror.

Terry stepped through the French doors and into the room, holding his big three-ring binder against his chest like a vicar with a family Bible. His mind reached for levity but he found none. Vera, pillow-propped against the headboard, hands thrust into armpits, legs crossed, Walkman plugged into ears, with a book open in her lap, stared unblinking at the ceiling. Terry stepped forward sharply and pulled her toe so that she jumped, yanked out the earphones, and said, "You broke my reverie, you brute."

"I hope you were thinking about Jumping Jack Flash."

"I wasn't. I was listening to Marilyn Monroe Classics as it happens. *Diamonds are a Girl's Best Friend,* and you better believe it, buster, because you're bloody useless, you."

"Liar! You were thinking about Jumping Jack going in and out of you like a massive piston. Go on, admit it."

"You know, women don't think about that sort of thing."

"I know they say they don't." Terry laughed. "They'd rather admit to more intellectual pursuits, like listening to some half-witted, iconoclastic bimbo with a voice designed to excite pedophiles." In a Louisiana accent Terry said, "Oh me oh my, I'd rather just be hugged all night!"

Vera laughed and said, "God, Terry, what in heaven's name were you writing?"

"Something related to what you were listening to actually. Tits."

"Why do you insist upon writing such rubbish? I keep telling you to write a good story that women will read. Only women read novels these days and they don't want to read about quivering body parts and flying sperm."

"I don't believe you. Besides, if I write about quivering body parts the world will listen. And men do read novels—just not simpering balderdash about relationships and feelings. They like action and ideas!"

"Pistonlike pricks and gigantic knockers?"

"Precisely."

"You've been writing that bloody book for twenty years and you haven't learned a thing."

"You'll eat your words when I win the Booker Prize."

"I'll eat my hat is what I'll do."

"Right, enough of this equivocation. I need a quick shower, then I might have to jump you."

"I expect you'll forget, but I'll endeavour not to move from my current location."

"Splendid."

As he showered, Terry could hear Vera moving about the room, opening drawers, closing the French windows. He sang a few bars of what he remembered of an Otis Redding song and then an aria Vera liked, made popular by Pavarotti. As he emerged, drying himself with the big white towel he sang: "A kiss on the clit might be quite continental, but candles are a girl's best friend."

Vera said, "Stop it, you fool. These walls are thin. This isn't Lambeth."

Terry loved her outrage. He felt like a young god about to cuckold Zeus. He rubbed himself exaggeratedly with the towel. Vera giggled as his penis rose. She covered her face with her hands and said, "Oh, dear, whatever next?"

"You see, Bridget," he said in an Irish accent, "me wits are on the wind and 'oy have a grand lust on me. So assume the position, woman!"

He wanged Jumping Jack Flash against the hands covering her face and, this time with the accent of an RAF pilot, said, "Will Madam kindly comply with instructions from HQ!"

"Dirty filthy goat!" Vera cried, but nevertheless turned and put her face in the pillow and her bum in the air. Muffled by the pillow, Terry heard, "Christ, anything to keep you quiet, you lunatic."

Terry huffed and puffed and Vera faked an orgasm.

He panted at her side, watching her eyelids tremor as she immediately fell asleep. She'd been crying before they made love, and, in his attempt to distract her with comedy and sex, he hadn't noticed. What a dolt you are, Langley. What could have upset her other than the usual?

He looked around the room. The drawer. He'd heard her open the drawer. She'd been reading his morning's work. His heart sank; there was something there she would be upset by, but he couldn't remember what he'd written. Quietly, he pulled on pajama bottoms and got the big folder out of the drawer and took it back out onto the balcony.

The voice in the book had increasingly become that of an old man, and where, when he was younger, there was a certain plotted vigor to the writing, there was now a tone of mere pamphleteering, usually triggered by whatever was going on in his life at that time.

The Spanish fountain gurgled and the sun shone on the north side of the courtyard. He had written:

> *The beautiful things that humanity creates have only become valuable to me in the twilight of my life. And in this twilight with so little time left I begin to see what I wish I had had the wisdom to see in my youth. Poor old Oscar said: "Youth is wasted on the young." All my vigor was packed into sperm sacks to be squirted into the guts of dubious women. At last I grew wiser and that wisdom helped me find my goddess, but after a short time of holding her close and healing from the disease of youth, my goddess began to crumble.*
>
> *And where are my dear wife's lovely breasts?*
>
> *Hey, you down there, are you wearing them? All these implants moving around on the wrong chests. A whole industry of stolen body parts! The unacceptable face of capitalism! Jehovah Himself is the marauder of body parts. You better keep your stinking maulers off Jumping Jack Flash.*

Look at that, Terry thought. I was just about to start emoting about the loss of Vera's breasts and I veer off instead into puerile diatribe. She saw that, saw that I can't handle it. I shouldn't have written that.

He gazed at the beautiful fountain and became the stone the fountain was made of, not the water that flowed from it; that way he could walk back into the room and minister to Vera and not require her to look after him.

He went back in to see her staring at the ceiling again.

"What's that damn thing you're reading?" he asked.

"Marty Kelso," she said, and held the book up to her chest protectively.

"I am slain," Terry cried. "I shall slit my jugular immediately. How can you read that turncoat, that cop-out, that Hobbit?"

"That bus driver."

"That nicotined nincompoop."

"That Booker Prize finalist."

"Where's my razor? Where is it?"

Vera laughed, jumped off the bed and kissed him.

* * *

Pym walked east to the river and along the levee, above the Café Du Monde, and all the way to downtown where the ferries to Algiers sail back and forth. On a whim he boarded a waiting ferry, ignoring a bum who stood on the gangway holding out his hand. The bum's reddish beard nearly touched a knotted rope, which served at his waist as a belt. He wore a filthy Saints cap turned backwards on his head; his eyes were bright blue but disconnected and unfocused. As Pym passed him, the bum dropped to one knee and pointed, singing, "Don't pay the ferryman. Don't even ask the price..."

A heavy-set member of the crew came over and told the bum to move off the gangway, to which the bum replied, "Fuck off, you fucking fat nigger—I'm not afraid of you."

The crew member spoke into a walkie-talkie.

"Whatcha gonna do, have some of your spade brothers come and rough me up, kill me, throw me in the river? Stupid blue-gummer, can't you see I'm already dead!"

Other crew members appeared and quietly picked the bum up and walked away with him, carrying him like one might a woman in labor, the bum staring off, straight-mouthed as if he were accustomed to such treatment. The heavy sailor who had been insulted gave Pym a wink and walked away, shaking his head and grinning.

Pym stood on the upper deck as the ferry pulled away from the Canal Street dock and crossed the Mississippi. The wide, brown river felt enchanted and tropical.

Ahead Pym saw small, pastel-painted houses, so different from the French Quarter, almost a ghost town. The facades of some of the buildings facing the river were nicely painted, but the sides were gray and decrepit. He felt hungry. A café nestled below the levee to the right, but he didn't want to eat there, so he took the next ferry back across.

He'd deal with Algiers later.

Tourists packed the Café Du Monde, most in shorts or sundresses, waiting for tables. The Asian servers bustled and yammered at each other in frustration. Pym nudged inside to use the toilet and see if he could find Lulu. In a place setting for two, sitting on her own, sat the woman from the balcony that morning. Pym found the men's room.

When he emerged back into the clatter of the café the woman still sat alone. She looked up and smiled. He strode over to her, checked his watch and said, "Good afternoon."

"How are you?"

"I'm getting used to this place. Where's your friend?"

"Eddie? He's at a convention downtown—be there till late tonight. I've been abandoned."

"I'm waiting for a table."

"Sit here why don't you?"

"I don't want to impose."

"Always so polite. Take a load off."

Pym sat, removed his jacket, and draped it over the back of his chair. The woman pushed a menu at him. He noted the arch-eye-browed way she did this—peculiar. It got on his nerves that suddenly nuances which never bothered him before presented themselves as readable, and in turn begged interpretation.

"I've ordered already," she said.

"Thank you," said Pym, and then held his hand out. "I'm Gilbert Pym."

"Hi," she said. She was doing something alluring with her eyes. "I'm Maddy."

"Pleased to meet you."

"Same."

Pym felt Maddy observing his hands as he held the menu, and he smelled her shampoo across the small table. The other times he'd seen her, always at a respectable distance, had produced the impression of beauty. Now, up close, he awaited a suitable moment to examine his initial perception of beauty. *This is all Terry's fault, with his little clever distinctions. And those cards of George's. I'm watchful and alert. Is it good or bad?*

Maddy looked up at a waitress squeezing between the tables and Pym looked at her over the top of the greasy menu. Her eyes weren't level and her lips were too big. A pimple had erupted on the left of her chin. If she had been Estelle, Pym would've insisted on popping it. Her teeth, which looked like a film star's from even a few yards away, proved up close to be slightly crooked. But still, she made his throat go dry. He couldn't help comparing her to Sasha, who was perfect, as she herself said—a work of art. And this woman, this Maddy, was someone else's girlfriend. A someone who hung on her, longed for her, ejaculated into her. Pym knew the lovemaking of the night before was still in her. He wanted to ask things he'd never bothered with before—how it feels for a woman the next day. Do they ache, have cramps, does stuff run out? But instead he asked, "Should I try one of these Po'boys?"

"Sure." She smiled. "You're not gonna get anything special in here. It's only good for coffee and doughnuts."

"What are you doing here then?"

"Been here all day."

"Why? It was a nice morning."

"I'm bumming a bit. I'll get over it."

"Fight with the boyfriend?"

"Something like that. It's a long and very old story. How about you? What brings you into this tourist trap?"

"Another long story. I'm down here looking for my stupid brother and I know he hangs out here, and there's a waitress that knows him who works here. And on a long shot, I'm hoping he'll just walk in, call me an asshole, and we'll go out and drink beer."

Pym liked the way Maddy's eyes watched him speak. They made him speak more. He wanted to keep speaking so she'd keep watching him. He knew he wasn't handsome, but he saw himself as big and muscular and honest and that at least was something. His words dried up and he just looked at her eyes. Maddy said, "You're very easy with strangers, aren't you? Why's that?"

"Nothing to hide, I guess."

"Hell, you ought to start a religion. What's going on with your brother?"

"He ran away. Couldn't stand the sports franchises any longer."

"Huh? Not even the Vikes? They were great this year. The Bears suck. Come on now, really? What's his problem? A woman?"

"In a way. Suffice to say he felt he had to get out of town in order to get away with a big change. I don't want him to go through that change, and came here to try and stop it, but I'm told by a friend of his that I'm too late."

"Bummer. I hope he's okay when you find him. It all sounds like the opening to a mystery novel."

"I never thought of it that way."

"But what happens next? If it's a mystery novel, that is?" She looked at him, laughing.

He wallowed in her peculiar aura of friendliness and the words just flew out of him without warning. "They fish him out of the river, and an old woman has a heart attack when she sees him." The sentence startled him so that his mouth dropped open and his heart pounded. A stranger, whose name he had forgotten, was reaching out to touch his hand as a sob broke from him.

"My God," she said. "We hit a nerve. Jeez, I'm sorry."

Pym couldn't stop it. He had his hand over his face so no one would see, and his face was hot and so was the water running through his fingers. This girl, Maddy, reached over the table and gripped his elbow. "And I thought I had problems," she murmured. "You poor thing."

"Sorry. I don't know where that came from. It's nonsense. I know he's okay. He can look after himself."

"It was on the news. That woman who found the body caught in her propeller or something. Yeah, it gave her a heart attack. You saw it on the news."

"Newspaper."

"You're an impressionable guy. It didn't happen. Your brother's okay. Screw mystery novels, they're bullshit."

"I've been down here one day and now I'm crying in the Café Du Monde in front of a beautiful stranger," said Pym, laughing through his tears. "What is this place?"

"It's just a town," she said. "It ain't much really. Just a dingy, dirty shithole full of little people with big dreams and no chance. That's America all over. I hate this fucking country."

"What?"

"Yep. I'd marry a rich Arab—if I could find one that wasn't an ass-hole—and get the fuck outta here."

Pym laughed, wiped his face.

"Or an Eskimo. Move to the frozen north. Rub noses and dry Caribou meat. Fuck this place."

"You're too young to be a hippy."

"They're fools too. I hate them."

"Did something bring this on?"

A waitress came to the table with a plate of blackened catfish and fries. Pym looked at her and asked if Lulu was around. "No," the waitress said, "Lulu didn't come to work today. Maybe she be here tonight."

Pym ordered and after the waitress went, Maddy said, "Okay. We're strangers sharing shit. Maybe I should get your call on my situation."

Maddy was a nurse and had been having an affair with this very married, but desperately unhappy anesthesiologist. Her constant discomfort with the situation had become even more a source of pain for him than his horrible, controlling wife, who was also a prominent Chicago doctor. Eddie was at a convention in town and Maddy couldn't go because lots of people knew his wife down here. His wife was at a convention in Vienna. Maddy loved Eddie, but she needed a life. "He's obsessed with me, morbidly territorial and possessive, but he won't leave his wife and kids. Says he can't trust me. Trust? What's that got to do with it after all this? What's not to trust?"

"So you had a big fight this morning?"

"I slept with this intern and Eddie found out. It was months ago now, but he can't get over it. It's killing him. I lied because I didn't want to lose him. I lied and double lied. Now he won't believe anything I say."

"He lies to his wife."

"Yes. Not the point though. I was special in his eyes. I've blown it. But I can't get out."

"Get out?"

"I can't. I'm all bound up with him. I can't believe I'm telling you this. It's unreal, sick. I must look like a whore."

"You can afford to let your guard down a bit away from home. This place feels unreal, like a dream. You let your guard down in dreams, don't you? All your shit's out of the box in front of you."

"It's not though, is it?" Maddy said, frowning. "We're sent shit by the universe, I think. It's too weird. You with your brother. Me with my Eddie shit. Pain, pain, and pain everywere. And this is supposed to be the land of milk and honey."

"Your fish is getting cold."

Maddy laughed. "That's my problem. I'm too much of a hot fish." She cut into the fry and ate some, shrugged. "It's edible."

"Eddieable?"

She laughed with her mouth full.

Pym liked the way she chewed. While she ate she watched him speak. He just kept speaking. He told her everything. The lost job. Laura and Ray. Estelle. George turning into Georgie. His food came and he ate and talked at the same time and told her all about Lulu and the postcards and last night and Sasha today and what a moron he'd been all his life.

When Pym finished eating and nothing more came out of his mouth, Maddy said, "So you're meeting this shemale tonight? This Sasha? Do you think she's after you?"

"I don't know, maybe a little."

"There's more going on here than meets the eye. Sounds like your brother's having one of those backstreet sex-change jobbies. I've seen some of the results of those—I'm a nurse, remember? Not pretty. You better find him. I think you're smelling a rat too, only you don't know what a rat smells like yet."

The tingling came back to Pym's scalp. The vampire image went on the rampage in his mind. Indeed, something felt very wrong. Maddy broke into Pym's thoughts with, "Take someone with you tonight… don't be alone with her. I'll try and get Eddie out—meet you at that mirror bar place, what's-its-name, you know?"

"Yes."

"End up there. Don't go home with her. She wants to do shit to you. You're vulnerable down here. Be careful. Make friends with that cop you mentioned. This ain't Minneapolis. It ain't Chicago either for that matter, so be careful. There's bad juju here."

"You're scaring me."

"Be scared, then you'll watch yourself. You're vulnerable, Gilbert. You're such a sweet guy. You shouldn't be hanging around with scum like us."

Pym laughed. Maddy laughed too, although he knew she'd meant what she said. "I'll find you in that bar tonight about three or so, and I'll come up behind, and if Eddie's not looking, I'll give your buns a squeeze and warn off this Sasha bitch. She's a monster. "'Course, if Eddie sees me do that you'll have another problem. I'm not sure which is the more dangerous."

They chatted until dusk, then walked outside. Starlings swarmed over Jackson Square. Round and round they swirled, small black stars, gathering all the strays into the main flock, one great black shadow moving like a tornado, and then, just before the sun went down, zoom, they vanished into the treetops. Maddy stood beside Pym, watching. She had goose-bumps on her forearms and hugged herself. Pym placed his jacket around her shoulders. Then they walked slowly back to the hotel amidst the shops closing and people bustling back to homes or hotels. Pym walked her upstairs and, outside his room, said, "You want to come in for a while?"

"Better not," she said. "It's been quite an afternoon, hasn't it? My head's pounding. Why do I only attract intense people?"

"We could have Sammy bring drinks to the balcony."

"Don't spoil it now. I'll see you again. But not now. I'll see you tonight, hopefully in that mirror bar. And if not, on the balcony for breakfast—about noon."

"All right. And thanks. I will be careful." Maddy kissed Pym on the cheek and went to her room. He watched her unlock her door, and she gave him a little wave before going inside.

He lay on the bed and heard her through the wall, bumping things. She turned on the bath taps and he imagined her undressing. He wondered if she would masturbate in the bath as he knew Estelle often did. He thought about doing so himself but resisted, not being sure if Terry and Vera were watching from somewhere. He laughed and let himself doze.

Someone had severed his head and placed it on a dusty shelf in a dark cupboard among jars of formaldehyde. He didn't know where his body was and he couldn't blink. It was an impossible dilemma. Head but no body. Stuck on a shelf. He knew the jars with which he shared the shelf contained unspeakable horrors. He kept trying to scream for help, but nothing came out of his mouth except dust, drawn up through his windpipe from the shelf. Someone moved around outside the cupboard. He opened the cupboard and saw the bloody eyes of the head and began screaming.

Pym sat up in the dark room and saw the wardrobe—a menacing presence against the wall. Music came from the street and the curtains blew inward. He didn't remember opening the French windows to the balcony. Muffled voices conversed—Maddy and Eddie next door. Pym switched on the bedside light, then got up, went outside to look up and down the balcony. Maddy's doors stood open; she talked quietly, explaining something.

He went back in and closed the doors. They came open again. He had to latch them. They'd been open all day. Anyone could've come in. Sasha knew why he was here. So did Lulu. And who in the hell were those crazy Brits? He would have to open the wardrobe to get his clean clothes. George's head would be on the shelf. Here, motherfucker, you can stop looking now. He went and pulled the doors open. Stupid fuck-wad. Nothing, of course. Paranoid. Talking to one weirdo after another until you become one yourself. Your body's buzzing. Calm down, your heart'll explode. What is this?

His intuition told him, like a voice from inside—George is dead, and Sasha knows. Who else knows? But you 'knew' there was a head in the wardrobe. Your imagination has never been your friend.

He showered, trying to shut out the voices and images. It was as if all the horror movies he'd ever seen came together and hit him with one big moment of terror. He imagined the water pouring off him, all the nonsense washing away, and imagined getting caught in the rain with Maddy and coming back to warm up in the shower. She gets in with him naked and lovely and slides down his torso and takes his penis in her mouth and just as he's about to come she looks up and it's no longer Maddy but Sasha, and he comes over her perfect teeth and she laughs and wraps her legs around him and fucks him standing.

Now he had an erection. Better than horror visions. Oral sex would be okay, wouldn't it? That wouldn't get me into too much trouble? He got out of the shower, dried off, and put on deodorant. He got his suit out of its plastic cover-all, which hung in the wardrobe to ease out the wrinkles caused by being stuffed into his sports bag. It was the light, double-breasted suit in which he'd been married. He'd brought a white shirt and red tie to wear with it, and with his good loafers he'd look pretty sharp. He had time to have a drink before picking up Sasha. He dressed and then tied his hair back in a stubby ponytail.

Murmurings continued from next door; Pym didn't like them. Maddy should be his girlfriend, not that shit-for-brains Doctor Quack. The phone rang and it was the bellboy, Sammy, from the night before, saying, "You comin' downstairs, Mistah Pym? English folk waitin' on you. I cain't make 'em leave till they see you."

Holding the varnished bannister, he descended the staircase to the lobby with its lush carpeting, where Sammy, last night a bell-boy, was now the barman. Terry rushed forward with his hand extended, bellowing, "Gilbert, my dear boy, awake at last. We couldn't raise you. Come, have a drink with us." He took Pym's elbow and led him to the bar where Vera sat on a high stool, her legs crossed and holding up an almost-empty martini glass in greeting. She looked young and gay this evening as she twirled a pearl necklace with her free hand. She said, "Terry's being a Graham Greene character tonight, Gilbert, please excuse him."

"The white suit?" asked Pym.

"Precisely. He insists. Tell him this isn't Havana."

Terry, obviously wearing contact lenses, stared at her with his blue Rutger Hauer eyes, serious and assessing, ready to leap afresh into extroversion. "He wants you to get pissed with him again, and he's hoping I'll poop out again and leave you all to it, but I won't. I'm determined to hang in and hang out."

Pym looked at Sammy and shrugged.

Terry asked, "Are you finished, darling? May I launch the evening? Or am I in for a few more psychological skewerings?"

"Launch away, you rotten lush... see if I care," said Vera.

"Do you hire these folks as local color, Sammy?" asked Pym. "Are they really just out-of-work actors from Baton Rouge?"

Sammy's brow thickened, went darker. "I be the only local color round here as I can see." And they all laughed.

"I'll take the first of the night, then, Sammy," said Pym. "A Budweezer."

"Oh, dear," said Terry, looking at Vera.

"What?"

"You've dropped in his estimation, Mr. Pym," said Vera. "He doesn't approve of Budweiser."

"Fuck him," Pym laughed. "It's the king of beers."

"You know nothing of beer," said Terry, his jowls dancing.

Vera said, "Dancer's so clever now, isn't he? He was an introvert when we met him. When was it, yesterday?"

"If you'll permit me, Gilbert, I'll find you good beer tonight and you'll only drink Budweiser to wash down your vitamins."

The phone rang and Sammy had to leave the bar and answer it at the reception desk. "Yep. He here. Fact, he right here. Phone for Mr. Pym."

Pym came over, frowning, and put the receiver to his ear. He heard only a dial tone and, after a few moments, replaced the receiver.

"Who dat?" asked Sammy.

"No one there."

Sammy and Terry and Vera all stared at Pym.

"Was it a man or woman, Sammy?" asked Terry.

"Couldn't tell. Didn't think about it."

"I'm going out now, Sammy. Keep an eye on my room, will you? Those French windows don't close properly. There's nothing of value in there, but keep an eye out just the same."

As he walked out the Brits followed him. Vera asked, "Are you sure everything's all right, Dancer?"

"No, but I have a sort of date—so they have to be all right. Do you think that cop will be in the mirror bar again tonight, Terry?"

"Rick? Yes, he said he would."

Pym noticed that Terry was subdued since the hang-up call. He thought, What's that about, but merely said, "I'll meet you there later, okay?"

"Yes," said Terry, perking up a bit. "Bring your date."

"I will. I want your full assessment."

"And you'll jolly well get it," adjoined Vera. "Won't he, darling?"

* * *

With Sasha holding his arm, Pym headed back into the heart of the Quarter. She had taken him shopping on Canal and Royal, and in his free hand he held a large plastic bag. The air had cleared his mind and when they got to the bar with the mirrors he looked for familiar faces but saw none. People danced to blues being played by a band on a small stage at the far end of the bar. The circular stand-up tables, built around antique, silver-painted columns, looked similar to the thin supports that held up balconies all around the Quarter, and the mirrors, arranged floor to ceiling, were separated only by thin strips of decorated tin. Pym thought it all very fine—as long as one didn't look too close. When Sasha wanted to sit on one of the high stools, a man moved for her and she placed her coat over the other stool and put Pym's bag of old clothes under it while he went to the bar. He bought a Budweiser and a Chianti. When he arrived back at the high table with the drinks, a black woman with very large eyes was talking angrily to Sasha. The woman caught sight of Pym arriving, shot an ambiguous glance at him, and disappeared into the crowd. He saw her again, looking out of the mirrors at him, but couldn't find her in the bar itself. After setting down the drinks and removing the coat so he could sit, he asked, "Who was that?"

"We took her chair," Sasha said.

They drank quietly for a minute or two until the band played a slow song and Sasha stood up. "Come on," she said, "it's time for one of these."

Aside from her large firm breasts pressed against him, her body was hard and slick. She felt like a power-pack of strength. Pym imagined rolling around on that nice bed of hers, the two of them pulling at each other. In his mind he had to make her simply an athletic woman, not one that had the muscle structure of a man—he had to not think about that. He thought of his fantasy in the shower and the erection came up and he had to hold her close so that it wouldn't show. She was whispering in his ear; he couldn't make it out, it was foreign, French maybe. He felt drunk again, the music deafened him, and that black woman with the big eyes he'd seen earlier kept looking out of the mirrors at him.

Someone grabbed his shoulders and squeezed real hard. "Holy shit!" Expecting to see Maddy, Pym turned, ready with a smile. But it was Terry. Terry, red-faced, totally looped in his white Graham Greene suit. He pulled Pym away from Sasha and tried to dip him, but Pym resisted, embarrassed. "Wait, wait, wait. Terry. Terry, this is my friend, Sasha. Sasha, Terry," Pym shouted.

"How do you do."

"Pleased to meet you."

"Stop this soppy dancing and come over to our table and have a drink."

Sasha shrugged—okay—and they collected their stuff and went to Terry's table. Terry had somehow picked up Maddy and Eddie—as Vera had predicted in the Maison de Veau—and Rick the cop and his lovely wife, Matilde, and two other couples, but Vera had gone back to the hotel already. Once Terry got them seated, he said, "Let the night begin. More wine!"

Maddy laughed at him and said, "You been saying that all night, man."

Eddie glared at Pym when Pym leaned over to Maddy and said of Terry, "He's crazy, you know, but he's ours."

"I know," laughed Maddy. "He won't go away. Does he get dangerous?"

"Only to himself."

Sasha sat beside him, her hands in her lap. Pym's attention had shifted to Maddy, and he couldn't look too much at her because of Eddie and he felt like a shit because Sasha was investing so much in him. Terry spoke Pym's thoughts. "Well, ladies and Gentlemen, we're living in the moment, are we not? What a nice little gathering. Whose round is it?"

And away it went again, the rounds of drinks, the shouting to be heard, the fuzzy-brained treks through the crowded bar to order because the waitress couldn't keep up with the party's demand. Pym noticed that Maddy more or less only spoke to the women and to old Terry, who didn't appear to present a threat to Eddie. They worked their way around to each other so that everyone had an intimate little yell into each other's ear.

After a while, Pym found himself talking to the policeman, Rick.

"How you doin', man. Find yo' brother?"

"No. This woman, Sasha, she knows him but doesn't know where he lives. And Lulu didn't know either. I'm stumped at the moment."

"Not much of a detective, are you?" said Rick. "You're at the end of your second day and no answers. By the way, man, you know what you're dealing with with this Sasha chick?"

"I think so."

"You know she ain't a she."

"Well, I reckon she is now. Take a look."

Rick laughed, "I hear you, man. I'm just sayin'."

Rick's wife, Matilde, was talking to Sasha and let out a cackle that made all those in the vicinity turn and smile at her. Rick looked at her and frowned. "She gonna start pissin' me off."

"She's great," said Pym.

"You don't gotta live wid her."

"That's probably what my wife was saying about me. Now she's with someone else."

"That's the way it goes, man. Say, you better call me in the morning and I'll run an APB on your brother."

"I'd appreciate that. Don't know where to start."

"You do what you do well and assign everything else to the experts. That's what I do. I use accountants, lawyers, and whores."

"All the same thing."

Rick nearly spat out his beer.

Pym was struck by the nature of bar talk. He looked at Sasha and she rolled her eyes toward him. *Let's get out of here*, they said. Rick was now talking to Eddie. Terry, holding a bottle of Budweiser, caught Pym by the arm and said, "You look as though you're about to dash off."

"Are you enjoying your Bud?"

"I'm drinking it in your honour. Can't get drunk on it. In London we call it gnat's piss."

"You were going to buy us real beer."

"I was, but tonight you obviously prefer far more exotic company than an elderly man and his beer fetish."

Mimicking Terry, Pym said, "I'm flattered that you're jealous."

"Ah—playing me at my own game."

"And a very good game it is."

"Ha! Now then, this Sasha, he has a marvelous figure. How will you escape him?"

"Maybe I don't want to. I've only just met her. Why's everyone down on her? She's okay. And yes, I know she used to be a man. She sure as hell isn't now."

"And she's rich."

"Ouch."

"Think, boy. Don't dip your wick."

Pym felt numb. Terry sped off somewhere.

Eddie went to the toilet, and Maddy came up to Pym and took her turn. "Sorry I had to have Terry startle you. It's just that Eddie's hyper insecure tonight."

"I got it. That guy's gotta go. He's a time-bomb."

"I can tell you're not heeding my advice about Sasha. No one likes her, you know. She's dangerous."

"Eddie thinks *you're* dangerous."

"I am to him. Because he won't do as he's told."

"I would. I don't have a wife anymore."

"But Gilbert, you have a brand new girlfriend."

"Not yet. Not consummated."

"If it gets consummated tonight you can forget breakfast in the morning."

They stared at each other for a long moment until Pym, again copying Terry's tone, said, "I will bear that in mind, my dear. Thank you for your candor."

"You be careful." She was holding on to his sleeve. He touched her arm and said, "You too. Christ, Eddie's much more dangerous than poor old Sasha."

"Here he comes. I'll see you in the morning, about ten, okay?"

"I see we've brought the time forward."

"You won't be sorry."

* * *

As Pym and Sasha slowly walked through the narrow streets to The House of Large Sizes, Pym found himself thinking of Maddy. The whole thing had become a sexual tug-of-war between man-made perfection, created by and for men, and nature's archetypal imperfection; the exaggerated womanly shape of the neutered Sasha versus the buxom seediness and easy promiscuity of Maddy—who made Estelle seem like Mary Poppins. Was this how Terry found himself a Vera? No, that was a product of wisdom, Pym suspected, and the integration of two choices. Sasha broke into his thoughts and asked what he was thinking. He told her he was thinking about George.

"Who was that nigger you were talking to?" Sasha asked.

"Nigger? Jeez, what's with you? He's a friend of Terry's, the Englishman."

"What's he do?"

"He's a cop. Why 'nigger'?"

"That's what they are. We try to keep it all separate down here. It works better. Rich white folk don't have nigger friends." Sasha laughed.

"That's nasty. I don't like that."

"You like these though, don't you?"

She pulled him into a doorway, opened her coat, zipped down her leather waistcoat and pushed out her breasts. Gently, she pulled his head down so that his face rested between them. People walked by laughing. "I want you to fuck me," she whispered. "I want you to come between my tits, I want you to come in my mouth. I want you to come up my ass."

Pym had his hands on her hips and felt Sasha trembling. He sucked on her nipples but they didn't erect, they remained soft and small, tasting of metal. "Come on," she said. "Let's go back."

At The House of Large Sizes, he dropped his carrier bag beside the door and followed her up the stairs. He watched her buttocks as before and decided he would go for it. What the hell... a new experience. He'd lie to Maddy in the morning and fuck her too. "I love New Orleans," he whispered. He had a slight concern though because nothing normal was happening in his nether regions. His brain wanted to have sex with Sasha, but his body wasn't convinced yet. She'll understand that, he realized; she'll know how to deal with that and will understand. She won't think there's something wrong with me.

A huge man stood in the kitchen with his back to them.

Pym felt a slight sense of relief as well as a sense of fear.

"What're y'all doing here?" Sasha said.

"Il faut qu'on parle," the big man said.

"Pas maintenant. Go back to Nadine! Nous avons convenu que c'est pour le bien de tous."

The man kept his back to them as he said, "Je ne peux pas."

"You must."

"Non. C'est toi que j'aime. Ma femme est folle et mon mariage est en ruine."

"You can't ruin it. Stick to the plan. Nous dépendons de votre stabilite."

"Je ne veux pas retourner à elle ce soir. Elle préside une cérémonie et je ne peux pas lui parler."

"Shit."

Sasha turned to Pym and said, "Did you get all that? Do you speak French?"

"I barely speak English."

"We have a problem. Come downstairs again."

Pym looked at the big old man but the man kept his back turned away.

Downstairs Sasha turned the lights on and rubbed her face. In the vicious shop lights she suddenly looked odd and fake, like an unhappy doll with perfect make up. "I have a problem to sort out," she said. "I'm caught between things here. I want to finish off our night properly but I have obligations to Duval."

"I understand." Phew, saved by the bell, he thought.

"You can come back tomorrow. Shit, I knew he'd pull something like this just when he shouldn't."

"Will you be safe?"

"Oh, yes... there's nothing to be done. I apologize."

As they talked, Pym walked around the square glass counter looking at the paraphernalia for sale. Most of the items were sex aids. "Do people buy a lot of this stuff?" he asked.

"It's amazingly profitable. You don't seem too concerned about all this."

"We were going to have a reasonable end to the night anyway."

"Yes, good. Come back tomorrow."

He could tell she was conflicted; she wanted him gone but she didn't want to release him.

"Thanks for the clothes, Sasha. And everything else. You spent a lot of dough. I appreciate it."

She smiled, stepped toward the door and said, "It's for a good cause."

"I'll see you sometime tomorrow but I have to find George."

"I thought we'd agreed to wait that out. Let him mend."

"I'm worried about him."

"He's fine."

"How do you know?"

"Well... I don't... he just will be. It's how it works. It's major surgery. You don't want people hanging on you."

A voice came down the stairs: "Sasha, Ou es tu?"

She rolled her eyes, called, "J'arrive!" Then, shrugging, she said to Pym, "I'll explain all this tomorrow."

* * *

Pym arrived at his hotel earlier than he'd expected. He found Vera, with no barman in sight, sitting alone with a cocktail and a book open in front of her. She looked up from the book as he entered and smiled. He approached and asked if she was okay.

"I'm fine," she said. "I appear to have taken over the role of bartender. Would you like a drink?"

"I'm about all drinked out. Do they have pop?"

"I should imagine."

A white and red triangular packet of Toblerone lay open by her drink. The pyramid-shaped white chocolate emerged from the triangular tunnel. He couldn't remember if he'd ever actually tried white chocolate. It made him think of veal.

Vera found him a root beer and wrote on a pad near the cash register. Pym was in the sort of mental state where even a dying woman in her early sixties could conceivably be a receptacle for a young man's pent up urges, but he pushed this impulse aside.

179

"Do you think, Vera," said Pym, "that a guy can be counted an asshole for having asshole thoughts, even if he doesn't act on them?"

"Quite simply, dear, the answer is no. Try not to act like an arsehole and you won't be one. Easy."

"Oh."

"Okay?"

"Right."

"Good."

"So, are you all right?"

"No, not really. Himself, the Terry, he can take care of. I just can't always sleep. I like to get in the light and read—darkness can be so cruel to the imagination."

"That's true."

"Are you off to bed now?"

"Yes, I should. So much has happened and it's only the end of my second day here."

"Go on then, young man. I'll see you tomorrow."

In his room he undressed, put on sweat pants and a T-shirt, and then, finding the room too hot, stepped onto the balcony and opened his arms to the cool air. Maddy's lights were on but her French doors were closed. Music came from many directions, all kinds of music. The veal restaurant was closed and Romano's cats were not at play. Pym stepped sideways along the balcony a little until he could distinguish the music playing in Maddy's room. Classical. Violin rhapsody type stuff—yearning plaintive gypsy melodies. Enough to break your heart if you thought of the woman you loved who was at this very moment having sex with that fuck Ray. Pym knew the piece but couldn't name the composer.

Then he realized that beneath the music a man wept. A continuous weeping man. Poor haunted Eddie, thought Pym. He became sad himself again for the same old reasons. Poor Maddy, taking care of sad men all day. Pym left his windows open and climbed into bed in his sweats, pulled the covers up. He needed a good sleep; tomorrow he would find George.

XV

A new suit, carefully selected and paid for by Sasha from a boutique on Royal and draped over the end of the bed, shocked Pym as he woke. His old suit, folded in a carrier bag on the desk chair, drew his eyes to the mirror above the little desk where he saw reflected the opposite wall with its *fleur-de-lys*. Annoyed that he hadn't noticed the pattern of the wallpaper before, he invoked Terry's voice to say, "You're only half-alive, mate."

He peed, cleaned his teeth, put everything away on hangers, then draped the garment bag that came with his new suit over his old one and hung it at the far end of the wardrobe, as far away from where the new one hung as possible. His father had told him that an orderly outward life encouraged an orderly inner one. He felt hungry, looked outside the door—no breakfast yet.

In the pocket of his everyday jacket he found George's postcards and Rick the policeman's business card. He placed both on the desk next to the telephone. He turned over one of the postcards. The Crescent City Connection bridge: blue sky, brown river, tugboat approaching and the Algiers ferries passing each other in the middle of the river.

> *Bro, across this bridge is your brother's destiny. I believe the first modern sex-change was performed in North Africa. Of all the bridges I have crossed this is the most significant. If you were here you'd stop me, wouldn't you? But you wouldn't know what you were doing and we'd fight again. I'm growing up now, thank God. I feel so much myself. Look at this old river! We lived all our lives along it, crossing back and forth, fishing in it. It's ours. -Georgie.*

181

"That's right, you're in Algiers," he said. "Sasha mentioned it too."

He picked up the phone and dialed Rick's number.

"Hey, man," Rick said. "How you doin' this morning? Headache?"

"No. Got an early night."

Rick laughed, "Good boy. You stayed outta her clutches."

"Things got pretty strange."

"You are headed for trouble with her, fool. Now, I guess you want me to find your brother, right?"

"Yep. How do we start? I think he's in Algiers—across the river there."

"Why you think that?"

Pym told Rick everything.

"I'll see what I can do. Call me this afternoon. You're buying dinner tonight. No women. I'm sick of them."

"Whatever," Pym laughed. "Thanks again."

Pym felt better for the promise of action. He telephoned for his breakfast, then went onto the balcony. He found the closed look of Maddy's door discouraging.

Sammy knocked, calling from the hallway. "Here you go, Mistah Pym, yo bre'fast."

"Thanks, my friend."

"I hear you was in early last night. New Orleans wearin' you down?"

"I was already worn down, Sammy."

He took the tray from Sammy rather than letting him in because he knew he'd never get rid of him. As Sammy held out his hand for a gratuity, Maddy's door opened and Eddie came out, wearing a suit and carrying a briefcase and a raincoat. As he passed, looking deep into Pym's eyes, he nodded curtly. Pym didn't want to know him. He closed the door without giving Sammy a tip and took the tray through to the balcony. He sat and poured coffee and didn't think of anything. Maddy's doors opened and she stepped onto the balcony in her dressing gown and stood, hands on hips, with her hair blowing in the warm breeze.

"Well?"

"Well, what?"

"You know."

"I was home early."

"Let's try again, Mr. Pym. Were you good or bad?"

"I behaved goodly."

She laughed. "Then I shall breakfast with you."

"Come on then."

"Tell me all about it."

He did so. When he finished, Maddy said, "I'm sorry, but I'm afraid this situation has to be dealt with. She can't be playing these games with you."

"Games?"

"Yes. It was a set up. She's trying to get you to want her. Making you wait. She wants you obsessed and under control. She's learned the woman thing real well. The old guy was going to be there all along and the French... that was a clever touch."

Pym tried to twinkle like Terry.

Maddy asked, "Are you listening to me?"

"I'm watching," he said. "I'm wondering how you're going to deal with this situation."

Staring at him, throat blotching pink, nipples erecting under her dressing gown, she whispered, "I shouldn't be doing this." He took her hand, ushered her into his room and closed the French doors. As Pym turned, Maddy's dressing gown dropped off her shoulders. He put his nose on hers and rubbed. She laughed, mashed her nipples against his, and then kissed him deeply.

"You mustn't fuck me," she whispered. "We can do everything else, but don't make me fuck, okay?"

"Okay," he said. "You're the boss."

She laughed, pulled his scrotum up with the palm of her hand and pulled him down onto the bed.

* * *

First came the sound of church bells, then the sound of sparrows chirping. Pym's head rested on Maddy's inner thigh, his cranium against her other leg, her vagina an inch from his eyes. His bladder throbbed. Maddy snored softly. She smelled sweet and fresh like buttermilk. She moaned and rolled away. Semen had dried in her hair and on the fine down of her upper lip. Pym thought of Eddie and then put him out of mind. He put George out of mind too, then Laura and Sasha and Estelle, while he observed this beautiful girl. "Don't wanna fuck, no fucking," she'd said again and again, "Don't let me fuck." And he'd helped her to numerous orgasms with his mouth and fingers. It seemed the same to him—didn't make any difference—but avoiding intercourse was an act of loyalty toward Eddie that Pym respected. She wouldn't have stopped him if he'd insisted. He knew that, but he felt pleased with himself for complying.

Careful not to wake her, Pym went to the toilet. As he peed, his hunger returned. He remembered the breakfast tray on the balcony. Birds would be pecking at it and the coffee would be cold. He went back into the room and said softly, "Hey, Madwoman. Let's go to that tourist trap for lunch."

Maddy rolled over and smiled at him. "Shower. Clothes. Twenty minutes, K?"

"Okay."

Then Rick called. Sure enough, a rooming house in Algiers proved to be George's last known address. "Do you know the place?" asked Pym.

"Not much occasion to go over there. Your brother musta wanted to live cheap."

"Should I take a cab over there or something?"

"Listen. I'll stick my neck out for you. I'll come over at six with an unmarked squad and we'll go take a look. Bring that crazy Limey widju. I like him, and he should see Algiers. He likes shit like that—the culture."

"I'll tell him he's coming."

Rick laughed, then said, "Okay, I cain't do no more today. Got a job, man. If George ain't in Algiers we'll try some other shit."

"Six then?"

"Affirmative."

Pym rang Terry and Vera's room. Vera answered, sounding oddly young.

"Good morning," he said. "This is Gil. Did that old fool come home at a reasonable hour?"

Vera laughed and said, "He came home."

"Is he awake? That is the question. I need him for something."

"Whether 'tis nobler in the mind to suffer the slings and arrows of Terry's outrageous torture, or to suffer him to be awake with a clanging hangover? That, my dear, is the question."

"I take it he's not, and you don't want him to be."

"You are clever, Mr. Pym."

"Why do you continue to call me Pym after all we've been through? Is it an English thing?"

"Have we been through something yet? I just like the sound of it."

"It does sound nicer when you say it."

"Do you prefer Dancer?"

"I like it when you guys call me that."

"Names are wonderful. Terry and Vera. Has a nice ring. That couple along the hall, Maddy and Eddie—that doesn't work very well—too much alike. Gilbert Pym. And your brother, George Pym. Nice. Names, Dancer, are wonderful."

"Vera, do you sit around thinking up this stuff?"

"Yes, dear."

"You've got too much time on your hands." After this utterance he took his tongue by the root with all fingers of his right hand—tasting Maddy—and pulled. Asshole, asshole, asshole.

After a slight pause, Vera said, "Yes, I do these days. I haven't really earned it. I've been awfully lucky. Look at what nice friends I have."

"That's because you're nice."

"Thank you. Now what is it you need Terry for? Which bar is he to sample next?"

"He's coming with Rick and me. Did you meet Rick? No? To find George. I've found his address and Rick says it's in a cheap part of town. We thought we'd take Terry over there and drop him off so he could tell them scuzzy folks how bad their beer is and that they're citizens of a colony."

Vera laughed. "You've pegged him."

"Tell him six sharp in the lobby, and no Graham Greene outfit."

"Right you are."

Pym pulled on a pair of soft jeans, a black concert T-shirt, and his bent-up loafers. He didn't want to shower again because he liked Maddy's scent all over him, but he washed his face, and, as he did so, saw her in the bathroom mirror, leaning in the door frame, arms folded. She said, "What a nice ass you have in jeans."

He went to her. She wore a print dress, a pair of brown Doc Martins, and had a bag slung over her shoulder. He kissed her. She slid down his body and opened his jeans and took him in her mouth. He could see in the mirror because she had her hair tied back.

She looked up at him with wet lips. "I'm ahead of you in the climaxes about eight to one." And then she went at it again. He couldn't see so well from above her. Her head was in the way. But in the mirror he could see the veins in his penis, wet, going in and out of her lovely mouth. Her eyes were closed and he could see the thin blue flesh of her eye sockets. Flesh that would soon wrinkle and crinkle like Vera's. He imagined Vera sucking his cock. Sasha, Lulu, George, yuk, get out of there, and laughing, stroked her head and remembered the sound of her orgasms that morning with his fingers spread in her.

Later, as they walked to the Café Du Monde, Pym imagined himself Maddy's boyfriend. She'd be perfect. Enough obsession. Just a plain good old American girlfriend, lots of sex and laughter and no thought of the future. Learn the lesson his mother had taught him after his break-up with Laura: If you wanted that girl to be an angel you should've given her heaven. Tell her you love her and mean it. Go to the opera if she wants. Bring flowers unexpectedly. But no shopping—fuck that.

Pym liked the way Maddy draped herself around him as they walked. Her miraculous entry into his life represented the great amalgam of his fantasies, and she knew it; she knew exactly how to manipulate the way men like him thought. Eddie couldn't take her gift, this easing into another's love; he wanted her to be his and his alone, but she only belonged to herself, like a chameleon.

She pulled him gently by the hand and showed him things in shop windows. Soon they felt spots of rain on their faces and looked upward, stuck their tongues out to catch it. Clouds rolled above, gray and waterlogged. On Decatur, Maddy looked up again and said, "I think we're in for it."

"Who cares?" Pym thought of the umbrella Sammy loaned him and wondered where it was.

"If this dress gets wet I'll get arrested."

"Serves you right."

"Hey, quit that, I'm good."

In the Café Du Monde, Pym immediately saw Lulu. He waved and she just looked at him. She had her hair pulled back and her glasses on and her breasts looked bigger. Maddy wanted to know how Pym knew the little oriental dude. Pym told her and she teased him about having a thing for transsexuals.

Whenever Pym beckoned Lulu over, she ignored him. Although he wondered what had upset her, he wasn't about to chase her down. He ate lunch with Maddy and then they went walking, navigating with Maddy's *Frommer's*. They looked in bookstores and antique shops in Pirate's Alley and Royal before walking up to St. Charles where they caught the streetcar over to the Garden District and found Ann Rice's house, Lafayette Cemetery, and Commander's Palace. Pym wanted to pull Maddy inside a big busted-up family tomb but, to his surprise, the abundance of tourists made her shy. It looked like it would finally rain so they caught the tram back to Canal Street and soon found themselves at Du Monde for late afternoon coffee. The rain held off. At dusk, Pym felt sad because he knew he had to return her to Eddie. They walked across to Jackson Square, sat in its north quadrant, and watched the faithful going to mass at St. Louis Cathedral and the swallows swarming before roosting for the night.

On their return to the hotel, they entered separately. From halfway up the staircase, Maddy looked down at Pym and a small horror ripped through him. A new face shone out of her… a hint of a smile, one bearing an attitude toward the world rather than any particular pleasure, one that wouldn't be at all in the way tonight when Eddie reached for her. She was just like him.

He sat at the bar and waited for Terry. Sammy popped up. "Mistah Pym, sir. You have a nice day with dat doctor's wife?"

"Have you been following me?"

"This is a small town, Mistah Pym."

"Gimme the first of the night, then."

"Bud?"

"You know it."

"He come home early, you know, Dat doctor? From his convention thing."

"Really? Do you know everything?"

"Know what I need to keep the peace."

"Was there any sort of problem?"

"No, but Doctor go out seeking his wife an' came back all pissed-off."

"There's one thing you don't know."

"What dat?"

"She's not his wife. She's his mistress. He has another wife."

"Who tell you dat? Her? Maybe she jus' bored. Anyway, you be out tonight with Mr. Langley. And I reckon that a pretty good thing."

"Langley. Is that his name? That's my middle name."

"That so? Common enough name."

"I suppose he told you everything when you took up his breakfast this afternoon."

187

Sammy chuckled. "Sat on the balcony and visited with him and his lady. Fine English people and no mistake. But I don't like you goin' over to Algiers at night. There's good and bad over there, but I gotta feelin' you headed toward bad."

"Why do you think that?"

"Reckon you be gettin' in over your head. Maybe your brother don' wanna be found."

"Man, you've got the whole story, haven't you?"

"As I say, I jus' try to keep business tidy and look after folks so's they come back. I wanna see you again next winter, Mistah Pym. Don't you go gettin' yourself kilt now."

"I got a cop along for the ride."

"I know. Don't mean nothin'. He killable like anyone else. That's all I'm sayin'."

"Will you call my mentor's room and tell him I'm here being frightened half to death by the bar staff."

Sammy went over to reception and called Terry's room.

"He be right down." Sammy sidled closer and his unusual green eyes looked seriously at Pym. "You bring double trouble around here. You makin' more noise than you think."

Pym felt his face reddening. He never could take being told off. "I'm just trying to find my brother. You'd do the same. Gimme the next Bud."

"In other words," muttered the old man, "shut da fuck up, Samuel."

"I'm hearing you, Sammy."

Pym didn't know exactly what to ask next. His stomach roiled—he wasn't sure why.

Terry showed up and had hardly opened his mouth when Sammy said, "What the fuck that outfit, man—you look like that Australian cat. What's his name?"

"Crocodile Dundee," laughed Pym.

"Hot damn, that he! Lordy, the things I see in this town."

Terry, quite put out, got one Bud down him before Rick arrived with the car. He left it parked outside, the flashers clicking.

* * *

They rode across the river on the Algiers ferry. Rick stayed in the car so he could study the street map while Pym and Terry stood on the passenger deck and looked up and down the river at the lights of New Orleans and the impressive Crescent City Connection Bridge and the warships anchored up-river and the paddle steamers docked like floating wedding cakes.

Terry remained quiet. He leaned on the railing and looked at everything through his thick glasses. "When do we pay the ferryman?" he muttered. Pym said, "This is free, I think. At least for cops." Terry laughed. He was about to speak, but they were across the river quickly and had to hustle back to the car.

Navigating for Rick, Terry held the map and followed every turn. Close to the river, in a historical area undergoing a renaissance, the houses were quaint and well kept. It was residential but not well lit and Pym saw no one walking around. He saw no cats. It resembled a seaside town closed up before a hurricane hit. Within blocks, the gentrification gave way to shab-biness. After crossing Opelousas, it was rubbish caught in the high weeds which displace the paving of the sidewalk; it was burned-out shotgun hous-es, and stripped, glass-shattered cars with jungle-weed and moss reclaiming the metal. A few residents idled on porches, their faces following the prog-ress of the car as it passed.

Terry missed a street sign. They drove a block too far and had to back-track to Lamarque. Rick found the address—the cross street on Atlantic. An imposing hacienda-style building on the southeast corner of the junction was in design not unlike the hotel in the French Quarter where Pym and Terry stayed, though this looked seedy with patches of stucco crumbling away and only a few outside windows—none lit. Mature weeds, saplings almost, with smooth trunks as thick as youthful arms, disarranged the side-walk alongside the structure like a premonition of judgment day. Across the street on the porches of the small Haitian-style bungalows, people watched from the shadows as Pym emerged from the car.

The Spanish styled structure made Pym think of the Alamo. What was that all about? His history—heroes and expansionism. This place changed hands between the Spanish and French. You could see it in the mixed styles of the neglected architecture. It came as a sort of shock to him that he him-self was an architect, but what different designs he lived by, or now, didn't live by. He had designed nothing of consequence, only that which would make money, short term, superficial function. Shame stung his scalp.

They walked through a rounded archway, Pym in the lead, that opened into a spacious, brick-laid courtyard. A red light illuminated what proved to be the main entrance above a once-stately portal, in front of which a large old man sat on a plain chair, toying with two kittens by making them leap and spin after a tiny silver bell on the end of a stick.

A cream colored Mercedes and another car, rusting, with fins—a Plymouth perhaps—and a dented blue van with a flat tire parked next to a dormant fountain, practically filled the courtyard. The cats leapt and mewed, fast, efficient, sleek. Duval, oblivious to anyone watching him, spoke kindly to the cats in French.

The square courtyard was surrounded by three stories of apartments with a running balcony at the second-floor level. Dim lights shone from windows... only a few of them. And the light was dingy, almost greasy in the pallid, sickly atmosphere. A gnarled palm tree grew beside the fountain and looked like it sometimes supported some sort of cabana at its base. Rick walked to it, stopping for a second to grind some charcoal from some sort of fire underfoot, and, shaking his head, touched its trunk. There were three other patches on the brick where fires once burned.

"Poto Mitan?" Rick asked the old man.

Duval looked up, startled, became still. The cats pounced on the wand, ripping at it.

"Pour une hounfor?" asked Rick.

Duval glared at him without answering.

"Pardon," said Rick, speaking as if the old man were retarded. "Nous somme chercher unit vingt-six."

No answer.

"M'sieu, did you hear me?" asked Rick. He took out his police ID, held it before Duval's eyes and then arranged it in the breast pocket of his jacket so that the badge showed.

"Nadine!" The man shouted. He didn't look at any of them. "Nadine! Arriver!"

"What's all this noise, man? I just asked you a simple question."

A woman suddenly stood among them. "You know he don't speak good English," she said. She was slim, with intense feline eyes, big bottom jaw, hair pulled tightly back. Pym knew her. It was the woman who glared at him the evening before as she spoke with Sasha in the bar, the one looking out of the mirrors. She wore a tight-fitting but rather worn summer frock with a chain belt at the waist, and attached to the belt were a bunch of keys.

"I didn't speak to him in English."

"I can answer your questions," the woman said. Then there was an interchange between she and Duval in French. The old man went back to playing with his cats.

"Why you tellin' him to keep his cool," asked Rick. "What he got to be uncool about?"

"Strangers—they spook him. Dis ain't no Garden District, you know. What is it you need in my part of town… officer?"

"We need to find one George Pym. Now don' fuck with me, girl. I know he live here."

She didn't answer but looked straight at Terry and said, "Who are you? You trespassing."

Rick didn't let Terry answer. Pointing at Pym, he said, "This here is George's brother. We're his friends. An' as you know, I am the po-lice. We don' want no trouble. Where's this George dude, Nadine?"

"I know who this one is," she said, pointing at the center of Pym's chest. Then turning and smiling at Rick, she said, "Georgie ain't here, Ricky. He been gone for days."

"So you monitor your guests?"

Nadine just looked at him, smiling with her big cat eyes, and the smile, despite being obviously sardonic, transformed her countenance from the formidable to the sexually sublime. Rick said, "Show us to Unit 26, please."

Nadine shrugged, started walking. Duval stood up and went inside. They followed Nadine across to the other side of the courtyard to a dark door that led up a flight of filthy, dimly lit stairs to Unit 26, one flight up on the left.

"Open it. Take us in," said Rick.

"I guess it would be stupid to ask for a warrant."

"It would be stupid because you'd be pissing me off."

Nadine sorted through her great bundle of keys, selected one, and opened the door. She put her hand into the darkness and switched on a light. Rick walked in first, followed by Pym. Cockroaches scurried and the room smelled like dried perfume. Terry bent at the waist like a butler and ushered Nadine into the room, resulting in a look of fury on her face; he followed her in and closed the door. Rick turned on more lights, but the room remained dim as though light failed to reflect from its walls, as though the light itself was going blind.

Pym recognized a George room anywhere, but his style had taken on a feminine quality. He'd draped some sort of gossamer material over a standard lamp and a bedside lamp. A bold cockroach waved its antennae from a corner.

On a shelf were pieces of George's life: his favorite books; a wedding picture of him with Estelle; a black and white of him and Gilbert with their heads under the hood of a car; a picture of Gilbert and Laura outside an Underground station in London; a picture of their mother, taken in the seventies, mini-skirted and breasts bulging, her long legs stretched out and crossed at the ankles... her long, luscious hair shagged around a half-smiling face that said, Come and get me, boys; a black and white of her and Michael Pym in their white baker's overalls, with flour on their hands; and a dozen or so of the hand-drawn cards from The House of Large Sizes slipped out of the cellophane of an open packet.

There was a poster pinned to a wall that advertised a comedy night with a caption at the bottom that said: "And introducing the hilarious Georgina Pym."

Terry stood gaping at the picture of Nina, which made Pym laugh.

"How long's he been away, Nadine?" asked Rick.

"Nearly a week."

At this, something jumped in Pym's heart: If only you'd gotten off your ass sooner.

"Is there anywhere else he might've gone?"

Nadine shrugged.

"His rent all paid up?"

"Hell, no. Peoples here never paid up wid rent."

"All his clothes and shit here? Nothin' been taken?"

"No, sir."

"You own this place?"

"You know who owns it."

"It's a shithole. Trash like you give Black people a bad name."

Pym didn't like the way Nadine glared at Rick, but Rick ignored it and said, "Who else you got living here?"

"All sorts."

"I bet. Any illegals?"

"No, sir. Hell wid you. Time to leave."

"We won't keep you much longer."

Pym went over to the window and looked down into the courtyard—a small girl stood beside the chair where Duval had sat. She stared up at Pym. The cats licked each other on the chair. He didn't like the girl's eyes.

"That your daughter?" Pym asked Nadine, to which she replied, "None of your goddamn business, golden boy." Rick laughed. Pym shrugged. Terry stood by the door with his hands in his pockets, looking grim, his eyes like big blue lanterns.

Pym examined the neatly organized closet, which smelled similar to Estelle's, finding only women's clothes. Make-up, medication containers, and pamphlets lay arranged on the top of a dresser. He looked for a mirror but saw none; he then sifted through the pamphlets—rapid weight loss, intestinal by-pass, liposuction, hormone replacement therapy, nutrition, collagen injections. Between the wall and the gossamer-covered lamp nestled a sort of deflated rubber mask that smelled like the inside of a snake's skin.

George kept important papers in the bottom drawer of the dresser—he'd always done it the same way. Pym opened the drawers, starting at the top one with its contents being mainly lingerie, stockings, and a set of vibrators in various sizes. In the next drawer down were some sweaters, a collection of magazines for transsexuals, and an elaborate wig. There was something inside the wig—clear plastic. Pym turned the wig over as one might a dead rodent, and a zip-lock baggy containing a tightly bound little leather bag, grayish in color, rolled out. Tied around it with a rubber band was a folded piece of paper. The third drawer contained neatly organized workout clothing, some with labels still attached. The forth drawer was empty, dry, smelling of cheap pine.

Pym looked up at Nadine, who glared at him. He said, "Someone's taken all his stuff—and don't give me that wacko look, Nadine—this is my brother! Where is he? You know, don't you?"

Pym felt a hand, Terry's, lain gently on his shoulder. Nadine didn't look like a woman moved easily. She'd changed from whom she appeared to be outside; now she looked overly thin and tall with a large head like a famished Tutsi.

"You got some sort of office in this complex?" asked Rick.

"Sure, why?"

"Let's go there. I wanna see what you got."

"You gonna need a search warrant for dat, man."

"You reckon I cain't get it?"

"While you getting it I be callin' my lawyer, asshole. Now all of yous git. I'm sick of you wastin' my time. What go down with Georgie Pym's none of my business. Out!"

While Nadine yelled at Rick, Pym took the plastic bag from the second drawer and slipped it into his pocket.

They sat in the car outside while Rick called someone on the car's radio. He was angry, but it was nothing about George... it was all about Nadine. Pym couldn't follow what was going on. The dialect and speed of the conversation bemused him. The little girl watched them cross the courtyard. Pym noticed her eyes were slightly crossed. In the bad light he could nevertheless see that she was half or perhaps three-quarters white. Pym winked at her but she just stared.

All the time he felt the little bag in his pocket. Rick said the bitch had something big to hide and it better be investigated quickly, but someone seemed to be disagreeing with him. This went on for twenty minutes.

Terry's personality had shifted to that of a quiet observer. Pym sat miserably, knowing something terrible had happened to George and gripped by the unreal feeling that all these strangers were actors in some cheesy sci-fi hologram designed to advance an individual's awareness. He just wanted George back and he voiced as much when Rick got off the radio. "This is like some twisted art movie," he said.

"In a movie," said Rick, turning to Pym on the back seat, "Denzel Washington would have the FBI here, the Marines, every motherfuckin' agency in America to shake down this operation. Me, I cain't get no fucker interested. Nobody's got nothin' on these assholes. You know the old Creole, Duval?"

"Yes, I saw him at The House of Large Sizes—he's something to do with Sasha."

"He used to be a big shot... now his daughter got the balls. What's he got to do with Sasha?"

"I think they used to be lovers."

"Sure, now it's all falling into place."

"They babbled away in French about something. And I'm the only fucker around here that doesn't speak any."

"Gotta get with the program, dude."

Terry broke in, shouting, "Christ Almighty! Look at that."

Fire licked the underside of black smoke that billowed upward. Pym and Terry got out of the car while Rick sat shouting into the radio. They ran to the archway that led to the courtyard and had to leap out of the way as the Mercedes shot through. It was impossible to see who drove, but the little girl looked out of the back window and smiled. From inside the courtyard they saw fire pouring from the windows and roof on the east side. No alarms sounded, no people, no panic, only flames and the gentle crackle of burning roof timbers.

"That was set deliberately," said Rick. "A gasoline fire for sure. Man, I knew she had something she didn't want me seeing."

Rick pulled the car into the archway and started blaring the horn. A few lights went on suddenly. A window opened under the fire and a woman's head emerged and looked around like a blind-eyed mole. Terry, in the middle of the square, pointed up with big gestures. The woman looked up, then quickly ducked back in. Moments later a bag flew out of the window, then a pillowcase filled with things, then another. Other windows opened; people yelled.

A portion of the roof exploded. People started to roll out of windows and the rickety French doors on the east side of the courtyard. People on the other side just watched or they came to the center where Terry stood on a mound of concrete foundation where perhaps another fountain used to stand. Rick arrived by Pym's side and said, "Okay, we've got these folks aware of what's going on. Now all we need is the goddamn fire truck! Look at these people. What are they? Freaks!"

The people collecting around Terry and looking up at the fire were mostly transsexuals in various states of undress. It was the time of the evening when people were preparing meals, or dressing to go out. A tall black man with large breasts and a swinging penis ran naked from one of the doors with his hair on fire. Terry and Pym held him down and wrapped a jacket around his head. Rick shouted at the people, "Get everybody out, get everybody out!" Terry turned to him and said, "Ricky, get your car out of the archway. They'll need a thoroughfare."

No sooner had Rick moved his car when a fire truck slowly began squeezing through, a fire marshal in full regalia walking backwards in front of it, guiding it in. At the same time water came spraying down over the roof from an unseen source, knocking hot debris into the courtyard.

"They're firing water cannons from the other side," said Terry to Pym. "Let's get this lot through the archway and into the street."

Another section of roof exploded and a wall collapsed; flames had moved to each flank of that end. "It's spreading," someone yelled. More people, loaded with belongings, swarmed from the portions of the structure as yet unaffected. The people were mostly black and thin and terrified, women and children, babbling different languages. Pym understood what Rick meant earlier when he asked Nadine about illegals; here they were and they'd been housed in a separate section of the hacienda from the transsexuals. An ambulance tried to push through the archway but was impeded by fleeing people. They swarmed now, like ants from a burning log.

Amid shouts and stink and sirens and air filled with red-hot cinders, the courtyard, only an hour ago a tranquil place where an old man played with kittens, now pulsed with disorder and mayhem. A fight broke out near the ambulance. A fireman fell to the ground. A window exploded, sending fragments of glass like bullets against the phalanx of escapees, cutting them. Pym couldn't see Terry. A hole opened in the side of the east building as a wall collapsed inwards.

"Holy shit," said Pym. "What've I started?"

Terry, standing behind him said, "You've only done what you had to do, son. You've uncovered something huge and rotten by the looks of it. Right now let's just help get these people out of here."

Pym and Terry shouted to the people not to panic—go slow, the only danger now is from panic. And, almost as soon as the last people had been ushered out of the square, the fire was out.

Soon the courtyard held police and medics. Pym stood at the center of the square, staring at it all until a uniformed officer gave him a violent push and shouted, "Leave! Now!"

Pym was about to explain why he was there but thought better of it and went over to Terry. Terry was right on it, saw the whole thing, and, shaking his head, said, "Come on, Sunshine, let's scarper."

They found Rick outside sitting on the hood of his car with no jacket on. A white van with an antenna on top stopped a few yards away.

"Can you believe it?" Rick asked. "Some motherfucker busted in the window and stole my goddamn coat. Got my cell phone, keys to the car— everythin' in it."

A small blonde woman got out of the white van and approached them. "What's going on?" she asked. Terry laughed and, pointing at the middle of Pym's chest, said, "Our boy Gilbert here was looking for his brother."

The blonde woman put her hand in the air and opened it, and a fat man came over with a black weapon-like camera on his shoulder. She asked, "Will you guys consent to an on-camera interview?"

* * *

The white television van pulled up outside the hotel with Pym, Terry, and Rick in it. The reporter, Cindy Sorensen, got the whole story during the ride back across the river. The cameraman, Pyke, drove, swearing at the traffic, disgruntled that the news team was being pulled out of its way to drop these people off in the snarled-up French Quarter.

As they prepared to get out, Cindy said to Pym, "You guys are heroes. You probably saved a lot of people."

Gravely, Pym replied, "We might've killed some too."

Cindy smiled at him. "Very Minnesotan of you," she said. *"I ain't gonna take no compliment, no matter what.* I'm from up there too, you know. Duluth originally. We'll have to talk."

Terry said, "Would you all like to come in for a drink? It's been a rather trying evening."

"No fucking way, Cindy!" shouted the cameraman. "We have to get out of this shithole and back to the station."

"I know, Pyke, don't worry. Sorry gentlemen, I must run. He's right… there's work to do. Can I contact you here?"

"Just talk to Sammy at reception," said Pym. "He knows everything."

Cindy had a charming smile and shook his hand warmly, holding her little blonde head to one side. Pym got out and helped Terry, who complained, "Cor, my bloody back's killing me and I could murder one of those Hurricanes."

Rick was last out and said, "You have a shower and a change of clothes first, man. We all stink of smoke."

Inside, the hotel lounge was crowded. A large Cajun woman assisted Sammy at the bar and the tall young man in a blazer, the one called Tibone, manned the reception desk. Everyone was well dressed, ready to begin hitting the restaurants and clubs. The clientele turned as the three walked in and the room quieted.

"Quick, Sammy, old chap," called Terry. "Three Budweezers on the house!"

Vera came toward him, looking him up and down. "You bloody fool," she laughed. "What on earth have you done now?"

Maddy stood at the bar in a black cocktail dress and high heels. She moved slightly behind Eddie and gave Pym a quizzical look. The way she styled her hair, thick and falling about her shoulders, made him want to go over and put his face in it. Eddie looked at Pym too; his hair was short and gray like the bristle on a wild boar, but he was dressed in a pinstriped, double breasted suit—not unlike Pym's old one, which Sasha told him was all the rage in Macedonia—and a black shirt and silver tie.

Someone tapped Pym's arm. "Mr. Pym," said Sammy, "I got an envelope for you. And you got mail. All at reception." He obviously wasn't thrilled by Pym's appearance. Pym sucked down his beer, nodded for another, and went to reception. Tibone handed Pym two envelopes... one fat, dirty, and hand delivered, the other crisp-edged manila and solidly postmarked from Minneapolis.

"You know who brought this?" asked Pym, tapping the thick envelope.

"Little oriental chick," said Tibone. "Cute."

"Lulu. I've seen her spooky handwriting before. Thank you, Tibone."

While he looked at the handwriting and shrugged, Tibone said, "You're welcome, Mr. Pym."

A powerful whiff of aftershave preceded Pym's comprehension that Eddie hovered behind him. Pym turned, crossing his arms over the envelopes. Eddie, face jutted forward, stood way too close. Lips barely moving, he said, "I want a word with you, pal."

They stepped outside onto the sidewalk. Pedestrians flowed past them, holding hands, laughing, sipping giant cocktails. Eddie looked up and down the street before saying, "I know you're after her."

"What?"

"I know what you want."

"You don't know shit."

"If you don't back off, I'll kill you."

"Look man. I..."

"Fuck it!" Eddie shouted. People kept walking by, ignoring them. Pym stayed quiet. "She's such a goddamn liar," said Eddie. "I've learned to work purely off instinct and I'm on to you. Now, make no mistake, I'm a smart man. I've seen it all, done it all. And you, you're a bum and a loser with a helluva lot to learn. If you just fucking keep away from her, you may live long enough to learn it."

"Come on."

"You got that, fuck?"

"You have this all..."

"Don't fuck with me! You got that?"

Pym felt the heat flush into his face. It was enough... he was going to start punching; he would draw blood from this bastard. Words garbling and stuttering, he said, "I'm not fucking with anybody, including your stupid girlfriend. Now, you fucking back off or I'll do some killing of my own."

"You can play the tough guy if you want, punk. But I'm warning you."

With the hint of a snarl, Eddie spun and walked back inside, leaving the powerful pungency of his expensive cologne. Pym stood battle-ready on the sidewalk, shivering with adrenaline, hands full of envelopes, and wondering why life had suddenly leaped into fast-forward.

* * *

In the shower Pym discovered cuts on his hands and neck, small scrapes really, scarcely noticeable until he got clean. He put on Dockers and a flannel shirt and sat down to examine his mail and the little bag he'd lifted from George's room. He wasn't afraid of an old fart like Eddie. Fuck him. George's incinerated room drew Pym's mind now. All George's weird stuff, all remaining evidence, the inside story... ashes all, except this funny little bag which Pym had the presence of mind to take.

He shook his head, held back tears. They were all shouting at him from somewhere, using his inner voice to get his attention, but they were all shouting at once—Maddy, Sasha, Laura, Estelle, Vera, his mother, Lulu, and the scary proprietor of the burned rooming house—Nadine. What the hell are you doing here, he thought. Go home, marry Estelle, give her babies, get a job.

Something was happening down on the street, crowds and music, and he wanted to get out there and lose himself in the revelry and forget the whirlwind of events that had overtaken him. He got up and opened the French windows so that he could at least feel some part of it. A single float was in the street—they were practicing for Mardi Gras, which was a week or so away. The float was all lit with colored bulbs, but he couldn't make out the theme. He went back inside and opened the rough-looking envelope. Pym slid the contents out onto the blotter pad. George's papers—his passport, an old photo of him, slimmer, with cropped hair and mustache. In the passport was an application, filled out in his immaculate script, for a new one, and the attached photographs—a pertly smiling man with cherub cheeks and long hair, wearing a hint of makeup.

There were rejection letters from several gender reassignment programs. There was one from the Minnesota Welfare Department rejecting his claim. There was a bank statement showing all his withdrawn savings; and there was a gray pamphlet with a photograph of Sasha on the front, the same one Mishawn had given Pym a few days ago.

The pamphlet promised a discreet, safe, and above all, economical way of changing gender without hassle. It clearly stated there were no frills, no counseling, merely the operation and a period of two weeks' convalescence.

Sasha, in her most seductive pose, deep bosomed, slender, hyper feminine, looked shamelessly at the camera like a Playboy pinup from Transylvania. A caption under the photo said: "This woman, an officer of our corporation, was once a man."

Several sub-ads accompanied the text, one of which was a detailed description of The House of Large Sizes in New Orleans. There was a description of Doctor Claude Duval, a brilliant surgeon in the field for five decades, trained in Paris, who would oversee all procedures.

In the other envelope was a note and an attachment from Mishawn. She'd obtained the address of the hotel from Laura and thought Pym should see the pamphlet he'd found among some papers George had left behind. It was the same pamphlet attached to a letter of acceptance signed by one Nadine Duval.

The phone rang. "Gilbert! Terry here. Are you joining us tonight?"

"I've got some weird shit in the mail. It's upsetting. I've got to sort it out."

"Is there some way I can help?"

"Don't know yet. Maybe."

"One drink will do you good. And a few laughs."

"Your answer to everything?"

"Most things. Life is short."

"I think they've killed my brother."

Terry stayed quiet for a moment, and then said, "We don't know that. But if they have, I'm afraid you're just going to have to stand up to it. I'd like to see this through with you. I've grown quite fond of you. Trouble is we're supposed to leave in a week, and I can't see it all being over by then."

"Terry, thanks. Look, maybe I'll turn up at that same bar with the mirrors later tonight."

"Yes, I was going to suggest that. I like that gaff. Young Rick telephoned and he'll be there too. He caught it from his wife, I'm afraid. And his police chief. But he tells me they've assigned him to some sort of case vis-à-vis the debacle we witnessed this evening."

"The plot's certainly thickening, as Vera might say."

"Indeed she would say that, bless her heart, and she'd be right. Make sure you don't become one of the littered dead."

"Jesus, I'll try not to."

"Report to HQ tonight, yes?"

"Yes, sir,"

"Carry on, then."

* * *

Pym put on the suit Sasha bought him and went downstairs with the intention of walking straight out into the street and to The House of Large Sizes, but the throng of guests turned to him and cheered as he descended the stairs.

"What's going on?" Pym called.

"You were on the news," Sammy said, in a bit of a huff. "You and Mr. Langley and that cop buddy of yours."

"What did they say about it?"

"It was that cute little Cindy Sorensen from Channel 2. You know, the usual, 'developing story' and all that. You was heroes though. Saved all da poor people while lookin' for yo brother. Very cool, Mr. Pym, very cool indeed."

"I better have a drink before I head out."

"Okay, but something stronger?"

"Like what?"

"Like champagne."

As the champagne happened, Terry came downstairs and was treated to the same appreciation. He had his contact lenses in. Pym loved how Terry worked a crowd.

Maddy was still there. Two tall doctor types flanked Eddie, and Maddy kept staring at Pym when Eddie wasn't looking. The two friends looked concerned for Eddie; they stood either side of him, talking into his ears.

After five minutes, Pym could no longer tolerate the tension, and, hot-faced and bloated with champagne, slipped unnoticed into the street and ambled slowly to The House of Large Sizes. He entered the deserted street to the echoes of his own footfalls, and, other than a small lamp lighting the balcony, noted with regret that the premises stood shuttered and dark. Without raising his voice, Pym said, "Is that you? Are you up there?"

Someone stirred but didn't answer.

"Sasha! Is that you up there?"

"No," came a man's voice. "It's me."

"Who's 'me'?"

"Darryl. Whose you?"

"Gil. Sasha's friend."

A shadow stood up and looked over the edge. Long hair, tight dress, cigarette between fingers. "She's gone."

"Where? I need to talk to her."

"Well, she just said she'd be gone for a few days and that I should mind the business."

"Can you come down or something? I'm getting a stiff neck."

Darryl left the balcony and soon opened the door of the shop and let Pym in. Darryl bolted the door behind Pym and then Pym followed him upstairs. As he did so his thoughts were thrown back to just a few days ago when all this started at the Gay 90's in Minneapolis—that unpleasant smell of cigarette smoke mixing with overthrown perfume and caked-on makeup. It activated a gag reflex in him.

"Don't you just love this place?" Darryl asked.

"Yes, it's unique."

"It's mine 'til she gets back, I guess."

As they walked through to the balcony, Pym noticed that candles burned everywhere, but the room was otherwise in disarray. It made him remember the state of his place in Minneapolis after Laura had left... like a college kid had moved in about two hours earlier.

Pym sat where he'd sat before on the balcony. There was one empty wine bottle, an open one, and one unopened one on the coffee table.

"Getting ready for the night?" Pym asked, pointing at the wine.

"Hot date coming over at midnight. I'm nervous."

"You'll be fine. By the way, I like your outfit."

"Oh, thanks. Can I offer you some wine?"

"Sure."

"I'll go get a glass."

Darryl wore Sasha's perfume, and possibly one of her dresses. When he returned and poured wine, Pym said, "So fill me in on some of this stuff."

"Sure. Whatever."

"So why's she gone?"

"Dunno. I just work here… do her artwork. I'm not clever like her. She took off in a big hurry though—with the old guy."

"Duval?"

"Yeah—Devil Man."

"What's Duval to Sasha?"

"I only know some of it—what they tell you when they've had a lot of wine—when they're fucking you—when you're in favor, that is. They're pretty secretive the rest of the time."

"Did you know the Duval complex across the river just burned down?"

"You're shittin' me."

"Nope. It was just on the news."

Darryl looked aghast and said, "That'll blow the whole deal."

"What whole deal?"

"I was going to…"

"I see. They do it real cheap, right?"

"Yeah, but they get what they can out of you. For instance, I work for Sasha."

"Like a slave?"

"Minimum wage."

"Quite a racket."

"For some of us, it's worth it."

"Do you know George Pym?"

"Sure—Georgie. She's somethin' else. She'll have a real challenge." Darryl winked. "She's your sister now."

Pym forced a laugh. "Did you meet her here, or out at the complex?"

"Both. She helped here too. Everyone does. Then they move you on. I'm not good at anything so I stay here."

"Sasha told me you were no good with numbers. That true?"

"That was cruel."

"Did you know how much she disdains you all? She told me a lot of stuff."

"You're gonna disillusion me, aren't you?"

"Not if you don't want me to."

"Well… I know I can never look like her. Duval and his team of little Asians didn't do hers, you know. Hers was legit. One of the big programs. And she was born with some of it."

"So that pamphlet's a fraud?"

"Yes. Nothing to do with me."

"So is Duval Sasha's sugar daddy?"

"No, it's more complicated than that. He threw her out when she wanted the change. He likes, well, drag queens. He's got this kink about dominating men. Sasha's the one that got to him. I couldn't get to him, although... He's lost interest now. Getting old. He just does what the witch tells him."

"The witch?"

"Nadine, his daughter."

"Ah, yes, I just met her. Quite a lady."

"No shit. Stay away from her."

"She's nothing. Her and her big set of keys."

"Nothin'? You don't understand. No one does. She's the real thing, man. Got her mamma's bones in a sack she keeps in the cupboard. Duval's wife was Voudon too. She looks so like Nadine that people think they're the same person resurrected. Might be true too. Little kid looks the same. It's voodoo, you know what I'm saying, with a twist. Duval's wife's mother was from West Africa where the magic is even crazier than here. They ran a lot of shit—you know, Haitian stuff. Scary. I shouldn't be saying this—too much wine."

"Tell me more."

"Duval's older than the hills. It's said Nadine keeps him young by feeding him the gonads of the boys they neuter. It's said that when one of us dies accidentally, the Duvals make gumbo out of the human flesh and share it among the hungry ones in the complex."

"Do you believe that stuff?"

"Yes. Well, no. It's kinda fun to believe. I know they're rich. A lot of guys like me that wanna be girls and can't afford it end up under Duval's knife and most are happy about it. He supplies a service and most of us are grateful. They've been upping the price though, and they make you live for a while on the hormone replacement they supply. They didn't used to do that."

"They're going legit, you mean?"

"I'm not sure what they do was ever illegal, was it?"

"No idea. Sounds shady. I'm no expert. I'm just a working guy from Minneapolis. What the fuck would I know? I'm just trying to help my brother."

"Sister."

"Whatever. So why've they all skipped town?"

"Don't know. They may have other concerns. Did the FBI burn the complex?"

"There were police there."

"I'd guess it was the illegals. They help the Haitians. That's been pissing people off. How do you know about all of this?"

"I was there."

"You're a cop, aren't you? I just caused myself a lot of trouble."

"I'm not a cop. Just a brother."

"I hope that's true. I wouldn't want to be on the wrong side of Nadine Duval."

A car pulled up across the road and parked half on the sidewalk. Darryl watched the car and frowned. The driver's side window rolled down and a black man looked up at the balcony. Darryl stood up and went to the front of the balcony into the light. The back window slid down too and someone else looked up. Then the car sped away.

"Spooky," said Darryl.

"Someone checking out the place?"

"Yeah. Not sure what to think about that."

"Did they see me?"

"If they did, they'd think you were Hank, who'll be here any minute."

"So I'd better go."

"I hate to say so, but yes."

* * *

Pym walked into the mirror bar and immediately saw Terry gesticulating like a monkey in front of a laughing Rick. Pym's heart warmed toward Terry, seeing the dear old fucker fooling around and multiplied into infinity by the mirrors. Rick's wife and Vera looked on, laughing, also arching away into infinity. Rick's wife saw Pym first and pointed. They turned and cheered; others in the bar did the same, not knowing why, just looped. As he walked toward them through the crowd someone put a beer in his hand. "Three days an' you taken over the bar, man." A young brunette touched his face as he passed. "I hope y'all find your brother, hon," she said.

When Pym got to his little knot of new friends, Terry put an arm around him and said, "You're an overnight celebrity. I hope you can handle it. I'll be your publicity agent."

"You can be sure there won't be any money in it."

"Ah, dear boy. Cynicism and resignation. These are not good qualities."

Vera said, "That little Sorensen girl was looking for you. She wanted another interview."

"You tell that hussy to stay away from my boy!"

Vera rolled her eyes.

Pym asked Rick if there were any new developments, and heard there were not as yet, but that they'd have to talk the following day. It sounded ominous and there was something in Rick's face Pym didn't like. It put a damper on his mood, but he got through it and went back to the hotel arm-in-arm between Vera and Terry. The hotel's bar was still lively and the Brits wanted to drink more, but Pym's spirit had been deflated by something in Rick's tone. He excused himself and went to his room, oddly confused about his feelings. Did he really want to find George? Did he really care about his brother's welfare that much? Or was it fear and loneliness? Now that he had friends, albeit very temporary ones, he didn't feel so lonely. And the purposefulness of his search helped too. Something to do.

He felt a sense of relief as he stepped into his room and closed the door. The telephone beside the bed blinked and he discovered a disarmingly cordial message from Cindy Sorensen asking for a meeting, but after an initial loin-tingle the prospect of getting into the chase with yet another woman just made him feel more fatigued. He opened the balcony door to let in cool air, took off all his clothes, and sat in bed naked, his head throbbing. He revisited George's cards. He wished he had a book to read, something deep with good language. He wondered about little Lulu. He wondered where this would all lead and if he was in any danger from these Duvals. He found himself worried about Sasha, Estelle, Maddy, Lulu—all of them. He felt stupid.

The cupboard burst open and his mother lunged at him with a knife. Bits of flesh clung to her and she was naked and had a knobby penis like a Greek athlete.

A ringing telephone woke him. He shook off the dream and lifted the receiver, noting the time—two a.m.

"I hoped I'd catch you," Sasha said.

He fell back on the pillow and closed his eyes.

"I know you probably think I'm mixed up in all this," she said, "but I'm not, really. I haven't done anything wrong."

"I think you've helped them do wrong things."

"I'm just driving down Esplanade now. Meet me outside your hotel."

"I'm not sure that's such a great idea."

"I'm alone. I'll explain all this if you give me a chance."

The voice that sometimes ruled him was screaming, Nooooooo! But he ignored it and said, "Okay—five minutes."

* * *

Sasha stayed quiet until they were somewhere in the middle of the Lake Pontchartrain Causeway. Then she started singing some old ballad. Pym found this incongruous and laughed at this human work of art that had focused its creative impulse on perfecting the form of femininity, singing a song of lost love from the point of view of a romantic Irishman. She looked at him and laughed too. "Do you know this song?" she asked. He sang her the next verse, then told her that his father, Old Michael Pym, was into folk music when they were kids—very different from their mother, who was a Jefferson Starship fan and a Grace Slick look-alike.

"Who's Grace Slick?" asked Sasha, "Someone before my time?"

"Before mine too," said Pym. "But you still hear it a lot in my family."

"Enough of music," Sasha said. "I want to know where we stand."

Pym looked around at the black expanse of the lake and laughed, saying, "In the middle of nowhere."

"Look, I've got some issues I need to explain to you. This is all more complicated than you can possibly imagine. It's like a big ball of barbed wire. And New Orleans is my life, my greenhouse if you like. I can't exist anywhere else. This Algiers thing threatens me. You don't mean me any harm, do you?"

"No. I don't mean anyone any harm. I just want my brother back."

"That *is* the harm, you see, baby. He put himself into that big ball of barbed wire, and the process of extracting him will loosen everything else that's caught up in the ball with him. This ball of barbed wire has been twisting and capturing and amalgamating since 1804. You follow my meaning?"

"What happened in 1804? Napoleon or something?"

Sasha sighed. "It was the Napoleon era, yes, but 1804 was when the Haitians rose up against the plantation owners. The whole Caribbean blew up. Many of the plantation owners fled here and brought a lot of their slaves. Don't you know any of this?"

"What the fuck's any of this got to do with Georgie?"

"It was the slaves, many of whom originated from what is now Daho-may in West Africa, who brought their religion to this part of the world."

Pym's head tingled. He hadn't taken it seriously when Darryl men-tioned it. "Oh, shit," he said. "Real voodoo. Shit."

"Something like that, yes."

The white line centering the road kept slipping by the car. Pym's scalp settled down but his face became numb as if a snake had bitten him. A flood of unwanted recollections tried to escape the storage bins of his brain and jam themselves all at once into his frontal lobe like starlings invading a tree. Sud-denly it was all there, settled and quiet, the panic over. It took until almost the end of the causeway and then it all fell into place. The inevitable dark horror of his childhood had returned as he always knew it would; meanwhile, Sasha drove quietly until finally she said, "I sense that you're upset."

Pym looked in the side mirror of the car and could see the lights of New Orleans illuminating the sky above the city. He turned around and looked properly and saw just how wide was the actual expanse of light. Sasha asked, "Are you ignoring me?"

"I probably have a Hollywood notion of what Voodoo is, but the men-tion of it frightens me."

"That's because you know something."

"What do I know?"

"You know there's more to it than people would have us believe. And you probably know that it's meant to be used for regular old life—just normal living—but that it's been subverted by charlatans and witches for their own gain. You sense that it's powerful stuff, and it is. Nadine Duval is the self-proclaimed queen of a new kind of cult that has morphed out of voodooism. She claims, among other things, to be a descendent of Marie Laveau, who died in 1881. Marie took possession of her during a ritual be-cause she was the exact right person, with all the right blood. And old Duval is descended from the Creoles and the old Hoodoos of the bayous. They're powerful people, creating something new."

"What's Poto Mitan?"

"Where did you hear that?"

"At the compound on Atlantic, in Algiers."

"You have good ears. It's the support pole in the middle of their temple, what they call a 'hounfor.' It's a metaphor for the snake of understanding,

Dambala, who joins Heaven and Earth. It's related to the Ouroborus imagery—the snake that eats its own tail, representing the cycle of life."

"Like the Womb-tomb."

"Wow, you've been reading, boyfriend."

"No, my brother has. I'm an ignorant slob."

"You're doing all right. Anyway, I'm surprised it was still there. Nadine doesn't hold with all that—she calls it mumbo-jumbo and chicken-shit and is phasing it out."

"It was there. It was something Rick asked about."

"Well, Rick would know all about that."

"I thought you didn't know Ricky?"

Sasha shrugged and said, "I know everyone."

"So they… this is nuts… have George under some sort of a spell?"

Sasha smiled and slowed the car behind a van. "Yes, a spell. But one originating in George. It is nuts, but only because human beings are nuts and not worthy of the rationality they possess. They crave magic. They don't want this life as it is and they create magic, and magic can be very effective for small things that lead to big things."

"You're more than just a pretty face, aren't you, Sasha?"

She stayed quiet while she thought. Pym wondered if she was giving him time to study her profile and adore her.

She said, "When Duval got me I was a mixed up senior at the University. I was studying history and comparative religion and was headed for the priesthood where I thought I might be able to still my longing to be a woman. Duval seduced me with his intellect, with books. I was a virgin. This is ten years ago. He was teaching a guest course in French history, which I was taking, and, during Mardi Gras, I met him by chance on the street in a downpour. He took me up to the apartment above the shop, which is now mine, and threw my clothes in the dryer. The only dry clothes he had for me to wear were his wife's because his were so big. He put me in her room and told me to try on what I liked and then he would have a glass of wine ready for me. I'll never forget putting them on. I'd never dared to do it before. I was lost to it all but trying to resist. I emerged in as neutral attire as I could find but not before I had tried on all kinds of lingerie. I loved the feeling of it on my skin and it made my ass pulsate and the back of my head vibrate.

"In his presence I blushed and he could see what I was. He said that because it was Mardis Gras I should let him put a little makeup on me. He had a wig there too, and when I saw myself in the mirror I was a skinny little Cajun girl. We played a game called Storyville, which we played a lot since, where I was this little Cajun harlot and he was the city mayor. He didn't do anything sexual to me at first. He was very clever. He waited until I begged him. I'll never forget that first time. I'll tell you all about it some time."

Pym laughed and said, "Oh, you want to save that part!"

"It makes me horny and I hate being horny when I'm with someone acting stingy, so we need to talk about other things you need to know."

"Okay, then."

"So, you can see from what I've told you that I have educated myself in these subjects, and you may be able also to see something of what Georgie was susceptible to."

"Got it."

Sasha made some turns once they were off the causeway and Pym was surprised to find himself in a pine grove. Pine trunks, illuminated by headlights, had always comforted him. Sasha pulled into a road off the main highway and quickly onto a gravel track that led to a big log cabin. Sasha got out, and Pym followed her to the entrance where she struggled to get the door open with the key. Pym didn't offer help; he couldn't stop yawning but kept looking up and over his shoulder into the huge, pine-darkness with a few bright stars shining in the narrow spaces between the treetops.

Sasha flipped a switch and the place became dimly lit, soft music began playing, and a fake-log fire voompt into life.

Pym laughed, looking at her incredulously, and said, "Instant atmosphere at the soul's midnight."

"Is it that late? Boy, you're grumpy."

"I've just been told my brother's mixed up with voodoo. I can be grumpy."

"I tried to explain. It's not that big of a deal. We all make contracts with the underworld whether we know it or not. Sit down by the fire and I'll bring you a drink. What would you like?"

"Just a pop of some kind. Any kind."

Sasha shook him awake and held the glass of orange soda in front of him. She sat opposite and crossed her legs. If she had been Estelle, he would have gone and wrenched her legs open and fucked her fast and then flung her to the floor and ordered her to masturbate and she would've done it. But he sat sipping his pop with Sasha looking at him over the top of a wine glass, which glinted with fake firelight. He didn't know why he was there and he had no idea what would happen next. Nothing moved in him despite a highly stimulating visual image presenting itself.

Simultaneously, he and Sasha said, "What is it you want from me?"

He laughed; she didn't.

Sasha sighed and said, "This is all such a mess. Plus, if I hadn't told you I used to be a man you'd be all over me."

"I'm not sure that's true. I'm a pretty horny guy and there's something that keeps me... I don't exactly know what it is. Maybe I'm trying to grow up and find some boundaries. Very unlike me, I admit, but this whole shifting gender bit, and the cross dressing and the voodoo, it's all making me sick. It's all so paltry and self-centered and meaningless. It makes me realize how meaningless my own obsessions have been."

"I'm sad."

"Sorry."

She shrugged, eased back in the chair and closed her eyes. She squeezed out the proverbial tear that ran down her cheek, which made Pym smile and shake his head as he sipped soda with the fire warming one side of his leg. After a while Pym saw the fingernails of Sasha's left hand creeping to the inside of her legs. The white trim of a slip showed under the hem of her skirt. Her right hand held the wine glass and she moved this down to her legs too and ran the base of the glass along the leg. Then she put the glass down and moaned slightly, always with her eyes lightly closed. With her fingernails she caressed lightly inside her thighs and her legs opened. Pym could see her breasts rising and falling with increasing arousal and he became alarmed because he had nothing stirring in him whatsoever.

"Hot," she said and pulled off her sweater so that her beautifully formed breasts bobbed before Pym's eyes like twin prehistoric fetishes doing an obese little dance. Sasha stood, gave Pym a martyred smile, slipped the rest of her clothes off and lay on the rug in front of the fire, rubbing her hands all over her body. Her form was magnificent and her hands seemed to be exploring the places Pym should admire. There was an unfamiliar smell, very faint. She opened her legs in front of him—she was letting everything rip, totally at his mercy—and he saw the refashioned version of paradise he'd been obsessed with all his life. If this had been Estelle he might have slipped onto the floor with her and muffed her till she came, but there was nothing to muff with Sasha—none of it looked right. She had her fingers in herself and said, "Oh, my pussy's so tight it aches." With her other hand she massaged her breasts. She slipped her middle finger into her anus and gasped. She began to move her fingers in and out, getting into it, breathing heavily.

She got up and straddled the arm of the chair she'd been sitting in earlier and stuck her buttocks in the air, her right arm stretched behind her, two fingers in each orifice, fucking herself. Her buttocks blushed. Her face was turned slightly sideways so Pym could observe her perfect profile, perfect teeth, and lips ready to receive a cock. "Oh, please," Sasha gasped. "Please."

Pym stood and undid his belt and stepped toward her. His penis hung like a dishrag. Her hand moved faster and she was groaning. "Fuck me as I come," she said. In a strangled voice, he said, "I'd rather just watch."

"Oh, God," she said.

"I want to just watch," he repeated. He felt cold in his genitals, a feeling of impotence he'd never experienced before.

"Piss on me, then," Sasha said. "If you won't fuck me then piss on me as I come."

Pym was amazed. His bladder was rather full. He laughed and she laughed too and that made it okay and he pushed and some urine leaked out and fell on her moving hand. This made her pump herself harder and then when Pym's urine flow increased Sasha went mad and started to come. He pissed over her ass and lower back and she turned around and made him piss on her breasts and in her mouth. She was in a frenzy, red hot, so that the urine steamed off her. One final massive convulsion made her scream and she slid to the floor face down, shuddering. Pym wasn't sure if she was laughing or crying. He shook himself, zipped up, and muttered, "That was different."

Sasha, exhausted, fell asleep, and Pym, himself dizzy with fatigue, placed a throw rug over her. He didn't want to stay, so finished his flat, odd-tasting soda and let himself out of the house.

As he walked in the dark back to the main road, lights from a car lit up the pine trees. It was a cab, which crept past him and then stopped, idling, while Pym caught up to it. The driver had his head ducked down, looking at him.

"Lucky you came along."

The driver didn't answer.

Pym got in the back, despite a vague sense that he shouldn't, and said, "Take me into town and drop me in the Quarter." His head spun.

The driver nodded and then spoke to his dispatcher in French.

Lake Pontchartrain was a massive black nothingness. A few stars reflected off it, and in the distance the constant fairy light of New Orleans speckled the dark water with bogus gaiety.

Sasha had taken him out of Nadine Duval's neon darkness and now he was headed back into it. He didn't know exactly why, but, despite his fear, he knew he had to go back and finish off the job he'd started. He'd felt safe on the other side of the lake for a couple of hours, even though they'd been rather strange hours. He hoped Sasha would be all right.

Pym sat at the center of the back seat so that he could see the driver's eyes in the rearview mirror. He wanted to stay awake but his eyes kept closing; he'd never felt so uncomfortably tired. His legs were spread out, numb, and his hands rested in his lap. Every few seconds, the driver glanced at him.

"I'm just going to close my eyes for a minute," Pym said.

The driver nodded. Through the windshield, the lights in the distance—a horizontal band of magic—made him smile with pleasure, and he closed his eyes.

A woman moved on top of him. She straddled him on the yellow couch in the Minneapolis house and he understood this to be a dream, one he often went to sleep hoping for but which always eluded him. He understood that he'd created an amalgam of his mother, Laura, Estelle, Sasha, Maddy, and Vera. He was having sex but it wasn't really sex. It was a struggle and he was doing something different with each of the entities. He was yearning for Laura while being molested by his mother; he was having a threesome with Estelle and Maddy and was annoyingly perturbed by the question plaguing his mind as to which one to ejaculate into; he was in a debate with Sasha and Vera, and Vera was winning hands down. Little Cindy Sorensen came into the room and behind her was a cameraman whom Pym suspected of being his brother George. A crowd waited outside the house, standing in the snow. Cindy narrated a news story and said, "This is what I meant, you see. The disturbed inside of an outwardly healthy human being. This is going to make or break." Terry came out of the kitchen with a can of beer and poured it over the amalgamated woman and she dissolved. "I don't understand you," Pym shouted. "Why would you waste that?"

Terry asked, "Your priorities, dear boy?"

Pym replied, "This dream is symbolic. I have to get out of it... there's danger."

"Big word for you," said Terry, and then Pym was pulling himself out of the dream as the cab bumped through potholes, shaking him awake.

He looked out at a dark crossroads with shabby, ghoulish structures at all four corners. The driver shut the engine off at the curb, got out, and slammed the door, taking the keys. Pym watched him walk to a dingily lit corner shop and go in. He yawned and sat back.

A dozen shabbily clad people emerged from an alley beside the shop and came toward the cab. Adrenaline pumped through him; his genitals shrank. It was like "The Night of the Living Dead" with African actors. Pym pushed down all four lock knobs on the doors and sat back.

The people approached cautiously, like wild animals might, and one of them, a man with a broken nose, slid onto the hood like a python and looked through the windshield. Ogling faces filled the windows. It struck Pym that this is what it would feel like to be a monkey in a zoo. Low at first, then louder, the people chanted—he couldn't understand it, but it terrified him. Everything that had ever frightened him was right there, right now.

A woman at the curb side of the car lifted her T-shirt and squashed her large dark breasts against the glass. A child crushed his face against the glass beneath the woman's breasts. On the road side of the cab an ass thrust against the window, the owner having pulled the cheeks so far apart that the sphincter was like a tiny pig's eye; a stringy bag of testicles hung below it. An implosive sound made Pym look up as the roof bowed inward.

The big-breasted woman turned around and pushed her ass against the window; her pink vagina opened like an orchid. Hands drummed rhythmically on the cab's paneling while other body parts gyrated against the glass, leaving smears of bodily fluid.

Pym shouted, "Fuck off, you filthy motherfuckers."

They hammered louder on the car. The men pressed their genitalia against the windows.

"You dirty scum, go back to hell!"

The pounding grew louder.

Pym thought he saw his brother's face but it was a black man with a mustache—the taxi driver returning with a bottle of water. Relief allowed him to sit back in the seat.

The people got out of the cabby's way as he pushed the long key into the door and let himself in, ignoring them as though they were spirits that only Pym could see.

As the fear left him, a realization leapt forward to replace it.

The genitals pressed against the window, the whole astounding sequence of the evening's events, the search for George—something was trying to come through his stupid, fogged brain. It was the little bag he'd taken from the drawer at George's deserted room. The gris-gris bag.

The little bag was a cured testicle sack. Probably George's.

"You bastards!"

The driver started the car; the people surrounding it adjusted their clothing and ambled back toward the alley beside the dingy shop. The cab began to move, and as it swung around the corner Pym immediately saw the buildings of downtown in the distance. He said, "Hey, what the fuck?"

The driver looked at him in the mirror and in a surprisingly light voice said, "I jus' speakin' wid a lady in da corner shop. She say she know'd you and say to say 'ello."

"Who was the lady?"

Reverently, the driver said, "Lady be Nadine Duval."

Pym stayed quiet, tried to calm his heart.

A voice in his head kept repeating: Run. Fly back to Minneapolis. Run for your life!

They drove under the freeway; Pym recognized Canal Street and felt relief as they passed the Radisson Hotel and a battered looking building that was a research facility for tropical diseases. The driver turned left on Rampart. "Anywhere here," Pym said, but the driver ignored him. The streets were deserted. The driver made a right on St. Philip, sped south for a few blocks, and stopped at the entrance to Pym's hotel.

Stunned, Pym got out and reached for his wallet. The driver looked him deep in the eyes and said, "No charge." Then he reached across his passenger seat and pulled up an umbrella, which he handed, handle first, out of the window. As Pym examined it, the taxi sped away.

The hotel door was locked. He leaned on the umbrella and thought he must be living a nightmare that was taking ahold of him like a virus. He looked up and down the street, seeing no one. A little white sign with a bell said *Concierge*. He pressed it.

Terry came through the lobby holding a drink and let him in. The skin of Terry's face had a hint of silver to it. Fatigued, he asked, "Out on the prowl?"

"What're you doing up? You're looking strange."

"Describe."

"Like the Tin Man."

"Ah, I see. You're beginning to shine."

"Don't start this, I've had a rough night."

"It's the beginning of the end of your childhood. You're dying, becoming new."

"Isn't that what happens to vampires. You'll be telling me next you're a vampire. Come to think of it I've never seen you in daylight."

"I certainly wish I could find a way to prolong life."

"Have you been worrying about Vera?"

"I couldn't sleep."

"Poor old Terry. How can I help?"

"Just keep shining brighter yourself." Terry laughed. "Christ, listen to me. I'm sick of myself. I've been saying the same things for years. I hate being so the same. I'm off to bed now. Lucky I was here—Sammy left ages ago. I'm knackered."

"If that means tired, so am I."

"See you tomorrow then. Sweet dreams, young prince."

"Wait. Something weird just happened. I have to tell someone."

Terry sighed and walked back over to the bar. "Fire away, m'lad."

Pym told him about the 'Night of the Living Dead' incident.

Pym watched Terry shapeshift into a professional. This transformation was marked by a benign frown, which altered the older man's face, and the silver texture under his eyes grew more pronounced.

After a while, Terry said, "It sounds like a dream or a hallucination."

"No. It happened. It just happened. I had a dream in the taxi, and then I woke and it was worse than any dream."

"Tell me about the dream."

Pym told it, and Terry laughed at the part about pouring beer over the amalgamated woman. Then his frown returned and he asked, "And what had you just been doing prior to all this?"

Pym looked up at the ceiling and blew out air. What is this emotion rising? What are these tears? Terry waited, frowning. A street cleaning vehicle scuzzed by outside. Pym couldn't speak.

Terry asked, "Have you disgraced yourself?"

Pym nodded.

"Ah—that Sasha got you, yes?"

Pym nodded, staring at his hands.

"Do you feel like crying?" Terry asked.

"No, I'm okay."

"Because it's alright. I see this all the time."

"I was going to try it. I was going to have sex with Sasha. But it wouldn't work. I couldn't do it. She wanted me to piss on her."

"And did you?"

"I did, yes."

Pym expected Terry to laugh, but he didn't; he just looked at the floor. After a moment he said, "In this sort of situation I usually find that the patient's boundaries are very thin. They'll do anything, and they come to me and try and manage the shame. It's why I want to retire. It's getting worse, not better."

"So I'm a patient."

"Well, at this moment I am being your psychologist in so far as you've loaded all this onto me and I'm producing a response."

"Okay, so go ahead and shrink me."

"Have you ever had any sort of psychological help?"

"I always thought it was for pussies who couldn't deal with their problems."

"Well, it is in a way. But the trouble is we're nearly all pussies. In your case, let's use pussy in another sense. You, I think, are a chaser of pussy, am I right? Have been for years?"

Pym smiled and said, "Yes."

"I see that notion pleases you. I remember that. It pleased me too until I understood why I was doing it."

"So why do I do it?"

"Basically, as we say in England, because you're a wanker."

The smile fell out of Pym's face. Terry's eyes blazed at him and he asked, "May I continue?"

Pym nodded.

"Sexual addiction is a form of impotence. It's usually traceable back to various kinds of negative involvement on the part of the parents, but a person suffering from sexual addiction is still responsible for his actions. You are responsible for yours and, as I understand it, there have been nasty consequences. Your brother, rather more complexly perhaps, appears to be suffering the same thing. Your dream, and your waking dream—which I have no doubt it was, unless Sasha is in league with the dastardly Nadine Duval and slipped you some Haitian hallucinogenic—your waking dream is a depiction of the world you've decided to inhabit. An obsessive, crude world centered on genitalia and orifices. You just got a good look at who you are, young man. You are what you saw, a slimy mayhem of genitalia. Aren't you sick of it?"

"So you think I'm a piece of shit."

"If you Americans could only learn a wider range of crudities we could truly customize a description of what you are. A nation of wankers. You're one of them."

"If you were younger I'd pop you for that."

"There, you see—no boundaries. I remember in the seventies we whined about the controls and boundaries, which appeared to be restricting us. As a society we got rid of a lot of those restrictions but have failed to replace them with anything new. We're a mess. You're a mess. I blame my own generation primarily. All ex-hippies should be shot. Except for me, of course."

"It wasn't a dream, Terry."

"Had to be. Who would do stuff like that and why?"

"I dunno, it was some kinda fucking voodoo shit."

"Well, this 'some kinda fucking voodoo shit' looks exactly like the inside of your—what we call in the shrink biz—psyche. That's all I'm saying. That'll be ninety pounds, please!"

"This isn't funny. They're after me."

"You didn't think coming down here was going to be a cake walk, did you? You come down here to interfere with your brother's intentions and think it's going to go swimmingly?"

"I didn't think a whole lot about it."

"I expect you'll be doing some thinking now, eh?"

"Yes, sir."

"Good lad. Now, may I piss off to bed? I'm bloody shattered."

"Go on then, piss off."

"Fuck you very much. Good night, sweet prince."

"Terry, you're the coolest old dude I've ever known. Good night."

* * *

For some reason the air conditioning was on in his room so Pym went onto the balcony where the moist air felt balmy and pleasant against his skin. Dim yellow light shone through the thin curtains of Maddy's room but no sound accompanied it. He saw no cats in the windows opposite. Pym still felt the cold shrinkage in his genitals, like he'd been freeze-dried down there. It was horrible, no joke at all. He felt an urgent need to receive heat, to know he could ejaculate into a real woman. He thought about this and laughed nervously, remembering Terry's opening sally that likened sexual addiction to impotence.

Pym drew Estelle into his thoughts and smiled, welcoming her. I should just throw in my lot with Estelle, he thought. She's a bit shallow, but she loves me and she's relatively normal compared to this bunch of crackpots. "We have a lot in common. I'm shallow too." He thought of Maddy sucking his cock. He desperately sought the imagery that would stimulate him, to no effect. Sasha hovered behind it all. No, stay out of this. Then she forced herself forward in all her remodeled perfection, and repulsion and attraction jousted like a black and white knight. Nothing. Cold. What would Terry say? Go to bed, sleep, stop being a wanker.

The goddamn French doors wouldn't stay closed, so he just left them ajar. He could barely keep his eyes open. I'll think it through tomorrow, he told himself. I'll even write it all down on postcards. George will never believe it unless I do. He got the postcards out, ready to study tomorrow, put his blank ones beside them, and in turn laid the funny little bag there too. He would not open the bag tonight. No more thinking. But he went to sleep thinking of his urine steaming off Sasha's sculptured body and the crazy people of the hood rubbing themselves against the window of the cab. He figured there must be a group home for the mentally handicapped at that dark junction, but he laughed at the thought that perhaps the whole city existed specifically for that purpose. No dreams, please—no more dreams.

XVI

But there were dreams. Pym slept a few hours inside the umbrous vortex of a slow-moving hurricane, through razor-sharp debris and crashing waves. His consciousness kept a feeler out in the live hotel room, preventing the efficacy of sleep from doing its work, and all the time the shifting, incoherent phalanx of thoughts and images kept registering their origins in his intelligence, making his body jerk and sweat and struggle for comfort. Since that Friday night on the Hennepin Avenue Bridge when the biting of his inner wit turned rabidly against him, this fevered quality had characterized his dreamlife, a quality which bespoke an outside, partly malevolent influence, one bent on burrowing deep into his inner core of self. And it seemed to him there were two selves, and that one of them was clearly up for grabs by the invading influence. He'd try to burst out and enter reality, but escape would only lead into another dream.

Then the woman he'd seen at the mirror bar, the one whose seat Sasha had allegedly taken, the one who kept staring at him out of the mirrors, the one with the keys at the Spanish house in Algiers—Nadine Duval—stood smiling beatifically at the end of the bed.

"As long as you keep smiling, you can stay," he said. "Have you ever slept with a black woman?" she asked. He said yes but meant no. He lied even in dreams. She brought all the dreams into a funnel, traveled in the funnel down the bed and sat on him, sucking his genitals up into her. "Let's have a truce while we get acquainted," she said. Then Nadine morphed into Dashiell with magnificent breasts and a python-like penis, and Pym had become Laura as the head of the python pushed through her lower torso cavity. He could feel it biting and masticating, feeding but also nesting. "What's this?" he kept screaming, "what's this?" He was suddenly a woman—Estelle now—and he didn't know how to come. "I can't come," Estelle told Dashiell. It was something Laura often said to Pym but not something Estelle ever said. Dashiell withdrew the snake and it took a long time and there was an unsatisfying void left and then a great cobra was thrusting in front of someone's eyes—whose eyes? Who was he? Dashiell grew huge and muscular like the demon that arises from Bald Mountain in *Fantasia* which had frightened Pym as a child. He spoke in a deep incoherent voice, a Pym voice, a voice as deep as the earth, hyper-male, deeper than deep, all the way down and way out as far as where there are no stars, and the cobra started spitting white venom, which hissed and burned on the beautiful breasts of Estelle. Now Pym was on top of Nadine Duval on whose face and lips glistened steaming white venom, and he held his little twelve-year-old cock in his hand like a pervert in a parking lot. He let go of her jaw. Pissed off, she tried to get up but he constricted her. She shouted, "If you're infected, motherfucker, I'll have you eaten."

Pym woke into more confusion.

Someone threw back the bed covers, climbed onto him and said, "All ready for me, I see."

Pym's mind deconstructed the end part of the dream into a warning about AIDS. Mixed with the vanishing atmosphere of the dream was perfume and cigarette smoke and the metallic smell of male skin, causing him to think for a second that the intruder might be the drag queen, Darryl; he was about to start lashing out, but his brain jogged fully awake and he found Maddy squatting over him, and she was no dream.

She'd come in through the French windows, just in her dressing gown. She shifted herself, took his penis in her mouth and pulled off the dressing gown as her head went up and down. She looked at him out the corner of her eye and winked. Laughing, he let his head fall back on the pillow. "You saved me," he said. "I was having nightmares." She mumbled something. After a minute she began licking up his belly to his chest until she straddled him. She found the head of his penis, and with a deft little movement of her pelvis enclosed herself around him and pushed down, shuddering as she did so. She put one hand on his solar-plexus, the other behind her on his thigh and rocked a dozen times before coming.

Breathlessly, she said, "Sorry. I've been thinking about this all night. I'll take longer with the next one." And she did it again. Pym watched her face. She stared at him as if to block everything else out, totally focused.

Finally, she stopped long enough to kiss him. "Now I'm yours," she whispered, "whether you want me or not." He could smell the odor of urine on her breath, reminding him of his full bladder, which had served a useful purpose for Maddy in that it had retarded his own climax and also sparked the painful thought that his brother's urethra might have been tossed into the gumbo.

"I have to pee," he said.

"All right," Maddy said. "But hurry."

He had to pee in the sink. He looked at the face in front of the head wherefrom the bizarre dream had emerged. To the face in the mirror, he said, "You are so fucked up." After considerable strain, he finished and went back into the bedroom.

Maddy stood in front of the wardrobe mirror, naked. She bent over, wiggling her buttocks at him. Something made his head spin, a seldom-used mechanism in the base of his skull. She looked around at him and he knew at once that she was some kind of demon that he was too weak to resist. Her lips moved as he closed in on her. "Just do it," she whispered. "Fuck me. Come in me." As he held her buttocks open he saw a small white scar at the base of her spine. He rubbed his thumb over it, and she gasped. "Is this where they removed your tail?"

She was red in the face, not listening, eyes glazed over.

* * *

After Maddy left, Pym showered and massaged moisturizer into his sore genitals. His chest felt like he'd sprinted ten miles. They were to meet at the Café Du Monde but were to go separately because Maddy feared Eddie might be having her watched. Pym was concerned about Eddie but Eddie was a flea compared to the Duvals. He looked at himself in the mirror, deep into his own eyes, and warned, "Stay in control, dude."

He called Cindy Sorensen and, surprisingly, reached the real her. "Hi, Mr. Hero," she chirped. "I gotta talk to you. We got a link with a Twin Cities news show that wants to air your story. They'll let me do it 'cos I used to work for them. Wanna give it a whirl?"

"I'm not sure. Can we decide later when I know more? I mean—sounds like they want one of those sweet stories. Maybe this isn't turning out that way."

"I hope it is. Look, let's do a prelim tomorrow. Then we can reshoot any new developments. Meanwhile, what are you up to the rest of the day?"

"Getting together with my cop buddy."

"I'll call you tonight and see if you're up to talking on camera. Okay? Look, I gotta jet."

Back to the mirror—not the face of a hero. Not at all.

While Pym waited for Maddy at Du Monde, and without paying any attention to the pictures on the front, he wrote postcards to George. He isolated each bizarre element and condensed it into a statement that would fit onto the back of a postcard. *Georgie, your friend Sasha likes to be pissed on. I think it's a holdover from her days as a college student. Her plumbing is not all it should be; I advise you to rethink the rearrangement of your own. Love, Gillie.*

Pym could see George sitting at home in Minneapolis, all decked out in Estelle's underwear, reading this card and cracking up. He would love the one about the night of the living dead too. George was a great lover of scatological humor—he'd appreciate the smeared shit on the cab windows.

Lulu wasn't in yet.

A big spider ran over Pym's foot.

A taxi clipped the leg of a horse and a furious street scene ensued.

Pym read the obituaries in the *Times-Picayune*.

A wooden Indian stood very still and people tried to make him blink and when they couldn't they put money in his pouch. An old black musician, a one-man band, played Duke Ellington numbers. A tough looking man with unfocused eyes wore colored balloons and fashioned animals out of them for tourist kids. A crowd of fat people with Iowa sweatshirts took over a whole corner of the restaurant and started talking loudly.

Pym discovered in himself no eagerness for Maddy's company. His hypocrisy surprised him; they were as bad as each other, but he disliked her unfaithfulness to Eddie. He could identify with Eddie's feelings. This kind of empathy also came as a surprise along with the epiphany of his own hypocrisy. How he hated Ray for seducing Laura, and Laura for favoring someone other than himself. How could she? Yet here he was, being the obliging other man. And Estelle—at least she had some rivals now in the area of the bizarre. In fact, she was looking pretty normal. A voice in his head said: "It doesn't matter how sexy Maddy is... you have to stop. You better tell her when she gets here."

He wrote on the postcard:

I found your strange little bag, Georgie. I wonder what it means. It's all that's left of your effects because the Duvals torched your place for some reason. I've got a nasty feeling that it's the sack your balls used to hang in. I hope I'm wrong. I hope parts of you haven't been fed to Doctor Duval. I shall be very pissed if they have. They will not want to be fucking with Gilbert Langley Pym if this is the case.

However hard he tried he could never make good cursive like his brother; it was embarrassing. He couldn't even remember the last time he handwrote anything. Someone stood behind him and he covered his writing like a kid in a quiz.

"Lulu. What's up?"

"Writing cards bad luck," she said.

"I hope not," Pym replied.

"People called Pym write cards in Du Monde then disappear," Lulu said. The whole side of her face was scraped and bruised. She'd cleaned up as best she could, but the scabbing looked sickening. She wore her oversized leather jacket.

"No waitressing today? Accident?"

"No accident. They try to kill me. I escape."

"Who's 'they'?"

"Le Voudon."

"Oh, shit. Now what?"

"Big trouble, Mista Pym."

"This is going to escalate, isn't it?"

"You get Georgie's things?"

"Yes, thank you."

"He gone, and shouldn't be. I get stuff for you from room before Duvals get it."

"Why didn't you tell me where he was?"

"Scared. No life other than this. But I like Georgie. I do him favor backtime—send you his cards, remember? Now he gone."

"You sent it all, didn't you? For some reason I thought it was going to turn out to be Sasha."

"Because Sasha sexier than Lulu?"

"No, because... I dunno why."

"Sasha take no time for stuff like dat. She fucking bitch."

"Is she deeply involved in all this?"

"Some. But not to harm Georgie. She just glamour person. Rake in lotsa cash from trannies."

"And what's the deal with she and Duval?"

"He love her. But eating his heart out because she no longer a boy." Lulu laughed and sat and lit one of her king-size cigarettes. "I say to her, too bad. Maybe old fart like it if you strap on dildo." They laughed. She wanted to talk more about the attack, and told how she had been set upon by a gang of Haitians as she walked to work the day before. It was obvious to Pym that no one was trying to actually kill her, just to hurt and frighten her, but she insisted they wanted her dead—and that she used Kung Fu on them to save herself, which made Pym suppress a smile. She didn't know anything else about George.

Maddy came in and waved. Lulu got up and left without saying good-bye. The traffic lights changed. Maddy got to the table radiant, her hair still damp. "That was a lovely morning," she said. "I love to get properly fucked."

Pym no longer liked her crudity. He faked a smile and then frowned before saying, "Look, I think my brother's dead." It surprised him to say it, but he found he did indeed think that. He had for a long time, but he said it now partly in the hope that it would send Maddy away. He didn't know who was worse, Nadine or Maddy; the evil, controlling witch, or the lying, unfaithful girlfriend with the voice of silk.

"Oh, come on, honey," Maddy said as she pulled a nail file from her purse. "He'll show up."

Maddy had bewitched Eddie just as much as the Duvals had bewitched George. So many people behaving in a manner contrary to what was good for them. Especially himself. Maddy filed the ends of her nails, totally engrossed. It was like she'd gone to sleep and hadn't been present to what he had said. "All right," Pym said. "Let's talk about you."

"Oh, pardon me, baby. I was waiting for you to finish off what I thought you were going to say and then I sort of drifted off into the Eddie situation."

Pym shrugged and said, "You know he threatened me the other night?"

"He told me. He wouldn't dare do anything—he has too much to lose."

"You seem a little off in all your assessments."

"Are we going to fight? Are you sick of me?"

"No."

"Good. Because after this morning I never want to fight with you. You're wonderful."

"Thank you. You're good at this, aren't you?"

"Good at what?"

"The whole love thing."

"Not really. I feel deeply and say what I feel. Life is very full but very short. I'm not about to be short-changed. I'm quite naive, I think. Did I ever tell you how I met Eddie?"

"Go ahead."

"It was a few years ago in Chicago. I was sitting alone at a table in the little plaza under the Hancock building, and I saw Eddie sitting in a patch of sunlight, wearing a white shirt. I could see his blue eyes from several yards away. I guess I was staring at him because I was suddenly on the receiving end of his blue gaze. I looked away but could sense he hadn't given up looking, and, after some minutes, chanced a quick glance between bites of cheesecake. Eddie locked into my eyes and wouldn't let go."

"Like a snake."

"Don't be so mean. No, he made this movement with his eyes that indicated that I should come and sit next to him. I ignored him. Then he did it with his hand. I looked up to heaven and said under my breath, 'What am I doing?' I took my cheesecake and coffee over to his table and have been at his table ever since."

"He's certainly no angel, is he?"

"No. I am though."

"Hmmmmm."

"You're kind!"

"Eddie seems pretty near the edge to me."

"Well, yes. He's upset with me. I can't always tell him the truth, and he has this wickedly good intuition. He can't just let things be. He constantly tries to dig the truth out of me, and I can't tell it because he takes it so badly, so I lie. He knows. Doesn't trust me. We came down here to get a break from all the tension. It was so good the first couple of days, but now he's deteriorated. I even gave him a fun toe but he ignores it now."

"What's a fun toe?"

"I painted his left toenail whore-red so he could think of it at his stuffy convention. It worked for a while. But now he's gone all haywire."

"What've you told him about me?"

"That we've had coffee, is all."

"Have you done this sort of thing before?"

"Good God, no. I can count the men I've been with in my life on one hand."

"All right. Well, look, I gotta call Rick at the police department. I don't know how my day's shaping up."

She looked at him, opened her bag, and took out a small lilac notepad and wrote her Chicago work address and telephone number on it. She drove it down into the top pocket of his jacket. "Just in case we get lost in the shuffle. I have my own little get-away in Lincoln Park. Come for a week-end—you'll like it. And, hon, I'm sure your brother's okay."

"Thanks. You're probably right." He thought for a minute while she gazed at him. Suddenly he found himself saying, "You know what? I gotta call the cops."

Pym went to a pay phone and called Rick.

There was an odd pause before Rick answered Pym's greeting. Then Rick said, "I gotta be a cop today, man. Okay?"

"Okay."

"I think we got George."

"I see."

"And I may be wrong, but I think we got him in the morgue. Better come on down and satisfy yourself."

* * *

While she read, Vera ate a large bar of Caramello.

"Hitting the old sweets a bit hard, aren't you, darling?"

Vera leveled a you-poor-fool glance at Terry, and replied, "I like it."

"I know, but will it like you?"

She continued to read, ignoring him. After a while Terry said, "Eating like a condemned person isn't going to help you feel better."

"I know, but I've never been allowed to eat enough chocolate."

"How are you feeling these days? We haven't talked much since arriving here."

"I'm sick of it, Terry."

"I know, darling. Is it, you know, feeling like anything?"

"Yes, it's here now. In my arm, especially. We'll have to go home soon."

227

Terry pulled aside the baggy, loose sleeve of her dressing gown and gently lifted her left arm. While he did this she sighed and said, "Oh, for goodness sake, Terry."

A large purplish contusion inhabited her armpit and the underside of her arm sagged with the first signs of swelling. He touched it with his right index finger and, inside the puffy sack, found it hard, meaning that it had been with her for some time without her drawing attention to it. Terry put her arm down and kissed her on the forehead. "You're naughty," he said.

Vera's eyes welled up with tears and she said, "It was lovely to come away with you one last time, but everything's getting a bit grey and irrelevant. I can't read for long, can't get into it like my old self. It's like I'm seeing what life really is, just a humdrum set of events strung together by my observance of them. I'm nothing but a machine designed to receive the five senses. I'm running down, turning into a black and white photograph."

"Oh, darling."

"It's not fair because I haven't reached the end of myself like I always thought I would. I'm angry and embarrassed. Sorry to intellectualize this but it's how I am. You'll experience it one day too. Only you'll do better than me because you'll go into pubs and tell everyone, and it'll all be terribly dramatic and important, like you're the first one to ever experience it."

"Am I really that shallow, Vera?"

"No, I just need someone to pick on."

"I'll go and get you more chocolate."

She covered her face with her hands. "I can't cope with this."

He put his arm over her shoulders. The telephone rang. "Oh, sod off."

"You better answer it, Terry, it may be your son."

The line was quiet at first—someone trying to control strong emotions. "Terry?"

"Yes, dear boy. Are you all right?"

Silence.

"Is there some progress?"

"They think so. I have to go to a morgue. I'm going to meet Rick there. I'm looking for a cab as we speak. I don't know how to do this."

Terry looked at Vera and said, "You poor bugger. I'd offer to come with you, old boy, but Vera's having a bit of a turn and I need to keep her company."

Vera vigorously shook her head in annoyance.

"That's all right," Gilbert said. "I need to do this alone, I guess. I just wondered if you had any advice."

Terry took the telephone over to the window, closed his eyes and saw flashes of a heavy boy sitting on the stairs, crying. He knew Vera watched him. He could barely speak without choking, but, very quietly, he managed to say, "If it's him, it's going to be extremely hard for you. You're going to go into shock and blame yourself and feel very angry. I'll be here."

"Thanks."

"Yes."

"I'll let you know. Bye."

Vera said, "What did you tell him that for? He'll think I'm some old tripe that needs a babysitter. He'll need you right now more than I do if what I overheard is what I think it is."

"Oh, it's probably not George. Let's not borrow trouble."

"Still…"

"No, no. Can't be helped, darling. I used you as my excuse to not drink today. I'm going to take a break."

"Christ, liquor stocks will go into a decline."

He stood holding the old fashioned telephone together with his thumbs, facing the courtyard, his shoulders quivering, so she'd think he was laughing.

* * *

Pym had no experience of morgues; he'd only seen them on television. Rick walked beside him. This morgue was old, its design created deep shadows, and there were cavernous corridors with yellow tiled walls and lots of stainless steel; everything was scraped and gouged at gurney level. Pym's head spun on the inside as he walked on numb legs.

Don't you fucking dare be dead. Please let's get this over with. His thoughts kept grasping at the moment of observation and practicing relief when he realized without doubt that the corpse was someone other than George. Yet he was also reviewing history: his first fistfight with George over a Hershey bar; the way George's eyes changed after he found out about Pym and Estelle; the way George laughed—a fat man's guffaw; the way little Pym spent so much time upon his brother's back; and the way his brother saved him from his mother before she went too far.

Pym felt a friendly warmth in his chest toward Rick, whom he knew didn't have to be doing any of this. Why were people so nice? Was it be-

229

cause of Terry? Something Terry was doing—creating cooperation and humanity in everyone? It could be that, yes. He wished Terry was here, and felt wrong for thinking of him first and not Estelle or Laura or even, God forbid, his mother, Nina.

They went into a room and looked around. It smelled like broccoli. A red-cheeked young man in green scrubs, whom Pym had hardly noticed, pulled a sheet off the face of a corpse. It was George—the broad forehead, pockmarked cheeks, mouth a small black hole, eyes not quite closed, white eyelashes with traces of mascara clinging to them, shoulder-length graying hair, highlighted with henna. Pym kept swallowing; a red corona invaded his vision. One of his first memories came insanely loose—seated, naked around George's huge shoulders as a little boy at a beach, being jogged about so much that he peed all down George's back.

"You stupid fucker," Pym muttered. Then he pulled the sheet further away; the orderly tried to stop him but it was too late. In an eyeblink there was the hole where George's genitals should be, all sewn and black-scabbed. Sacks of flesh slipped sideways down the ribs, and there were yellow and purple contusions where liposuction had trimmed away George's stomach and love handles; around his waist circled a livid ring of small blisters.

"Fucker! Stupid fucker!"

He slapped George's face.

"What've you done?"

George didn't move; it was like striking a huge piece of sculptured cheese. Rick and the orderly pulled Pym away. Rick spoke into his ear: "Easy now, man, easy."

"Holy shit," the attendant said. "I can't have this."

Pym stood back, stared at the palm that had struck a corpse; looked at the inert, unholy body, a body subjected to vicious self-loathing; looked at the dead George who would always be George from the past, always be his brother whatever foolishness obsessed his mind; looked into the shocked faces of the men holding him and saw compassion there.

Pym didn't know what to do with his hands; one of the hands had just struck the man who had chased Ma out of the house that day. He could barely see anymore. "George..." he whispered, and finally let grief overtake him.

Rick and the attendant held him, but now he wanted to kiss George, not hit him; he wanted to go to him, hold him, bring him back—he was in there somewhere. He'd always been deeply hidden. Pym strained against them, unable to see, the wet pouring from his face, blinding him.

"Jesus, Gilbert," said Rick, his own eyes watering. "Oh, man."

"My brother. Look at him—he's dead. George."

Rick held his shoulders gently, whispering in his ear, "It's okay, buddy, it's okay, my friend." Pym was bent forward, looking at his brother. He could sense Rick and the attendant exchanging glances. The attendant also had tears in his eyes.

After a while Pym said, "All right, guys. Okay. I'll be okay now. Thanks." Pym looked at the attendant and repeated it. He was released, allowing him to step forward, respectfully now, and examine George properly.

George wasn't fat any more. He was long and thin, and had shapely legs and arms. Only his rib cage was a man's, but protruding from it and smearing sideways were eruptions the shape of witches hats under his pulpy nipples. Where his genitals should have been was a space, a hole only sparsely obscured by rusty pubic hair and folds of sewn flesh amid crusted scabs. George's eyes were holes too—just slits looking nowhere. Separate from the livid scabs around his middle were small, moist holes. His lips were fuller, his cheeks sunken. His toenails and fingernails were painted dark red, and there remained those traces of mascara on his eyelids.

Pointing at the holes in George's stomach, Pym said, "Was he shot? Are they bullet holes?"

The attendant shook his head. "No, sir," he said in a soft Southern accent. "He's been through it, I'm afraid. Liposuction and a gastric by-pass and then a full..." He pointed at the mutilation between George's legs, swallowed, then pointed at the wounds and said, "Those holes are petechiae—his immune system crashed, causing a massive infection. When he died he was in the middle of a shingles attack too."

"He died of an infection, then?"

"We're pretty sure, yes."

Rick said quietly, "And I understand he should not have been operated on when he was. Is that right?"

"Yes, absolutely," said the attendant. "Whoever did this gender reassignment was not weighing up the risks. And the patient was in no shape to undergo it. God only knows what meds he was on."

Pym felt like a small animal with a tiger's jaws around its neck. All he could say was, "Can I wipe that mascara shit out of his eyes?"

The attendant, red-eyed, looked around, not knowing what to do. Rick said, "Come on, man. That's enough. It don't make no difference now. Let's get outta here."

Pym was asked to sign some papers, and then Rick led him down a passage, out into painful sunlight, and into a car. People walked along the streets not knowing that George Pym lay dead in the morgue. Rick drove. A radio sporadically spat police messages. Rick said something into the police radio about a positive identification. Pym didn't think. He saw a sign for Po'boys and felt hunger. A trolley went by. They were on St. Charles and then they were on Canal Street where pieces of paper blew around in the wind and idle men stood about on corners and watched the car pass.

"You ready to talk?"

"What about?"

"You're allowed to be fucked up, man. It's normal."

"So tell me. Why did he die?"

"Massive infection."

"No foul play, then?"

"Don't look like it. This ain't a murder case—medical incompetence, maybe even manslaughter—but you'll never get murder out of it, not in this town."

"Something went wrong inside his head. It's like he was altered. I don't get it."

"It's not so unusual, man. It's the American way. When we want something, we want it now."

"I wanna be a woman, right now," said Pym, mimicking George's voice. Rick looked at him and frowned, then laughed. Pym found himself laughing too, then had to hold back a sob.

"Medical Examiner say yo brother run himself down pretty low, losing weight and taking hormones and shit, all in a short period of time, and when Doctor Death come knockin' after his op, brother ain't got the immunity to fight him off."

"They did something to him—those Duvals."

"Maybe. But I reckon they'll claim that whatever they did he wanted done. But we'll keep digging in the shit pile."

"Are we going back to Algiers?"

"No, Gilbert Pym, my man, we're going back to your hotel where you gonna sit in the bar and have a big ol' drink with dem nice English. Me, I gotta be the po-lice. We got some folk in custody and I got a pile of work to do."

"Who's in custody?"

"We got Nadine Duval. She not too pleased widjou, man," he laughed. "Say it all your fault, cussing you every which way. She fuckin' crazy. Been in the asylum once already. And we got the princess in, too—the little girl, Fortuna, the next witch. I gotta find her a social worker. An' we got a coupla foreign nationals from Thailand who claim to be surgeons. But old Duval and your girlfren' Sasha done skipped the country. Border people check 'em through into Mexico. Musta drove all night. Very guilty-looking, but we got no evidence yet on anyone, so you gotta sit tight. Duval's the motherfucker we want—illegal surgery, maybe. Left a lot of these poor fools half done. Man, the shit that's in this town—you would not believe it!"

Pym tried to get his brain moving. It was like death itself, sludgy, a black and white photograph. "Slavery. You can get Duval on slavery. There'll be all sorts of things. Cannibalism even."

Rick frowned and said, "We're not sure yet what all's chargeable. We gotta work on it."

"Did you find a bag of bones?"

"Bag of bones?"

"Nadine Duval keeps her mother's bones in a sack."

"You watch too many movies."

Rick had more practical information. The New Orleans Fire Department found George in a makeshift morgue, an old meat locker, and George's wasn't the only body. The legs of an accompanying corpse were badly burned, and another was all but unidentifiable. The NOPD figured faulty wiring in the old meat locker caused the fire. Knowing this sent Pym back into his thoughtless funk, and the next thing he knew he was being gently walked inside by Vera and Terry. Sammy brought him a strong drink.

They all knew. Maddy sat next to him and patted his knee. He liked her smell and thoughtlessly reached over and ran his hand through her hair. Everyone sat around the circular table, quiet. Pym expected Maddy to start in about her relationship with Eddie, but she just kept looking at Pym with concern.

"Where's your old man this afternoon?"

"Still at his big convention." She smiled. "Thanks for asking."

The meanness went right over her head. He was about to cry, but he didn't want to do it in front of anyone.

Pym downed his drink, stood up, and said, "Sorry, you guys, I need to be alone for a bit, okay?" And he dragged himself up the stairs to his room with the image of his brother's half-closed eyes skidding across his emotions. He felt their eyes watching him move up the stairs. He could see himself walking up the stairs like an old man in a blonde wig trying to look younger than his years. What was he going to do with the body? Should he keep the bones in a sack? Take them home? Do magic with them?

The door to his room was flung wide open and bedclothes lay mounded on the floor. The maid came out of the bathroom and looked at him, smiling. "I'll go for a walk," he said. He took the stairway down into the courtyard so he wouldn't have to speak to the others.

He walked up to Bourbon Street, took a left, and looked at the shemale joint with the swinging legs outside. In the doorway four black teenagers surrounded a shemale who laughingly allowed them to look at her breasts and up her skirt. Many of these would have been Duval's clients, no doubt; or, maybe not… they were too good looking.

Pym walked on to Canal Street. It started to rain. Paper and grit blew around. He walked all the way down, drawn by the waving of palms, and entered the casino. He entered the plastic palace, put a quarter in a slot machine, pulled the handle, and walked on. The air smelled of stale cigarette smoke. Ugly losers sat with bowls of quarters in their laps, plugging money into machines. It was what George liked—glitz; it was all he could ever see. The things George had come to value were all wrapped around this pursuit of looking good in the middle of the glitz. What happens when the glitz disappears? What if there's a big war? What happens when you get old? So I'll have a funeral down here, thought Pym. Screw it, we'll cremate the idiot in New Orleans where he completely lost touch with who he was. Take his ashes back to Minneapolis where his trouble started. Yes.

* * *

On entering his room, Pym noticed that the maid hadn't shut the balcony windows. He closed them; he didn't want anyone in the street hearing if he started crying again. These pseudo-voodoo crazies could do anything they wanted to him; all his doors were left open. He was clueless, jobless, luckless. What the fuck—lower than low, and alone. He had slinked back in unnoticed past his friends in the lobby—they were all still there, Terry, Vera, Maddy, Sammy, boozing away as if nothing had happened, albeit more quietly than usual.

Pym took out the papers he'd had to sign at the morgue and placed them on the little desk with the newspaper from the first day and all his accumulated bits of crap: the mysterious little bag, Maddy's slip of paper with contact information scribbled on it, Cindy Sorensen's card, a pen with lint clogging the ball point, the postcards he'd been writing to George.

He took off his jacket and went to the wardrobe to hang it up. As he opened the wardrobe doors, a snub-nosed gun barrel was placed between his eyes.

"Keep still, you piece of shit. I'll blow your brains out."

"Eddie. Eddie, take it easy, man."

"To the chair. Sit in the chair. Move, motherfucker."

"Holy shit, Eddie, what are you doing?"

"Sit, fuck. You fucking..."

Pym sat in the chair in front of the desk and saw himself in the small mirror—terror in his eyes. A thought rocketed through him about privacy, then got obliterated by the recollection that Eddie had vowed to kill him if he didn't leave Maddy alone. Downstairs this minute, Maddy, all full of his semen, drank with the English.

"Put your hands behind your back. Do it! Through the chair slats like that! Yes. Be still."

Pym felt handcuffs click around his wrists. And in an instant Eddie had duct taped his ankles to the chair legs. Then Eddie jammed a sock into Pym's mouth and wrapped tape around his cheeks.

Within seconds, he panicked, frantically heaving oxygen up his nostrils. His face witnessed it all in the mirror and his inner voice asked: Why didn't you struggle? You just let it happen.

Suffocating. He imagined answering his own question later in an interview when it was all over and he was safe. "You just don't," he said. "You think you would resist. But you just don't." The interviewer was Cindy Sorensen. If he could escape this thing, please, God, one chance, he'd ask her out and not care if she said no. He'd be good forever, he'd settle down. He'd be nice to Estelle.

"Now how do you feel, lover-boy?"

Pym used eye contact to try and ask Eddie to let him go.

"I guess you thought you were a smart motherfucker. Well, here's how smart you are." Eddie held the gun to Pym's temple and stood away, straight-armed. Pym could only see Eddie's arm and the gun in the mirror.

He tried to implore with his eyes, tried to make the chair jump, but he saw the hammer rising on the gun and falling—anticipated the split second of seeing his brains flying out the other side of his head and his face distorting, but you couldn't experience that, could you, because the brain would already be gone and he'd be the one on the slab at the morgue. And the hammer was down and the barrel still pressed into his temple. The hand and shirtsleeve remained in the mirror. Pym's face flushed; he felt and saw the heat. His heart fired like a machine gun and he'd wet himself—he could smell it.

"A little Russian Roulette, Pym? You like?"

Pym shook his head.

"One more try?"

Pym shook his head vigorously and roared inside himself.

"I warned you, didn't I? There are times when you need to listen and not be a fuck. Maddy's destroyed you, just like she's destroyed me."

Pym shook his head again.

"You want to speak?"

Pym nodded.

"All right. If you cry out, I'll cut your throat immediately."

As Eddie pulled the tape from Pym's mouth and pulled the sock from it with one hand, he held a silver scalpel to Pym's jugular with the other. After gasping for air, Pym choked out, "Eddie, listen."

"Careful, son. That's what Maddy always says when I'm on to her. Listen, Eddie, I can explain it all. Fucking lying bitch!"

"No. No. Look. They've found my brother. He's dead. I'm sorry about Maddy. I didn't get it all till today. I see what she is. I've been punished for all that. Something else punished me. If you kill me, how can I learn?"

"You don't normally talk this much, do you, Pym? Maddy said you're the strong silent type. You look more like the scared shitless rabbit type to me—a wriggling, scurrying rodent, a manipulative wretch out to save his own skin at all costs. No honor, no reflection, no wisdom. Your life is nothing... I'll be doing you a favor ending it."

"I just wanted to give you the option of not being a murderer. You're supposed to save lives, aren't you?"

Still with the scalpel touching Pym's throat, Eddie said, "I'll let you live on one condition... that you answer my questions with absolute honesty and I mean absolute. And clarify when you know you should. Holding back information will result in death—it's the same as a lie. I know a lot already and you don't know what I know. Agreed?"

"Yes."

"How many times have you fucked her and when?"

"Only this morning. She came through those doors and jumped me."

"Did you come in her?"

"Yes."

"Up her cunt?"

"Yes."

"Up her ass?"

"No."

"Did she suck your cock?"

"Yes."

"When?"

"Yesterday. A couple of times. And this morning."

"Did you come in her mouth?"

"Yes."

"Oooooooh..."

Eddie sat on the floor so Pym could no longer see him. He could hear Eddie wheezing. Pym had the sense that the room was full of a chemical called grief and he was breathing it.

"Ooooh... jeez. Why did you have to fucking tell me that? Oh, Jesus— why? I can't fucking... handle it... I'm so fucking stuck... stupid motherfuck- ing motherfucker."

Pym watched himself listening, watching his own eyes, asking wisdom and control of himself. "You wanted the truth," he heard himself say. It just came out. The tone was a borrowed one, that of Terry. "She lies to you because you can't handle the truth about her. If you're going to have a mistress she's probably going to be a bit loose, and you're going to have to accept that about her."

"Mistress? Is that what she calls herself? I knew all that, Pym. I'm not stupid. I've been in therapy for two years. It's that she lies. She says she's so goddamn pure. She told me at first she could count the lovers she'd had on one hand. I've got it up to about thirty at the moment and had to fight her on every one of them."

"You're making that your business. I wouldn't give a shit."

"She wants me to stay with her. How can I stay with someone I can't trust?"

"I hear that. I'd get the fuck out of it if I were you. I won't be seeing her again. She's dangerous. You'll get no more trouble from me."

"Did she want you to fuck her in the ass?"

"Yes."

"Did you?"

"No."

"She cleaned your dick with her mouth after you fucked her."

"Yes."

"Have you any idea how this kills me?"

"I'm sorry. She thinks about you constantly. There's no doubt she loves you."

"I believe that. God, what is she? You know, I think she likes me to dip my cock into other men's cum. She's punishing me. I'm screwed with her."

"Eddie, you're not. You can leave her."

"Yep. I will do that now. This is the living proof I've needed. I'm grateful for that at least. Oh fuck!" And Eddie began crying again.

"Release me from this chair, Eddie. I'll help you."

"Not yet. You're still not out of trouble. You should die. I'm sorry about your brother, but maybe he was a stupid, thoughtless, self-serving idiot, and by killing you I'd be culling the population of a family of fucks."

"Come on, you don't mean that. You know I've been vulnerable too. You know I needed some comfort and Maddy chose me because of that, to pile a little more revenge on you. My wife, who I still love, is living with a man who seems to understand her better than I did. I call him a fuck too, but in my heart of hearts I know she chose him because he's a good guy. Get me out of this. Come on, Eddie."

"I don't know how you can love someone and still do this shit to them," Eddie said.

"It's not about love, man. It's about sex. You get that, don't you?"

No answer came from the floor behind Pym. The weeping started again. Pym looked at himself in the mirror and frowned. With his lips he mimed, "You stupid fool. Look what you've done to this guy. Idiot. No more of this."

Eddie cleared his weeping and stood up. He went into the bathroom and Pym heard him run the tap. As he came back, Eddie opened the doors on the balcony and an aroma of roasting coffee entered the room. He had brought a glass of water with him and put it up to Pym's lips.

"Thanks," said Pym.

"I guess it isn't so much your fault. I've been blaming other people all my life. It's me who's the fuck."

"Well, I shouldn't've been messing with another man's woman. I won't do that again—ever. If she'd wanted to be rid of you that would've been different, but she doesn't. She loves you. I'm real sorry, Eddie."

"And you're also motivated by self-preservation."

Pym's heart increased tempo again as electricity pulsed in his hair follicles. "I want you to let me go, yes. But the deal was that I tell you only the truth and I've done that, and will do it all night if necessary."

"I've got all the truth I need. I know what to do next. I'm going to cut you loose, feet first. Then I'll undo the handcuffs. Don't even move a muscle until I've left the room. You got that?"

"Got it."

* * *

Pym tried to remain calm as he walked down the stairs to the hotel bar. His clothes were drenched and stank as if he'd been swimming in a cesspool. He had sat for a long time in front of the mirror, thinking it all through. His heart refused to believe he was out of danger. As he descended the staircase, the smell of the carpet, the smell of ozone from the rain coming down outside, the feel of the air on his moist skin, made his heart leap with the joy of life. His friends still sat soberly around the table nearest the bar. Sammy stood beside them, holding a tray. It was Sammy who looked up and saw him. "Mistah Pym back down."

Pym approached, took one look upward to make sure Eddie wasn't training a gun on him, and then said calmly, "Well, Maddy, I guess Eddie didn't go to his convention today."

"Oh my God," she said, and stood. They all stood. Terry stepped forward. Pym said, "I've just spent half an hour having my life flash before my eyes, first with a gun to my head, then with a scalpel at my throat. But here I am, alive. He's up there with a gun."

"Unreal," Maddy said.

"No, very real. Not at all like a movie, either. I pissed myself."

Maddy's face paled. A thought Pym didn't like spoke in his mind: Your turn now, chick. Pym sat down and, one by one, drained all their drinks.

"What did he say about me?" asked Maddy.

"That you're killing him."

"What's this all about?" asked Vera.

Terry leaned into Vera and whispered in her ear, to which she responded with raised eyebrows. Maddy said to Sammy, "Would you please call our room and make sure he's okay? I don't think I better go up there right now."

"Sure, Ma'am," said Sammy and went to reception.

"Are you going to press charges against him?" Maddy asked. Pym found himself answering "No" without hesitation. He kept blowing hard as if he'd just done a hard day's labor. Terry sat across from him, staring, and said, "Quite a day, young man."

"I guess," said Pym. "Quite a few days. It's like the earth opened up."

Vera, who sat on the other side of him, said, "Poor little bugger."

Sammy came back, eyes big, and said, "No answer."

"Oh no," said Maddy, and took off up the stairs. Sammy followed her, hollering, then up went Terry.

Vera shouted, "Terry! No!" But he ignored her and kept going. She looked at Pym.

"Oh, shit," Pym said, and went after Terry, Vera following.

In the hallway, Pym saw Maddy struggling with the key. Her hand shook too much to get the key in the lock. Sammy took it from her, got the door open, and pushed it against a chair set in place to jam the entrance. Pym opened his own door and looked in. The wardrobe doors gaped. The French windows stood open. There was his chair with the tangled duct tape and the smell of coffee. He looked back into the hall.

"Come through here," Pym said. Maddy flew through his room and out onto the balcony followed by Terry. The doors into her room off the balcony were open and Pym went in behind Terry. Maddy screamed and sank to her knees in front of the bathroom door. Sammy was there, and Vera, holding her hands up to her face.

Terry said, "No one touch anything. Sammy, you better call the police."

Eddie crouched comfortably, head across the toilet bowl, with his upper chest and forehead supported by neatly folded white towels. The raised toilet seat had shit spots on its underside. From where Pym stood he saw one staring blue eye, the left one. He stepped closer to see the toilet bowl filled with blood. Eddie's hands, a little bloody, finger-locked under his stomach. He wore a white T-shirt, black sweatpants, and his feet were crossed. The big toenail on his left foot was painted red.

Maddy crouched on the floor, face hidden behind her bony hands, and Vera knelt beside her with an arm around her. Terry said to Pym, "Let's go to your room."

As they walked between the French doors they could see people eating in the veal restaurant. People walked, laughing along the sidewalks, careless of the rain, holding hands, sipping those huge cocktails. It was after the fact that Pym smelled the blood—rusty, salty. He laid across his bed—no feelings.

It suddenly occurred to Pym that this whole thing could have been made to look like he had murdered Eddie and tried to make it look like a suicide. He sprang upright.

"You've had some rough days, man," Rick said. He stood in the French doors. "I think we better get you out of town before anything else happens."

Pym tried to laugh but couldn't. He pointed at the duct tape on the floor. Rick shook his head and said, "Later, man. No sweat. Let's all just cool off."

Terry came through the French doors and sat next to Pym on the bed. He put his arm around him and pulled Pym tightly against him. "You poor old chap," he said. "I'm afraid we've managed to bugger you up quite severely, haven't we?"

Vera came and sat in the chair that had only a few minutes ago held Pym captive. Rick stood with his legs apart, frowning. Vera looked intensely at Terry and said, "It's time." Terry looked back at her and shook his head. Vera looked at Rick and shrugged. Rick smiled and said, "If you need me, I'll be next door."

Pym said, "Can this all just stop now? Enough!"

* * *

An extraordinary experience, Terry thought. If you wrote it like this, some fool of a critic would whine that it was too incident rich. Only the public like non-stop incident, which means it's bad art. He sat alone on the balcony, watching the fountain bubbling in the dark, attractively lit in green from under the water. He never saw so much blood. Vera had—she'd been a nurse. And poor Gilbert, having to witness this only hours after visiting his brother in the morgue. Brought it all on himself though. Still, the boy was not unlike him when he was younger, but he'd never had a series of lessons quite this sharp. We don't improve through the generations, we decline—the human race tumbling toward Darwinian extinction. What does it matter? We die, each of us in his own little apocalypse. Poor Vera—her turn next.

He should have told the boy. Vera said so. But he felt at the time that it would be too much. Now he wished he had said it, because the next bombshell was that Maddy was indeed Eddie's wife. She was just bored. Beautiful woman though. Jesus—the young Terrance Langley would not have resisted, no indeed. Like father, like son. Should've told him, get it all done at once.

You are my son.

Oh, please. How melodramatic can you get?

But it's true!

When real life becomes too melodramatic, English people ignore it. It's too embarrassing when it's done badly. Too American. Imagine it going like this:

Terry and Vera stand silhouetted against the French windows like Grant Wood characters, and announce: "Gilbert, boy. We gat sumthin' to tell yooo..."

Or, in a Basil Rathbone voice: "Look, old chap, I have something frightfully difficult to explain, and frankly I'm at a loss as to how to proceed, so the best thing is to just spit it out and have done with, what? Jolly good. Well you see, back in the seventies I was one of those blasted hippies and visited America and rogered the lodgings out of your mater before buggering off back to Blighty, and, sorry to say, you are the result. I am, in short, warts and all, your father. I realize there are disturbing parallels to the ghastly incident which recently occurred, but I thought it best to get everything out in the open once and for all."

Or:

Terry says, "There hasn't been a good time to say what has to be said. Everything's been moving so quickly for you and, you see, I never had the right moment. We expected more help from your brother, George."

Gilbert pulls away, wiping his eyes and looks quizzically at Terry.

"Bugger it all, Terry," says Vera. "Get to the bloody point, man!"

Terry sighs, puts his hand tentatively on Pym's knee, and says, "Gilbert, I'm your father."

Gilbert faints.

Then he wakes up and says, "Langley."

Terry smiles and nods. "Nina gave you my surname for your middle name."

Gilbert's eyes glisten. Everything's falling into place. Life is on the verge of renewal. Looking very troubled, Terry says, "George told you the story of your mother and I. He told me you were angry at him for doing so."

Vera says, "He was very concerned for you. Your brother loved you. He felt you were headed for a precipice of some kind and made an effort to contact Terry in England. Your mother helped. And your ex-wife."

"Wait a minute. So this was all staged—getting me to New Orleans?"

"Yes," says Vera, "in a way." She looks at Terry as if to gain permission to speak. He nods to her and takes off his glasses to rub his eyes. "It was supposed to be a big, wonderful reunion," Vera says. "George assured us you'd be a good sport about it. He knew you'd be missing him. We were so excited. It was an amazing story. Terry laughs, and Vera smiles. "Then," she continues, "in his dotage, Terry gets this telephone call from New Orleans, USA, and suddenly he has a son. And the son's going to witness the trans-formation of a brother into a sister. There was a big shindig planned here at the hotel. It's all such a shame. It would've been like a fairytale."

This isn't a bad scenario, thought Terry—keep going:

"But then George didn't turn up to meet us at the airport and never contacted us. The party was all paid for by George, and we sort of took it all over when he dropped out of the picture. That's how we met Rick. Terry had a bad feeling and called the police, and we got lucky with Rick who is a wonderful human being."

"So he knew all about this too?"

"He was already trying to find George when you arrived."

Terry says, "Gilbert, I'm sorry."

Pym crawls over to him and puts his hands on Terry's knees and says, "Don't be sorry. I'm numb from all this right now, but I know I'm going to find a way to be happy about it at some point. I don't know when."

No no no! He wouldn't say that!

Try:

Gilbert's not prepared for my arms to encircle him, so he's stiff at first. We both control emotion, and, to cover it, Gilbert says, "Does this mean I have to start eating kidneys?"

* * *

243

That night it took Pym a long time to fall asleep. He kept waking up to the reality of George's death and then would be startled at the reality of Eddie's. And he thought about how Maddy used him; and he would weep into the pillow and fall asleep only to wake again and think of Nadine and the voodoo, and pissing on Sasha, and wanting to murder that bastard Duval.

A rattling of bones started all around him. Nadine stood in the dark in front of the wardrobe, casting a spell. He wanted her to do it. He wanted to make sure he would wake up and find that it had all been a nightmare. As payment, he had to take his brother's body to a bayou and feed it to the alligators. He stood beside the water and rolled a body out of a white sheet. It was his wife Laura's body that rolled into the brown water and immediately sank. He frantically waded in to recover it and kept trying to ignore something coming at him from under the water. It got him by the genitals and he screamed, trying to pull away, so that the head came out of the water and it was Nadine with his cock and balls in her mouth.

They struggled in the water-battle and, love entangled, he tried to push into her and kill her at the same time. The more they fought the stronger he got; she kept morphing into different people to try and give him the slip but he wouldn't let go of her. Finally, she became Laura and he relaxed his grip and she was instantly on him—a snarling black demon with red eyes and salivating fangs. He called on his fathers, and his fathers sent him strength, and he got the demon by the neck and squeezed and pushed it under the water and held it there until its struggles ceased.

He let go and Nadine's body drifted down the bayou. Other bodies drifted with her. A little girl, the one from the Spanish house, stood on the riverbank, glaring at him with her half-wit's eyes. He could read her mind. When she grew up she would become her mother and cause him to have bone cancer. He leapt out of the water and chased her. She turned into a cat. He caught the cat by the tail and lashed it against a tree and then flung it into the bayou where alligators tore it apart.

He was naked. A contingent of police arrived on horseback and arrested him for indecency. He rode on the back of a horse with his arms around a policeman. They took him to Baton Rouge and rode right through the door of City Hall. The building was like the Minnesota State Capitol. They took him to a room full of women and threw him in.

He knew a few of the women, but mostly they were friendly strangers. None of them spoke his language, but he rolled around with them, pushing his cock into as many as he could, and when they understood what he wanted they all vied for a turn. He thought he was in heaven. They bathed him in warm milk and combed out his hair and delicately pushed out the detritus that had collected in his pores.

He became alarmed when he saw his mother trying to hide herself in the crowd of women. She was trying to find a way into the milk bath, and he knew she'd have her knife concealed somewhere on her. The doors of the chamber flew open and the cops stood and looked at him. They weren't cops anymore; they were men in ridiculous looking cloaks. The women looked at each other and the men just stared at him.

His mother hovered in the crowd of women. He knew he must go to the men and he tried to stand, but the women held him tightly and rubbed their breasts against him. The men ran forward and shouted at the women and the women ran away, calling them sexist pigs.

One of the men said to him, "Pull yourself out of the goddamn milk, you fucking pussy." He got out and they put a cloak around him and they took him out into a corridor and then into another room full of men. There was an aisle ahead of him and he walked down the aisle with the men watching, and an elderly man and woman sat on big chairs and looked at him. He ran to them and fell at their feet and started weeping so hard that the building shook and dust fell from the rafters. The man touched his head and pulled him to his feet. One of his teeth fell out and the place where it came from bled profusely. The old man gave him a new tooth and he turned with it to show the men, and the men laughed and then started to cheer as if he'd just been victorious in a boxing match.

XVII

Pym didn't want to wake from the dream. But the men marched him out of the building to where a horse waited for him and they rode with him as far as the border, the hooves of the Clydesdales thundering, and he woke up laughing. He looked around the room, happy.

The dream hung on him, vivid and constant, and it didn't go away even when he thought of the horrific experiences of the last few days. Even the terrifying notion that he was being psychically blasted by Nadine Duval from her jail cell shattered under the force of the dream. He hadn't been able to shake the silly notion firmly upon him that she sent him poisonous dreams, mind-altering nightmares. But the dream of the men in cloaks came from inside him. It felt true and gave him direction. His heart felt cleansed by it, and he was through with something or other... he wasn't sure quite what. His addiction to the tit? Was it about growing up?

Pym pulled the sheet up to his chin and listened to the hooves of a horse walking under his balcony. In your waking consciousness, you lumber ahead evenly, experiencing, thinking with this narrow window of perception, whereas when you sleep, a deeper, nonlinear perception takes place. Who needs movies when we have our own dreams?

He looked at the cracks in the ceiling. In his dreams his mother always carried a knife and came after him with it. In real life she had always been pretty nice to him. What did her aggression mean? It flashed on him pleasantly that he could ask Terry. He tried it on aloud: *Hey, Terry. Explain dreams to me.* The voice that sometimes spoke to him stirred itself and said: You don't even tell the truth in dreams. Happiness receded and he was spiraling downward. It was his mother. She was beside the bed, telling him some sloppy drunk fairytale and toward the end she lost the thread of the story and her hand crept under the blankets and she was saying *Ah, my sexy little prince, how does the story end?* And then she was licking the sticky stuff off the palm of her hand, saying *That's how it ends, my dirty little bastard.*

"What'll I be dreaming up next?" Pym whispered. And he immediately knew. It was always there, where he was able to avoid it, locked in one of his cupboards, the day she was rubbing him on the yellow couch, the house smelling of dope, Dad at work; her, home alone with him, bored, drunk. Come on little man, come on, honey, let's see what you got for mama. His little cock sticking up and her about to lower herself onto him, giggling, 'don't tell anyone or Momma will be in big twouble'; and him aching to do it, to have it slip in there, and then big George shouting 'what the fuck are you doing, you crazy bitch.' Then screaming and shouting and slapping, and Mother running out of the house, and nothing ever the same again.

The telephone rang and his heart jumped.

Cindy Sorensen said, "Gosh, Gilbert, I'm so incredibly sad about your brother and the suicide guy. I heard all about it. That's a lot of grief all at once."

"Yes, I seem to be stepping in all kinds of shit."

"Well, anyway. Just thought I'd call."

"Thanks. Look... I'm wondering if you've had breakfast yet."

"At about 5:30 a.m." Cindy laughed.

"Jeez. Well, I feel kinda goofy, but I'd like to see you."

"Okaaaaaaaaay," she said.

"Come on here, help me out."

"No way," she said.

"Do you get, like..."

"Now you're sounding like me. Valley Boy."

"Okay. Meet me for lunch."

"Sure. But only because you must need some cheering up."

"I do. I want to talk to someone normal."

"That wasn't so hard, was it?"

"You mean asking you to lunch?"

"Yes. Guys are so weird."

"You don't know the half of it."

"And do I even need to?"

"You've made my day."

"That's sweet. You been to the Café Du Monde?"

"Ah, yes. Somewhere else maybe?"

"French Market. Crab cakes to die for."

"That's just down from here, on Decatur?"

"Sure, that's it. Noon. Gotta jet. Pyke's breaking my balls to start taping some crap about Mardi Gras. The dude is intense."

Pym's inner voice went into full throttle; the damn thing wouldn't shut up. Who do you telephone first, Estelle or Laura? Pym dialed Estelle's number. He got her answering machine and left the number of the hotel. Laura would be at work. He stood in the shower and cried for George as the water pelted him. He kept seeing George laid out on the gurney and Eddie's red-nailed fun toe. Pym's penis still ached from Maddy's treatment of it the morning before. It was like she hadn't wanted anyone else to use it. He was sick of maniacs. He cried hard all through his thoughts as the water roared in his ears. Was this little Cindy going to turn out to be another crazy person? Why had he been so scared to ask her out? She reminded him of Laura. She was the Laura type. Not beautiful, not pretentious, but earnest and balanced, with a tendency to put on a little weight in the hips. She didn't have big spectacular breasts or a waspy waist. As he dried himself, looking in the steamed up mirror at his red eyes, he said, "Just a lunch with someone normal. That's all. Please."

The phone rang and he lay naked on the bed and said hello.

"Superstud!" said Estelle, "I been lustin' after you, workin' my finger to the bone."

"Stella," Pym said, beat, his eyes rolling back.

"I can see your eyes rolling back in your head like they do."

"Hold up a sec."

"Okaaaaaaaay. What?"

"Are you sitting down?"

"Yeah yeah—what? Oh, my God."

"George is dead, hon."

Her astonishment resounded palpably in the line's silence. At last, softly, the sexy gravel vanished from her voice, and she said, "I can't believe it. Are you trying to teach me some sort of lesson for being a crude bitch?" It could've been a little girl on the line.

Pym closed his eyes tight and said, "No, babes. He died of an infection. We have to have a funeral."

"Of course. Oh, Jesus. Did he suffer?"

"Can you get down here?"

"Yes. When?"

"Now."

"Gimme the details. Gil, I'm so sorry. I was so mean to him. God-damn."

"We'll talk it through when you get here."

"Please don't go yet."

"I have to. There's so much to do—you have no idea."

"Gil, God. I'm so sorry we lost him. Please don't go. I got no one to talk to."

Pym nodded to himself. He was angry with her. He was always angry with her. On a very real level he'd always made it her fault that they had an affair, and the fact was that it wasn't her fault, it was his. "I'm sorry," he said, and aping Terry again, said, "Forgive me, Estelle. This is all very trying."

"Of course it is, sweetheart. But we'll get through it."

"Yes. Look, you better tell Mishawn all about it. Give him the number here. There's a lot of people who will want to know, that should know—fast. Mishawn's the one to tell them."

"Okay, I'll tell him as soon as I hang up."

"You think you can find my mom and tell her?"

"I'll find her."

"Cool."

"Don't say *cool.*"

Pym pushed out a laugh, then said, "Go on then, away with you."

Estelle started crying—she never cried. "Gil, don't leave me."

He winced, knew it was coming. She was on the verge of blowing it. Gently, he said, "Don't say anything else for now. Hush. You need to feel this and think all about it—get clean in your head. Hush. Don't talk any-more."

Estelle hung up gently.

He looked at the ceiling cracks. One made him imagine a road through the Amazon. The road crossed a river and then petered out at the bend of the river. You have to get on a boat now, he whispered to himself. The ceiling was a white map of an uncharted country.

He rang Rick.

"I want to talk to Nadine Duval."

"You a brave man or what, Gilbert Pym?"

"There's stuff to clear up. My head's all muddled and I learned from that Sasha chick all about the voodoo thing with Nadine."

"Shit. I wanted you to stay out of that."

"It's been all in my head. Weird dreams and thoughts."

"Yep."

"I need to see her again—make her a flesh and blood person. There's no such thing as all this Voodoo crap. It's all in the head. She's just a good psychologist."

Rick remained quiet for an uncomfortably long moment before saying with a resigned sigh in his voice, "Okay, man, you got it. I'll set it up."

Pym hung up, then called reception and asked for coffee. Sammy brought it up personally.

* * *

Cindy was thirty minutes late. Pym sipped his second beer and, from the safety of the balcony, watched the same menacing bum he'd seen at the Algiers ferry a few days ago, panhandling on the corner below. The bum, in a voice deep and cracked, sang the well-known parts of popular songs as people approached him.

Pleased to meet you,

Hope you know my name...

He'd hold out his hand as they passed, invariably to no avail, then he would take a swing at the person in the air with his fist and start in singing again as the next prospect approached. He never sang a whole song, just parts. Pym understood this; snatches of songs were all he could ever remember.

What would you say if I sang out of tune?

Would you stand up and walk out on me?

Along with other diners sitting on the balcony, Pym accompanied the bum in the next two lines:

Lend me your ears and I'll sing you a song,

And I'll try not to sing out of key...

Cindy Sorensen coat-flapped toward the bum and looked up as he crouched, pointed at her and shouted *Hey! You! Get offa my cloud!* She laughed and put something into the bum's hand before looking both ways, crossing the road, and passing out of sight under the balcony. The bum looked at what was in his hand, frowned, crouched again, and pointed after Cindy, yelling, "I've seen you. You got no tits. Make that goddamn TV station buy you some tits. There's no excuse for a pretty woman these days to not have nice tits. They're cheap."

Having completed his critique of Cindy, the bum dug around in his layers of oily clothing for a place to stash the coin. He looked down the sidewalk of Decatur and then up Ursulines, found that no one approached, and sat down.

Cindy rushed along the balcony, smiling. "You must think I'm such a jerk," she said.

"He's the jerk—him down there. You're here, aren't you? Or is this a hologram?"

"I may as well be a hologram the way this station runs me around. I've got an hour is all and I'm starved. Him? That's Liam Toth, a crazy man."

"When I was a kid, my folks had this album by Jethro Tull, *Aqualung*. You know it?"

"Bit before my time probably."

"There he is down there, Old Aqualung, snot running down his nose and eyeing little girls with bad intent."

"He's harmless. His story is that he has a doctorate in English from Tulane, but he couldn't get a professorship anywhere because he's a white male. So he set about having a life-long tantrum and took to the streets."

"That's sad. He has a good voice."

"Maybe. He's consistent with this place."

This is normal, Pym thought. This is a nice normal conversation.

The sky was overcast, but a warm breeze blew off the river. A waiter arrived and they ordered the crab cakes and a plate of shrimp. Pym wanted to try the crawdads but Cindy told him they were overrated—messy to extract and rather flavorless meat. "I feel bad eating them too," she said, "it's like ripping a child apart just to eat its heart."

"A child?"

Cindy laughed and said, "Cindy needs coffee. I was up so early I can hardly see straight. But what about you? How are you doing with all these horrible experiences afflicting you at once?"

"I'm relatively okay. I'm trying not to dwell on it."

"Then we'll avoid it," Cindy said. "Sounds like Minnesota. If it's nasty don't think about it."

Pym laughed.

A paddle steamer pulled by slowly and its horn blew, so that Cindy, who sat with her back to the river, jumped and shrieked.

"I hate those damn things."

The bum on the corner shouted, "Shut the fuck up, you asshole. I'm trying to work here!"

Pym wanted to laugh but felt he shouldn't. But a part of him was happy; he couldn't help it.

"That's the American Queen," Cindy said, pulling a face. "It does the run up to Minneapolis. Talk about a slow boat to nowhere."

Pym's mirth jumped out of him and he laughed. His face felt flushed. "If it's going to Minneapolis it'll need an ice breaker to get through."

"That's right. I'm out of touch. Maybe it only goes as far as St. Louis this time of year."

"I hear it's expensive."

Cindy didn't answer, just looked at him seriously, then finally said, "I can't believe what just happened to you. It's like unreal."

"Ruins your story, doesn't it?"

"It kinda does. At least the nice one. I wouldn't mind a crack at it though. If you let me do it, I might be able to farm it out freelance to a station in the Twin Cities. People up there should know about this. Sitting up there, fat and happy in the snow."

"I'm not sure the story's over yet."

"I'm not going anywhere."

"Will you come to the funeral with me?"

"Wow. Like *with* you? Not covering the story?"

"Only if you want."

Across the road an old-time jazz band, elderly men in straw hats, started playing for the few tourists who sat outside a sidewalk café. Cindy looked at them, smiling. "It's so cool, isn't it?" she said.

The bum, Liam Toth, exploded into invective, foaming at the corners of his mouth, and throwing his arm as though releasing thunderbolts at the band, then shuffled off along Decatur, elbowing people aside and roaring his fury. "Purple-dicked old bastards, ruining a man's livelihood, playing that boring crap for numbskulls and nitwits. I hate this fucking town. Time for the levees to burst and drown us all. This is Sodom! This is Gomorrah! A plague on you all!"

Cindy stared after him as the band played on.

"He doesn't think it's so cool here, I guess," said Pym.

"Poor guy," said Cindy. Then she turned her face back to Pym and said, "Gilbert, I've got to say I'm a bit scared of you. I mean, as someone to get close to. I know most of the story. Got the rest of it today—and it was only a couple of days ago you were having it off with the doctor's wife." She giggled, and then said, "And now you're asking me out—sort of—to a funeral. What's that about?"

Pym sighed and looked up at the sky. She peered at him as one would at a child who refuses to acknowledge an adult's gaze. Pym found his face getting warm. He looked at her quickly, frowning, then glanced away. "It's not as bad as it looks. It's this place. Wild shit happens here. I mean, I've not been a saint or anything, but Maddy, well she was, I don't know..."

"Smarter than you?"

"Well, if you consider getting someone's trust and then pissing on them 'smart,' then I guess she was."

"She told you she was Eddie's mistress?"

He nodded.

"What was your first clue that she was a shit?"

"I guess I'm just used to people like that. You give them the benefit of the doubt because they're all you've got, and they're sexy. My mom..."

"Please, no blaming parents..."

"She was like that. I'm comfortable around people like Maddy. I know what they want. But I've learned my lesson."

"Well, I'd bore the hell out of you. I'm normal. I never lie about anything big and I have a great relationship with my parents. I don't have affairs and I've sworn off pre-marital sex."

Pym looked at her to make sure she was serious, then said, "You're like my first wife."

"Didn't she leave you for someone else?"

"I reckon we weren't as good a fit as I thought."

"So what makes you think we'd get on?"

"The law of second chances."

"That's a convention, not a law."

Using Terry's voice, Pym leaned forward and said, "I feel bound to express my opinion that you and I would formulate a splendid union. And it's apparent that you, at the very least, are considering my invitation."

"Considering," she confirmed, while ripping the tail off a shrimp. "And only because you're so ruggedly handsome and packed with boyish charm. And, you've had a rotten time of it, so I feel sorry for you."

Pym laughed, cleared his throat, and announced, "Gilbert Langley Pym invites Cindy to his brother's funeral in the hope that she will supply supportive companionship. He promises to no longer be drawn into the web of dangerous women."

Cindy laughed. "Okay, but only because I'm a sucker for public displays of idiocy. And with the understanding that you know I'm not a collectible."

"Boy, that was hard—to get you to come to a goddamn funeral! What if I wanted to kiss you?"

"You'd have to wait for my period."

Pym, shocked, spat out beer, to which Cindy laughed and clapped.

Cindy left without eating her crab cakes. Pym watched her clipping down Decatur. His interest in her felt no more than a grasping at straws that harked back to Laura—empty. He wanted George to sit across from him and snatch up all the left-overs. The still-warm crab cakes were too good to leave; he wrapped them in a wad of napkins, slipped them into his pocket, left money under a plate, and then went down into the street where he headed for the House of Large Sizes.

Darryl slouched in the window, sketching on a pad—he was a boy today in faded jeans and gray sweater. Maybe he was the boy on one of George's postcards. Darryl smiled as Pym entered. "Hey, it's that nice man from the other night. Did you find Georgie?"

Pym thought for a minute and said, "Yes, Darryl, I found her."

"That's wonderful."

"How did your date go?"

"Hank? Real good. I'm in love."

"It'll be a lucky person who ends up with you. You're so talented."

"Thank you."

"Is the boss back?"

"Go right on up, you know the way."

Pym was surprised. He came to ask Darryl questions, but Sasha was back from Mexico. As he walked up the stairs he heard the sound of a calculator being used along with a slightly familiar aria, something Laura used to make him listen to, a woman's beautiful high voice, full of sadness, and the sadness backed up by a huge, yearning orchestra. He stood on the top stair and saw through the book-lined living room to the balcony. Sasha sat at a small table, absorbed in accounting. He called and she looked up, frozen for a second, and then said, "I'm sorry about George. I had no idea."

"I know. Can I come through?"

"You will anyway."

"Like Sherman. Big nasty Yankee."

"Don't try to make friends. I could bite you."

"I'm sorry I left the other night. It wasn't my scene."

"Not your 'scene,'" she sneered. "What funny things you say." She lowered her voice and laughed, "You got off on golden showers."

"No, Sasha—*you* got off on golden showers."

She looked at him like a guilty schoolgirl, then got up and went into the kitchen. "Sit down," she said. He sat in a sparse canvas chair that felt surprisingly comfortable. He spoke a bit louder because he couldn't see her from where he sat.

"So how was Mexico?"

"How did you know I went there?"

"The cops."

"Fuck them, they got nothing on me. I had to get Duval out of the country. He freaked out, but it turns out they got nothing on him either. We have lawyers."

Pym, confused, swallowed his outrage.

She came in, handed him a mug of tea with a napkin. Then she went back for her own and sat with her legs crossed, holding the mug as if to warm her hands.

"Look," Pym said, "I brought you a tiny offering. They're delicious." And he gave her one of the crab cakes from his pocket. It was still slightly warm. She accepted it, and said, "What a strange man you are."

"Eat it."

"Is it poisoned?"

"I don't do sneaky things like that. Eat."

Sasha gave him a long sly look, then bit into the crab cake. She closed her eyes and chewed. "I haven't tasted this in years," she said. "I don't permit myself such food. It's delicious." She indulged another bite, holding her hand under the cake to catch crumbs. "God help me, it's fabulous."

Pym switched their teas around and Sasha laughed, mouth open, food showing in her teeth, and Pym discovered a trace of the crude boy who had once inhabited her. Laughing at the ease and prettiness of the moment, he said, "I love your city."

"You're thoughtful. Okay, what do you want?"

"I want to know how to talk to Nadine Duval."

Sasha's eyes widened. She shrugged, then appeared pensive while she chewed. She licked her fingers and rubbed her hands with the napkin, then sat back and crossed her arms under her breasts. Pym's interest fluttered a little. He liked the bracelets on her wrists, but he remembered the coldness he felt before and that threw the rising interest into chaos. She squinted and at last said, "I'm not sure what she can do to you. You're a paradox. Did you ever see *Planet of the Apes*?"

"Charlton Heston's classic overacting?"

"Do you remember why the cerebral monkey defense system wouldn't work on the gorillas?"

Pym laughed and said, "Got it."

"I'm serious."

"It's because I'm from Minnesota, isn't it?"

"You don't need anything. There's nothing you really want."

"Sure there is."

"No."

"I want my wife back. I wanted Georgie back."

"That's not the sort of thing. It's obsessions."

"Women. I like to fuck women."

"That was put like a true gentleman."

"I apologize."

"That's how she'll come at you—the sex thing. And your weakness and fears—she'll know them."

"I'm not sure why I have to see her. It's all over. She's up on numerous federal charges. She'll be away twenty years."

"Don't bet on it. And if you go to see her she'll try and find a way to use you for something."

"Like what?"

"I dunno. Heck, you don't even know why you want to see her."

"Dreams. I want them to stop."

"Go on."

"I have a little bag I took from Georgie's room."

"Oh."

"When I left your cabin I was picked up by a taxi and he took me into a dark part of the city and the car was surrounded by people doing weird shit."

"She's already riding you."

"What's in the bag?"

"Good. You didn't open it. That's a start. Tell me what you would expect to find in the bag."

Pym shrugged.

"Just examine your mind and tell me what you think George would want in the bag."

"I don't even know why he would want a little bag made out of his own scrotum sack."

Sasha winced, "Ooooh, well there's a start."

"Come on, explain this."

"You'd be best off to go drop the bag into one of those tourist bins where they have piles of fake ones for five dollars. Someone will take it off your hands and never know the difference. It's yours right now because you took it from the dead. You have something of Georgie's and whatever she wanted it for is still at work in the bag. It won't work the same way for you. It *will* continue to work, but in a very distorted way."

"I fucking hate this. What was it for?"

"I'll tell you after you've spent two hours as my sex slave."

"Sasha."

"Just my little joke. Lighten up. I'll tell you, and you're not going to like it. Let's see..."

Sasha sat back, closed her eyes and recited, "These are the powers of the Minkisi—to cause sickness in a person and to also remove it. To destroy, to kill, to benefit. To impose taboos on things and also to remove them. To look after their owners and visit retribution upon them. The way of every Minkisi is this—when you have composed it, observe its rules lest it be annoyed and punish you. It knows no mercy."

Pym's guts fell through him as if he'd just heard that a comet would collide with Earth. "What the fuck! Minkisi? Do I have to be a goddamn linguist to know what's going on here?"

"That wouldn't do any harm. To live fully in the world one should educate oneself in the ways of the world. All the ways. You're waking from the dream of childhood. Consider yourself lucky—most humans who've lived through the cycle never wake up, never even get the opportunity. The sad thing in America is that we have ample opportunity to do so, but we choose to remain oblivious and ruin the rest of the world with our ignorance."

"Thanks for the lecture but what do I call this thing?"

"Around here we call it a gris-gris bag. It's French."

"I hate this stuff. How does it work?"

"The magic is self-seeing. The poor fools in the throes of narcissistic pain will literally give their souls or anything else for this magic. They want to look into a mirror and see the image of the person they want to be. They want to think that their real body is just a disguise. Georgie wanted to be a combination of his mother and his ex-wife. Having sex with his wife meant he had to go somewhere else in his head, to be in a convincing world of make-believe. He was probably thinking about having sex with his brother..."

"No way."

"Yes way, absolutely yes way. I hear it all the time. It started with him wanting to be his mother and then got transferred to... what's her name?"

"Estelle."

"The affair you and Estelle had angered him, but it was also a way to get you and she together, his two objects of desire. He wants to be her getting fucked by you. It was a catalyst for him to break free of his commitment to her, in order to pursue becoming her. Every man he's fucked since doing this has been you—trust me. Here's something you don't understand—when a person wants someone to fuck them it's very different from wanting to do the fucking; being acted upon is very different from being the actor. You may not notice such distinctions, but we do. George had been waiting so long... he was already over forty—no time for long treatments and therapy. Do it now with the Duvals, with the Thai surgeons. Do it all, transform overnight like magic. If you want magic, you better find a witch."

"Nadine."

"She asks a price. First, cash for the surgery, lots of it. Second, the life of a loved one. The life sacrificed has to be equal to the desired object. Who will you give me, George, that you may yourself become enough of a witch to formulate your true self and move through the world at will?"

"This is against nature."

"Don't be such a prude. It's in nature, therefore it is nature. What do you know about nature? You live in America."

"Who did he sacrifice?"

"I don't know. Someone very dear to him. Nadine would know, but you can't get her to ever tell the truth. He loved you on every level a man or a woman can love another man. I could see into his heart. It was amazing. But there's his mother, and of course, my main rival, Estelle."

"Your main rival? Estelle?"

"Yes. She's your obsession. I'd like to be getting the attention she has—and so would George, wherever he is."

"He's on a slab in the morgue."

"Don't bet on it."

"Oh, here we go."

"As you wish. Have you been having extremely strange dreams? The gris-gris will open you to them. It will open you to the truth that most people don't need to see, the truth of what we really are, us humans. There are vampires of course, but they're not what people think. If you're smart, you'll realize they're much scarier than those romantic Ann Rice constructs. Although I wonder about her sometimes—she knows her stuff."

"Whose side are you on?"

Sasha laughed and said, "I'm on my side. Have you any idea how hard all this is to keep up with?" And she displayed herself again with her hand. "It's an insult that you wouldn't give up your soul to have this—given your own obsession with the female form. I can only think you must be a disguised version of your brother."

Pym looked at her for a moment, then laughed. "You are clever, but I'm on to you. You won't get me that way. There may be a way to get me, but it won't be that way."

Sasha frowned. "I've been very nice to you."

"I've said that to women, hoping for some small favor and they just laugh."

"Are you laughing at me?"

"I wouldn't dare."

"That wouldn't be wise. Tell me what I have to do."

He looked at her and thought for an instant that he saw the same desperation his brother displayed during their argument. "I'm not promising anything. As you've seen, I'm turned off by the idea of you being a man underneath all that. But help me understand all this. Get me out of the gris-gris curse thing, and I'll forgive your involvement in the death of my brother and try to be your friend."

She stared at him, smoldering. He was afraid of her but kept the tough look on his face.

"You're a cold-hearted prig."

"Spill."

She sighed and said, "Tell me what you'd expect to find in the bag."

"Objects and stuff belonging to the object of desire?"

"If you wanted, say, to get a connection to Gilbert Pym and Estelle Pym, what would you put of them in a little bag made from the cured scrotum of George Pym?"

Pym closed his eyes. "I hate this."

"You're cleverer than you think, come on."

"Stuff from the bed they'd just made love in. I'd scoop up those tiny cells that the skin's casting off all the time. I'd find hair and fingernails. I'd get a pair of undies that Estelle wore after sex and cut out the part that my brother's semen had dripped into. I'd find a thread of clothing, a baby tooth, a watch they'd worn. Hair from a razor... shit..."

Sasha laughed and said, "Go on."

"I'd collect it all in a sandwich bag and breathe into it and press the seal together."

"You're one of us... you've been fooling me all along."

"Stop playing games. Is that what you meant?"

"It's exactly what I meant—and it's probably exactly what he did. Then Nadine would add her juju."

"He was one determined motherfucker."

"You can think of this as a metaphor if you prefer, or you could imagine someone doing the job for him, breaking into Estelle's house in Minneapolis. Perhaps Georgie herself would fly up there and do the job. Perhaps Nadine sent one of her niggers up there."

Pym winced and then frowned at her word choice.

"You need to live down here for a bit, Gilbert, and broaden your experience. I'll look after you."

"I bet you would."

"I'll get you in the end, you know."

"That's what I'm worried about."

Sasha laughed.

Pym said, "I still don't know what to say to Nadine."

"There's no way to prepare. She'll know a lot of your mind—she's very clever. But," Sasha said sarcastically, "there's no such thing as magic, so don't worry. Right?"

"More of your double talk?"

"What are you doing tonight for dinner? You wanna try another cool restaurant, say Antoine's?"

"I think I need to spend some time with family tonight."

"Of course. I'm sorry."

"I'll let you know what's going on."

He left and felt Sasha's eyes on him as he went to the stairs and again when he was in the street. He purposely crossed the street to a position where he knew she would have to watch him walking away. He was learning their little games.

* * *

Pym felt he had neglected Terry. He knocked on the door and Vera answered and took him out to the shaded balcony, which overlooked the quaint courtyard. Terry lay back on a chair with damp balls of cotton wool in his eye sockets. Pym had never observed the courtyard properly and was surprised at its private luxury. He sat next to Terry and said, "God help me. Despite everything, I love this place."

Terry said, "Is it because you've never traveled in the tropics?"

"I guess."

"The tropics produce that impression on the novice traveler. Then you find out that nothing works and everyone's corrupt and there's disease everywhere. Winters, dear boy—thank your lucky stars for northern winters."

"Winters are for holing up in bed with buxom women," said Pym.

Terry lifted his hands in front of his face as if he were praying, pulled away the cotton balls, and gazed over the courtyard. Vera cleared her throat and said, "Gilbert, we have to have a word with you about something. To put it Terry's way, you're what the ignorant masses of the British Isles call 'cunt happy.'"

Shocked, Terry said, "Vera, only I can use foul language."

261

"No, no, I am your equal."

"Dear Lord."

Pym felt discomforted that they had been talking about him. He could only say, "I haven't heard that one before." He felt himself flushing and the top of his head itched.

"They used to refer to it as being over-sexed." Vera grinned. "I always thought that was a rather too complimentary term for it. Now we call it sexual addiction."

Terry said, "If sex gets in the way of your life too often, trips you up, alters you negatively in any way—this is not dissimilar to other addictions—then you know you have a problem. I'd say that's you... don't you agree, boyo?"

"Sex isn't supposed to be such a big deal," Vera added.

Terry said, "It's an interesting measure of our decadence that the more affluent we make ourselves, the more we fall prey to addictions. Too much leisure time and nothing serious to do with it."

"There it is," shrugged Vera, her eyebrows arching. "Idle hands are the Devil's workshop." Then, giving Terry a shove, she said, "And, I may add, being a fanatical Arsenal fan can be an addiction too—Terrance!"

"Don't start. I can't help it. It's in my blood. Passed down from father to son."

"Nonsense. You're a bastard. You've been in fights over a bloody football team. You punched that man last year. You're a geriatric hooligan."

Terry laughed.

Pym said, "Wait. What are you two talking about?"

"He's an Arsenal fan!"

Pym shook his head.

Terry's mouth dropped open. "You mean you've never heard of the greatest football club in the world?"

"Soccer club," Vera translated.

"You Yanks are so bloody insular. You have no idea what's going on beyond your own borders. Arsenal—in the real world—are much bigger than, say, the New York Yankees—"

"Oh, no, we've set him off! Get chloroform, quick!"

"—and cricket! Let me tell you about cricket."

Vera screamed.

"Cricket is a much bigger game globally than your silly baseball, which started as a game for girls. Rounders! Before America was even discovered."

Vera leaned into Pym and said, "What Terry really hates is that we English invent all these games and then the rest of the world beats us at them."

"Damn you, woman, we will win the next World Cup."

"We will not. Winning is decidedly vulgar."

Terry laughed and said, "A very American trait."

They both started laughing and Pym had no idea what was happening.

Terry wiped his eyes and said, "Look, seriously now, football may be a bit of an addiction—she's right, Gilbert, I confess—but it's far less destructive, say, than your brother's addiction. His was a habit of mind. Imagery so increasingly erotic—to him—that only a short sharp burst of adulthood could've brought him out of it. He created a sexual maze around the image of femininity and then lost himself inside it, as opposed to where you've got lost—outside it. At least your addiction doesn't require surgery."

Pym wanted to say something clever, but all he spoke was, "George couldn't handle being a guy. It's hard. It even scares *me* sometimes."

"Yes and no," said Vera. "I've treated a lot of these folks in Europe and it's not that simple. Your brother's a whole study unto himself. And as far as life being increasingly hard for men, they certainly seem to be creating their own paradox—the more they invent, the more redundant they render themselves."

"Oh, darling, let's get off this subject otherwise we'll quarrel."

"All right," said Vera. "Suffice to say then, that when bogus religion finds its way into the hands of charlatans and science finds its way into the hands of the unscrupulous, the human race will go the same way as the dinosaurs. Responsible people need to do their bit to maintain the balance between the world as it's seen by the opportunist and the world as it is seen by the enlightened. It's all about growing and finding balance in a perpetual cycle that will never cease until the planet dries up like a prune."

"Bloody hell, where did that come from?"

"I've been meaning to say it."

"I think you better write it. It sounds like a sermon."

"You swine."

"Oh, Lord. I'm in for a curtain-lecture tonight."

"Indeed you are."

"May I have a stab at the global problem?"

"Who could possibly stop you?"

"An excellent philosopher I recently read," said Terry, "whose name of course slips my mind, put it this way... and I hope I can do him justice. The underlying problem of our time is decadent man's pursuit of phantomatics. The overall impulse, once we've solved our animal economic needs, is to become discontent with the way we're made and rebel against it, trying to escape the accident of our bodies and the accident of our humanity, instead of reveling in the life we have, the ability to see and feel, which is miracle enough, that we were born at all. Handling consciousness by gaining maturity of thought is the only antidote to this frightening disorder of phantomatics, produced by fear of death, in the guise of mysticisms of various kinds. If we're to survive as a species, and it doesn't really matter whether we do or not given our true place in the universe, we must step out of the infantile shadow of the Middle Ages and exist as merely sentient beings who go forth bravely in a brave new world."

"Bravo," laughed Vera, "you just said what I said except more pompously."

Terry laughed and said, "Thank you, darling."

Bewildered, Pym brought the remaining crab cake from his jacket pocket and unwrapped it. The lightly fried aroma, a touch of lime mixing with crisped fish and breadcrumbs, activated his salivary glands. Terry and Vera both leaned forward to look. "I had one left after lunch with Cindy," Pym said. "I brought it for you." He broke it in half, the savory smell exploding in the air under their noses, and gave them each a piece.

"Blessed are the peacemakers," said Terry, and Vera laughed, biting into the cake. "My God," she said, "This is delicious." Terry and Vera ate quietly.

XVIII

For his visit to see Nadine Duval in the City Jail Pym wore the suit Sasha had bought him. He brought Sammy's umbrella, but wasn't sure why. His heart pounded, like nerves before a race. As soon as he was shown into the private visiting room that Rick had arranged and saw Nadine sitting, attired in an orange jump suit, he couldn't figure out his own feelings. It was like before he'd started waking up; he was slipping back and being the same old puerile him. There was a shape to Nadine Duval's mouth that drew his eye, and then his imagination.

She watched him looking at her mouth.

It was a big primitive mouth, the lips pursed like tropical leaves. Her beautiful eyes shone, alive with intelligence and, as he drew closer, he noticed what she did with the pupils—expanding and contracting them like tiny heartbeats. She was magnificent and, despite all he knew, he felt immediately drawn to her. The old calculations began, designed instinctively to wind up between her legs. But she slammed into him like a cobra, her voice high and hysterical.

"Only reason I couldn't get to you, motherfucker, is that you too stupid to know I be watching you."

Pym took his time to sit across from her. He was acutely aware of the slim tape recorder Rick persuaded him to slip into his jacket pocket; perhaps she was aware of it too—she was so sharp.

"Obviously no introductions necessary," Pym said.

"Spare me your lame sarcasm, you white devil."

"I'm not too stupid to know that you're a phony. You're not capable of magic, Nadine. It's just psychology. You're a charlatan, and they're going to put you away for a long time."

"They ain't got nothin' on me. I'll be outta here, an' on yo pink ass before you know it."

"You learn about people's insides. You feed on their pathetic lack of self-control. You understand what people want to be, and then you have power over them. I read all about it. West African witchcraft, the Voudon and the rest of it. Just another pile of shit for gullible saps like my brother to get duped by."

"Sasha musta tell you all that, 'cos you ain't no big reader, Gilba Pym—I know that. She gotta big mouf."

"You may not be a real witch, but you sure are dangerous—and you are about as evil as a human being can get."

"Please, white boy, quit this moralistic bullshit."

"You should be locked away forever."

Nadine twisted her body sideways and sneered. She acted as though there was someone invisible beside her who instructed her. "That won't work," a voice said, a voice different from a moment ago, its signature someone else's altogether. "You'll have to kill me. Otherwise I'll always be after you. Jail's no barrier to me attacking you and everything that's yours."

"What's this shifting voice thing? Maybe it works up in the Projects or Algiers, but I have a mother who does that as a party trick."

Nadine closed her eyes, then sprang them open again—the pupils had invaded the entire iris so that she looked at him with shining opals. It sent a chill through him, but he held on to what he knew she was doing and resisted activating his childhood fears. Coolly, he remarked, "Spooky, but nothing more than clever acting. You got nothing on my ma."

Her gaze was indeed that of the cobra… narrow, moist and unblinking, the whites becoming blood-shot. She proffered her hand, palm up, as if it held something. "In my hand you see nothing," she said in a sort of French accent. Then she blew the nothing and he felt her warm breath in his face. "But through your eyes you taste our souls." A voice to die for, a voice you could make love to as a disembodied entity.

He wanted it up close to him, speaking into his ear. He struggled away from it and said, "You mean to do me harm. Why?"

She shrugged, did a total body shuffle, didn't answer.

"Why do you have such trouble with me? I just did what I had to do. You'd do the same."

"Perhaps." It was a new voice, rational like Sasha's. "But your brother gave you to me. I refuse to surrender what's mine."

"What do you mean?"

She sat back, put her hands behind her head and spoke in a Midwestern accent. "To accomplish the deep magic of in-seeing, you have to sacrifice the soul of a loved one, preferably a family member. You have to give up something as big as what you want. I'm sure you know all about that now from your ever reliable information source."

"I don't believe George would do that."

"You don't know how badly he wanted to be his mother."

"You are one nasty person."

Nadine frowned as though she'd never thought about that before. "'Nasty,'" she mimicked, shifting persona again to that of a cynical white person. "Gal, that's a knockout punch. You sure know how to hit where it hurts, good buddy."

Pym couldn't help laughing. "You'd make more money on the stage than you do as a witch. Tell me, Nadine, why do you need to cause such havoc in the world? Life's fabulous without all this intrigue and pain. Can't you just live?"

"Haitians like us don't just live. The rich eat us, live off us. You are the rich. I will eat you first."

"Me, rich? You're delusional."

"Ah yes, you white trash think you're poor and underprivileged. I've heard this shit before. All whites are rich and privileged—you just want more. Go to Haiti—see what poor is."

"Okay, I'll grant you I don't know what real poor is, but I'm just trying to live—no different from you. You can't blame the ants for where the ant colony was built."

"And you all learn 'debate' in high school so you can justify your greedy culture. Then you all go to college and your parents pay."

Leaning forward, Pym said, "I put myself through college and so did my brother, who you killed."

"Your momma sucked cocks while you put yourself through college. She give your brother money, he give you money. You didn't send none to Haiti, did you! Your momma still suck cock, and she suck yours too if you let her."

Pym stood up, "You're beyond sick. I hope you're one of a kind."

"Ha. Asshole. There's millions of us."

Leaning over her, Pym said, "So if you hate us whites so much, why is Duval your man?"

"He's my daddy."

"As if that isn't sick enough, but I guess I'm becoming immune to the goings on in this cesspool."

She shifted again, became regal and said, "Ah, Duval is very special, and I deserve someone very special. He is my Bull of Heaven. And he is mine—oh, yes."

"But he loves Sasha. What's that all about?"

Another shift to an unidentifiable entity. "You heard about the size of his cock? Ain't no good you bein' in the world when there be cock like that around to be had."

Laughter came from behind Pym. He looked around and saw the guard cracking up. The man looked at him and shrugged.

"All right. I guess all my college didn't teach me to fight as mean as you do. Are you saying Sasha only likes him because of the size of his cock?"

"Don't forget, she's really a man. Men of all persuasions are obsessed with cocks."

Pym laughed again and looked around at the guard who was wiping his eyes with a handkerchief. Pym said, "You're something else."

Nadine shrugged, displayed a proud little smile that he couldn't help liking. He asked, "So explain how you got George brainwashed so fast?"

"Fast? He done brainwash himself. All his life he be drunk on pictures in his own mind. As he grew older he get better at it and then it take him over and he become it. He wannabee his momma—sucking cocks and getting fucked in the ass. I'm surprised you didn't have the same thing. Maybe you do, and just hide it good."

"You'd like that, wouldn't you?"

"I would. I'd dress you up like Sasha and have Duval fuck you till the brains come out your nose."

"I think your mind has turned to shit."

"Activate your shadow, sugar. Take a walk on the wild side."

He tried to look intelligent, but he had no idea what she was talking about.

She looked into him, her eyes luminous, shining black. "Let old Naddy give Gillian Pym a biology lesson. Every man is made from the caste of a woman. It's witchcraft right from the start. Destined for womanhood, an egg is punctured by impudent spermatozoa—filthy, wriggling tadpoles, stinking of testosterone. She would rather perish whole than be punctured, but the scum sometimes break in and a battle for the soul of the egg takes place. 'We will march on,' the spermatazoa cries, and the egg unwillingly submits. It's the first rape."

"Oh no!" Pym laughed. "You're one of *them!*"

She held her finger up and continued. "The egg continues to fight. If the invader is successful, the female parts transform according to the will of the invader and the entity grows as a boy. If the invader is repulsed, the entity develops as a girl. Occasionally the battle is close and the entity grows with a longing for the lost half so narrowly missed. The bodies of men are as they are because of the witchcraft of the Great Spirit who tries to transform everything into the masculine. We are here to resist the domination of the Great Spirit."

"Fascinating claptrap," said Pym.

"All men are made from women and the stinking part always yearns for some sort of return. You want to get back up inside us, to start again. You want to go back to the breast and fuck your way in like you did to the egg. It's your curse to want our safety. You long for the oblivion of return. You long for the safety of the womb. Some of you want to *be* the womb. Ha! And when you can't have it you take it away from us, make our lives hell. You have those stupid hanging sacks of jism—stinking bags of oppression—vulnerable and tender. I want to bite them off!"

"Me-oh-my. So you're a witch-feminist?"

"You've understood nothing. Feminists understand nothing. They're a bunch of spoiled little white girls who long to join the oppressed. We'll cut their throats too when the time comes."

"You've created a fantasy world for yourself, Nadine, and you're living in it. You're swallowing your own crazy medicine."

Nadine snarled and shook her head like a wolf. The guard laughed nervously. "You better run hide, little motherfucker. Hide under a rock." Her eyes became those of a leopard, her nostrils flared, and her teeth gnashed. It was a challenge to fight. It released something in Pym that he understood. He wanted the guard to leave so that he could kick the shit out of her and put her properly in her place.

He leaned into her and whispered, "I have a better idea, you fucking arrogant bitch. I'll take your earlier advice and have you killed."

He got up and turned his back on her. He was performing a little act himself now; he was that mercenary with nothing to lose. What the fuck, we'll just finish this.

"All right, see here," Nadine said in the reasonable voice, which caught his attention, so that he slowly turned around. There was another person present, a witch with integrity this time. "Your brother dead," this kind voice said. "It weren't supposed to happen. As white folk go I liked Georgie. He was decent—you hear what I'm saying? Just really screwed up—like nothin' I ever seen before."

"Are you saying you're sorry?"

"Sit down."

"Don't be manipulating me now."

"He's dead. You're free. But if he was alive you'd be mine." She put her head to one side and smiled, and he saw the woman who smiled in his dream. "I coulda made you into somethin' special, somethin' perfect." Quietly, so the yawning guard couldn't hear, she said, "You wouldn't mind belonging to me one bit, sugar."

Her lovely brown eyes shone; her breath smelled sweet and moist, like fresh cookies. He remembered how she felt in the dream, but the voice that sometimes spoke in his head decided to speak out in the world today and he heard it saying, "It might have been quite an experience, but it's not for me. I'm just a regular guy and I don't want your stuff. I love what I am. I'm perfect as is—hairy, flawed, and stupid. I don't need any alteration. I want to be what I already am."

Nadine drew back slowly and he felt the warmth of her attention withdraw, that emptiness of withdrawal he'd felt in the strange dream, not unlike what he felt with the loss of his wife and brother. What power was it that she wielded? He stayed leaning forward. Was it just like the power he himself had over Estelle, or was it actually something mystic? Whatever it was, his face was hot and he had an erection.

Nadine smiled.

Pym sat back, stubborn, saying, "You are something else, aren't you?"

"Cain't do you no good in here."

She spoke his thoughts, watched his face, then said, "You know'd me. Dream or real, no different."

"You know me from inside my dream? Is that what you're claiming?"

"Sure do."

Pym did a little shapeshifting himself. He became Terry, and said, "You're the ultimate in the exotic. You're what the obsessive mind longs for—the feminine that exists between heaven and hell and rebirths the sick

living slave every day. No thinking required. Is that what zombies are...
addicts at the end of the rope?"

Nadine's eyes got big and she smiled and said, "You signifying, Gilba
Pym. I can use you. Duval gettin' old."

He sat back, shaking his head. "You nearly got me."

"I'll always be there, baby, right on your ass."

"You can't be everywhere."

"You know that I was with Georgie when he passed out of his body?"

"I didn't know that."

"Death vigil. Just me and him. He axed for you and then his wife. He
wanted his momma, but all he got was me."

"And what did you do for him?"

"Saved his soul."

"What the fuck are you talking about?"

"His last breath. I got it right here. I sucked it right down like you
suckin' on yo momma's pussy, and he come in me all in a rush and I got him
wid me right now, listenin' to dis whole ting. He part of me, one of me."

Nadine's pupils dilated and her eyes shivered. Pym sat a long time
looking into her eyes. He felt her strength. It didn't matter whether or not
George was really in her. What mattered was that she had *said* he was.

Pym, his tongue feeling blistered and dry, said, "How do I get him out
of you?"

"Duval wants him. Fresh soul keep Duval young."

"You people are crazy."

"We people do as we please."

"You're claiming my brother is alive in you?"

She did her little twist, then said, "Gillie, stop messing around, you
wretched boy. Remember how I saved you from Mother? Now you must
save me. Trust Nadine, she'll show you what to do."

Goosebumps came up all over Pym's body. He could hear his own
heart pounding. George must have confided everything to Nadine. He trusted her. She was a brilliant mimic of the human voice. Pym said, "So what is
it you're saying I should do?"

"I want payment."

"What?"

"I tell you later, when I know for sure."

"From in here?"

"I told you, this place cain't hold me."

"So whose side are you on now?"

"Mine."

"What do I do in the meantime?"

"Teach Duval a lesson. I tell him to stay away from Sasha and he won't. Besides, he let Georgie die. Do that and I set you and George free. You no good to me now."

"Please clarify."

"You kill Duval."

"I won't kill anyone. Not even to save my brother. There's nothing that would make me kill anyone, not even that creep Duval. George wouldn't want that either."

"You don't know your brother so well."

"You're full of shit, all of you."

"Sasha told you too, didn't she?" And back came the Midwestern accent. "It's true. He'd give up even you to live out a paltry obsession. Hard to believe, but true. Of course, you pissed him off. Maybe you'd do the same thing."

"Never."

"You live in a dream yourself, Gilba Pym."

"Then I'm going to wake myself up."

"You want your brother back?"

"What do you mean?"

"I can give him back to you."

"He's dead. No one can bring back the dead."

"I can. I told you, he's right here. You heard him."

"Ventriloquism, trickery."

"No. Come closer."

Pym moved in closer and smelled her warm skin, felt her sweet cake-breath as she spoke quietly, friendly, reasonably now, reminding him of something pleasant from childhood. She whispered, "I know how to do this. I always have."

Pym looked around at the guard who yawned, looking at his hands, then looked back at Nadine and her nose almost touched his. Her lips were parted, ready to be kissed. Somehow he managed not to kiss her but said, "And what would be the price?"

"One night," she said.

"Why?"

"I want you."

"Why me? You can have anyone."

"It's a long story, and why does it matter? I'll put all your nonsense to rest. All your longings. You'll be able to move on undistracted by infantile concerns and you'll have your brother with you. Help get me out of here. Don't press charges over holding your brother's corpse illegally. That's all they've got me on, nothing else. Don't sleep with that monster Sasha. Sasha's a man, a freak. And here's me ready to love you. You've been waiting for me all your life and now I'm here you're afraid. What do you think all those fantasies were about? All that philanderin'? You were trying to find me, and here I am. I am not your mother, sugar, I am *the* Mother."

He was breathing her breath. Nothing mattered. Her eyes had turned blue. She pulled away and he stayed bent over ridiculously, panting.

"That hoodoo you stole from Georgie's room?"

"The gris-gris bag."

"Give it to his wife. Don't look in it. Don't let her look in it, ever."

"Why?"

"To get your brother back. You have my word."

"All right, what harm can it do?"

"None to you. But remember that you owe me a night of love."

Nadine touched his face gently with her fingertips and pulled away.

He said, "You are something else."

She frowned, laughed, and said, "You need to find another phrase to describe me."

"Okay," he said, "How about this. I'm going to fuck the shit out of you."

She opened her eyes wide; they were green now. He smelled her excitement coming up from below the table; something primitive throbbed in the back of his head.

"You are a strong man. I'll pray for you."

She looked like a nun. He had to sit down.

Pym laughed. He looked around and the deputy was laughing too. The deputy came over and said, "Looks like you two resolved your differences. I'm afraid time's up."

"We have more to discuss, Deputy," Nadine said.

"Sorry, your majesty, it's time for your breakfast."

Nadine stood up quickly and went through a door with the deputy without looking back.

In the cab his skin buzzed, his mind filled with Nadine Duval. He could barely breathe and the base of his skull ached. He'd forgotten his name. The cab stopped at a light under a line of palms and people streamed out of a tourist bus into the casino. "What's my goddamn name?"

The cabby laughed and said, "How'd you like my town, mister? Killing enough brain cells?"

"This town is fucking me up."

"Where to, my friend?" the cabby asked. "You're obviously a sucker for punishment."

"Thanks. Just drive."

"Yes, sir, Mister No Name."

The inner voice brought him back to center: Your name is Gilbert Langley Pym and you're a fucking idiot.

* * *

There was a message from Cindy Sorensen at reception. Sammy grinned real big like an asshole who knew everything when he handed it over. Pym ripped open the envelope and read:

> *Since we are now friends, would you like to come to the House of Blues with me tonight? There's a band I want to see and we can use my press pass. We can have dinner at my favorite restaurant first. Call me on my cell. Cynthia.*

The inner voice said: This is stupid. What will you do about Estelle?

He went to his room and took off his new suit. The little tape recorder fell out on the floor. He had completely forgotten it and it was still rolling; he turned it off. In his boxers, he went into the bathroom to piss and when he pulled the shorts away pre-cum dropped in strings into the porcelain. He squeezed the glans of his penis and more came out, great wads of clear lubricant dropping onto the porcelain and into the water where it spread out like fine olive oil.

He looked at himself in the mirror and saw a drawn, shocked face. His annoying inner voice wanted to speak, but he suppressed it and said instead, "No. You fuck off. This is the ultimate. I've never felt anything like this."

Someone slipped you Viagra. Sasha perhaps. They're all in league together. This isn't real; it's a con job. They still want something and you shouldn't give it to them.

"Fuck off. God, I have to fuck her, I have to fuck them all."

He picked up the phone and called Cindy.

She was breathless and in the middle of something, but she was nevertheless perky and efficient. "I'm going to be working right up to the last minute," she said. As she spoke, Pym watched his glistening penis rise. He was about to suggest she simply come to his room and he'd supply wine and appetizers and soft music, but she said, "Meet me at Nola. It's right there in the Quarter—534 St. Louis. I have reservations under Sorensen for seven-thirty. They know me and they'll seat you if I'm late."

Pyke shouted something at her in the background to which she responded, "Okay, okay. Jeez."

"Should I bring a book?"

Cindy laughed and said, "No, bring those little cards you write on. It's so cute."

"Cute?"

"Yah."

"Christ."

"Gotta jet. See you tonight."

Talking to Cindy got his mind off Nadine for a while, but she came flooding back in. He loved thinking about her; she was like mind perfume. He knew it was some kind of madness, but he didn't care.

Pym called Rick, and Rick came over to the hotel instead of hitting the gym. They went for a long, slow run all around the city. Pym was amazed at how much there was to know about Rick, and Rick was amazed that there wasn't more to know about Pym. "Man, you gotta get out more. All you done all your life is chase pussy. Ain't no career in that less you gonna be a gigolo."

Here was a very together guy, Pym thought. He has a job he loves, a beautiful wife, and a fit constitution that can just go out at the drop of hat and run with a buddy. And a minister on the weekends—amazing. And running without socks. They ran out to Audubon Park and back to the hotel via St. Charles.

"Where's Duval? I know he's back in town."

"You bein' some kind of gumshoe?"

"I have my sources."

"Indeed you do, my man. Yeah, he back in town."

"Where's he staying? His place in Algiers is destroyed."

"Dunno where he staying, but he be going to mass every evening at St. Louis Cathedral. Then he'll go eat somewhere in the Quarter, usually where there's French spoken."

"You're kidding me?"

"No. Duval's a big-ass Catholic, a real idolater, upstanding member of the church community, make no mistake. But his English is shit and he clears his conscious of wrong-doing every day."

"Where is that church?"

"Jackson Square."

"Oh yeah, right by the Café Du Monde, where the starlings live."

"You don't go messin' with him now."

"No, just curious."

"What are starlings?"

"Birds that act together like they've got one brain."

"Kinda like white people."

Pym laughed, punched Rick on the arm, and said, "Kinda like all people."

"I hear that," laughed Rick.

The running and talking pulled Pym's pulsating libido into some semblance of normality, and he finally asked what would happen to Nadine. "Not much to charge her with so far," Rick said. "But we're working on it. She's got good New Orleans lawyers though."

"She said I shouldn't press charges against her for holding the body of my brother illegally."

"She said you shouldn't? What the hell were you talking to her about?"

"I think she wants to fuck me."

"Man!" Rick stopped dead, with his hands on his hips. "Are you crazy?"

"I have it all on tape."

"Right, the tape. I need that. Did she get to you?"

"Somewhat."

"What dat mean?"

"It means yes."

"She gone too far. She's gonna give us all a bad name. She gotta go!"

When they got back to the hotel Rick was hobbling with blisters on both feet. "Man, I never ran that far in my life. Figured I could keep up wi-dju. Damn, you one crazy running motherfucker."

Rick showered in Pym's room while he stretched and did crunches. It felt good to run again. Rick was only under the shower a few minutes, then emerged toweling off and asked for the tape recorder.

"Bedside drawer," Pym said. He watched Rick cross the room naked and noticed the long taught brown muscles quiver as he moved... the lean, muscular torso, the hard bubble butt and swinging pudendum. It was something he saw all the time in gyms. Would he ever want to make love to that? To be in some sort of embrace with it? It didn't compute. How could his brother have been attracted to someone of his own gender?

"I'll listen to this and get back to you," Rick said.

"I warn you, it's pretty wild in places."

"You just go out with that nice Cindy chick and forget all about Nadine Duval. You find you a nice girl, not some crazy-assed bitch from fucking Disney World bullshit woowooland."

"Yes, officer."

"Man, I am worried about you."

* * *

Cindy continued to read the menu.

I might indeed have some sort of problem, Pym thought, because when he looked at a roast chicken passing by the table on a platter he immediately thought of Estelle's buttocks raised in anticipation of a rear entry. He laughed, and Cindy looked up and said, "Sorry, I never know what to order here." Then he felt bad. He was addicted to Estelle and had now been without her for several days. His crotch got so tight that he had to shift position.

The Nadine thing had lifted off him. He remembered the heat of it, but it didn't affect him now. She was insane, good at what she did. It meant nothing, but Estelle was in him like a computer program. There had to be some way to erase it, to replace it with a Cynthia Sorensen program; and then the next task would be to replace the Mister Shithead program with a Mister Nice Guy program. He now understood what Terry had meant that most men only find one goddess in their lives; Pym's was Estelle. Getting hooked up with someone else's goddess was either worthless or dangerous—witness poor Eddie. Terry had said, "If you consort permanently with the goddess, you are either immolated in her light or are forced to become a god yourself, at least briefly, until such time as nature quietly explains that gods and goddesses are just metaphors."

Cindy Sorensen had a very pretty face. Not beautiful or handsome, just pretty. Her hair, bobbed and shiny blonde, showed off nice ears, sporting plain gold rings in each delicate earlobe. Intelligent, reasonable, and healthy, she was solidly career oriented. Please be my goddess, Pym thought. An answer came back: She can't, and you won't. This is the only opportunity to have Estelle. She loves you, but will go to someone else like Laura did—like your mother did—if you don't act. If you don't act the time will never be right again. But the reason you like Estelle is because she's so like your crazy mother, and you need to escape that. But as he thought this he remembered her calling on her cell and singing "Have I told you lately that I love you," and he wanted to weep.

He excused himself and Cindy smiled up at him and asked him if he wanted her to order for him if the waiter came while he was gone. "I want the free range roasted chicken," he said. Cindy made a face and said, "Want to share that?" He shook his head and she smiled. Pym had to push his way through the bar area, and when he got to the toilets near the kitchen he noticed a bank of telephones. He checked to see if Cindy could see him, then put in his credit card and dialed. As Estelle's number rang he was thinking, I am not a nice man, I am not a nice man at all. She answered after ten rings.

"What are you doing?" Pym asked.

"I'm on the other line with someone."

"Tell them to piss off."

"No, Gil. Stop. I've given up on you."

"I need to talk to you."

"What is this? Usually you hate me."

"I love you some, I guess."

Pym expected her to be quiet but not for as long as she was. He said finally, "Is it too late now?" He didn't know what she knew about Maddy and Eddie. Tread carefully, boy.

"No. I'm scared though. My heart's going ballistic."

"Who's on the other line?"

"It don't matter."

"Good. You know what not to do, then?"

"Yes, master."

Pym laughed and said, "All right, I think we've got it."

"Oh, I hope so… this time."

"I just grew up, I think. Some at least."

Estelle laughed and said, "We'll see."

"We will—we'll see. Maybe you could try it."

"So I'm not to go on a date tonight?"

Pym didn't reply. A disturbance registered in his bowels. Estelle already taking advantage of a shift in the power structure between them. It amazed him that he would even think of this. He could stomp her right now, or he could let her be herself. He stayed quiet.

Finally, she said, "I guess that would be no."

Icily, he said, "Have you forgotten you already have a boyfriend and your husband just died! Are you kidding? But hey, do what you need to do."

"Life's gotta go on, Gil. I'm lonely and sad and I love you, but I'm sick of being insulted. I think you might have caught me just in time."

"Don't start fucking with me now."

"Okay, okay."

"You better quit while you're ahead."

"Got it. Relax."

"I have to piss now."

"Very romantic."

"I'm working on it."

"Let me hear you say it again, then."

"It would be too much for you all in one night."

"You're right. I'll go out now and have fifty guys say it to me as they try to brush my boobs, and I'll know I gotta boy in New Orleans who loves me for my soul."

"Your soul and your boobs."

"And you can only say you love me once, right? And that was just it?"

Pym laughed and rubbed his eyes. "I want to try it face to face."

Now she was quiet.

Pym said, "When the time's right I'll tell you all the time."

"I'll see you tomorrow night, Gil. I love you."

"Same," he said, strangling. "Safe journey."

Cindy smiled as he sat down and he felt like a heel. Some old men sang a ballad in French. At that moment a big man in a beige suit passed the window in the street. Pym went to get up but Cindy held his hand. "You're antsy tonight. Sip a little wine and relax."

He sat back and spread the napkin in his lap.

"Gil, I have to tell you something." She held his hand tight as she said this. Pym looked into her face. "I just wanna be buds, okay. There can't be anything physical. I like you, but there just can't."

Had she overheard him talk to Estelle? Was everyone psychic around here? He shrugged, "I'm not sure I..."

"If you want us to continue being friends don't say anything defensive."

"Okay. I'll be quiet. I'll just listen."

"Let me say this and then let's have a great evening, okay?"

"All right."

"You're not my kind of people, Gil. You're very cool and all, but I'm not into the bad boy thing. A lot of women get off on that, but I think they're idiots. I guess I'm just holding out for the young Republican type."

He looked around the restaurant.

"Does this make any sense?"

"Yes."

"Are you okay?"

"Yes. Now let's continue our evening, shall we?"

"Thank you."

"You're paying."

"Okay, deal."

Cindy sat back relieved, like she'd dodged an execution.

Pym felt rejected; it was odd how it hurt; but it was also a relief. Estelle. He could have Estelle free and clear. And was that Duval that just walked by?

"I feel like my body's changing. I can't seem to sit still. I'm sad about George all the time, but it's under the surface and there's another part of me that's excited about the future."

Cindy lifted her wine glass and held it at mouth level. "Here's to being human," she said.

"Yes," he said, "Thank you." And they clinked glasses.

* * *

At the House of Blues Cindy talked heatedly with three women near the bar. They all gesticulated madly over an issue of local politics. Bored, Pym wandered off. Away from the bar the music deafened him. He explored upstairs and found Sasha sitting at the end of the left balcony just above the stage where the music was loudest. She sat under a light reading a book. It struck him suddenly that Sasha had asked him out and he hadn't given it another thought. He felt oafish and wanted to make it right. He got close to her and saw yellow earplugs stuffed in her ears. He tapped her on the shoulder and she looked up at him. "You're strange!" he shouted. "You go to hear a band and then plug your ears."

She took out an earplug and pulled his head down to her mouth. "This is the warm-up band. It's tuneless, boring shit. The band I'm waiting for are very innovative. You won't like them though."

"Oh, and why's that?"

"Because you're a barbarian."

"I'm sorry I didn't get back to you."

Sasha shrugged, set her face as if to say, *You have no idea what you just did.* Then she said, "Anyway..." and the pounding music suddenly stopped and she waited to speak while the warm-up band left the stage to polite applause.

"You're not a good person to hang around with anymore."

"Now what?"

"There'll be retaliation for destroying the Duval empire."

"Like what?"

"Like bones rattling outside your window at night; like the dead eyes of zombies sent to kill you and make you one of them—as unstoppable as a mob with machetes. There's no escape if they decide to pursue you. I just hope it's not you they'll want. You may have to get something to protect you 'cos it sure isn't gonna be me."

"Why?"

"Nadine made bail this afternoon."

Pym had been staring down at Sasha for an indeterminate period when a light dig in his kidneys made him turn from her. Cindy stood behind him, looking up with a slight frown. He turned back to Sasha and said, "Gotta go." Sasha shrugged.

Cindy said, "Come on, stud. Buy me a drink."

Sasha lifted her book.

Pym followed Cindy to the bar where she whipped around and asked, "Why are you talking to that hideous cross-dresser?"

"She's a friend, and not a cross-dresser... a transsexual."

"They are so out of it, those people. They've sold their souls."

"Like my brother?"

"Oh, sorry."

"Well, you're probably right, but they have to live too."

"Not near me, they don't."

"Is the young Republican rampant in you tonight?"

"I'm just watching your back. You're naive—a babe in the woods. Everybody's after something. And don't produce the old cliché of asking me what I'm after."

"I have to know though."

"A beer. A nice dance. Simple Minnesota girl."

"I'll dance a tango with you, shall I? Or would you prefer a foxtrot?"

Cindy laughed, "Take it easy, Mr. Pym, this place is hot. Get me a cold one."

Pym stood behind people and caught the barman's attention with his eyes. He never felt this tall in Minneapolis. He handed Cindy a bottle of Dixie.

She said, "I was only kidding."

"About what? Wanting a beer?"

"About the trannies. They're fine. I wanted to see if you're one of those creeps who'll agree with a girl just to get into her pants."

Pym's thoughts tore around inside his mind like electrified ferrets. Nadine was on the loose. He wanted Estelle now, he needed his brother, and he wanted Eddie back alive again. He felt sorry for Sasha, he missed Laura, and now Cindy was admitting way more than she realized. She's mine if I want her, he thought, and one of George's bullshit pronouncements from their youth, one now monstrously ironic, asserted itself within him: *Every one you turn down, is one you'll never have.* He looked down at her, sipped from his own bottle of Dixie, and shook his head with feigned disgust.

"Stupid of me," she shouted.

"Drink your beer."

"Well, anyway, you said all the right things."

Pym couldn't help it and said, "So I can kiss you now?"

"I guess," she said. "After all, it is my period."

He put his arm around her and squeezed, immaturity oozing out of him, letting her feel his strength, like when someone grabs a man's bicep and he feels compelled to flex it. Under the soft layer of her superfluous weight he felt tiny bones, like a bird's, and immediately felt ridiculous. He said, "So that's why you're being nice to me. You're safe."

She turned away, blushing.

The band set up and got started. It was a glam band—*Pretty Ponies* or something, made up of tall musicians dressed as fishnet Valkyries, whose gender was tricky to determine from the back of the room. Pym recognized their musical style. It was something like an old favorite of his mother's, David Bowie. So this was all going on back then too; I guess it's always been with us. Cindy pulled him out to dance. They held their beers and danced among the fetishized population of New Orleans whose costumes, droll and predictable, did little to set them apart from the general population from whom they alienated themselves. In their pursuit of individuality, they all looked alike.

Pym was 'Dancer' again, letting it all hang out with nice little Cindy. He unselfconsciously danced away all his worries for a while until he happened to glance up at the balcony to see Sasha dancing strangely on her own, staring down at him, as though parallelism and hypnotism worked in some weird, dreamlike accord between them. Cindy pulled him to her and set her head under his chin. He danced like this for a while, feeling confusion in that Cindy had apparently changed her mind about him—just when he didn't want her to.

After a while he looked up again—no Sasha. Then he saw her a few feet away being dragged through the dancers by Duval. Gently, he disentangled from Cindy and followed Duval's tall figure as he pulled Sasha through the patrons. They were out in the alley by the time Pym was able to catch hold of Duval's arm.

The old man kept pulling, as though he were distracted, not quite present.

Sasha stopped, and her action caused Duval to turn, startled. He stood still, his eyes dead, looking down at Pym.

Pym asked, "Sasha, are you okay?"

She hesitated, then said, "I'm fine. Go back to dancing."

"You're being coerced."

She cocked her head and said, "It's just our game. He's going to be getting what you could've had. Go back and jitterbug with Susie homemaker."

Duval, sneering, pulled Sasha's elbow and she started to leave.

"Be careful," Pym said. "Don't trust these fuckers."

Sasha, walking backwards, said, "You're the one I should not have trusted." Then she disappeared with Duval into a gaggle of black men wearing gold chains around their necks.

Pym found Cindy ordering beer. She asked, "What the hell was that all about?"

"Sasha was a friend of George's. She's that old fucker's sex slave. I tried to help her but she wouldn't have any of it."

"Yuck. How do you find these scumbags?"

"I think it's a question of seek and ye shall find."

"Now there's a quote taken gloriously out of context." Cindy handed him a bottle of beer. Pym said, "At least I'm trying." She put her arms around his neck and started dancing. He felt foolish. She was drunk and he didn't like it.

On the dance floor she was just starting to press some pelvis when Pyke broke through the crowd. He wore a light blue shirt and Indian jewelry. He shrugged at Pym, touched Cindy on the shoulder, and said, "Sorry. We've been called in. Gang shooting on Poydras."

There came Sorry sorry sorry and the rest of it, and suddenly, not far behind Cindy and with a never-before-experienced sense of relief, Pym had left the House of Blues and was dodging tourists on Decatur where a group of drunken Chinese girls walked ahead of him, getting obnoxious in a way they'd never dare at home. Cheap cheap cheap, tacky tacky tacky. His head ached from the noise and beer at the House of Blues. A huge cargo vessel, its masts lit up, passed beyond the levee, and a streetcar loaded with tourists passed in the opposite direction.

The girls stopped and he had to walk through the middle of them as they parted, giggling, but too afraid to touch. Opposite the closed gates of Jackson Square, the wild bum Liam Toth stood in the middle of a flower bed abusing tourists, mules, police officers—all who wouldn't listen. "What the fuck are you guys doing here? Trying to get laid? Dream on, fatso. What are you looking at? Hey, Mule, don't fuckin' flick your ears at me, you dumb bastard. Officer! You're supposed to arrest me for this! God I hate this place. I'm dead. I'm in Hell. Stupid niggers and white trash, moving like shoals of tuna fish." He pointed at some women wearing Iowa State sweatshirts and sang, *Fat bottom girls you make the rockin' world go 'round.*

Pym couldn't walk between the park railings and the waiting buggy rides because of the wads of tourists, so he crossed the road. As Liam Toth's wide blue eyes picked him up, Pym registered it and stopped. They stood still for a moment, looking at each other.

Toth shouted, "I know you!"

Pym saluted him and Liam grinned, revealing the knocked-out history of his big mouth.

* * *

In fading light, he tried to write a postcard for George, or was it Cindy? Without a table he found writing difficult. The note pad kept listing and his writing made no sense. He wanted to condense a message about the men on horseback who had saved him from the women in the milk bath. He wanted to find the men again and be with them.

In the dark of his hotel room, Pym struggled with something resembling a pencil before being stopped by what sounded like the rustling of a wedding dress. He remembered the sound of Laura as she walked up the aisle with him. After Laura left him, she'd said, "God, Gilbert, who invented love? I should marry his executioner." Was this Laura in the room? Surely not. He heard the dress slip to the floor and the bed covers lift. A warm, velvet-skinned woman, moist from the humidity, rolled onto him, kissed him, and tweaked his nipples.

He tried to joke, "Cindy, I thought better of you..." But he couldn't continue because his mouth filled with tongue.

She rode him in the dark before he could wake up properly. She whispered. "Don't worry. Just come in me, you deserve it. I've been a bitch." When he came, it triggered her, and she seemed to fly around the room, shrieking. Then she laid quietly on top of him, kissing his mouth, smelling of cookies.

Pym woke into light and at first felt pleased that a life-long wish had been granted—that one could get properly laid in a dream. But his inner voice registered alarm, and an old word, *succubus*, lodged somewhere between the text of the dream and an identification of the anxiety which frightened him, causing him to throw aside the bedclothes. He gasped at the bloodstained sheets. He immediately thought of Eddie—the darkness of the blood... hardly red, more black, but red at the edges. Was it Maddy last night? The blood was everywhere. Was it Cindy? How would she have gotten in? He startled suddenly and felt for his balls. They were gone. He looked down to understand that the blood was his. No they were intact, still there, just shrunk deep inside his torso from the terror.

He showered; it was a weird shower. He couldn't get clean—the blood was caked on like burnt okra. He called down and told Sammy about the problem.

Sammy said, "Mr. Pym, you din't hurt no one, did you?"

"Of course not. I had a nose bleed."

"You gonna drown in blood."

"Say what?"

"We takin' care of you, motherfucker."

"What's going on?"

"We want you out."

"Sammy, is that you?"

He went and looked at the sheets. There wasn't as much blood as he thought. He must have just freaked out. The blood had relocated; it covered the room—symbols scribbled on the walls. His brother's corpse lay in the bed with its jaw slack and gaping, just flung there. Pym couldn't stop shivering. He opened the French windows but there was no light in the street, just a wall of utter darkness. He looked along the balcony and saw the darkness creeping along the railings, devouring everything. He ran inside, closed the doors, started backing up as the darkness seeped under the door like black powder. He lifted the phone but it was sticky and viscous. George started sitting up in the bed, turning his eyeless face toward Pym. His face was crumbling, but he was freshly made-up like a harlot. There were spirits in the room. He could feel but not see them. "Wake me up! Somebody wake me up!" he screamed.

"This is it, Gillie," said George. "This is Hell."

Pym flew across the room to the door and tried to open it. He had to pull hard. It was like someone held the handle the other side. His brother used to do that. George crawled toward him across the carpet like a dog with a broken back. Pym yanked the door open and a woman in a wedding dress leered into his face. The darkness inhabited the hallway and people he loved struggled, suffocating, in its noxiousness—Terry, Vera, Sammy, Laura. The woman reached out for him, muttering in French. He flew backwards, sat atop the wardrobe. She started gnawing on George's face; George screamed, wet shit bubbling out of his ass. She pointed at Pym, rustled toward him with blood staining the front of her dress. He flew to the French windows, threw them open, and stepped onto the balcony, breathing in the darkness. He started climbing the railing, preparing to launch himself, preparing to fly to the river and follow it home to Minnesota and the safety and oblivion of Estelle, but the old bride's icy hand came up through his legs and pulled his cock off.

"Don't jump, old chap. You'll hurt yourself."

Across the narrow street stood Terry, looking up at him.

"I see you can't wake up," Terry said. "Well, the only thing to do under such circumstances is to take control. Read the symbolism. It's all you. You've not been allowing yourself shame. I can only be proud of you if you tell the truth to yourself."

"But supposing I'm dead? What good's the truth then?"

"It would be the text you'd take to the grave. Here are the remains of one Pym—he told the truth at the end."

"Fuck!"

"I find it appalling that you even use that word in dreams."

"I'm having trouble learning."

"It can get worse, you know."

"Oh, no. Please."

He was awake.

His whole body shook. He had never been so afraid. It was a chill, emanating in the spine. His heart pounded. The dream had released him at last and spat him back into the temporary safety of daylight. The French windows were open... sparrows chirped outside. He looked around the room. It was more frightening than being tied up and threatened by Eddie—he'd choose that any day. Cut my throat, but don't send me a dream like that again.

The face, the old bride's face rose from the end of the bed. "No one sent the dream," she said. "Remember!"

He started screaming again. He ran along the wall, out of the window, up and over the roof; he leapt into the sky and swam through the air. He could see her down there on the balcony looking up at him. From on high he could see the water gathering out of the blackness, a great frozen tsunami that could break any second and swamp the city. Who could he save? He could only carry one. And the old bride would be down there. He would face her, if he could save just one. Who would it be? A terrible decision. It would be one who still lived. It would be old Terry. Yes, Terry. He swam down through the black and into the courtyard the opposite side of the hotel from where the old bride stood on his balcony. He landed hard, *thump*, on the balcony outside Terry's French windows and started hammering on them so that the glass rattled.

A light went on. He kept hammering, calling out.

The door opened and Terry stood there, Vera behind him.

"What the bloody hell's going on?"

"Terry, get him inside quick. Something's happened."

This felt different. The hands touching him contained warmth, like real hands. His cock was still there although it did indeed have blood on it and was shot through with pain like someone had thrust an umbrella down his piss-pipe and then opened it. He stood naked and shivering in Terry and Vera's room. Screams still came out of him; he tried to stop them.

Terry took him in his arms and said, "It's all right, boy, you're all right, son."

Terry held him tight. Pym smelled his aftershave, his skin, and perhaps a trace of Vera's soap in his hair. "You're all right, son," Terry said. "Just calm down now."

His heart, a drumbeat before execution, began to slow. His mouth tasted of old coffee. A chill ague oozed from his spine.

"I flew here," he said.

"We all did," said Terry, patting his shoulder.

"He's somnolent," said Vera. "He's stuck in a dream."

"Why's he naked?"

"Perhaps he's been mugged. See it all the time in Lewisham."

"He's got blood all over his John Thomas."

Vera pulled him from Terry, wrapped a blanket around him and sat him in the chair beside the desk on which lay a thick ring-binder with pungent, yellowing pages. She asked, "Should we take him back to his room?"

Pym looked up at her and said, "No fucking way, man. I'm not going in there." He started weeping.

"My God, okay, okay, you can sleep in here, what's happened to you?"

"We have the extra bed. How fortunate."

"Shut up."

"I've been such a jerk. I didn't realize. I don't know how to put it right."

"I'll make tea," said Vera.

She made tea with the standard coffee paraphernalia that comes with hotel rooms.

"So this is real? Am I outta the dream?"

Terry stroked his head, tears in his eyes, and said, "Some say life's a dream that we wake up from only in death."

"Oh, Terry," shouted Vera, "For God's sake! Lay off, will you? You'll send the kid back into the horrors."

"Are you suggesting he dropped acid? Some sort of hallucinogenic?"

"Well?"

"Bad trip?"

"I remember those well. Now I only have to put up with you."

"Thank you, darling."

Pym laughed, wiped the water away from his eyes, and said, "Now I know I'm back into reality. You two are bickering."

"Were you smoking the wacky-backy, old son?"

"No, sir."

"Mushrooms?"

"No, sir."

"Any pharmaceuticals at all?"

"Not that I'm aware of. I've never experienced anything like that. It was so fucking real. I just got my ass kicked."

"You look like the Dying Gaul before he fell."

"That's enough, Terry!"

"As I said earlier, drawing down the wrath of Hera..."

"Don't you dare identify me with Hera, she's a harridan."

"Dreams are all we're made of. Hopes and terrors that make themselves monstrous in dreams are reflections of who we're being. What the hell have you done to get blood all over yourself?"

Pym looked down, saw the blood caked there, and had no answer.

XIX

Terry watched from the chair by the bathroom as Pym woke up. Vera, a great breathing pile of bedclothes who had taken over the whole bed, still slept. The boy's bleary gaze rested on her, no doubt wondering where he was. "Good morning, sport," said Terry, so that Pym turned his head. "How are you feeling?"

"Embarrassed."

"I expect you are. Like when you wet the bed."

"Oh, a lot worse, trust me."

"Did you imbibe anything? Tell the truth."

"Hell no. Only a few Dixies."

"Ah well, there, you see—American beer."

Pym laughed. "Am I going nuts?"

"I don't know, but even in New Orleans you can't be running around naked in the middle of the night."

"I wasn't running."

"What then?"

"Flying."

"Oh, that's much clearer."

Pym laughed.

"Big day for you today. Perhaps that's what brought it on."

"What's 'it'?"

"In layman's terms, some form of anxiety-spun sleepwalking, I expect. Very nasty, but ultimately harmless. However, you've told me about a number of dreams that seem to be pretty powerful. I'm getting a bit worried about you."

"You were in the dream."

"I didn't give you permission to put me in your dream."

"You were spouting wisdom, as usual."

"Phew." Like a pompous thespian, Terry wiped his brow and twinkled, trying to send the message that Pym's nightmare had been disarmed and was meaningless, but the young man's face remained long and haunted. "Now," Terry tried, "you have an entourage arriving from Minneapolis today, and a cremation to attend. Are you up for it?"

"No."

"I'm not sure we can postpone it."

"I'll get through it. I guess."

"Indeed you will. Then this can all start fading into the past."

"But right now it's in the future."

"Stand in the future, my boy, and it will become past soon enough."

From under the bedclothes Vera grunted. Terry and Pym grinned.

* * *

Estelle thought people would dress a lot better in New Orleans. She sat up front in the airport limo, next to the Caribbean-looking driver, and watched the people on the streets. Nina, Mishawn, and Dashiell laughed about something in back; it could've been the driver, who, Estelle supposed, might seem handsome to them. Others from Minneapolis had promised to come to the funeral but they hadn't shown up. Dashiell surprised her with his presence; she wondered what it meant.

She ached for Gilbert. His words on the telephone, all jammed up as they were, encouraged her. Everything would work out between them. No more sneaking behind people's backs… just she and Gil together. They'd build a life, have a kid, a perfect one. She'd have one of those caesarian sections. New Orleans reminded her of West Saint Paul—pretty shabby. She couldn't imagine why George loved it so much. Love can sure be a dangerous commodity, she thought.

* * *

A lot of people Estelle didn't know accompanied the little funeral party across the Mississippi in the big ferry. It was formal and sad. Estelle liked how wide the river was here. It was the same river she lived in the middle of in Minneapolis, but it didn't at all feel like the same river. Usually, when people weren't talking to her she didn't think, but she had to think all the time now and her head ached.

It struck her that she hadn't been consulted on the cremation, but she didn't linger on it. The service for George was held at a small funeral home on Teche Street in Algiers. Estelle had no idea who set it all up. There was a small brass band of old black men in strange uniforms to walk with the coffin from the ferry. It was pleasant enough, not what she would've liked, but many people whom she didn't know walked behind her in the procession, which George would've liked.

The funeral sped by and felt anticlimactic and meaningless. Estelle, walking behind the coffin between Gilbert and Nina, arms linked with them, loved the way her clothes felt on her; she wished she could see herself. There was something damn sexy about funeral attire. And here she was getting the best of two worlds: the sorrowful widow, and the coy fiancée. She could hardly believe the way it was all turning out, and she was amazed by all the people present, especially those who had traveled from Minneapolis with her to say goodbye to George.

* * *

When Estelle entered the hotel lobby Terry let out an involuntary whistle, which resulted in Vera giving him a whack on the arm. Sammy and Rick turned as Estelle walked in and their mouths dropped open. Cindy, who was getting ready to rush away with the cameraman, Pyke, sat back down and frowned.

It was now evening, and the mourners gathered in the small lobby of the hotel and clustered around the bar, where Tibone attempted to meet the demand. The Langleys had not attended the funeral since Vera felt unwell. Estelle should have arrived hours ago with Pym's mother, Nina. After the service they avoided speaking to anyone and then stayed over in Algiers to walk along the levee. Nina was upset. She couldn't bear showing that sort of weakness and needed to walk with Estelle in order to compose herself. Estelle would take her mother-in-law back to the Richelieu to change, then meet up with the others.

Pym laughed.

Asking Cindy to go with him to the funeral was an act of insanity, which he'd only been saved from by Cindy's lunatic schedule. Estelle looked at him, sad. An emotion shot through him—it was relief. She wore a plain charcoal suit and pumps, and her hair was pulled back conservatively; she could be selling cosmetics or pharmaceuticals, but the effect of her unmistakable shape, the tight rolling roundness of her hips, the inward curve of her lower spine, the proudly pushed up chest, the long neck and powerful jaw, was phenomenal. Pym imagined Sammy's tongue lolling out onto the floor, and he laughed more. Through his laughter he said, "For those of you who weren't at the funeral, this is my sister-in-law, Estelle."

Terry stood and stepped smartly up to her, extending his hand. "Oh, my dear," he said, "I wish we were meeting under happier circumstances. I'm Terrence Langley—Gilbert's... friend." His usual slump had vanished and he stood tall, above Estelle, looking down into the deep pillow of her breasts; he seemed to be breathing in her essence. Vera winced with cynicism and shook her head. Pym heard her mutter, "Oh, how the mighty fall."

Estelle inclined her head and smiled. At-a-girl, thought Pym. Just don't open your mouth. But then he became aware of the absence of his mother. He frowned and asked where she was.

Estelle shrugged and said, "She sent me ahead. She'll make her own way later."

Pym noticed Vera holding Terry's hand tightly.

Cindy Sorensen looked at Pym and frowned and then smiled. It was like Laura's pissed-off smile. Pym wanted to laugh even more because it was the same technique that Laura would use to indicate disdain and intimidation.

* * *

Vera sucked in her breath, causing Terry to look around the hotel lobby to discover the gaze of a white-haired woman. The gaze came from eyes, large and blue, set a little too close together, and the woman's forehead, high and square, displayed the arched eyebrows of someone telepathically adept. The long hair, gathered like a cumulus cloud around her square shoulders, produced in Terry the immediate impression that he was being looked upon from heaven. The woman's eyes shifted to Vera and registered shock.

Vera muttered, "It's her, isn't it?"

When the truth struck, that before him stood his decades-old obsession, Nina Pym, Terry felt a sensation akin to a heavy bell dropping through his torso. His left hand hurt from Vera's grip, causing him to glance at her and predict with uncanny accuracy what she'd say next.

293

"I knew this would happen one day."

Nina Pym stood still, her hands and feet pressed together, until her son Gilbert saw her and went over to greet her. He bent to kiss her on the cheek, feigning a touch with both hands on her back, then withdrew farther than a son normally would from a mother before leading her to a chair by the window. As she walked with him she looked over her shoulder at Terry.

Vera said, "I knew that bitch would take your breath away."

"Darling, don't be silly."

"Silly! Don't be such a prat, Terry. Here's me with a puffy arm and no breasts. Why am I being silly?"

"Because your immediate assumption is that I'll skip away with the wicked witch of the west and live craftily ever after."

"Don't try to be funny."

"It's been thirty-two years."

"I know you too well, mate."

"Come on now, stop it."

"You're a bastard... I know you."

Terry slid his arm across Vera's shoulder, pulling her a little closer, and said, "Who's your old stick, then? Come on, give us a kiss."

"Don't try to make friends."

He laughed and said, "Oy never done nuffink, yer Honour."

"Yes, you did. You let her cattle-drive your libido for three decades."

"Darling, you are clever. I wish I'd said that."

"You will, Terry, you will. And everyone will know how clever you are."

"Thou art a bitter fool."

"Thou art a stupid old git."

"Come on now... Vera? That rational person I love? I call thee forth. Away with Bitch-Cow, the beastly Terry-hater."

Vera laughed.

They finished their drinks.

Vera stiffened again minutes later when Nina Pym stood and moved tentatively across the lounge toward them. Gilbert chatted to Estelle and Sammy, after introducing them, and didn't appear to have noticed his mother making her move. She kept coming until she stood above where Terry and Vera sat. She gazed, fascinated, for a few seconds at Terry, then looked to Vera and with a beatific smile and asked, "May I speak with him?"

Vera looked at Terry, shrugged, and said, "Of course." She rose, hiding her puffy arm under her pashmina and went upstairs. Terry stared after her, willing her to look back at him as she ascended. When he turned his attention to Nina, her smile was slit-eyed, pout-lipped, and lascivious.

"Hello, Nina," he said. To which she replied, "Hello, your highness."

Terry laughed and said, "Not these days."

Nina sat, never taking her eyes off him. "Your lovely wife has warmed the seat for me."

Terry gazed at her. "You amaze me. You're just as much trouble as you always were."

"I'm worse now. You left me to stew for thirty years. You look fabulous."

"Vera can lip read, you know."

"She's gone."

"She'll be watching from somewhere."

"I never stopped loving you."

He wanted to say, *Nor I you,* and take her in his arms, but instead he clung to his integrity despite a rude blush invading his face. He tried to turn this high emotion to anger, and said, "Still no boundaries, I see."

"You were never much for boundaries yourself. My god, those thrusts..."

"That was then."

"You still light up a room. A day hasn't gone by since you left me that I haven't wanted you. I always wanted you... you know that."

"I'm not sure what to say."

"Keep quiet then. I'll talk for both of us. Losing you didn't help me like that stupid fucking husband of mine obviously thought it would. It just got worse. I could've been faithful to you, but Michael Pym got you on his side, didn't he? The Pyms are all bastards."

"Even Gilbert?"

"Gil's a Langley, as you very well know."

"You're extraordinary. Thirty years and you sound the same, even say the same sorts of things. You're still an agent of chaos, aren't you?"

"Only to those who can't handle me."

"And who are they?"

"Everyone but you. I was your faithful mare. You should've ridden me into the sunset."

295

Terry wanted to say he still could, but what came out was a lame pacification. "Well, Nina, thirty years is a long time, a lot of water under the bridge, and the sunset's—"

"It's not a long time, not really. We look older but we don't change inside. You walked away from your perfect match. You had to be bad to get me and you didn't want to be bad, but you ended up bad anyway by hiding away in England without me. I would have taken over that country."

Terry laughed and said, "Yes, you'd go down well over there."

Nina's eyes sparked with mirth and she gave him a little slap. "Go down? Ha! You're still a sicko!"

He could smell her skin. It would be natural just to begin making love to her here, right on the carpet. He still knew how she thought; he could predict the words going through her mind. Thirty years was indeed not very long.

"Did you think of me?"

"What do you think?"

"How much?"

"Nina, it's not right to talk about this. Not this way at least. I have Vera, and I have to look after her."

Nina stared, mad blue eyes skewering into his, and gently touched his face. "That just made it worse," she said. "You come over here to help out a boy who doesn't even know you're his daddy, and even though you must be longing to jump my bones, you're steadfast in your loyalty to Vera. You're a prince—just what I knew you'd turn into."

"After all that frog kissing you did."

She laughed, but her eyes filled with water.

Terry said, "Come on now, Nina, let's change the subject. What about George? What about Gilbert?"

"Gil's out of his mind and George left the building."

"How are you feeling about that?"

"He thought he had the wrong body, so he got rid of it. He's around somewhere. He's all right, I'm sure. George is very resourceful."

"Is this how you really think or are you in some kind of denial?"

"Ah, you're still a skeptic. I'd forgotten how frightened you are of the spirit world."

"We had some interesting talks about that, as I recall."

"Yes, and you were always a blind fool. Don't you get the sense that people are still around after they die? George is around here somewhere.

And Michael Pym... he's hanging around, watching and judging me—and still can't get it up."

"So what happened to Michael?"

"Threw himself off a bridge."

"Bloody hell."

"Couldn't handle me."

"So you haven't told Gilbert about us?"

"Not yet. George warned me not to. He said you wanted to handle it yourself."

"So you must've spoken to George as recently as I."

"Yes. He yelled at me. Gave me my orders. Told me I was a stinking, rotten mother and that everything's my fault. Then he demanded a thousand bucks to tide him over. I wish I hadn't had kids. They're a pain in the ass, especially when they die before you."

Her face went blank, sort of elongated, and Terry detected something going on in her, perhaps a virus protection program kicking in to keep agony at bay. He patted her shoulder, and she snapped out of it and smiled at him. Terry asked, "So what are you going to do about poor George's ashes? And how should I best handle Gilbert?"

"I forgot that you never ask one question at a time."

"That must be something I only do around you."

"I bet there's a lot of things you'll only do around me."

"Jesus, Nina."

"Thirty-two years I've been waiting to talk to you, so I sure as hell ain't gonna bother with small talk."

"I'm English. Small talk's our speciality."

With the sound of Nina's laughter came a flood of pictures—their morning trysts on the yellow couch, the way she held him stable when he drove around those steep freeway intersections, the taste of her vagina, the sound of her orgasms, the funny way she shopped but seldom bought anything. All this oozed from her laughter and his heart surged with the old pent-up longing for her.

He looked around the lounge and saw that Vera had somehow come back down and joined Gilbert and Estelle. They were glaring at Nina. He waved to catch their attention, and then called, "Come over here, you lot." Nina looked too, betraying a trace of disappointment, yet retaining the smile while Vera and Gilbert walked over to them. Estelle bent to say something to Sammy.

"We're all sorted," Terry said. "Aren't we, Nina?"

"I guess," she said. "Whatever that means."

Gilbert frowned, uncomprehending.

"Let's have a cocktail."

"The universal British solution."

"The British are coming!"

Nina laughed, Vera frowned, and Gilbert asked, "What the fuck's going on?"

* * *

What's this? thought Pym. Ma going after Terry?

It astounded him. In New Orleans for her son's funeral and she's shamelessly hitting on the most exotic thing in pants. Fucking old bitch. He tapped Estelle's arm and said, "Look at that." Estelle laughed, then stifled it, alerting Pym to Vera's sudden presence beside them.

"I may need a drink soon," Vera said.

Pym sensed Vera stiffen and felt immediately protective toward her so that with some severity he asked, "What's going on?"

"All in good time, dear boy, all in good time. Off you go and order us a round of Hurricanes."

Estelle took his arm and said, "Come on."

At the bar Pym said, "How do I put a stop to it?"

"She's barely human," said Estelle.

"Poor Vera. Someone should kill my stupid mother."

Tibone mixed Hurricanes with one eye on Estelle's breasts. Then, in the mirror in back of the bar, Pym saw Nadine walk into the lounge and stand still, looking around. The shock of seeing Nadine caused a sensation in him like a greased javelin thrust up his anus. Nadine, her dreadlocks hanging, wore a black dress, heels, and carried a large shoulder purse. She resembled a normal person out for a drink at a nice lounge. Old Sammy went over to Nadine and gave her something small, which, without thanks, she accepted and slid into the purse. Her eyes found Pym in the mirror. He sighed and turned to face her. She glanced for a second at Estelle and then back at him. A warning tried to get through in the guise of frightening images. He'd seen a movie once where a vampire had gone into a room like this and massacred all present. Or was it that Edgar Allen Poe story where the personification of the plague enters the sealed environment and infects everyone. The javelin effect in his bowels screamed of extreme danger, but he didn't know what to do about it. He remembered that he was charged by Nadine with killing Duval and looked around for Rick, but Rick was gone.

"Who's that?" asked Estelle.

"That's Nadine Duval. Our resident Mambo."

"Oh, jeez."

Pym asked, "How does she do that with her eyes?"

"Do what?'

"They seem to be changing colors as I watch."

"Looks like a dingy old bag to me," said Estelle.

"That's because she doesn't want to alert you to the presence of a rival."

"Her? A rival? Like, for you? Your head's up your ass, bucko."

"She wants my baby."

Estelle guffawed, "Stop. You're killin' me."

"I'm serious. She's a truly insane person who thinks my mother qualifies me to father a mambo child with her. It's unbelievably bizarre and George set it all up in some weird way I haven't figured out. We're in for some sort of trouble, but I'm not sure what yet."

Estelle smiled, shrugged, and said, "Why don't I just go and rip her head off."

Pym couldn't help laughing and that made Nadine glare at him. Without taking his eyes off her he put his arm around Estelle and said, "Hold that thought, it might not be such a bad idea at the end of the day."

He wished he had a cell phone. He'd call Rick. Nadine had every right to be there; she was out on bail, there was little evidence against her. And she stood, waiting for him to give in and come to her. The barman shoved the drinks forward. Pym charged them to his room, and, with Estelle's help, took them over to the oldsters, who, all three, sat owl-eyed and nervous.

"Ah!" shouted Terry, "The cavalry."

Nina laughed. Pym glared at her.

Estelle wandered off as she liked to do, and Pym sucked down his drink in seconds. He was about to get another one when a tall transvestite accosted him. It took him a while to recognize Darryl from the House of Large Sizes.

"You have to come with me," Darryl said. "They've hurt her."

"Who's been hurt?"

"Sasha. They've hurt her. You have to come."

"Shit."

Pym didn't know how to do any of this. In films it was easy. People didn't have real emotions, and there weren't real consequences for violence and promiscuity. The body count mounts and no one cares. But this, this real life, was unbearable. "What do you want me to do, Darryl?"

"I don't know, Mr. Pym. She liked you. And you'll know what to do. I mean, you're kinda The Man, aren't you?"

Pym turned to Terry and said, "Sasha's been hurt. My presence is requested."

"Oh, don't get mixed up in anything, son."

"I won't, but she helped me a lot. I owe her. Just keep an eye on Nadine. She just walked in."

"You must be joking. Where is she?"

"You'll see her. I'd just as soon leave if she's here. If she says anything to me, I'll probably slug her and do more jail time than her."

"If we're not still down here when you get back, come to our room. I have to explain something important to you."

As he walked around the outside of the hotel, he could see in the windows and noticed Mishawn holding a drink and standing alone. She wore her little glasses and cardigan and khaki Dockers. She'd come down with Estelle and Nina, but Pym hadn't spoken to her yet. He saw Dashiell talking to the barman, and then saw Estelle talking to Nadine. He stopped and looked in the window at them. "Now that's not cool," he said. Estelle had her back to him and moved her hands around animatedly. She held a cigarette. Nadine saw him through the window and turned her face slightly with an expression of sufficient arrogance to make Pym want to smash through the window to get at her.

Darryl said, "We better hurry, Mr. Pym."

"Christ, this is all getting way out of control."

Pym walked under his own balcony and thought of Maddy and Eddie. That tragic incident, only two days ago, aside from being all his fault, was still, or should be, a present incident, yet it now seemed way in the past, as did his peregrinations through the streets of the Quarter with Sasha and Terry and Rick. It all seemed like a memory from long ago. As with the incidents in Minneapolis, he realized that there were always going to be consequences for egocentrically driven and untenable liaisons. He wasn't sure when it happened, but at some point before coming down to New Orleans he had committed himself to being a good guy. He'd forgotten that promise to himself and almost immediately his backsliding got punished with serious consequences. He stopped and looked up to the sky, which surprisingly was full of stars. "Okay," he said, "Okay!"

Darryl, clipping along beside him, laughed seriously, and said, "I do that sometimes."

"I guess we all do it. Tell me, Darryl, does life ever just start going too fast for you?"

"It's got about one gear for me, Mr. Pym. Nothin' ever goes smooth in this town. It's always like this. People fuckin' around all the time. I hate this goddamn place."

"You're not the first to tell me that."

"Everybody's stupid and obsessed and self-centered."

"So now tell me what happened to Sasha."

"Old Duval was there. Yelling in French. It was like a scene from that cartoon Beauty and the Beast. It all was about you. After a while Sasha came and told me to leave and lock up after me, which I did. I went to the café to tell Lulu. She was just getting off her shift, so we went back there and all the lights were off. I let us back in with the key, and, I don't know why, but I thought I better go upstairs. And there was Sasha, sitting in the dark, not moving. I got scared and came back down to the shop. Lulu stayed there while I came to get you."

"You didn't call the police?"

"Cops don't help the likes of us."

It took only minutes to get to the shop and sure enough, there was little Lulu crouched in the dark doorway, crying. Darryl kneeled to give comfort. "It all over," Lulu said. "We fucked now."

"No," said Darryl, "they'll get it all going again, wait and see."

Pym entered the dark shop, the other two following as far as the stairs where they stopped and let him go up alone. Sasha sat in a chair, all the lights off, backlit by the stove-light in the kitchenette. Pym couldn't place the funny smell in the room. He turned on a small standard lamp.

Sasha was all ripped up as though a leopard had mauled her. If there had ever been a Glamour wrapped around her it was gone now. She didn't acknowledge Pym's presence, just stared ahead like a body without a soul. Naked, save for a bloody beige blanket wrapped around her, she neither twitched nor shivered. Plopped on the carpet, resembling stranded jellyfish, lay two milky plasma sacks. Pym opened Sasha's blanket and saw where someone had slashed her breasts to remove the implants. He looked for other wounds but found none. This was enough, he realized. This was like killing her.

Pym looked for a phone but found none. He called to Darryl and Lulu. He gave Lulu Rick's card, but Lulu gave it back. "I not call that asshole." Pym took the card back and thought for a minute.

"Quick, Darryl, get an ambulance. Lulu, get more blankets. Sasha's probably in shock or something. What do you do in this situation? I've never heard of people getting their tits sliced up. Christ!"

He started to lightly tap Sasha's cheeks. "Come on, hon. Come back to us. We're gonna get you fixed up."

"It no good," said Lulu. "She got the dust in her. Make her stay like that."

"What dust? What are you talking about?"

Lulu shrugged and left to find blankets.

He understood; his brain clicked into gear. Time to stop being an oaf. He'd heard about the blowfish dust the Voudon used to make zombies. And here he was, in the middle of his worst nightmare, the very scenario that would stop him sleeping at night as a child. All the insane stories his mother told, and all the horrible films he was allowed to watch. And it's real. Oh, not in some supernatural sense, but certainly all done in the pursuit of the supernatural—a supernatural, however frightening, vastly preferable to the horror of oblivion. Nothing is more frightening than the despicable acts humans visit on one another.

He waited for an ambulance and watched Sasha's eyes staring off into nothingness, trying not to look at the blood; it reminded him of Eddie, and it was all his fault. Sasha, who despite her argument with the God she still believed in, remained a Roman Catholic and went to mass in Jackson Square on Sundays, mostly to be seen. He felt an uncomfortably great sorrow for her. And this was in some similar way the aftermath of his brother who had also died from a mutilation he put himself in the way of. Why do we not think of what lies ahead when we embark on our insane quests?

If I beat the shit out of Duval, I'll probably draw the wrath of this whole Voodoo community, and maybe even get prosecuted by the police. But if I don't, he thinks he can get away with this. Who will stand up for my brother and Sasha, and big old Darryl, and poor little Lulu? Who will stand up for the good-natured Mishawn? When, in their mania, they get this far beyond the pale of normality they need help, protection, support, but all they find are predators. I have to go after Duval. And Nadine. She should die. People like her are too dangerous to be allowed to live. Duval too. "I have to kill them."

It was like the voice came from somewhere else, not from within him, and it woke him out of his reverie. He found he was serious; he had decided to kill the Duvals. It was extraordinary—he'd never felt anything like it. The power of deciding, all on your own, that it was right to kill. How could it be right to kill? But here it was, the permission from nature itself, to take the law into your own hands and accept a deed for which no one else has the stomach. Before the death of George, Pym wouldn't have had the stomach either. But in the last few days he had seen dead and maimed bodies, and now he was ready to create some more.

* * *

Estelle felt so nervous she bummed a cigarette from Dashiell. Dashiell lit the cigarette for her and then sauntered away to impress the handsome barman. Nadine stepped in front of her. "So, you must be Estelle," Nadine said.

"Yes, and you're Nadine."

"That's right. I reckon he's told you a lot of bullshit about me."

"Which he? George or Gil?"

"George wasn't a bullshitter. That's why I'm here to pay my respects. Gil is a bullshitter. Georgie, she my friend... we trusted each other. You don't think George was easily fooled, do you?"

"Well... no."

"How about you? Are you easily fooled?"

"Probably."

"How many girlfiends you think Gilba Pym should have?"

"One."

Nadine thrust her face upward and laughed. "You crazy. You think a boy like that gonna change for you? Hell, he be fuckin' the whole city before he done."

"You're wrong about him. He's got a good heart."

"They all say that. Ask Old Sammy how Gilba Pym been fuckin' some Chicago chick so bad after like a day here, and her old man done went and kill hisself. Ask about Sasha, and the TV reporter chick he be sniffing after."

303

Yeah, he got a good heart in him for sure, sugar. He supposed to come down, find George, and he go hog-wild for pussy."

"What are you trying to do to me, telling me all this shit? You think it ain't enough to have George die and then have to drag his mother down here too? And organize everyone? And you start talking to me with your creepy agenda. I know all about you, you're a fucking lunatic!"

"You gonna zap someone's eye with that straight, baby."

"Fuckin' A."

"I hear you, I hear you."

"Like hell you do."

"Nobody appreciate you, you're all strung out, and here's a skinny nigger bitch talking trash about your man. It ain't nice of me, but I never said I was a nice... I ain't. But you are."

"What do you mean?"

"You try hard, don't you? You make your body just so and people don't notice the small details, like those delicate muscles in your neck, so strong yet feminine. Gilba don't notice that, huh? You're dynamite, and they take you for granted. I know... I been there. It's why I ain't so nice anymore. Bein' nice don't get you nowhere 'cept pregnant and alone. It's all bullshit."

"Well, you're right about people not appreciating what I do. You can't exactly draw attention to yourself by telling them."

Nadine laughed and said, "You go to Catholic school?"

"Yep."

"Sheeeit," said Nadine, placing her hand on Estelle's forearm. "Me too."

Estelle cried and laughed simultaneously.

Nadine said, "Come and sit down over here, girl."

Estelle sank into a soft sofa with a view through the plate glass into the street and watched the staggering crowds while Nadine went to the bar to get her a drink. The grief had started to hit her. All the organizing had kept it in abeyance, and then, when she arrived, Gil whisked her straight to his room and they made love gloriously, like people celebrating their right to live. She never before experienced such ardor from him. It was like he'd been drowning and her arrival saved him. She could feel his semen in her, and that had made her happy until Nadine's words took all the magic out of it. The son-of-a-bitch.

A bum pressed his face against the window, smearing his big lips and tongue and cheeks sideways. Estelle put her hand on the glass and gave him the finger. He pulled away and vigorously yessed his head. "In your dreams, granddad," she said.

Nadine was quick with the drinks, already on her way back, edging her way past people. Estelle was surprised that Nadine and Dashiell were acquainted. She wondered what the deal with Nadine would be. What was the angle? She'd play it out… wait and see.

Nadine handed her the big red drink and said, "Here you go, sugar."

It looked delicious. Estelle took a pull on the straw. It tasted amazing, almost psychedelic. "This is great," she said, and took another big suck of it.

"When we're done with these I want to show you a couple of places where George hung out. It'll interest you."

"I should probably stay here."

"The Quarter's only small, all within a five-minute walk. You'll be fine. You're with me, and this is my town."

Estelle shrugged, finished her drink greedily.

* * *

Pym caught a cab back from the hospital, and when he walked into the lobby-lounge he found several of those who had come to pay their respects to George still drinking although it was close to 3 a.m. Dashiell leant at the bar laughing with Tibone and turned to look at Pym as he entered. Tibone nodded at him. Mishawn curled like a cat on a sofa while three others, unknown to Pym, talked animatedly around her, seated at a low cocktail table. His mother, Terry, and Vera were gone. He was glad there was no cowboy—what was that guy's name?

He needed a nightcap after what he had just experienced. He went to where Dashiell stood with Tibone and said, "A brandy Manhattan, stirred not shaken."

Without looking at him, Tibone said, "Yes, Mr. Pym."

"How you doing, Pym sibling," asked Dashiell. "I'm so sorry about Georgie."

Pym looked him in the eyes and said, "I reckon you ought to be. It was your idea he come down here." He kept his gaze on Dashiell. A white anger flowed in him. He thought of what to do, how in a few viscious strikes he would destroy the monstrosity standing before him. Dashiell's mouth dropped open a little and he backed away slightly, glancing quickly at Tibone, who kept mixing the drink. A sort of swelling took place in Tibone's forehead. Dashiell said, "Hey, you know people make their own decisions."

"And that's the only reason why I'm not going to hospitalize you."

"Gee, thanks."

"You're not worth going to jail for. You're a piece of shit. You and people like you."

"Georgie was my friend..."

"Crap! You used him, you son of a bitch."

Tibone pushed the drink across the bar. It was on a small white doily. Pym picked it up, took a pull from it and then put it down again, missing the doily. He still needed to hit Dashiell and Dashiell knew it. Pym could smell the fear coming off him.

What the fuck, Pym thought, just one good punch. But Mishawn stood between them before he could let fly. She asked, "How you doing, Pym sibling?"

"Really, really badly," he said, still not taking his eyes off Dashiell. Mishawn touched his arm and said, "Come on, hon." Pym looked at Tibone and said, "You know who Sasha is? The Queen of the Quarter?"

Tibone nodded.

"They cut her breasts out tonight. The Duvals. I got her to the hospital. She nearly bled to death. She's in some sort of waking coma. It could happen to any of you. You better all make sure you toe the line." Tibone stared at him, blank.

Mishawn said, "Hey, Pym sibling, I reckon it's bedtime."

* * *

Pym entered the dark room, found his way to the bedside, and turned on the lamp. Estelle slept and didn't stir. He undressed and showered. The room could've been from a hundred years ago. He heard noises in the hallway—someone drunk. Estelle's eyes looked sunken; she was feeling all this much more than she showed. He would be a good guy now. He would marry his brother's widow like in the Old Testament and make sure she's happy. No more bullshit. This shit is the result of bullshit. Chaos, horror, and despair. He lay down and thought through the chain of events and found himself the main link in all of them. In a while he'd be over it, not feeling so bad. Try to do better.

Estelle barely breathed. She seemed to sink into the bed. She smelled like she'd been working out and hadn't taken a shower. Wide awake, Pym's mind lingered in the ER. He'd gone with Sasha in the ambulance and had one of the cops that turned up call Rick, who found him there later. The experience condensed down to a few awful moments: The lead medic asking what relation Pym was to the injured party and the resulting confusion as to what his relationship actually was with Sasha; the consternation in the ER when the doctors could find no reason for her catatonic state other than shock; seeing Sasha without her powerful Glamour was heartbreaking—she wasn't a she anymore, just a washed up Tranny who still looked like a man. Pym fancied that somewhere in her trance she was free, maybe walking along a beach naked, just a normal woman. He hoped so.

XX

The babble in the hotel lounge grew so profound in Terry's ears that he got up and fled suddenly into the street, where he sucked air gratefully. The walls are crumbling, he thought, must escape, be away from this for a while. Once a plunging young Paris, sweeping Nina out of the arms of her ponderous husband, he himself now resembled a gaunt, compromised Priam, impotent even to save his saintly Hecuba from her burgeoning arm.

All full of hurricane juice, Terry loped into the night lest some fool haul him back inside the hotel. His bladder nagged to be emptied, but he ignored it. To Pat O'Brien's I shall wend my un-merry way, fleeing like Aeneas from the tectonic squeeze of ancient obsessions. Quiet this clatter in your mind. If you ever wrote down anything, it would help. Too lazy, like an inept chthonic god lost in dreams and paralysis when the deadly new order declares war. Good-for-nothing bastard. Lucky is all, fell on your feet, otherwise no fancy job you'd have, a tramp you'd be—Psychology all-the-rage back then. Heal thyself? Reality catches up, and you find yourself running naked in the storm like the old mad king who did everything wrong. Nina, Nina, Nina, why did I leave you?

He wept as he negotiated the raised sidewalks—revelers gazed at him.

It's something to avoid, something to explain carefully to my Gilbert. What do I mean by 'it'? I mean don't walk away from passion until it's truly spent, otherwise it'll sit in you like a horseradish plant, expanding annually, hot and deep-rooted until it chokes out everything else in your garden. Gilbert mustn't lose his Estelle. It's plain they magnetize. What is that term for positive and negative clapping together like they do? Curious that I remember so little.

Terry wandered to St. Peter Street and stood outside Pat O'Brien's. Nothing remotely Irish about it—a tourist trap. Need some sport. Don't get

punched again. Tease the Irish if they're there. Usually find them everywhere, looking for an easier life, then sulking about exile and the loss of
home. Loads of them here, New York, and Boston. And Liverpool stuffed
with 'em since. Niggers of Europe, Lennon said. Isolated on the fringe,
drifting ever toward tribalism and song. Good folk though; love 'em really,
only ones with the craic like me, only ones who get my jokes. Their blood
in me from my father so bastardly absent... bloody fucking abandoning git!

Terry went into O'Brien's and found the toilet.

Bathroom they call it. Restroom. I'm going to rest. Have a bath. Toilet
sounds rude to their ear. Puritanical nation, bristling with weapons of mass
destruction. Antipersonnel devices. Orwellian future maturing like a tumor.
We could all see it coming—no one really running the show, just a Zeitgeist
in a suit and a plastic haircut. No, I am no Nostradamus, nor was meant to
be, just a... what is it... deferential something-or-other... glad to be of use.
Ugh, your leaky brain! Muck out the Baaaaaathroom. Herculean hoof, clean
up after the sheep. Your thought process will one day produce an aneurism
and you'll suffer premature mortality in a paroxysm of neurology. When
your son visits you in Hades he'll find you aphasic and drooling, playing
Solitaire with Ronald Ray-Gun, with no clear advice except stay out of here
as long as possible—a shade of yourself.

At the piscine, Terry voided into a pile of ice and laughed at the luxury, as if pissing into ice could cool you off. Some fat bastard stood two
down, staring at the ceiling, unable to piss. The equestrian potency of Terry's stream no doubt made it worse for the poor man—funny how we associate an inability to piss while being watched with a lack of manhood. When
Terry's stream ended, pre-cum remained present. My God Nina, what have
you done? He pressed his glans and more sticky stuff rolled out, clear and
glistening, a solution he hadn't seen in years. He had to go into a stall and
wipe himself with a tissue.

When he came out, the fat man still stood, trying to piss, with veins
standing out on his neck. "You need to get your prostate checked, mate,"
said Terry.

The man turned on him, wild eyed, and said breathlessly, "Fuck off,
you faggot."

He fucked off rapidly, then selected one of the many bars in the
O'Brien's complex and entered, painting on his approachable grin. A group
of fat people sucked something out of the head of a child through straws.

No, not a child, but a multi-gallon receptacle full of booze. Mindless Americans sucking hurricanes from the brains of angels. Me next. Lobotomize me, oh Lord, in America Thy dwelling place. He retreated into the street. He'd seen another pub on his travels, more authentic. Where? Ah, south of a French city. Bordeaux, Marseilles. Ridiculous bloody memory. He walked over an odd-looking manhole cover, bumped into a very solid tramp coming the other way, turned right, walked straight ahead, searching hard for the right word. How can we even pretend to have lives when we remember so little? Barely alive in this illusion.

O'Flaherty's on Toulouse, that's it! Ah, see—lucky. Luck of the partially Irish. Irish when I'm partial to being so. A sign said: "Premiership football and full Irish breakfast served all day." Irish eyes beguiling, begob.

He went in, stood inside the door, and looked at the pool tables, low-slung lampshades and dart board; smelled the spilled beer and cigarette smoke. A black-haired waitress sat on a stool, smoking and talking to a shaven-headed barman decorated with tattoos and silver piercings. They both looked at Terry and then looked away. In a corner a knot of men seated at a round table turned to face him. They looked British but he wasn't sure why. The music wasn't too loud—Mary Black singing an old sad ballad. It isn't hair or eyes or shape of face that distinguishes them. What is it? Genotype. He's drawn to them like a squid to light. Think of what it is, perhaps ask: Why is it I can clock you cunts at a mile yet you all look different? Better not start with that.

"God save all here," said Terry.

They looked startled. One cocked his head and said, "And may the Lord God also protect you."

"I'll need bloody saving soon… this town's killing me."

"He's one of us," said the meatiest.

"He's another Brit," said a bald one, "trying to fraternize."

Another, red tufted and freckled, thick bespectacled like himself, said in rough Glaswegian, "That's cuz there's nay cunt in this toon tae talk tae."

A tiny one, Jagger-lipped and sozzle-eyed, with a layer of dandruff on the shoulders of his black concert T-shirt, punched the sweaty-sock lightly, and said, "Ay, and what cunt wud understand you?"

They all laughed.

"Ah," said Terry, "my ears ring with the mingled accents of our fair green isles. May I join you, gents, or are you a closed unit?"

"Price for joining," said the first one, an eye twinkling mad and green, "is a shout, and a damn good excuse for your toffee-nosed accent." They all laughed.

"The latter first," said Terry, bowing. "Greatly against my will, I was sent at a tender age by my mother to Roedean School."

"Sassenach bastard."

"Half Kilburn, half Islington."

"Poor sod!"

"Catholic and Protestant am I, Celt and Saxon and Norseman all. And when they place the pennies on my eyes none of it will matter a Tinker's damn."

The Glaswegian let out a guffaw, and said, "He's gud, he's gud."

One of them said, "I suppose we're all that here. But we need more assurance that your pusillanity won't infect us with gobbus flagmaticcus."

The bald one gaffawed and said, "Ya drunken feckin eejit, what ya talking about?"

Friend, thought Terry. A man my own age who makes up words and has no idea what the hell he's talking about. Could do with a male friend... never had one, all women. He said, "No, I am indeed of the gutter like yourselves."

"Thank God for that."

"This is a ridiculous conversation."

"Different though, innit."

"In reaction to growing up a dim-witted dope, I over-educated myself and am now stuck in a poncy profession."

"No professions mentioned tonight, please."

"Welcome to the round table, oh grizzled, four-eyed wanker."

"Leave your lance by the door, please, sir."

"The Guinness is crap here, but I'll have one."

"Mine's a Jammy's."

"One ay they hurricane bastards fur me, mate."

"Do they do them here?"

"When you're buying, yes."

Terry raised an arm to the waitress. She nodded, put her cigarette down, shook out her hair and strolled across, shorter and stouter than she looked when sitting. In the same instant, Terry noticed a man with a big nose and pockmarked cheeks standing in the doorway, staring at him. The waitress took their orders, shaking her head and making them repeat everything, smiling reluctantly at all the shit they gave her while the pockmarked man continued to loiter in the doorway, looking, Terry realized with slight alarm, at him with considerable malice.

As the waitress rolled away, the Glaswegian said, loud enough for the guy to hear but probably not understand, "Wha's this cunt in the doorway lookin' at?"

"Hey, Gaddifi! Are we making too much noise?" asked Slab-Face.

The pockmarked man's eyes narrowed venomously, but he slid backwards and disappeared.

"That was a queer one."

"Ominous."

"He was givin' oor Sassanach the evil eye."

"Shall we go out there and kick the shite out of him?"

"Later, maybe," said Terry. "Let's have a drink for the nonce." And away it went, the lovely brain-numbing splurge of clever intellect spilling from the mouths of men adapted to bar stools and dart boards. The topics leaping from the sickness of America to its finer points, but quickly turning to football—Arsenal's dominance, Man U's moneybags, Liverpool's fickle form, but mention of Celtic and Rangers well avoided lest fists fly, for no one apparently knew yet to which ilk the Glaswegian belonged. And all the time the cornucopia of cheap American luxury being shouted for and delivered. Until finally someone sensible, and it wasn't Terry, said, "Fuck's sake, can't you bastards talk about anything but football?"

"No."

"What else matters?"

"I mean, after they put the pennies on ya eyes, who feckin cares?"

"There you go."

"But here we are gathered in a decadent outpost of the great American empire as it moves forward in history in its wasteful and unconscious vigor, polluting the future, and all we discuss is football. Shouldn't we be discussing strategies for curtailing the power of the great Satan?"

A man had entered while Terry spoke, bringing cool air into the bar. He sat alone at the next table, staring at them, his sweatshirt emblazoned with an identifying emblem from the other football, the pride of his state, Wisconsin.

The others looked at each other after Terry's statement.

"Bit heavy for me."

"He's right, it is the great Satan, and this town is Satan's arse."

"They'll blow themselves up eventually. Need no help from us."

"Trouble is they'll take us with them."

"Say," the Wisconsinite interrupted, "Are you guys Australian?"

"No, we're fucking Bolivians."

"Fuck a littler duck."

"Oblivious."

"Stupid fecken Septic."

The Septic laughed nervously and skulked to the far end of the bar.

The glasses piled on the table; the ashtray filled.

In walked a well-dressed black man, wearing dark glasses, and looked around the room. One of the lads said, "Stevie Wonder."

Terry included, they all looked at him, laughing, but seeing something familiar. The man frowned, then grinned, showing a rack of big white teeth, and ambled over, saying, "Awright, lads? 'aving' a good night, are yer?"

They laughed and opened a seat for him.

"Now all we need is a Stani."

"An' a sheep-shagger—we're missing the Welsh."

"Have a drink, sunshine."

"'Oy, why doesn't he have to justify his Sassanach accent?'"

"Affirmative action, mate."

"An' cuz 'ee don't talk like a nancy-boy."

Where's our new mate from? Streatham? Shoulda guessed. Who do you support? Crystal Palace? Fuckin' hell, they're crap. I hate them. Jagger-mouth supports Donee Rovers, who are magically re-emerged from the hell of the Football Conference. Kennedy, predictably is Celtic. The two Kilarney boys have Liverpool season tickets, and the other one, who turns out to be an Ulsterman, supports Glentoran and draws gob-smacked stares at the admission. Terry's championing of the Gunners draws a round of boos—the Magnificent Seven, The Seven Dwarves, Seven Against Thebes, Seven Amigos, Severn Bores, the Seven Tossers of the Apocalypse.

Terry discovered only two of the Irish were together. The others, tourists all, drifted to this place for the same reason he did. Each sought his own kind this evening, each had troubles to escape, each constructed a hard facade to hide from the world a hurt so unspeakable that only the warmth of a pub and the laughter of like voices could get him through the night. Each evening new assemblies would meld and then sadly disperse when this island bastion amid Big Easiness stopped serving, to drag themselves, antilocuted and inebriated, back to power-hungry wives and lovers, fuming alone in untidy hotel rooms.

Kevin from Streatham laughed so hard that he had to stretch backwards to relieve his diaphragm. He kept laughing until it became infectious and Terry found himself doing the same, trying to ease the pain of out-of-control laughter. And in the ridiculous midst of it he thought of his dying wife and his under-threat son, his own invisible father, the looming breasts and lusting pelvis of Nina, and the frightening power of the Duvals; and yet he still laughed, the laughter parting all before it and filling the starved parts of him with the joy of being alive. And in that moment he loved what he was, not just a repressed old Englishman, but a man from the peculiarly shaped pair of islands in the North Sea, greened by the Gulf Stream, its inhabitants far more homogenous than they pretended to be, but retaining the loyalty of their regions and their dialects to the point of death. Here he sat, happy, among friends and enemies alike, locked together by language and libation in Fat City, Louisiana, the Casablanca of his dreams.

So it continued until time came for closing. Terry felt what he had predicted—sadness. If there is a heaven, he thought, let it be this. Let me be assigned to a corner of a pub with a mix of every one of us, religion, colour, and creed notwithstanding, and let me drink and laugh and talk about football until the universal cows fart their way home, and God, that bastard that doesn't exist gives a thumbs up for the fat lady's swan song. The compaction of the universe... phurrrrrrrrt.

Drunk now, Terry slurred, "I am an aging Lancelot..."

"No, you're not. Yoor pissed. Which of us is gonnae take the old cunt home?"

He heard their kind words, but the song came rolling out accompanied by tears and then they joined in as they lifted him to his feet and pulled his arms over their shoulders.

> And it's no, nay, never,
> No, nay, never, no more,
> Will I play the wild rover?
> No, never, no more.

"Oh, dear, once more into the breach..."

Kennedy took charge. "Och, he's a depressing auld fucker. Sooner we get him hame the better."

Terry wanted to tell him what a good lad he was despite his lack of teeth and bolloxed eyesight, but he couldn't form the words. They walked and walked and when they arrived, seemingly in minutes, in front of the familiar entrance to his hotel, he realized they were all with him, old Conner leading the way.

"Dis must be it, lads. Let's take him in and have the last one before we depart in pieces."

Lights spinning, the grain of the pavement looming up, Terry said to Sammy, "I'm drunk, Sam." There was another of those queer manholes between his shoes. "Gargoyles," said Terry, sweeping his hand over the manhole cover, "may I present the entrance to hell."

"I'll take him now," said Sammy.

Terry found himself at the turn in the staircase, looking down at his new friends, who stood at the bar, none as drunk as he, and at odd angles to each other like cows seen from a hot air balloon, or maggots in a Petrie dish. "Good night, boys!" he yelled and they looked up, laughing. "Tibone, their money's no good." Also standing in the doorway, glaring up at him, stood two men. One, black and muscular, had large eyes; the other, white, but swarthy and pockmarked with a large nose looked at him with such malevolence that it unnerved him. It was the Gaddifi look-a-like from earlier. I wonder who they are. I must have insulted them tonight and they don't know how harmless I am.

Sammy noticed them, pointed at them, and shouted, "Hey! Get the hell outta here!"

The swarthy one sneered and stood his ground, the other backing up a bit. Sammy looked at Tibone and Tibone began to move. Chuckling foolishly at this show of machismo, Terry looked again to see the men gone. "What was that about, Sam?"

"Nothin', Mr. Langley. Just street scum. Let's get you to bed."

He moved along the dim hallway in what felt like hundred-year-old light, helped by the tiny Sammy. The wallpaper felt rough on his left hand, and there was his door being opened after a brief knock, and there was Vera's lovely face.

"Oh, Christ. Thank you, Sammy. I'm so sorry."

"No problem, ma'am. Happens all the time."

"Nevertheless..."

"You be okay with him now?"

"Yes."

"Have a good night."

The tugging of his clothes, the acid taste in his mouth. He said, "Put your lance by the door, please, sir."

"I know what this is about," Vera said. "I bloody know exactly what this is about."

We are from Roedean
Good girls are we
We take a pride in our vaginity...

"Stop it. Stop it now. You'll wake people up with your nonsense. That horrible woman might come and try to help. She's mad... she's completely mad. Oh, how I hate this."

The side of his face on the cool pillow, the window open and the warm moist air so fresh entering his lungs. Vera moving about the room, his eyes closing, not at all afraid of death when you expect to wake soon. Poor Vera. Furious at me for knowing what will happen next.

"Now don't start weeping," Vera said, as she climbed into bed beside him. "I simply won't have it."

Terry turned and groped for her, squinting against the bare light bulb showing under the rim of the bedside lamp. She was a shadow, a silhouette, all sharp and flat. "Darling," he asked, "Where are you?"

Vera didn't answer, but he felt her darkness leaning over him. She pulled the sheet up to his chin.

XXI

It was early, he'd barely slept, and the forecast said to expect heavy rain so Pym brought Sammy's umbrella. He knew Duval went to the first mass at the cathedral. Get this done, he thought, and then, under his breath, said, "Where are you, Terry, you old bastard?" He felt a rockslide of panic building in him and needed an ally. Somehow he had to put all this right. The Duvals would threaten everyone close to him now; he couldn't allow that. He couldn't dispel the picture in his mind's eye of Sasha having to undergo the brutal slicing of her breasts. And the vacant look in her eyes that she now had as she sat, yanked out of her fantasy life and into the surgical reality of an emergency room. One of the nurses remarked that a skilled surgeon must have done the wounding. What would the monster do to Terry or Vera?

Pym headed for Pirates Alley where there was a café and a bookshop—the center of Terry's universe—at the back of St. Louis Cathedral where old Duval would take confession. Pym entered the alley off Royal and pushed through a clot of tourists listening to some guy dressed in eighteenth century garb lecturing about duels that used to be fought in St. Anthony's Garden. During his walks at night, Pym had stopped to admire the eerie, arms-spread shadow of Christ cast by flood-lighting against the back of the St. Louis Cathedral. Men had died in there while dueling for their honor.

A sign on the door of the bookstore said closed, but an old man stood inside, looking out the window. Pym glared at him and the man frowned. Another alley led to the right and several men played chess outside a café. One of them looked at him and then quickly looked away. There was a smell of disinfectant and urine and an old-fashioned drainage trough ran down the middle of the alley, filled with rainwater. Pym sat himself at a vacant table and watched the little side door in the Cathedral from which he hoped Duval would soon emerge. A waiter had to ask him several times what he wanted before he ordered coffee.

The tour group gathered by the railings in Pym's line of sight, and he hoped Duval would not appear yet. The guide spoke loudly of ghosts and vampires, and most of the sleepy-eyed tourists yawned. Pym laughed bitterly at the irony of all the supernatural nonsense that people believed in when in reality far worse crap went on every moment beneath their noses. In so few days the darkness of life had opened to him and he was about to become part of it.

The waiter brought coffee as heavy raindrops fell.

The chess players moved inside, and Pym took their place under a large umbrella. The waiter came out and asked him if he would be okay outside, and he nodded yes while sipping his coffee.

The rain came harder, and the tour group moved quickly to Jackson Square and turned left. Thunder clapped overhead like a bomb blast and seconds later a deluge fell. Pym moved deeper under the table umbrella and opened Sammy's umbrella to the side against being splashed.

When he looked up, Duval stood in the small doorway in the side of the church. He was slipping on a big plastic poncho, which you could pick up free in the bars of Bourbon Street. He pulled the clear plastic hood over his head and stepped down into the alley.

Pym stood, holding the umbrella over himself so that the rain streamed around him. In a few strides he stood before Duval and said, "Do you know who I am?"

Duval shrugged, gave him a dazed look through the rain.

"I'd like to talk to you about George Pym."

Pym wanted Duval to hit him first. He said, "You look like a fat condom in that thing, you piece of shit."

Duval processed the words slowly, then smiled, and said in strained English, "You are so young. Like your mother just birthed you." There came a faint gesture to touch Pym's arm.

Up close all the details of Duval showed in his face. He had a big nose and a deep upper lip. His brown eyes bore a crescent of white around the iris. A sort of disconnection took place in Pym, a kind of hollow whiteness, and, as though a film spun out ultra-close to the action, he thrust the umbrella at Duval, and then his arms and legs began firing outwards, connecting with Duval like an octopus underwater. The mangled umbrella bounced away like an injured buzzard. The giant collapsed against a fire hydrant in a pool of dark liquid, which ran away down the alley. Beautiful scarlet color poured from his mouth and nose.

Duval held his stomach, coughing.

Pym's body buzzed. What had he done? What is this? Did I do this? It felt as though someone else inhabited his body. His leg extended out again and kicked Duval in the side of the head, toppling him sideways. The other leg extended, although Pym tried to stop it, and kicked the old man in the stomach. The old man wretched and then wretched a second time so that a foul-smelling protrusion of vomit ripped from his mouth. He convulsed and more of it came; livid lumps shot from him, the stink like offal. Pym gagged and stepped away.

Duval muttered something in French. It got louder as he panicked. Between his incomprehensible utterances, bigger lumps violently regurgitated. He rolled on his stomach, which was so protruded that if Pym had kicked him in the head again he would have sent the old man spinning. Pym was in the air suddenly and then landing in the small of the old man's back. As he landed he stamped, and stamped again. He felt the deep joy of viciousness; it was glorious, the blood inside him roaring for more, like a thousand hungry apes, and then stop stop stop enough enough calm... calm... dear Christ, what am I doing?

Pym stepped away, horrified, as blood and vapor flew from Duval's mouth like scores of ghosts let loose in the wet air. Duval said something in French and Pym knew that it meant *You've killed me.*

"I don't want to kill anybody," Pym said.

The old man lay still, looking up at him blankly. Pym felt sorry for him. This could be his father, any father that makes mistakes. He wanted to help him up and take him to the hospital but instead he gave him another kick.

Someone stood a few paces down the alley. *"Attention!* Puju!"

"Hey, what's going on?"

Now two big men stood facing Pym.

"What have you done to him?" asked the one called Puju.

The old man wept.

The other man flicked open a knife.

You're running now, thought Pym. This is why you run. This is what terror is—when you see a knife open and you've done wrong. This is not a dream, this is not a film, you're going to have a knife stuck through you and you're going to die. He ran down the alley and then right into St. Peter Street. Tourists stood in doorways out of the rain so he could run straight along the sidewalk on the right side of the road. At the corner of Royal he looked back and they were nearly on him. He leapt across the road in front of a mule and sprinted another block to Bourbon Street without looking back. Then he swung right and dodged through a gaggle of men looking up at a balcony. One of them said, "What the fuck?" and took a swing at him. As he ran farther, he looked back to see his pursuers knock over the same drunks. A woman said, "Look! They're making a movie. Cool." He turned on the jets and ran to St. Ann where he turned left and sprinted up the middle of the road and swung right on Dauphine. He was about to swing right on St. Phillip and sprint down to his hotel where, for some inexplicable reason, he thought he might be safe, when a car pulled across him and he ran into it, bouncing backwards. The taxi driver from the night he left Sasha on the other side of Pontchartrain stood in front of him and he knew his life was over... there was no way around.

He turned to face his pursuers, but they had stopped and stood a few paces away at the corner. The back door of the taxi opened and a brown hand reached out and beckoned him in. The big taxi driver nodded at him. He looked again at the other two and they were backing up. He got in and was enveloped by the familiar smell of the taxi. Someone there in the back seat—Rick.

"Shit. You."

Rick smiled while the rain tapped on the taxi's roof and said, "It's a delicate thing, man, but I ain't your normal everyday cop. And on weekends I ain't your normal everyday preacher."

"You're Voudon."

"Sorry, man. It's not exactly something you go around telling new acquaintances."

"Is everyone here more than one thing?"

"Everyone everywhere's more than one thing."

"So I'm a dead man."

Rick laughed and said, "Not if I have anything to do with it. You safe for now, but I ain't fucking Spiderman. Cain't be everywhere at once."

"So who were those guys?"

"The black brother's Pascal. Used to be a good boy till Nadine got ahold of him with all her bullshit. Don't know the white dude but he'll be a hoodoo."

"Puju, I think."

"How you know that?"

"I heard him called that."

"Why they chasing you?"

"I beat up Duval."

"You fuckin' idiot."

"What have I done?"

"You lucky to have Jean-Baptiste looking after you, man."

The driver turned and smiled.

"Did you kill him?"

"Of course not. I don't kill people."

"Old folks die pretty easy when you beat the shit out of them. If you don't wanna kill old folk don't be beating on them. He probably dead, and you be up for aggravated murder. Not a good situation under Napoleonic law."

Pym's legs felt numb. They shook while Jean-Baptiste drove slowly through the Quarter's deep puddles.

"You quiet, man. Unlike you."

Pym still said nothing.

"Lucky you got friends that understand the situation. Our religion is a wonderful thing. It's nothing like what this crazy Hoodoo bitch Nadine trying to do with it. She gone too far now, way too far. She all over the place like an old mamma's shit."

"You said that on our run."

"I did. But that was before she start slashing peoples."

"Sasha didn't deserve that."

"Man, now I'm mad. Nadine be fucking up my town."

"She's fucking up my family."

"She's gone too far, man. This ain't gonna be pretty."

"You keep mentioning 'hoodoo.' What is that?"

"They're descended from the swamp people. The *Traiteurs*. Healers, not Voudon. Mostly white trash from before the Louisiana purchase. Old Duval nothing but a traiteur with a degree. White trash fusing with psychotic Haitian and you get Nadine. Fucking crazy bitch. Hoodoos be cool mostly, except Nadine Duval has co-opted their shit for herself. She think she got Marie Laveau inside her."

"The Voodoo queen."

"So called. But to us she's a saint. Nadine insulting us. But we put up with the Duvals. In this town you have to live and let live. But we all done with that now."

Pym rubbed his temples with cold fingertips. Rick, shrugging, said, "You know, man, voodoo, isn't what it used to be. It's always evolving and never was what Hollywood made it. Forget that 'Serpent and the Rainbow' Papa Doc shit. It's a religion for the general good."

"Just like the Mormons, eh?"

Rick put his head back and laughed. "No, brother, not like them," he said, "No milktoast here. All we really are is the cattle belonging to an indifferent, insensitive god, and among the cattle walk spirits that help or hinder the cattle according to the cattle's observances. Our sister Nadine was just a conduit for the spirits to mount and talk to us. She was real good till her craziness get the better of her and she go off on her own and do all her shit."

Pym, feeling a great weight of fatigue, said, "Old Terry would have a different call on it all."

"He sees only one reality. Anyway, he English—they burned all their gods a thousand years ago in favor of the Christian cult."

"Good old Terry."

"Crocodile Dundee."

Pym put his head back and closed his eyes. And the word that symbolized it all, the word that was about to ruin his life, the word that in his limited American vocabulary had taken on myriad meaning, stretched out of him like a stale, old, ineffective fart—"Fuck."

* * *

Terry woke into an unusual silence. Outside, New Orleans was quiet. The time didn't matter. He seldom suffered from hangovers, but the side of his head hurt as though some traitorous Hebrew had driven a nail through it. You shouldn't try to write with a skin-full, he thought, as he got out of bed and opened the big folder.

"I'm still drunk," he muttered. "This is bad."

He scribbled something into the margin of the section about the biological and evolutionary need for humans to keep exploring, to have purpose, and, at first, the flow of the writing pleased him. Loosened up by this most delightful mistress, he thought, my mistress beginning with A. But he soon remembered how such writing seemed in the morning—utter drivel. Drink is a substitute for madness and when you're mad everything you say and do is useless. He put the pencil down, not wanting to perpetrate the madness of continuing something he knew to be futile.

He laid the painful side of his head against the manuscript for a moment and smelled its agedness, like something a grave robber found in a tomb and kept handy for an arse-wipe. He closed his eyes and felt the stab of pain, thinking maybe a brain aneurism would take him before Vera. Please don't have the next thought, please please, but it came anyway—two connected items: insurance money and Nina Pym. God in heaven, why don't you strike me dead?

Somebody stood behind him.

Hair follicles darted away from his head like small reef fish at the approach of a shark. Something dark behind him, a woman, inches from his skull. "Please don't touch me." He knew who it was. How did he know who it was? How could he? Only a dream surely, but the terror remained. He looked sideways and glimpsed her gaunt form in the mirror, not attending to him at all but leaning over the sleeping Vera. He leapt up to batter it away but found the room empty. He looked in the mirror again but only saw himself.

"I've killed her," Terry said. "All these years of stress. Her knowing Nina might arrive back in my life. All my stupid talk she's had to put up with."

He knelt beside Vera, touched her face.

She frowned, whispered, "Don't wake me up, you bloody old fool."

He started crying and she roused herself. "Oh, darling, whatever's the matter?"

"It's me. I've done this to you with all my nonsense. You've been an angel to put up with my idiotic life."

Vera wiped tears from his face with the sheet. "Terry, dear," she said, fully awake now. "I don't know what's brought this on, but I forbid you to blame yourself. I'm an old stress bucket just like my mum. It took her too, didn't it? You've been brilliant, Terry. It was decades of comedy—even when you were being serious. You've made my life this rollicking old London pub song… sad, romantic, but always with a giggle at the end. So stop this, and come in bed with me."

As soon as he closed his eyes he saw Nina, white haired and dangerous, and the blood coursed into his penis against Vera's thigh. She sighed and said, "You always get like this when I cry."

IAN GRAHAM LEASK

He made love to her, but he couldn't keep Nina out of his mind. Doing so would have brought impotence. He let go and allowed the imagery to take him, and when he ejaculated it was as if champagne flowed. An almost pleasant pain engulfed the back of his head, accompanying the pain in his temple. You're still trying to breed with this wretched old sperm.

Vera wiped herself with a wad of tissues. She turned to him and whispered, "Thank you, darling. You're wonderful."

He grunted and patted her head. She giggled.

"Cheer up. It's no fun for me having you mope."

"I can't imagine you gone. I suppose I just haven't faced this. I'm crushed by my own... I hate it so. It's like some disgusting demon that holds sway over us. Oh, if I could only take a swipe at death."

"Best revenge is to live, darling. I'll feel better knowing you're looked after and continue to annoy people in the Lord Nelson, or running around with that crazy Pym woman."

"What?"

"Yes yes, you'll get your chance when I'm gone. As long as you're happy I suppose that's all right. Just keep her away from me in the meantime."

He held her, nuzzled his face into her neck. She smelled like vanilla ice cream. They stayed very still.

Soon Vera snored exhaustedly. Terry began to drift off, thinking perhaps there was a hint of dawn in the air, and, as he sank into oblivion, the dark goddess stood at the end of the bed again, her nostrils flaring and eyes blazing, her breath putrid with the compacted stench of a billion trillion souls. He understood the metaphor now. The fury of death stood for dark matter, made up of the magnetic space between molecules, and waited for the aneurism in Vera's swollen arm to pop and darken her like the dying of a sun.

XXII

Pym came back into his room to find Estelle still in a deep sleep. He shook her roughly and said, "Come on, wake up. Man, I was about to call an ambulance. I've never known anyone to sleep like you."

He watched her drag herself from sleep like an exhausted child and look around at the strange hotel room, bewildered. She pushed herself up with her arms and when her eyes rested on his face she scowled. The small of her back curved naturally inward and she threw her shoulders back with no affectation other than a morning stretch—so naturally feminine, gorgeous. He said quietly, "We're meeting Ma and Terry and Vera for breakfast. We're late already."

"Fuck it."

"Fuck what?"

"This. Us."

Pym understood and said, "Someone told you about Maddy."

"Yep."

Pym looked at his hands.

"I don't get why you do that."

"Me neither. Stupid."

"I was expecting you to blame your mother."

"You have no idea..."

Estelle swung herself to the end of the bed and, pulling the sheet around herself, asked, "I'm never going to be enough for you, am I?"

"Yes, you are. Estelle, the lesson is truly learned. A man is dead—partly because of my thoughtlessness. How could I not learn?"

"Bullshit. How could you do that when you yourself were still so hurt over Laura getting a new boyfriend? You'll never learn. Guys don't. You're all liars."

325

"And women don't lie?"

"No. Look, I think Laura had the right idea. This ain't good for me anymore."

"Why? You got the best deal on the planet now. I'll never stray again."

"Until the next time."

"Come on, don't resort to clichés."

"You like your variety."

"I'm done with all that crap. Lesson more than learned."

Estelle sighed and pulled the sheet up under her chin. "Yeah, well."

"Yeah, well what?"

"I dunno now."

"Well, fuck you."

She looked at him, her color rising. "Do you want another ass-kicking like I gave you last week?" Estelle asked.

Pym laughed, and grinning, replied, "Like you could with your little pussy arms." He expected her to laugh with him but she didn't. "I think you're trying to forgive me," he said, "but there's something stopping you."

"I'm just a mug."

"No. You hung in with me through the storm and now it's all over. I'm sorry, but I guess I still had to finish some things off. I apologize, Estelle. You'll get no more trouble from me."

"Why can't I break up with you?"

"Because you love me."

"Do you love me too?" Estelle asked. "I don't think you do. You're so cool about this. It's not what I expected."

"Basically, I've been in love with your tits."

Estelle laughed and said, "Better than nothing I guess."

Pym laughed too and said, "I sure learned a lesson about that. America is all about tits... about glamor, youth, slimness. Trouble is we get old—most of us without gaining any wisdom—and the men get prostate cancer and the women get breast cancer and then we all feel like we're fucked. But we're not, we're still here—like Terry and Vera. Look at that! That's what I want. I want to love you even without those things—like Terry loves Vera."

Estelle's eyes watered, but despite her emotion she laughed and said, "This is all shit. You been coached by Terry in what to say. Either that or you're possessed. Where's 'shut-the-fuck-up-you-fucking-bimbo-bitch' gone?"

"It'll be back."

"And worse."

"I won't let you down. We've both screwed things up pretty good. Let's not do it again."

"You got it, man. Now, back to the love."

"You're relentless."

"I want to know if I'm loved or not."

"Or what?"

"Or I'm outta here."

"Is this a threat, bitch?"

"See, I knew you were in there somewhere."

"You fucking stupid bimbo."

She looked at him, startled.

He laughed.

"Christ, Gil."

"I love you, Estelle. You're going to have to relax and let me learn how to do that better than I've seen it done."

"Have you any idea how much I love you? Right from the start, as soon as I saw your pink, green-eyed face. Love. It made a bad girl of me."

He kissed her and said, "I think we got a good ending to what's usually a nasty and predictable story."

"This Maddy thing certainly turned sour on you fast, didn't it?"

"Sure did. Wake up call."

"You could do worse than have me the rest of your life."

"I know it."

"There's a few other things to discuss."

"One thing's ending, another's beginning," Pym said.

"We have to draw out the ending a bit," Estelle said, "so the new beginning will make sense."

"Yes," Pym said, "I guess that's necessary. You are clever."

Estelle smelled a bit raunchy from her night on the town without him. "It's you that's clever," she said, and snuggled next to him. "But you gotta quit wasting your time, babe."

He didn't want to annoy her by saying she smelled funny, so he said, "I need a change. I wanna move here to New Orleans... live in the Garden District."

"Leave Minnesota?"

327

"We'll sell the St. Anthony house and rent out the island place, put little Mishawn in charge of the salon, and get outta Minneapolis."

Estelle's left arm lay across his shoulders, the nails of her fingers gently caressing his earlobe. Pym thought of his brother and held back a sob. "Georgie loved it here. I do too. And I hate to say it, but you'll be getting some insurance money."

"Is that why you love me?" She laughed.

Pym felt his face flush with anger, but she pulled down on his earlobe and kissed the end of his nose. "Money don't mean nothin' to me if I got you."

"Same."

"But leaving Minnesota may be a bit much."

"You could do with a change too."

"I want a baby at some point, Gil."

"I wondered when that was coming."

Estelle said, "It's only natural," and then watched his face while he thought.

"It would be a whole new life," Pym finally said.

He could feel Estelle looking at him, but kept his eyes cast down. Cautiously, she said, "I know it would be great. If we need something different it's a little kid to look after. God, how great would that be! Dontcha think?"

Pym nodded, frowning, and let a minute pass before saying, "And in that regard... I want to move to New Orleans."

She gritted her teeth and tugged his ear.

"Ouch."

"Our life's in the Cities. We're from there."

"Exactly. We need to get outta there before it's too late. Before I become cold and scared and watered down. The land of ten thousand politically correct neurotics." Emotion rose in him. It took him by surprise... a fury from the past and a nostalgia for something he didn't yet have.

Estelle withdrew her hand from his ear and said, "George set you up so's you'd start thinking again. George called this place 'The land of the dead.' I don't really understand it, but explain to me what it means when you've suddenly got a jones for emigrating to the land of the dead. It don't sound too wholesome to me."

"He meant it as a metaphor. You know what a metaphor is?"

"Of course I do... I ain't stupid."

"My dumb little dingbat."

Estelle jumped on him, legs straddling him, holding his face in her hands. With her nose on his she said, "And you, you think with your dick, you pea-brained motherfucker."

She was right. His cock rose and started pushing at her, but she squirmed away, saying, "What's the matter with you? Dontcha think I'm gonna need a little time?"

He put his hands by his sides and said, "You're right, I'm sorry. Take all the time you need. Pull some jeans on and let's go get breakfast."

"Not yet. I want to discuss this baby."

"What baby?"

"The one we're having, dude."

"There's a ban on making love but we can discuss offspring?"

"You got it."

"Well, I'm not sure, Stella. If we were to have a kid... I'd want to be a happy dad—not like my dad. I feel like I already reside in the land of the dead, you know. Minnesota's a great place, but I don't think I'm cut out for all the cleanliness and order and having to say the right thing all the god-damn time."

Estelle laughed. "Bull-shit! You didn't answer the question. You been yabbering on about metaphor, but me and baby don't want no metaphoric answer. What do you actually mean?"

Pym laughed and said, "Okay. Let's see. I have one life to live. I'm not going to put up with any more punishment for something I've already paid for. There's no reward afterwards, so I'm going to live unafraid of sanctions. I'm going to be good because I'm a good person and for no other reason. I need a new place to do that in."

Estelle put her hand over his head and said, "Please forgive him, Jesus, he's clueless."

As she moved back onto him he caught a whiff of something he couldn't identify and said, "You smell different. What were you doing out on the town last night, catting around?"

"I told you... I went dancing on Bourbon Street."

"On your own?"

"Why not? You just wandered off somewhere. Why can't I?"

"It's different, and you know it."

"Dashiell and some of the others took me out. They took pity on me after I heard about your shenanigans."

"Who told you?"

"None of your damn business. You get to be sorry and keep your trap shut."

"All right, all right." Pym thought he had better divert the subject, so he said, "Anyway, my point is New Orleans is a real city, one I feel more alive in. You can walk places. They have streetcars, sidewalk cafés, palm trees. I love palms."

"You get murdered here. Maybe turned into a zombie or something."

"It's warm all year."

"A city with shitty public education that will sink like Atlantis with the next big hurricane."

"A city where you can have a drink on the street without some high-minded hypocrite giving you a ticket. There's the symbol of freedom and personal responsibility right there. I don't like being controlled by anal retentive Teutons."

Estelle laughed. "That's the deal then, is it? I get a baby, and you get to move us to the most dangerous city in America so you can booze on the street?"

"Yes, Estelle, I'm afraid that has to be the deal."

Estelle laid one hand on his shoulder and another on his knee. "Private school for the kid, then," she said. "We go to the Catholics."

Pym shrugged. "Fine. It's all the same to me. I'll simply tell him the truth when the time comes."

Estelle frowned. "I never thought it would be like this. Why did I have to get myself hooked up with a family of deep thinkers. You're a pain in the ass."

Pym shrugged again. "It'll only get worse in that regard."

"So, I'm hearing we can have a baby if we move to New Orleans?"

"Tentatively, yes."

"And we can bring her up Catholic and send her to private school?"

"Okay."

"And then another one?"

"Let's start with one."

Estelle turned on the waterworks.

"I'll build a hair salon for you in the Quarter. Take a look around, there's lots of buildings to renovate. You see them all boarded up, waiting to be loved by a good architect. We could live over the top of one, have a nice balcony with tropical plants. Then, when we can afford it, we'll renovate a little mansion in the Garden District. Or there's always Algiers. I've always wanted to live on a street called Pelican."

Wiping her eyes with the sheet, Estelle said, "Oh, how sweet."

"On second thought, we'd better stay out of Algiers."

Estelle frowned, uncomprehending.

Pym continued, "We'll have a salon and live above it, and I'll go to graduate school and get my brain back."

"There'll be scads of salons."

"Yes, but none of them will have the likes of you in residence."

"It won't be that easy."

"We have friends down here."

"Right, fucking crazy pagans."

"Better than nothing."

"I have to shower."

"No time. We're late."

"Then don't break my balls for smelling funky."

Estelle laughed, pulling on her tightest jeans.

* * *

Estelle's rectum hurt. It was not an unpleasant pain, and it made her ultra-aware of the way her buttocks rolled, made her walk tall, head high, which in turn hollowed her abs and pushed out her breasts. As she strolled arm-in-arm along Chartres with Gilbert, passers-by stared openly at her. Estelle smiled without looking at anyone—as a beautiful woman should.

"Where are we going, Bubba, that Café Du Monde place George always talked about?"

"No way," said Gil, and kept walking.

"You're way too quiet, boyfriend. That worries me."

"I'm thinking about everything."

"Then stop," she said, turning to him. "Look at these."

Gilbert put his face to the sky and laughed, tight-eyed. Estelle pulled his arm in closer and kissed his cheek, pleased with herself for having made him laugh. She tried to remember her widowhood, but felt too happy about her victory to feel it.

They turned right on Ursulines and had to step into the street because a fat man with a cigar stub stuck in the side of his mouth used a hose to spray the sidewalk outside his store. Everything felt so different in New Orleans and Estelle understood why Gilbert liked it so much. She liked the little shops with flower-laden balconies above, and the narrow, intimate streets. Not a Lutheran in sight. But for all its foreignness it was shabby and cheap—she'd immediately noticed the city's tackiness while cabbing into the Quarter from the airport and again, last night, while out on the town with her new friends.

Gilbert crossed the road and showed her a closed store with a sign: *The House of Large Sizes.* "George shopped here," Gilbert explained. The unlit window displayed cheap, sleazy lingerie and fishnet in triple-X and high heels designed for giants. Estelle laughed, fascinated. Chained leather, inflatable dolls, and sex toys lay around, revealing someone's complete lack of merchandising flair. The whole display reminded her of last night and a slight scent of sex drifted to her nose from between her breasts; with the ache in her rectum and a blush gathering, she pushed last night out of her mind. They crossed back over the street and walked to Decatur where a wild-looking bum, gesticulating on the corner at pedestrians, accosted them with a courtly bow. It was the one she had given the finger to last night. Today Estelle curtsied instead, which surprised the bum and made him laugh. Gilbert handed him a five-buck note. Gil and the bum smiled at each other. The bum's mad blue eyes swept over Estelle and then back onto Gilbert, and with comically raised eyebrows, he sang:

It's your birthday!

Happy Birthday to you!

The sun tried to break out from behind gray, pregnant looking clouds as Estelle held Gilbert's hand across traffic-filled Decatur to French Market Place. Terry and Vera sat at a round table under the awning of a sidewalk café. Terry stood, kissed Estelle on both cheeks, and shook hands with Gilbert. They sat and ordered coffee from a glum gay waiter with slicked back hair, wearing a really cool burnt orange sweater with a wide neckline.

They waited for Nina.

Nina had to come from the Hotel Le Richelieu and couldn't ever be on time. She always had to make an entrance. Why would someone of that age, after all this shit, still have to be angling for approval?

Sure enough, after ten minutes Nina pulled up in a horse and buggy and was helped down by a driver dressed as a confederate officer. Nina wore a white dress and straw hat, an outfit way too young for her. If she'd only get herself to a gym regularly she wouldn't look too bad.

Nina tried to pay him, but the driver refused and helped her onto the pavement and toward the café. Terry stood up, waiting to greet her, but Gilbert sat still, all white-cheeked and mad. The Confederate officer tipped his hat to Estelle and winked while Terry kissed Nina on both cheeks and helped her to a chair. The minutest of nods occurred between Nina and Vera. Most of the Confederate officer's teeth were missing. As handsome as he was, Estelle wouldn't want to kiss him. She liked teeth.

They ordered Creole eggs and biscuits, none of them ever having tried that before.

"So, Gilbert," Terry said, "your mother and I have something to explain to you."

Gilbert shrank a little and looked around nervously, not knowing where to put his hands.

Nina cocked her thumb at Terry and said, "He's your daddy."

Gilbert sat quietly. Just looked at them.

Terry nodded seriously.

Vera took hold of Terry's arm.

"You were that roadie George told me about?"

"Yes," said Nina. "He was the roadie. And I don't want any shit from you, Gillie. It was what it was."

"Ma, shut up."

Gilbert stared at Terry and Terry stared back. It went on like that for five minutes. Rain fell suddenly in a noisy torrent and then stopped, giving way to blinding sunshine. They all donned sunglasses. Everything clicked with running water and cars whooshed through puddles. Estelle gave Gil's hand a squeeze but he ignored her. The slick waiter brought eggs, poached in a red Creole sauce, and laid out the warm yellow biscuits. He must have had a bad night because he only smiled with his mouth.

Estelle didn't doubt it was true about Terry being Gilbert's dad. You could see the likeness. What a mess a bit of sex can cause. She suddenly flashed on what had happened last night when she went out on the town with Nadine and her friends. She couldn't keep it out of her mind and the memory made her blush. She wanted it to be a dream, but it wasn't one, not at all.

Her backside ached because at the end of the night's proceedings she had let Puju slide his big porno cock into her ass and fuck her hard like a dog, while she straddled Pascal, with Nadine and Lulu licking and sucking on her. Like a ball of passion, thinking as one, they strove for the ultimate climax and achieved it in a tangle of shrieks, drumbeats, and hot sweat. Kissing a woman for the first time had sent her through the roof. And to be hard-fucked professionally by Puju! The thought of it made her face burn as she devoured the spicy eggs.

She'd had her revenge. She wouldn't break Gilbert's balls anymore. She'd done it all, taken a walk on the wild side with the United Nations. Two men, a woman, and a tranny. She laughed to herself.

Gilbert looked at her sadly and said, "Yep, I guess it is pretty funny."

Nina laughed but Terry and Vera didn't. Terry said, "I don't think it's funny at all, Gilbert. I feel terrible that things worked out the way they did. But look at it like this—here we all are, still kicking."

"The survivors," said Gil.

"That's one way to put it," said Terry.

"It isn't you I blame," Gil said. "I've seen you in action. You're a terrific old dude, Terry. I may even be able to get used to you as some sort of dad. But her! Ma." He glared at Nina, and said, "You are just a lousy excuse for humanity. This whole fucking thing goes back to you."

"Ah crap, ya big baby. Take responsibility for yourself. I never told you to act like me—in fact, I tanned your goddamned hide when I saw too much me emerging in you. The sooner you get over having me as a mother, the sooner you'll make a decent man."

Nina sat back, proud of her outburst. Terry appeared to be nodding in agreement. Gilbert looked at him. "Yes?"

"I'm afraid she's right. Blaming parents won't get you off the hook of your own conscience."

"I always knew that. But still."

Nina, her mouth full of biscuit and sauce, said, "I was a lousy mother. Still am. Boring old Michael had to have me, didn't he? Thought he could keep me safe by knocking me up with George. Then this guy..." and she hooked her thumb again at Terry, "comes along. Sorry, Vera. And all bets are off. And then guilt sends him away again with you a secret inside me. Mister Integrity." She gave Terry a little whack with her free hand. "Christ, it was hard."

Estelle watched them eat and talk. Good, she thought, my Gil has a father again. An English one this time. Now we'll be okay, the English know how to do everything right. After a while she zoned out of the conversation and thought of all the tricks Lulu had taught her.

After breakfast the five of them strolled along the Moonwalk without speaking much, past the huge but quiet riverboats docked at the Toulouse Street Wharf, and then boarded the ferry to Algiers. They ambled to the little funeral home on Teche where they'd been at the service the day before. George's ashes were ready for pick-up and an old black man in a light blue leisure suit handed them to Nina. Nina handed them to Estelle who handed them off to Gil. They strolled to a big, shabby, half-burned building a few blocks away on Atlantic… a structure not unlike the size and layout of the hotel she was staying at with Gil; it took up most of the block like some institution for the insane, and, George being such a neatnik, it amazed her that he could abide such a place. While they walked, Terry narrated the story of the fire and what he thought he knew of Nadine's schemes and George's death. Estelle didn't listen; she thought Terry was turning out to be a bit of a blowhard.

They looked at the charred damage for a while and then started back toward the river. Aside from a few quaint streets near where the ferry docked, Estelle thought Algiers a horrible place with its shabby little houses, wandering dogs, and weed-strewn sidewalks. On the way they saw the Mardi Gras floats being decked out nearby. The big, colored faces sticking up high in the air reminded Estelle of George, and she cried a little. Gil gave her a squeeze and said, "It sure must've been hard, hearing all that."

"Poor George," Estelle said. "He'll always be in me somewhere."

As the ferry pulled away from Algiers, Vera took the ashes under one arm and Gil's arm in her other and walked the long upper deck, talking intimately to him with her head bowed. Estelle thought they should dump the ashes into the river right then and there—get it over with. Put him where he wants to be. But no, Gil wants to bring him back to Minneapolis. Stupid. They'll wind up dumping him in the river anyway. People are always holding George back from what he wants.

Nina stood with Terry at a railing and Estelle heard her say, "We'll stay in touch this time, yes?"

"Of course, I hope we've all learned our lessons."

"Because the last thirty-two years has been a real bugger."

"I know, but as I said earlier—here we all are."

"At last."

"Yes."

"How's Jumping Jack Flash?"

Terry burst out laughing.

The ferry pulled out, engines shuddering underfoot, and turned against the running current of the river. Estelle felt the warm humidity on her skin and turned her face to the sun. In the middle of the river the other ferry approached as Estelle leaned on the railing a few yards from Nina and Terry, who muttered, heads close together.

Estelle stood straight suddenly, covering her forehead with her hand against the glare of the sky. Across the expanse of water that divided the passing ferries, on the upper deck with wind blowing her hair, stood Nadine Duval. Estelle waved and Nadine turned her face toward her and just stared. Perhaps she didn't have good eyesight, or the sun's glare made it so she couldn't tell who waved at her. Puju and Pascal stood near her. Estelle smiled—the UN delegation. On the car deck below Nadine, old Sammy from the hotel stood looking upward as if he could see Nadine right through the sheet metal. He looked a bit crazy.

In the first seconds of seeing her UN delegation, Estelle's mind jumped to Pym's suggestion of living here in New Orleans. Nadine and her crowd would be Estelle's friends. She didn't have many friends, never had. These new friends understood her, appreciated how much work went into her body. They were lovers and losers like her, taking pleasure when they could. Her heart warmed toward them. Yes, she'd move down here with Gil. No doubt he'd start something with that flat-chested reporter chick. Why does he like these washed out plain-janes?

But where was poor little Lulu? They'd made her do everything, like a slave; she was so smart and delicate, and knew eroticism backwards. Estelle would have her little secret life with them... she could be their goddess. The memory of last night sent sensations through her she'd never felt before. A queer buzzing and shudder down deep, inflaming, pulsing. A sex-worm in her mind firing up the drumbeat of her heart—a sudden shortness of breath. Was it dirty, pornographic? No, it was just loneliness and love.

When she thought Nadine could see her properly she raised a hand high in greeting. Nadine continued to stare at her, the eyes menacing, cold and distant. Embarrassed, Estelle felt the smile deflate in her face, replaced by a mild stinging in the hair follicles of her scalp. Puju and Pascal loitered near Nadine, Puju smoking, Pascal with his nose in a book. Nadine just stared, like, who the fuck are you, bitch? She dropped her hand to the rail, understanding in an instant that she'd been duped in some way. Her gut hurt.

* * *

Nadine Duval, out in the morning light, a rare treat for her, stood on the upper deck of the Algiers-bound ferry. The river wind blew through her hair and the ferry headed across to where she belonged. Lulu had made them Vietnamese coffee before they left, and they'd reviewed with considerable mirth the videotape made the previous night, recording their team-handed seduction of the giantess. What a film it would be.

Today she felt safe from the cruel Zandor who reside at the bottom of rivers and lakes and forced her to previously cross the river via the Crescent City Connection. She had used their help many times but never paid them back. Today she felt as powerful as them.

A glow ran through her, her multitude rejoiced, each entity glowing in its Govi within the dark city. There would be continued life, a new mother. Struggle led to strength and success. And now she was headed back to the Spanish house to meet contractors who would put it all back together with insurance money. Clever old Duval. The structure was worth next to nothing, but the insurance was high. Duval and his dodges. End of the road for him though. She would soon put the frightened old fool on a plane to Port-au-Prince where he could live out the rest of his days at a nephew's plantation. Plenty of pretty little brown boys there for him if he ever recovers from the beating he took this morning from the Golden Boy. Ha! Gilbert Pym, my prince, I have your wrigglers fighting for entry into my egg. Lulu is such a clever slave.

The other ferry approached from the Algiers side. Her heart rode high on the waves and the smell of ozone was in the spray. And there they were on the upper deck of the approaching ferry—the Pyms! Nadine was much amused. The Goddess and the Loa surely conspired to arrange this.

As the ferries passed, she saw the Giantess leaning on a railing, and the fool waved at her. We suck you dry of your lover's juice, and you wave at us like we're soul sisters. You are finished, girl. Wait till Golden Boy sees what you did.

He won't recognize me in the film. My clever little Lulu saw to that.

What idiots these people are.

And there's the Englishman, making honeyed word-love to the old mother. That threw me off pretty good. Clever old George—bringing in a Protestant. Not an idolater, you see—impossible to frighten. I don't understand his business in all this yet, but I will soon. And his mangled wife talking to my Gilba Pym. It'll take a little more time to get you, because of your double-dealing brother but you haven't seen the last of me, Goldilocks. After this baby's born, I'll slap a paternity suit on you and get you down here again, and then, yes, then there'll be, yes yes yes instead of no no no.

She could feel the sperm Lulu had sucked out of the giantess and spat up into her; it crawled and wriggled inside her toward the life force of the Mother. The filthy male sperm, battering at the wall of her egg in their obnoxious vigor. The multitude inside roared on the fighting sperm like Romans in the Coliseum. Let one in Mother, yes, a girl one only though, yes.

All was well. Little Fortuna slept safe at Lulu's apartment.

Nadine smelled Puju's Russian cigarette smoke. He was pleased with himself because Nadine had given him some attention—all show for the giantess. And Pascal read like a fiend, training to be a hounsi-kanzo. Puju's contentment with himself astounded her. What disgusting hyenas they both were, despite their loyalty.

The ferry docked and they walked up the metal ramp to the street, Nadine leading, her hounsi Pascal and Puju a few steps behind. The taxi waited. The driver sped down Bounty and Teche streets, took a hard left on Lamarque, and accelerated the four blocks to the hacienda. "Welcome me home, little neighborhood," Nadine said.

The driver pulled into the courtyard of the Spanish house and, after stopping, turned, and in Haitian French, told Nadine it was the end of the line. Before she could speak, other men, attired as Ton Ton to cause fear, surrounded the cab, opened the doors, and pulled Puju and Pascal out. She heard them being beaten and kicked.

She laughed at the brothers all dressed up in black, but she stopped laughing when she saw The Baron stalking around behind them in his skeleton suit. Her nephew, Tibone, attended too, arms crossed, glaring at her with his red eyes.

Ricard the Hougan—she'd know him even behind his dark glasses— leaned into the cab and frowned at her. In an instant she read everything in his countenance. In a wild panic she screamed, "Zandor away!" while fashioning a ward-off-evil sign with her fingers. The hougan lifted his hand and blew a fine dust in her face, then slammed the door. She knew the dust well. The goddess came flying forward. The others doors slammed shut.

The dust penetrated her eyes and ears and clogged her mouth and nostrils so that she coughed and spat. Her eyes streamed with tears and she began hiccoughing and feeling immediately numb as she gasped for breath.

Uproar struck the dark city inside her; her entities whirled in terror, all suffering with the clear knowledge of what was to follow. They pleaded for the Calm One to come forward and handle this, but he too was afraid, so that the host, Nadine, became a kidnapped little girl shuddering with terror.

The Ton Ton opened the doors after a few minutes, pulled her from the cab by her hair, and threw her onto the cobblestones. She couldn't blink; her eyes remained open, still streaming with water. Someone ripped the keys from around her waist and others lifted her legs and began stuffing her into a body bag. Dizziness enveloped her but she could smell the men's sweat and traces of ozone in the river air. She regretted everything and tried to say, spare me, I'm pregnant, but nothing came out of her mouth. She cursed the Voudon in her mind but knew it wouldn't scare them unless they heard her. Entities flooded forward like cards being dealt, but each shrank away in horror at what was befalling it.

They tied the top of the bag and her eyes saw only brown darkness. Then they drove a long way. She felt nauseated. She could hear but not speak and her limbs became stiff, as though viscous glue invaded her veins and joints. She wanted to transform into a snake, but nothing worked. She tried to scream, but nothing came out of her mouth. Her lungs stiffened, her heart slowed. Only her tear ducts worked. Poor little girl. What would become of Fortuna? Would she be safe with Lulu? Would Lulu know to send Fortuna to Duval?

They carried her onto a boat; she felt it rocking. Then she heard the boat's engines start, smelled the diesel, and after a while felt the idling engine vibrating under her. The engines roared and the boat bumped through water for a long time.

A man laughed, saying, "Do a witch float or not float, mon?"

Another replied, "Shut up. Dis Boko drop like an anchor. Don't touch no part of it."

She smelled their cigarette smoke.

She smelled their unwiped asses.

It fascinated her to hear the Zandor speak.

At last the great dark one came forward, the bon ange of the Zandor ancestor, who had hidden in her since birth—the one responsible for all the glorious bad. Vicious it was, but strong, and careless of life. "We're going to join the others," it pronounced. "All is saved and we will rise again from the depths to wipe men clean from the face of the earth."

They lifted her, swung her three times and tossed her into the water. As she sank, she bent in the middle and understood that weights were tied around her. The throb of the boat's engine faded and the dark grew darker and quieter, and in her mouth she felt water but her sense of taste failed to detect whether it was fresh or salt. She assumed river because little time had passed. If it was river they had made a grave mistake.

Down, down she sank to reside with the Zandor on the bottom, to linger with them and become more and more powerful. She lay at an angle on some rocks, alive but not breathing. Soon she felt curious fish touching her. Incompetent fools! She laughed inside herself. They had paralyzed her lungs so that she couldn't drown. Hold off the terror. She would wait for the Zandor to come... for the ancient Nephilim to claim her. Then there would be hell to pay. She imagined the giant who would take her to wife. She imagined the semen of the Nephilim, sustaining her like the buttermilk her mother fed her. She wanted her mother.

XXIII

It was the kind of day in Minneapolis when people drive with their windows open and start looking for the budding fuzziness that inhabits trees when the first penetrating warmth emerges from the spring sun. The snow melts quickly, leaving only stubborn piles of grainy ice, packed down and left over from early winter.

Double wrapped and not sharing the enthusiasm of his passengers, the Ethiopian cabbie, who appeared to be highborn and proud, dumped their luggage on the sidewalk, shivered while Estelle paid him, then drove away, closing his electronic windows.

When Gilbert and Estelle opened the front door to his house the full force of a stomach-turning stench assaulted them. "Whoa," said Pym. "What have I done now?"

Estelle dropped her bags, backed out the doorway, and vomited in the frozen flowerbed. Pym threw his bags inside, carefully placed George's ashes inside the door, just around the corner, and went to help Estelle. "Stella," he said, "this is unlike you."

"I know. Holy Christ." She retched more, but only strings of bile emerged. Pym held her head, took out a napkin that he'd inexplicably kept in his pocket during the flight from New Orleans, and wiped her mouth.

"Sit on the step and I'll see what's up."

Trying not to gag, Pym took the bags inside and placed them at the foot of the stairs between the end of the yellow couch and the banister. When he looked around he realized that the living room had been torn up as though a ferocious beast had gone mad in there. The stuffing of the yellow couch spilled out like pus and in places the pinewood frame showed. The carpet's pile was ripped up and the wallpaper hung like dreadlocks with plaster clinging to it. The stair carpet, ripped and soiled with vomit that spread all the way up, gave Pym a clear indication of what he should expect in the bedrooms. Holding her hand over her mouth, Estelle came behind him and put her arms around his waist. "It's that cat that adopted you," she whispered into his ear.

"Hell, I never thought about that."

"Poor thing. I forgot too."

In the kitchen they found a lump of bloated fur and teeth in the middle of the floor. Estelle said, "It was just a cat. Christ, how could it cause this mayhem?"

"It's been locked in for more than two weeks."

"I feel terrible. Just a poor little kitty."

"It doesn't look much like a kitty now."

"It looks like a dead demon. It's all teeth and claws."

The creature had sunken eyes and looked wet as if it had been sweating after death. "It smells like a boatload of rotten cheese." Estelle went to the sink, retched up bile, and then turned on the tap.

"You okay?"

"Sure. Just get the poor thing outta here."

Pym opened the back door, went onto the porch and brought the snow shovel into the kitchen. He took a wad of paper towels in his left hand and held the neck of the snow shovel with his right, trying to slide the creature into the well of the shovel. "Estelle," he said gently, "hold the door open."

As she stepped over the creature it suddenly elevated into the air, liquid flying off it. Pym leapt away. Estelle screamed. The thing tottered for a second before settling again into a splayed heap. Estelle screamed, "Still alive, still alive!"

The stink increased as the creature's stomach split open slowly like a loose seam and its guts oozed out with a flatulent sound. It laid still.

"Christ."

"Find a new oath, for crying out loud."

"Stop. Don't start on me."

Pym slid the mass of animal and guts onto the snow shovel and, retching, took it outside and laid it in the snow by the garage wall where Laura used to plant morning glories in May. Estelle came behind him with a garbage bag. "Here, put it in this."

"I just put it down."

"Come on."

"Is it dead or alive? Damn thing!"

"Poor thing, Gil. Come on."

"Did you see what it did to the house?"

"The house needed gutting anyway."

Pym laughed and said, "That's true at least. It'll be good to get rid of the old couch."

Estelle, holding the palms of her hands on the sides of her head, said, "What in the name of the risen Christ is going on here?"

They spent the afternoon and early evening cleaning the house and throwing stuff in the back alley for the garbage men. It took an hour to haul out the yellow couch; it resisted every doorway and corner as if reluctant to leave, and, seeing it placed out in the sunlight by the garage, Pym wondered why he hadn't thrown it out long before. Aside from being an eyesore it brought back disturbing memories. Good riddance. Because the house still stank, they left all the windows open and decamped to Estelle's place on Peter Pan Island, fixed a light supper, and then went to bed.

They made love with the vanity mirror pulled up beside the bed the way Estelle liked it. During the act, Pym watched Estelle watching herself. His hands held her hips and she felt taught and dense, incredibly heavy compared to the light and lithe Maddy. If she stopped working out she'd put on a lot of weight. He feared where that kind of change would send him. He loved the new little cocoon of integrity he had built; it felt like he'd had it for a lifetime.

After he came he fell sideways like a man shot with an arrow. Estelle laughed and said she hadn't worked him that hard.

"Don't ever change," he said. "Stay like this."

"I'll try," she said. "But it's a lot of work. I'll need incentive."

"I'll give you incentive."

"You better. After all this."

"I know."

Estelle fell asleep, smiling.

Her side of the bed sagged. Pym found himself continually rolling toward her. It was as though sleep doubled her weight, like she was suddenly filled with magnets. When he nudged her she felt solid, immovable.

Even in the mirror above the round bed he could see the sag to the left. Either her muscle density had expanded greatly or the mattress was shot.

He imagined his brother bouncing around on it in his slinky perversions and decided that a new mattress would be appropriate—throw the old one out like the yellow couch. He saw himself in the mirror and felt guilty. The inner voice said: Get that shit-eating grin off your mug. What are you laughing at, you cruel son of a bitch?

Peter Pan Island, the west end of it at least, reminded Pym of the gentrified part of Algiers—the modest clapboard houses with white picket fences and wooden outside staircases; the uneven sidewalk slabs with sinuous weeds undermining the concrete with their imperial ambitions of returning everything to forest; the humid river air; a great city looming up across the flow… spectacular at night.

When Pym told Estelle, *yes*, he would move into George's house with her and rent out his property in Northeast, she was so happy she jumped backwards and did two flips, whooping like a rebel. Pym smiled and felt a great warmth come over him. She had no guard up—she was completely honest, revealing herself entirely. You can love this eccentric woman, Pym thought… you can make this work. You can avoid fuck-ups and you can live in the future, not the past.

They'd worked hard that day, moving things in from Pym's house, and they'd spread George's ashes in the flowerbed that George himself had laid out last year around the front door. They'd had to remove the last crunchy vestiges of snow and rake away the flattened mulch before sprinkling George into the earth. They opened a bottle of Merlot and poured a glassful into the dirt, mostly around the base of a perennial, so that the dark brown earth and grey ashes and red wine all mixed together and looked like a porridge that could any minute re-animate and turn into a brain. Pym remarked as much, laughing, whereupon Estelle punched his arm and said, "Ish, that's morbid."

Pym had not had the heart to dispose of the gris-gris bag. He thought about walking across the road and throwing it into the river as Nadine Duval had once said he should do, but, when Estelle went inside to phone for a pizza, Pym took a garden trowel, lifted a wedge of wet, recently thawed turf beside the gate, scooped out a damp hole, and slid the gris-gris bag into it. He put a little of the earth back over the top of it and then patted down the sod. "There you are, brother. Bring us luck."

George had already brought luck. There was a large insurance policy, split between him and Estelle and another that paid off the mortgage on the house. Pym was surprised George had left him anything. It was typical of

George to think of others in this way, and Pym silently resolved to follow his brother's example in that regard. An overwhelming anxiety about the future, which had always prevented Pym from actually allowing himself to advance into it, was suddenly taken away by the death of his brother. There was Estelle, and there was money, and there was suddenly a very sane mother, making settle-down sounds.

Pym had kept in touch with Terry to check on the progress of Vera. At eleven o'clock CST on a Friday the phone call came from Terry in London.

"Vera died this afternoon."

"What happened?"

"Aneurism caused by that swelling under her arm. It came on quite suddenly."

"Oh, jeez, I'm sorry, Terry."

"Although she was clearly headed downhill, we thought we'd have a little more time together."

Pym started crying. Estelle came up behind him and put her hands on his head. She kissed the back of his neck.

Terry said, "After the aneurism hit it took only a week. I can't believe I'm even saying this."

Wiping water from his face, Pym said, "I can't believe it either. Seems like I just had cocktails with her at the hotel."

"*Momento mori.* Here today, gone tomorrow. It'll come to all of us."

"How are you holding up, man?"

"I'm calling you. I'm in a mess." Terry laughed. "Being English, and trying not to show it."

"I wish I were there. Do you want me to fly over?"

"No, of course not. You've got your own bereavement—lots to sort out there. I'll be all right."

"But she's sort of... my stepmother."

"Ah, you're a lovely man, Gilbert. That was the right thing to say. I'll tell you where to send some flowers. We all have our griefs to deal with just now. You stay put, boyo."

"Where are you? There's a weird noise in the background. You sound like you're under the sea."

"I have you programmed into my mobile, old son. I'm on Waterloo Bridge."

"Don't jump."

"Too many bystanders."

"I can hear the traffic. Makes me nostalgic."

"Gives me hives."

"Is it on the way home? You should go home."

"Easier said than done."

"Have you got someone looking after you?"

"I'll be all right."

"You're all alone, aren't you? It was just you and Vera."

"I have plenty of support. Remember I'm in the mental health business. In fact, I'm headed to the office right now for a spin dry."

"And lay off the liquor."

"Yes, young prince."

"I can't believe this happened so soon."

"Neither can I."

"I'm so sorry. Poor Vera. Poor you."

"How's Estelle?"

"She's forgiven me. She's right here."

"Better hang on to her, mate."

"That's probably right. We'll see."

"We shall indeed. And how's Nina?"

Pym laughed. "Well, seeing you again has had an effect on her. She's working out with Estelle at our gym. On a big health kick. She's quit swearing."

"No smoking, no swearing? She'll be taking holy orders next."

"Yeah, right."

"I've always loved your mother, you know."

"I know."

"I'm so sorry."

"It's all right. It all worked out."

"I'm not sure it did."

"How do you mean?"

"It makes Vera's passing a rare kind of hell. I know Nina's pretty flighty, but if you love someone you're blind to their faults."

Pym frowned, not understanding.

Terry continued, his voice on the edge of a sob. "You see, I feel so guilty. I've never stopped thinking of your mother. All these years. And yet I loved Vera so deeply, she was so good."

"She *was* good. And when someone you love dies there are always these weird mixed emotions. I've got the same thing going on with George. Estelle and I just got the insurance money, half each. It's weird, somebody's death setting you up. We're rich all of a sudden. I don't know whether to laugh or cry."

"Yes, I have the same situation, and... oh, this is too hard."

"Just be with it, man. It'll all settle down."

"Into what?"

"A great life. You can finish your book. You can come here and write it in peace. You can do another one after that. You're not that old. And I want to give you George's brilliant set of postcards. Only you would know what to do with them."

"Thank you. And you and Estelle must come here too. On your honeymoon perhaps. You can stay in the house. I'll bugger off somewhere."

"Listen, call me tomorrow, okay?"

"I will."

"You must. I have all your numbers, don't I? And you have mine?"

"Yes."

"Be sure to call me tomorrow."

"I will, yes."

* * *

Standing in the middle of Waterloo Bridge in the warm afternoon sun, looking southwest at the conglomeration of monuments and magnificent architecture spanning four millennia of human history, Terry dropped his mobile phone into the deep left pocket of his slacks. He hadn't eaten in two days and the extra weight he'd added to his waistline in America had dissolved, and Vera with it. He felt himself shrinking commiserate to his grief. He had rung Gilbert in Minnesota. Mission accomplished. He should have said, "Yes, please fly over and look after me." But his native reserve stopped him. His stupid, annoying, so un-American response was: "I'll be all right. I have plenty of support." For all his attempts at extroversion he was still an Englishman. What complete bollocks!

He didn't know exactly how he'd arrived in the middle of Waterloo Bridge from St. Thomas' Hospital. Was it Belvedere Road, then Jubilee Gardens and past the Royal Festival Hall? He couldn't remember any of it, but he must have come that way. He wouldn't have come along the Embankment. Would he? A new experience—total blackout without the aid of alcohol. And Vera lying cold with a sheet over her, gone, never see her again. How is that? Can't be. Here one minute, gone the next. And the river underneath. Look at this hand with its veins, blood running through it, dirt under the nails, scars, liver spots, that cigarette burn from childhood. A small cunning wart. This numbness I've never felt. For Vera I feel. And me, alone now, and aging. Vera kept me together; now I'll fly apart.

Terry leaned on the white tubular railing and looked into the river, the same rich fetal colour as the Mississippi in New Orleans. He looked into the river as if it could see back and recognize the indictment gathered together in his face. "I'm boring you, aren't I?"

He struggled to keep his voice inside, to not be seen as a Waterloo nutcase, to not yell out loud: You have no time for this infestation on your banks. You don't even know we're here. The original builders of this town, when it was nothing but a market for nomads and tattooed vagrants, worshipped you as a god. Oh, thou indifferent geologic water groove. The river of life, the way you flow like our lives, as corporeal as water forming streams and flowing toward the sea to be fortified with salt.

The words wouldn't stay inside anymore and he shouted, "Silt and salt is the promise, is it? All these passage graves and standing stones. Henges and megoliths. Snakes and ladders. Cosmic fucking Tiddlywinks. Bleeding Neolithic maidens tossed into your waters at Battersee because of the fear of their fathers. Fertility at the delta? Sarfend Pier? Flesh of sacrificed maiden feeds codfish and cockle beds! Heavenly substance? You can kiss my saggy pink arse! You're nothing but a drainage system!"

Singing, cockles and mussels, alive, alive oh!

A group of noisy women, holding each other's arms, approached, heading for an early hen night perhaps, and passed behind him as though he didn't exist; he waited for them to be gone before speaking to the river again. "But nothing begets nothing as we reach the estuary. That's the real truth, isn't it? Was Vera right all along? That the only meaning is the small one in the here and now? If she was right, then all those wars I used to rage against were worth something after all—they were struggles to gain momentary meaning, buying time for evolution. But can we handle it? How many times has this grief been written and explained? Yet still we cling to the straw of the supernatural as though our intellect itself has a flight or fight response to the ineluctable loss of consciousness that awaits us. We cannot pay the price for the gift of consciousness, we are incapable—the price is that we acknowledge our mortality. If Vera's right, then let's be the Borg from Star Trek—let's live through each other, live through the future that the ones coming behind us build on our shoulders... a brave new world. This place is already a bloody great hive!"

Spent, his throat hurting, Terry ambled north on the west side of the bridge and stopped, overlooking Savoy Pier and the Queen Mary of Glasgow with the Strand Underpass roaring behind him to his right. There stood Cleopatra's Needle, dark and pitted, surrounded by tourists. She's left that. We nicked it from those fez wallahs. Vera liked to sit and watch the river from there; sit her bum on sandstone carved by ancient hands. She marveled that those hands were gone but that the purloined obelisk bore witness to their existence. London she's left, zipped into the underpass to never see the light again. How could any of us? I mustn't weep, not here. It'll stop traffic, get reported on Capital Radio—"Terrance Langley Can't Take It!" But her, under that sheet, tattoos and all. Nothing in her face. Not her anymore. That mouth I kissed.

Sitting beside Vera at the last, Terry had said, "Despite what I know you believe, I expect to see you again, darling." She had opened her eyes... focused them. "Don't be so stupid," she whispered. "I've resisted that clap-trap all my life. Not going to cave in now. Face it like those before me. Hold my hand, old stick."

Then, much later she said, "Terry, I'm afraid."

Then the last breath and an inward collapsing and that snake tail sound in the sternum. His mind went into orbit, a thousand words a second, every emotion clashing like a rugby scrum. Calm down, Vera would say, You're letting your thoughts race again. Calm down and get control.

That Irish nurse: "Are you going to be all right, Mr. Langley. Can I bring somethin' for yus?"

"Yes, ring that bastard God and make Him give my Vera back."

"Come and sit for a bit, luv. Come on. Can I get a priest, a pastor or someone? No? How about a cup of tea?"

Broughton came out, knelt down in front of him, and looked into his eyes. "We're all so sorry."

"Yes, I know. Thank you. You did all you could. I know that."

"Good. And, if it helps a bit—she didn't suffer."

349

He held up his mobile phone. Broughton took it and handed it to the nurse. "My secretary," said Terry. "Minnie. In the address book. She'll come and get me." He spun inside. The room stayed still in his vision, but inside his brain the synapses danced in a maelstrom.

He didn't know how long he waited for Minnie. They said she was on her way, but he couldn't sit any longer—he was full of fireworks. When he rushed out of the ward he forgot his jacket. They couldn't stop him, but the Irish nurse had the presence of mind to slap the mobile into his hand. Then what? No recollection—like being dead yourself for a while. And poor Minnie would be out searching, clumping along in her black shoes, jangling cheap jewelry. She doesn't own a mobile. Inconsiderate. Forgive me she will.

A 'City Cruises' paddleboat passed underneath the bridge. Big Ben, lit up in the sun, chimed three times. The paddleboat had a red hull and white traces of Louisiana on its upper decks that made Terry think of Gilbert holding George's ashes as they crossed the Mississippi on the Algiers ferry. Should've deposited them into the drink right there. Gilbert, Nina, both handling the death of a loved one so much better than he. Nina firmly believes in the survival of the ego. She would, of course. And Gilbert, my savagely practical son, just gets on with things despite his innate sensitivity. Savage practicality from mother, debilitating sensitivity from father. Healthy savagery overriding potential paralysis. Gift of the Goddess. Terry flung his arm at Whitehall and, in a loud American accent, shouted, "There ya go!"

Little green pods packed with tourists turned slowly to the end of their ride in the gargantuan sovereign that is the London Eye. What if it should break loose and roll down the river, flattening bridges, all the way to Shoeburyness, explode the USS Montgomery, and break all the windows in Essex and Kent? See the damn thing from space. City symbol—coinage.

London pounded with traffic despite rush hour being two hours off. Cop shop behind—Thames Police. Waterboys. Vera's ashes in the river, I think, yes. She loves this river. Empty them off the Millennium Bridge, the newest one she loves so much. We would walk up to the cathedral from there, sit in Paternoster Square and eat crusty baguettes while guessing the nationality of tourists.

"I better go to church—it's been years," Terry said to the river. "Horrid old agnostic suddenly seeks Jesus. Vera would say 'This'll be interesting.'"

Terry turned, looked east, and muttered, "It's over there, St. Paul's. Wren's nest."

The annoying work of a contemporary architect, a Norman Foster creation, pointed at heaven like an atomic suppository. And those old domes, St. Paul's and the one in Rome, mosques too, with erect nipples on top are appropriate structures under which one such as Terry should worship. Naughty—have respect. Can't. Bloody well try—Vera's dead. Yes, darling, I will obey.

"Let's start hoofing it, Langley. Come on, off to church with you."

As I was walking by St. Paul's

A lady grabbed me by the...

He didn't want the Embankment—sick of the river. As he turned right at the stoplights, crossing in front of a bus at the end of the Strand, his mobile started pulsing in his pocket. He stood on the corner outside Pret a Manger in the midst of rushing pedestrians, most of whom would outlive him, lifted the phone to his ear, and said bitterly, "Terrence Langley. Man of flesh and bone."

"Always fooling around, even at the worst of times," said the voice.

At first he thought Vera spoke; no, American—Nina Pym—his ear for accents desensitized by the fortnight amongst them.

"Nina," he said, "Bloody hell."

"How you doing? Are you in the subway?"

"I'm in London. This is what it sounds like."

"But are you doing all right?"

"No."

"I'm coming."

"No, Nina, don't."

"I don't care. I'm coming. Nothing will stop me. You need me."

Buses went by and he strained to hear what she said next. "You're going to be hurting and I'm the only one who can soothe you and let you grieve at the same time. I'm the only one who can show you that death doesn't really matter."

"It matters right now. It matters terribly."

"Vera's fine. Stop worrying about her. She doesn't want you in pain."

"I'm just walking to church."

"Pray for me too. I'm terrified of flying."

"You shouldn't come."

"I'm coming. The next available flight."

"Do you even have a passport?"

"I've had one at the ready for thirty-two years. Only used it for Mexico."

"I don't know what to say. Perhaps it's too soon."

"No, it isn't. You'll like it. I'll arrange it all with my rich son. I'll be in touch."

"Dear oh dear."

"Don't be afraid to let it out. Don't bottle it up. You'll blow your mind."

"Thanks, I'll try to remember that."

"I can't wait to see you. I'll help you with everything. I'll be in touch. Hang in there."

Nina Pym hadn't changed. She cut like a scythe through all boundaries. It was brilliant in a way, thoughtless and infuriating at times, but nevertheless vital, life affirming. No worries. Terry tried not to think of the old saw *Beware of what you wish for,* but it cruised around his brain with impunity. He started down the Strand, passing Somerset House with its yawning archway and blue railings where births and deaths used to be recorded. A sign advertised "The Gilbert Collection" and he had to remind himself that coincidence means nothing. There is no message.

* * *

Pym's mother insisted upon flying to London to comfort Terry. Nina had mellowed out considerably since seeing Terry again, and Pym thought he might be able to tolerate her presence in his life now. Estelle, who only knew some of the background, encouraged him to forgive his mother. "Women should be forgiven," she told him repeatedly. Pym admired Nina's courage; it was a romantic risk, a rebound situation, and she hated flying. He bought her a ticket and, on a lovely May evening, put her on the flight from Minneapolis-St. Paul International Airport to London Gatwick. Mishawn had colored Nina's hair to make it a lush, middle-aged brown with blonde highlights. Nina had worked hard to get her figure back and looked like a film star, but when he held her, kissed her good-bye, he felt her trembling against him. For the first time in his adult life, she smelled good to him.

They'd all changed hairstyles. Pym wanted to try his like his dad's. They had the same hair. And Estelle had some voguish cut that made her look like a model. On the way back from the airport, Estelle pulled a little box from the glove compartment—it looked like a small white coffin. It was a pregnancy test kit. She held it up for Pym to see as he drove.

Smiling guardedly, she said, "Positive."

Pym drove quietly, frowning slightly. His inner voice started up like a crooning old grandmother: A new little soul, how amazing, a new potential so easy to nurture, all we have to do is love it. Then the opposite response: Also easy to terminate at this stage—I'm not ready for this—another generation of crazy Pyms into an overpopulated world.

Estelle touched his right knee and looked ahead as he turned north onto 35W. Traffic slowed, it was the tail end of rush hour, and once they'd made the turn onto the freeway, downtown Minneapolis came into view, a gleaming cluster of modernity in the evening sun, and the traffic came to a stop. "What the hell's going on? Rush hour should be over."

"Twins game tonight," said Estelle.

"God, why do they bother?"

Estelle didn't laugh, but said, "I tell you I'm pregnant and you start bashing the Twins. What's that about?"

"Avoidance."

"Gil, you promised we could have a baby."

"Are you sure we're ready for this—a very different life?"

Estelle frowned, kept her eyes on Downtown. Cautiously, she said, "Absolutely. We discussed this in New Orleans. No changing your mind on me now. Remember? I get a baby, and you get to move to the rectum of America."

Any other time he would have laughed. He let a minute pass before saying, "I still want to move to New Orleans. But the reality is different from the theory."

"Told you so."

"I'm referring more to parenthood than getting out of this place."

Estelle withdrew her hand from his knee. "So what are you saying? We abort this one and wait awhile? If we do that I'll be in the land of the dead forever."

He looked at her, surprised. He thought for a minute or two, before saying, "The timing's all wrong. Something feels bad about it. Like maybe we were infected by all that shit going down with George and the Duvals and the rest of it." He continued, laughing nervously. "I wonder if you made a pact with the Devil to get me or something."

"Please forgive him, Jesus, for his black thoughts."

"It was a pretty weird time. Do we want a kid born out of that?"

"Yes."

"Oh, okay. Don't even think about it."

"I don't need to. It isn't the kid's fault."

"No," Pym sighed, "I guess not."

"I love you, but you're a cold son of a bitch sometimes, Gilbert Pym."

"I'll warm up to it. It's just a lot all at once. Can't you see that?"

"Yes. But I see it all like a final battle, you know. There's lots of action and then you win and it all settles down for a while until the kid becomes a teenager."

Pym laughed. "And starts smoking."

"And gets hormonal. Okay, let's abort now. Just kidding." Estelle put her arm around him and said, "You'll have your faithful girl, a secure future with a newly sane mother, a wise English dad, and a gorgeous healthy baby to bounce on your knee."

He drove the car almost a hundred yards before having to stop, and then said, "You're right. It was all agreed. Sorry."

Estelle squeezed his knee. "Start saving for private school, dude."

Pym shrugged. "Don't forget my addendum, Stella. I'm having no part in any stupid religious nonsense."

Now Estelle frowned. "Your atheism is going to be a problem."

"You can walk home if you like."

"It might be quicker. Look, are we going ahead with this?"

"Okay, yes."

"Jeez," said Estelle, her eyes welling up, "I thought this would be a joyful moment, instead of ponderous Pym-gloom."

"Sorry, darling."

"Don't start that Terry shit."

In Terry's voice and with a slight inclination of the head, Pym said. "You've got your wish, my dear. We'll welcome this whelp into the world. Now for Christ's sake shut your bleedin' cakehole."

Estelle burst out laughing and crying at the same time.

A woman in a white Volvo glared at Pym and tried to look at Estelle sympathetically. Pym said, "Look at this one," alerting Estelle to the glaring woman. "She assumes I'm an abuser, a wife-beater. We gotta get outta here."

Estelle laughed and shot the woman a middle finger.

The woman changed lanes.

"Do you love me?" Estelle asked.

Pym laughed. "Here we go again." He drove as far as the 48th Street exit before being halted.

"We talked all this through that day, remember?"

Estelle sniffed. "A woman needs to hear it more than once."

"Why is it that men have to be the way women want them? I'm uncomfortable professing love all the goddamn time. Now get the fuck outta my face!"

Estelle cried, "There's my Gilbert! I knew you were in there somewhere. Asshole."

"You're relentless."

"I want to know if I'm loved."

"You are."

"Good. I suppose that's it then until New Year's Eve."

"I reckon so. Deal with it."

"I'm moving to Paris."

"Right. Minneapolis bimbo hits the Champs Elysee. Tit alert!"

Startled, Estelle said, "You're not funny. You're just a bastard. In fact, that woman was right, you are an abuser. I should go live with your dad—he knows how to treat a woman."

He laughed, and said, "Ma's already got him, I'm afraid. You'll have to find another gentleman."

"Christ, Gil, lighten up."

"I must obey."

"I love you. Okay? I ain't afraid to say it. You been a piss poor boyfriend, but I forgave you everything. Now be nice to me."

"I must obey."

"That Maddy creature you got into trouble with... is that the kind of girl you prefer?"

"No, ma'am."

"Then be nice to me."

"How do I know you're not like her?"

"Hey! Don't be a jerk. You know what I'm like."

"Steady as a rock?" Pym laughed.

"Exactly," Estelle said. "Don't ever question that—or forget it."

"Or you'll rip my nose off?"

"I love your nose."

They were passing by the Metrodome now, a stadium that struck Pym as rather outmoded, like the Superdome. Pym asked, "Who dat?"

Estelle frowned. Her left arm lay across his shoulders, the nails of her fingers gently caressing his earlobe. He thought of his brother and held back a sob. Estelle said, "You're clever. You're thinking straight, looking after us. I love the way you've got everything arranged so we can move to New Orleans and not lose anything here. It's smart, like George."

They crossed the river, got off on the University Avenue exit and drove back to Peter Pan Island.

At bedtime, Estelle felt too tired to make love and there remained an awkwardness after the preceding hours of emotional head banging. But Pym was pleased to find that it felt normal; it was okay; you don't have to make love every goddamn night. Estelle slept on her back, naked, barely breathing. Pym looked at her flat stomach. He yawned and thought: Baby in there. Miracle.

He smelled her hair, kissed the smooth cliff of her cheekbone. Up so close he could hear Estelle's eyeballs moving behind their lids; he watched them, wondered what she dreamed.

Cindy Sorensen had talked him into doing an interview about unsanctioned gender reassignment and how families were impacted by it. He had a little preparation to work up for her, but he couldn't concentrate. She would be flying into Minneapolis in a few days to tape it at a local affiliate. The story was over; he wasn't eager to reopen it.

Through the open curtains he saw the giant, yellow-lit Norwest building looming like some glittering night deity, Marduk or Baal, no, the aloof Mawa of the Voudon overlooking the city with its inimical demon face; a mouth grimly turned down with squinty Samarai eyes and a suggestion of pointed ears. Local Fundamentalists thought it represented the Beast 666. Pym's recent adventures clearly showed the inside of things to be very different from how they appear outwardly.

His reading, and his notes on yellow legal pads, lay piled up beside him on the bedside table. He let himself sink until the very silence itself seemed to be whispering. Was he awake or asleep? Is life waking or sleeping? It hardly mattered. Was it a New Orleans jazz band in the distance? Was it voices outside the window? Was it the wind, or an aircraft approaching? He thought he said: Where am I now? There was something he wanted to write, but he couldn't move. He strained his ears, listening. He didn't want that dream to come back—the old woman at the end of the bed. He wasn't in the mood for flying. The very molecules of the air were making words—they said: *Gillie it's me, I'm here. It's me.*

He looked upward at the round ceiling mirror and saw that Estelle had her eyes open and was looking at him in the mirror. A shock drilled his spine from occiput to anus. His heart was a base guitar. Estelle's lips moved.

Roll on me. Gillie, roll on top—nail me. Do it. Nail me good.

Pym pulled to his side of the bed. Estelle was an anaconda filled with devoured men. The faint, aspirated sound, coming from the bottom of her lungs, was not Estelle's. In the mirror, Pym saw her stir, turn to him and bring her mouth close to his ear, the tongue flicking; he watched her hand enclose his genitals and the sinews flexing in her forearms. She smelled fresh and sweet like rubbed herbs. He felt her warm breath in his ear as she pulled the blood into him, saying *Gillie, you old silly,* and then slipped onto him, opened herself with two fingers and guided the head of his penis into her vagina. *I'll do it, then,* she whispered, *I'll do the nailing.*

An expression of ecstasy appeared on her face, or was it relief—a mission accomplished—Pym couldn't tell. He was confused. All he could do was watch the powerful muscles of her back and buttocks sink, lunge, and sink repeatedly. Her face flushed red and she turned her head slightly to the side. Pym thought he heard her say, *I'm home, Gillie, I'm home.*

He woke propped up in bed with the legal pad in front of him and the light still on. Estelle snored daintily beside him. "Those jerks are still in my dreams. Life's too short for more of this crap."

He looked over what he had written in preparation for the interview with Cindy:

> *If you have a family member going through this you have to make sure you listen to them, draw them out. They may be enacting something that's simply become a habit of thought in their minds, an overwhelming longing, and they don't know how to see the truth. They stop seeing straight. They think they may have been born in the wrong body. Except for a few cases there's no real evidence of that. The truth is it's simply an obsession, a sexual preference, and in that sense perfectly legitimate, at least if one's of a tolerant*

> *frame of mind. They have to seek help, and then a legitimate gender reassignment program, not rip-off psycho scumbags like my brother got mixed up with.*
>
> *Our whole culture has to do a better job of waking up to reality. We think kids shouldn't swear so we ban swearing and all sorts of books in school. We allow lots of killing on TV but not sex. We think we're holding to standards, but the standards don't exist. We get this one shot at being alive and we're made the way we're made. What a mess it causes to try and alter our skin. My experience with my brother George led me to blame a lot of this on the magical thinking of my mother. Getting magical thinking under control is imperative. Otherwise you become a candidate for the nuthouse. You will have weird things going on in your imagination, but it isn't God, or Satan, or spirits. It isn't your ancestors talking through your blood. It's this wonderful gift you have called imagination.*

Is this what I really mean? Pym thought. He turned off the light and went to sleep satisfied that it was.

The queer dream in the night made Pym get up early and call Rick in New Orleans. Rick didn't get who it was at first, then said, "What do you need, man? I'm just headed to work."

"Couple of things."

"Shoot."

Taken aback by Rick's coolness, Pym didn't ask about the strange dream, which was his main reason for calling. Instead, he said, "I miss it down there."

"Don't. It sucks here."

"Hey, dude, you're my spiritual adviser."

Rick laughed, but it wasn't a friendly laugh.

"Seen anything of Nadine Duval?"

"She nullified, man."

"I suppose that's good. I shouldn't stay revengeful."

"Don't you be worryin' none about revenge."

"Okay. Is she in town?"

"You still a running fool, Gilbert Pym?"

"Estelle's pregnant."

"You cool wid dat?"

"I guess. Enough so's we're thinking of moving to New Orleans."

"No way. You stay where you are."

"Are you serious?"

"I am real fuckin' serious, dude. You stay the fuck outta this town. You fine in the place you're at. Or maybe you go live wid your daddy in that big ol' London town. You be safe there. This place is fucked up. It'll chew you up and leave you a husk of yourself."

"How's Sasha doing?"

"Staring at a wall."

"And Lulu?"

"Running The House of Large Sizes. Playing Tiger Shark to the Thai surgeons."

"Lulu running the House of Large Sizes! Very cool."

"Scotch one snake and another motherfucker takes its place."

"She's a good person though, isn't she?"

"I gotta jet, man. Remember, you a cold weather monkey. Stay where you belong. Look after yourself, man."

When Pym put down the phone he found Estelle looking at him from the doorway. He asked, "What's the matter?"

"Nothing."

"You look scared."

"I'm hungry."

Estelle was ravenous and wanted to drive around to Kramachek's to get breakfast meat.

"Why this hunger?" Pym asked, and she replied, "Eating for two."

"That's how it starts," Pym grinned.

"What?" Estelle said, pointing at his nose.

"Getting porky."

"You may have to put up with a little pork for a while."

"I guess."

"Coming with?"

"No. I'll meet you back here in an hour. I have to go around to the house and fix the belt in the dryer for the new tenant."

"I'm impressed. Mister fix-it-all-of-a-sudden, mister self-sufficient. Or is it because our new tenant's an attractive Irish lady?"

"No, Stella, it's because the dryer quit working."

"I'm just shitting ya, babe. Sort of."

"Stop this, it isn't funny."

"I'm scared you'll find someone smarter than me. You're doing all this reading. I can't keep up with you."

"Your job is to have our baby. And make one of your breakfasts."

"And fuck you like a whore."

"Let's not lose sight of the basics."

They kissed and she looked deep into his eyes. She thrust gently against him. "I may have to get you after breakfast."

* * *

Siobhan Moody stood in the doorway as the handsome landlord approached, carrying a tool bag. "Sorry," Siobhan said. "I'm away to work. Is there anything I need to help you with?"

He walked up to her, smiling, smelling of soap. "No, you're good." He laughed. "I have the tools and the how-to manual."

She stood aside as he stepped in and looked around the living room. He was very big, towering over her, powerful under his work shirt, and had blonde hair swept back like that Irish writer who moved to Paris and whose name she could never recall.

"You settled in quickly," the landlord said. "These new furnishings make it look so different. I like it. You have excellent taste."

"All rented for me by the Pillsbury Dough Boy." Siobhan laughed.

"That's right, you can walk to your office from here, can't you?"

"I'm from Dublin. I like to walk everywhere. Detest driving."

"Smart woman."

If she didn't have a meeting to prep for she'd hang around and watch him work. Hand him his tools. "Oh, by the way," she said. "There's some post for you." She took his mail from a side-table and handed it to him. He frowned, pulling a fat manila envelope from the small bundle and rattled it against his ear. Siobhan saw that someone with extremely poor handwriting had addressed the envelope. After a moment, the landlord said, more to himself than to her, "Huh, weird—Lulu's spooky script."

"Who's Lulu?"

The landlord laughed, looked at her, and said, "A transgender person in New Orleans."

"Well, I never. Fair play to you for being broad-minded, Mr. Pym."

He laughed again, rather nervously, she thought, and said, "She's harmless—seems to be there to show me what I need to see." Then he sighed, a bit painfully, and said, "It's a long story."

He opened the envelope and pulled out a black, videocassette labeled *Estelle and friends*. He stared at it, frowning.

After a moment Siobhan said, "You're welcome to use the video machine if you've a mind."

He broke into his beautiful green-eyed smile, obviously delighted by her simple commodiousness. "Could I?" he said. "That would be great."

"Help yourself, love. I'll be off now. See you soon, yeah."

"I hope so."

A lovely man, Siobhan thought to herself as she walked in the beautiful blue spring morning toward her office. It's a pity he's lumbered with that daft cow of a girlfriend. What did he mean by 'I hope so'? I wonder if he likes me.

FINIS

About the Author

IAN GRAHAM LEASK was born and raised in the London area. He is lucky to have had an unhappy childhood. He started writing at fifteen and has never stopped—his office is full of notebooks. He traveled. After a year in Germany, where he worked as a meat porter in a schlachthoff and wrote dull poetry at night, he settled in Minneapolis, graduated from the University of Minnesota with degrees in English and writing, and narrowly avoided becoming a professor. He has thrived as a teacher, literary consultant and publisher, and is the author of *The Wounded and other stories about sons and fathers*. He co-hosts KFAI's literary radio show "Write On! Radio" and lives mostly in Minneapolis with frequent spells in London.